A Widow's Courage

Also by Anna Jacobs

THE BIRCH END SAGA
A Daughter's Journey

THE ELLINDALE SAGA
One Quiet Woman
One Kind Man
One Special Village
One Perfect Family

THE RIVENSHAW SAGA
A Time to Remember
A Time for Renewal
A Time to Rejoice
Gifts For Our Time

THE TRADERS
The Trader's Wife
The Trader's Sister
The Trader's Dream
The Trader's Gift
The Trader's Reward

THE SWAN RIVER SAGA
Farewell to Lancashire
Beyond the Sunset
Destiny's Path

THE GIBSON FAMILY
Salem Street
High Street
Ridge Hill
Hallam Square
Spinners Lake

THE IRISH SISTERS
A Pennyworth of Sunshine
Twopenny Rainbows
Threepenny Dreams

THE STALEYS
Down Weavers Lane
Calico Road

THE KERSHAW SISTERS
Our Lizzie
Our Polly
Our Eva
Our Mary Ann

THE SETTLERS
Lancashire Lass
Lancashire Legacy

THE PRESTON FAMILY
Pride of Lancashire
Star of the North
Bright Day Dawning
Heart of the Town

LADY BINGRAM'S
AIDES
Tomorrow's Promises
Yesterday's Girl

STANDALONE NOVELS
Jessie
Like No Other
Freedom's Land

ANNA JACOBS

A Widow's Courage

Birch End Saga Book Two

HODDER &
STOUGHTON

First published in Great Britain in 2020 by Hodder & Stoughton
An Hachette UK company

1

A CIP catalogue record for this title is available from the British Library

Hardback ISBN 978 1 473 67783 8
eBook ISBN 978 1 473 67784 5

Typeset in Plantin Light by Palimpsest Book Production Limited, Falkirk, Stirlingshire

Printed and bound in Great Britain by Clays Ltd, Elcograf S.p.A.

Hodder & Stoughton policy is to use papers that are natural, renewable and
recyclable products and made from wood grown in sustainable forests.
The logging and manufacturing processes are expected to conform to the
environmental regulations of the country of origin.

Hodder & Stoughton Ltd
Carmelite House
50 Victoria Embankment
London EC4Y 0DZ

www.hodder.co.uk

Dear readers,

This is the second book in my new series. I do hope you enjoy reading it. Once again, I've thoroughly enjoyed writing another story set in the middle village in Ellin Valley, my imaginary Pennine valley.

This time, it's Stella's story. I liked that name on sight. I have a list of first names from the 1920s and I looked at those before my other lists and 'Stella' stood out. I not only have other lists but several books of names, because I try to choose either a classic name that goes on and on or else a name particularly popular in that era.

We also continue Wilf Pollard's story. He's a bit like my maternal grandfather, Fred Wild, who could turn his hand to anything. Even though those grandparents lived for many years in a one room up, one room down terraced back-to-back house, my granddad still managed to put a lathe and workshop in the cellar.

Those back-to-back houses had only one frontage and were built against a similar row of one-sided houses. Theirs opened at the back, on to a big yard, with toilets at the other side of it, each shared by two or three houses.

The housewives were ferociously clean, in spite of not having a bathroom, only a tin bath (kept in the cellar) set out in front of the fire. The bath water came in buckets from a gas water heater over the kitchen sink. And the 'kitchen', with only sink, cooker and draining board, was at the top of the stairs leading down to the cellar. Chopping food was done on the table in the only room downstairs. But as I said, everything was cleaner than most houses today, in my opinion – even the paved path outside the door was washed regularly and coloured by stones that left yellow traces.

I could still walk round that house, I remember it so clearly, because at one stage we lived in a two-up, two-down house (also without built-in bathroom) in the next street. Even when we moved away I often visited my grandparents, walking a couple of miles across town to get there so that I could save my penny busfare to buy books with.

The cottage my heroine falls in love with in this book is much grander. I hope you enjoy her story.

A quick reminder, if you'd like a complete list of books in each series, please visit my website, where there is a complete list and other lists too. Just go to:

www.annajacobs.com/seriesList

Happy reading!

Anna

A Widow's Courage

I

Lancashire, November 1931–34

Stella Newby woke with a start as someone yelled in the street. She sat up in bed, puzzled by the flickering light for a moment, then jerked fully awake as she realised what it was. She shook her husband. 'Wake up, Derrick! Something's on fire.'

He was out of bed in a flash, peering out of the window at his side of the bed. 'It's next door, love.'

Someone was shouting for help and he called, 'Get out of the house!' as he ran from the room.

Stella grabbed their clothes from the chair beside the bed, not waiting to put hers on because flames were flickering near their bedroom window now.

Coughing and spluttering, she raced downstairs and risked going into the kitchen to grab her handbag and the pot containing their rent money from the mantelpiece, before running out to the front. She gasped at how hot it felt there.

'This way.' Someone pulled her away from the house and along the street towards the corner shop, outside which people were gathering. She looked around for Derrick but couldn't see him.

There was a clanging sound and a fire engine turned into the street, slowing as people in its path scattered.

Stella stood there in her nightdress, clutching her bundle of clothes, looking for her husband.

'Here. Put your coat on, love. Good thing you grabbed it, eh?'

She let the owner of the shop help her put it on, then picked up her bundle again. 'Have you seen my Derrick?'

'No.' Mrs Lilley turned to yell, 'Anyone seen Derrick Newby?'

People shook their heads or murmured 'No'.

Stella was really worried now. Where could he be?

Someone down the street was having hysterics, calling out a name again and again.

A man came running to join them. 'There's a little lass missing. Anyone else not accounted for?'

'My husband.'

He stared at her. 'Tall chap? Thin?'

'Yes.'

'I saw him run into the house that was on fire, saying he'd get the little lass out.'

Stella felt sick and dizzy as that sank in. When she managed to gather her thoughts, she found she was sitting on a chair, surrounded by faces. The electricity had gone off but there was plenty of light from the fire.

Someone else came up. 'Number seven's caught it now, gone up like a torch, it has.'

The woman next to the man jabbed him in the side and pointed to Stella. 'That's her house.'

He stared at her in shock. 'Eh, lass. I'm that sorry. I didn't recognise you with your hair down. You allus look so neat.'

'Has anyone seen my husband?'

'I'll go and ask.'

The neighbour didn't come back for a while, not till the flames were starting to die down as the firemen got things under control. A man came with him, the curate from church. He knelt beside Stella and she knew then, knew before he even said the words.

'I'm sorry, Mrs Newby. I'm afraid your husband's dead.

He got caught by a falling beam. He was a real hero, rescued a child.'

What did she care about that? She wanted Derrick back, alive.

'Come through to my back room, love,' Mrs Lilley said. 'You'll want to get dressed.'

Stella looked down at the bundle of clothes, not even knowing what she'd grabbed in her haste to leave. The neighbour helped her sort them out and she got dressed, staring down at Derrick's outer clothes.

She cried then, sobbing and clutching his shirt. But what good did that do? What good did anything do now?

When the tears dried up, she felt numb, as if she was made of stone.

Stella didn't feel anything till she found out that Derrick had let the fire and life insurance payments slip. There was no money even for a proper funeral. She'd been left to start life all over again at the age of twenty-seven, with her dreams shattered and owning only the clothes she stood up in.

One of the firemen had found a slightly scorched wedding photograph of her and Derrick, saved by its glass and the fact that it had fallen down the back of the chest of drawers. Stella couldn't bear to look at it.

She stayed with Mrs Lilley for a few days, sleeping on the rug in the kitchen. Derrick's workmates from the factory and the people in their street took up a collection for her. Two days after the fire they presented her with a little drawstring bag of coins. She hated being the object of charity, but she took it. She needed to buy clothes and other necessities.

Once she had Derrick's death certificate, she went to the Post Office Savings Bank accompanied by the curate to prove who she was and get access to their savings. Not that there was much, just a few pounds.

When they came out, he asked gently, 'What are you going to do, Mrs Newby?'

'Find a job and somewhere to live.'

'I know a lodging house with a vacancy. I can vouch for your respectability.'

She heard of a job in an office and got there at seven in the morning, to find herself fifth in a queue of hopefuls. The second one got the job.

Next time she heard of a job she got there at four in the morning and was the first in the queue. She got that job because she had good office skills and could prove it.

People from her old street went on with their lives and the quiet evenings began for her. Stella didn't like living in lodgings with other people and sharing all her meals, but she had no choice. She missed cooking for herself and was a far better cook than her landlady.

One thing she hadn't expected was that some men assumed she missed the marriage bed and treated her disrespectfully. She'd been shocked rigid the first time it happened, because the man to do that had been a neighbour of theirs for years and should have known she wasn't that sort of woman.

If her granddad hadn't taught her ways of protecting herself when she was younger, the man might have succeeded, too, because she was small and slender, and looked weaker than she was.

As the months passed, it happened again. Several times. She learned to kick out and kept a hatpin handy for a weapon of defence. It certainly made a man yelp to be jabbed in the arm with one, or to scrape your shoe down the front of his shin or, as a last resort, kick him in a vulnerable place.

After a few months, she left Salford and moved to Rochdale to work for a friend of her employer, who was moving to the south. She didn't keep in touch with anyone, not even the cousins who were her only close family.

By now she had enough money to hire a room where she could share cooking facilities on the landing – two gas burners and a sink.

She didn't tell any of her new friends and neighbours about losing Derrick. Better to pretend to be a colourless spinster whose elderly aunt had just died. She was small and found it easy to dress plainly and stay in the background.

Three years later, Stella waited outside the newsagent's for her friend to buy a coupon for the football pools, as she did every week on payday. Stella knew Lena had been doing that for over a year but had only won once, though it had been a nice little sum of just over £5.

Stella would have saved that money, but Lena had insisted on paying for them both to go to the cinema in the best seats and had spent the rest on new clothes and a handbag.

As months passed with no more wins, she tried to show Lena the sums that proved she was wasting her money gambling. Her friend had just laughed and said she got her sixpence worth every single week in the dreams of what she'd do if she won a big amount.

Today it seemed to be taking longer than usual to buy the coupon and Stella was about to go in and see what was wrong when Lena came out, beaming at her.

She held out an envelope. 'Here you are. Happy birthday, love!'

'Oh! I didn't think anyone knew.'

'I found out when I was waiting for you in the outer office at the laundry a few weeks ago. It was in the ledger with all our details in it, sitting open on a corner of Miss Marlow's desk. I couldn't resist having a peek.'

'Well, it's very kind of you to buy me a card but—'

Lena chuckled. 'It's more than a card, love. There's a present in there as well. Let's go and sit on that bench while you open it.' She led the way across to the small public garden and plonked herself down, looking smug.

Stella sat beside her and opened the envelope. The card had a bunch of flowers on the outside and was garishly bright, as you'd expect of anything Lena bought. There was something inside it as well, so she opened it and her heart sank. When you worked hard for every penny, it hurt to see even the smallest amount thrown away.

'Oh, Lena! You shouldn't have wasted your money.'

Her friend got that stubborn look on her face. 'It's not wasted, and it's only sixpence.' She put an arm round Stella and gave her a hug. 'You've been very down in the mouth this week and I wanted to give you something happy to dream about. I've filled it in for you already because my cat knows more about football than you do.'

What could she say other than 'Thank you for your kind thought'?

Something suddenly occurred to her. 'I won't know how to check whether I've won or not!' From what she'd heard, it was something to do with whether the teams had scored draws or not, but what difference that made, she hadn't a clue.

'I'll come around on Sunday afternoon and help you check, then if the weather's fine we'll go for a walk. I can borrow Alistair's newspaper because he'll have checked his pools and be fast asleep on the sofa by two o'clock.' She wagged her forefinger at Stella. 'You have to promise me that you'll dream about what you'd do if you won.'

'All right. How much am I going to imagine winning?'

Lena thought about this for a moment, head on one side, then said firmly, 'A thousand pounds. You might as well have a big dream as a little one. It is your thirtieth birthday today, after all.'

'I can't imagine having ten pounds to spare, let alone a

thousand.' Stella managed on what she earned and all she really cared about these days was looking decent, having books to read and making occasional visits to the cinema. She not only borrowed books from the local library but also bought herself a novel every month from the tray of cheap second-hand books on one of the market stalls. She'd always wanted her own bookcase, but Derrick hadn't been a reader and said it would clutter up the room. Now she had made one very cheaply out of planks balanced on bricks and had filled two whole shelves with books.

Lena stared at her, head on one side. 'You're hopeless, Stella Newby. Look, you could dream about buying a whole pile of your beloved books. Brand new ones, mind, with bright, shiny covers, not those tattered second-hand ones. And a new winter coat. Yours is shabby.'

They parted company at the end of the street and Stella walked slowly home. She let out a huff of disgust as she went into the untidy hall where someone had kicked off their muddy shoes and left them lying near the foot of the stairs. She wished she could afford to rent a house of her own again. She still missed the privacy.

The previous Monday had marked the third anniversary of the fire and that was what had made her sad. She was a different person now from Mrs Derrick Newby, living a quiet life, enjoying her simple escapes into films and books.

But she remembered the happier days and Derrick's loving smile. She always remembered. He'd been a quiet sort of man, really kind. You needed kindness in a hard world.

Well, life went on. One day perhaps she'd manage to find a more interesting way of living and to achieve her dearest dream: a home of her own. But she couldn't afford to rent a whole house on a woman's lower wages, so it remained just that – a dream.

★

She hadn't intended to do any dreaming about winning the pools, whatever Lena said. But the dingy room made her feel unsettled, as did the sound of her neighbour splashing and singing tunelessly in the bathroom just along the landing. Jane paid the landlady an extra sixpence every Saturday evening for a bath and made it last as long as she could. The singing always got on Stella's nerves but there was nothing she could do about it.

Imagine winning a thousand pounds, Lena had said, and dream of what you'd do. Before she knew it, Stella was working out what she'd do with a hundred pounds because she simply couldn't imagine winning a thousand. Find somewhere nicer to live, for a start.

'Oh, you stupid woman!' she said aloud. 'Haven't you learned what happens to dreams?'

From then on till she went to bed she managed to stop her imagination running riot because she had a new library book by Angela Thirkell, her favourite author, and she couldn't put it down.

But who can control what happens when you're asleep? Certainly not her.

She woke up in the morning feeling angry and unrested, wishing she did have a thousand pounds, because she'd buy the beautiful little cottage she'd owned in her dreams, the sort of place she and Derrick had talked about buying one day.

By the time Lena arrived on Sunday afternoon, Stella had got her irritation under control and stopped herself from indulging in any more stupid, impossible fantasies. She kept reminding herself that her friend had meant well as she got out her tin of special biscuits. Lena was the only guest she ever had, but that didn't mean she had to be mean with her.

She was watching out of the window as Lena walked up

the street and her anger evaporated at the sunny smile on her friend's face. Who could stay angry at such a kind, cheerful woman?

She ran down the stairs and opened the front door before the knocker went.

Lena brandished a newspaper at her. 'Here we go.'

'Come on up.' She saw the curtain of the downstairs room move slightly and knew her landlady would be checking that the visitor wasn't a man.

When they got up to her room, Stella said firmly, 'Sit down in the chair and I'll sit on the bed. I'll make you a cup of tea in a minute but first, I want to get one thing clear: if a miracle happens and I win a pound or two, I don't want anyone knowing about it.'

Lena flattened one hand across her chest. 'I'll keep your secret if you tell me what you dreamed about.'

Stella sighed. 'Oh, very well. I dreamed I'd won enough to buy myself a little cottage to live in all on my own.'

'You didn't dream about meeting a handsome hero as well?'

Her heart clenched at that but she hoped she hadn't shown it. 'Good heavens, no. I'd rather have a cat than a man, thank you very much.'

'Trust me, a man is more fun! But you're such a quiet little thing, you don't even try to attract anyone's attention. Get your coupon out and we'll go through it. My Alistair won this week, and it'll probably be about five pounds. I have a feeling it's a lucky week and you're going to win as well. Got a pencil?'

'Yes. Here you are.' She had it ready on the mantelpiece.

Muttering to herself, Lena used the newspaper to go through the football results and mark them off on the paper. Stella didn't bother watching her but sat staring into space, wishing her friend would hurry up then they could go out for a walk in the fresh air.

When Lena squealed and grabbed her by the arms, she nearly jumped out of her skin. 'Stop it, you fool. You're hurting me.'

Lena's grasp slackened but she was staring at her as if Stella had suddenly grown horns. 'You've won.'

'I don't believe it. Check again.'

'I don't make mistakes about this sort of thing.'

'Check again. Please.'

A few minutes later Lena gave her a smug look. 'I checked. Same results. Happy birthday, lucky lady.'

'How much have I won?'

'You won't know for a day or two.'

'You said Alistair had won five pounds. How could you tell?'

'I said *about* five pounds. You'll have to wait for the exact amount, but I can tell you now that you'll have won a lot more than that.'

'How much more?'

'A hundred or so.'

'Oh, dear heaven!' Stella's legs gave way and she sat down abruptly on the edge of her bed.

'We should celebrate,' Lena said.

'No! You promised you'd not tell anyone.'

'But Stella, all your friends at work will want to share such good news.'

'You're the only real friend I have. The others are just . . . workmates. All they'll want is for me to pay for a celebration and I'm not doing it.' She took a deep breath. 'I think we ought to share the win.'

'No. I bought it for you. I think it'd be wrong to take your money.'

Lena had that stubborn look on her face Stella had seen before and she knew her friend wouldn't change her mind. 'If you're sure about that?'

'I am. This is *your* piece of luck.'

'All right. But please don't tell anyone. If the local news-paper gets to know about this, they'll go ferreting around and probably find out about my husband as well.'

Lena stilled. '*You have a husband?* You never said.'

She clapped one hand to her mouth, wishing that hadn't slipped out.

'What did he do? Run away? You get such a sad look sometimes. I always want to hug you.'

'He died. In a house fire. He was a hero. Saved a child's life. Only he lost his own doing it. Our house was next door and burned down, too. I lost all our possessions.' She hadn't meant to tell her friend about any of that but once she started it all poured out.

For once Lena didn't squeal or shout, just took hold of Stella's nearest hand. 'I knew there was something sad in your life. That must have been so dreadful for you.'

Stella could only nod. 'Last week was the three-year anni-versary of my husband dying, and that's what upset me. Please don't tell anyone about this. I hate people pitying me.'

'Only Alistair. And he'll keep it a secret.'

'All right. Look, it's a lovely sunny day. Let's go out for our walk now.'

After their tour of the park, Lena went home and Stella sat down at the small table squashed in between her bed and the window. She stared outside at the row of houses across the street, thinking she should be happy. The money would make a wonderful difference to her life.

She was happy, wasn't she?

Of course she was.

A hundred pounds or so, Lena had said. It sounded like a fortune.

Only . . . she was surrounded by people struggling to make ends meet. If they knew she'd won money, they'd be pestering her to help them. And you couldn't help everyone who needed it, much as you'd like to.

Besides, she wanted to feel secure more than anything else, and if that was selfish, she couldn't help it. She would save the money because she hadn't felt secure since Derrick died, was terrified of falling ill and not being able to pay her rent.

She stared blindly out, blinking away the tears, and suddenly the world came into focus. Dark little soot-stained houses. Not much smoke in the air today because it was a Sunday, and there weren't as many mills as there used to be anyway, because some of them had gone broke and closed down.

But there were still enough mills left to dirty the air you breathed and any washing you hung out came in speckled with smuts. Suddenly she longed for the countryside. She and Derrick used to go walking on the moors sometimes. Fresh air, open spaces, birds calling in the sky above you. They'd both loved that.

And then it came to her, the best dream of all. If she had won a hundred pounds, she'd use it to move to a small town or even a village, somewhere close to the moors. She'd be careful, find a job before she moved. Working in an office was boring but she had more skills than most typists, what with shorthand and being able to understand accounts, so she should have more chance of finding employment than most women did.

But she wouldn't know what she'd won for a day or two, so for the time being she'd just carry on as usual.

Sometimes that was all you could do: carry on.

2

Wilf Pollard hesitated as he got ready for work. Enid was looking chalk white this morning and had hardly opened her mouth, though she'd got up as usual to prepare his breakfast.

'Are you feeling ill again?' He spoke hesitantly because she'd snapped at him for the slightest thing lately.

'Just a bit off colour. It'll pass.'

'You've not seemed well for a while. Maybe you should see the doctor.'

'I have done. He said to take a tonic.'

'Perhaps you should see him again?'

'And waste our money being told to rest? I've enough to worry about and will leave wasting our money to you.'

He breathed deeply and managed not to snap back at her. She was being so careful with money lately, he wasn't finding the meals satisfying and he was sure the children ought to have more to eat. 'It's not wasting money to see a doctor.'

'It is for people like us. Doctors are for rich folk who have nothing better to do than lie around in bed and coddle themselves. He says my problem is women's trouble, if you must know, and it'll pass once my monthlies stop.'

'That's what you said when you asked me to sleep in the loft so that you could get up if you needed to in the night without waking me. It's been months now and you've not got any better.' And he hadn't heard her get up very often but had heard her groaning in her sleep as if she was in pain.

Enid had changed during the hard years he'd been on the tramp looking for work anywhere he could find it, and she now kept all her feelings to herself. Sometimes he felt as if she was a stranger, not at all like the lively young woman he'd married. It didn't stop her being a good wife and mother in the sense that the house was always clean and so were their clothes. But the food wasn't plentiful and sometimes he was left hungry.

'Enid?' he prompted when she didn't reply.

'Yes, well, it helps to sleep on my own. I get very restless. The best thing you can do for me now is leave me in peace till I get past this time of life. I'll have a lie down this afternoon for an hour. That'll help more than anything. You know I can't abide people fussing over me.'

'If you're sure there's nothing I can do to help you?'

Her voice was sharp. 'You can get off to work and leave me to look after our home and children.'

Wilf shook his head as he got into his van and set off down the valley from the village of Ellindale. Enid was the most stubborn person he'd ever met, and was getting worse as she grew older.

He stopped just down the main road to pick up his helper and chatted to Ricky for the rest of the drive down the valley. With a sick mother to support, his young assistant was desperate for work, and although things were improving gradually, jobs were still scarce around here. Wilf wished he could give Ricky steady, full-time work, because the lad was a hard worker and a quick learner. But building jobs came and went.

Smiling, he drove through Rivenshaw and on to the farmland south of the town, patting the steering wheel affectionately. He'd bought this van earlier in the year and what a difference it had made to his life. He could find better building jobs now and more of them because he could travel further to get to them.

Enid had made such a fuss when he borrowed the money to buy it, but he'd proved her wrong by paying the loan from Charlie Willcox off in three months rather than six. A successful businessman like Charlie had believed in him, but his own wife hadn't.

Enid had tried to make Wilf promise never to borrow money again, but he'd refused. He wouldn't borrow money to spend on anything risky and she must trust him to know about that.

He hoped she wouldn't speak sharply to the children as she got them ready for school today. She loved them, he knew she did, and it had been her idea to adopt them when their parents died, because she and Wilf hadn't managed to get a child of their own after ten years of trying.

Maybe he should see the doctor himself and ask about Enid. No, the young doctor who'd come to the valley a few years ago had left recently, and the old doctor was stuck in his ways. There was a new doctor, but Wilf doubted she'd agree to go and see him.

Wilf forgot his domestic troubles as he worked on the stone barn he was rebuilding for Farmer Tidsworth to use for storage. It had been in a bad state, with the roof half collapsed, but the stone walls were still basically sound and able to be repaired. With a few new roof beams to replace the rotten ones that had given way under the weight of snow, most of the slates could be reused and the place made waterproof again.

Whoever had first built the barn had put in decent foundations, which folk hadn't always done in the old days. He wondered why they hadn't put in better roof beams while they were at it. Perhaps someone else had done that, someone who built shoddily like Higgerson did. Wilf scowled at the mere thought of that man. He might be the town's biggest builder, but he only put an effort into homes for his richer clients. The houses thrown up for poorer folk were very badly put together.

At midday Wilf and Ricky accepted the offer of a bowl of broth from the farmer's wife with real gratitude. It was not only tasty with chunks of meat in it, but it warmed you up nicely. And it'd save him nipping out to buy extra food to supplement what Enid had given him tonight.

When she saw the piece of dry bread, which was all Ricky produced for his meal, Mrs Tidsworth took it off him and buttered it, adding a few shreds of ham and topping it with a slice of her own bread before putting another ladleful of broth into his bowl.

Some folk could be so kind to those who were having a hard time, while others took advantage of them. This farmer and his wife were both decent folk.

When they'd finished their meal, Wilf led the way back outside into icy winds and a much damper feeling in the air. He got the sacks with tapes sewn to the corners out of the van. He'd oiled these sacks himself to make them fairly water-proof. They would put these round their shoulders if it began to rain and that'd keep the worst of the moisture off their bodies. It was no use buying fancy mackintoshes when you were doing this sort of rough work.

He sighed as he looked at the lowering sky. Long months of winter weather always seemed to loom ahead of you at this time of year, and it wasn't even the shortest day yet.

He called an end to their work earlier than he would have done in summer, for sheer lack of daylight and because the rain was setting in. When he stood up after using the last of the mortar, he eased his back and studied his work, nodding in satisfaction. Whether jobs were large or small, he still liked to get them right, and he'd sorted through the stones that had loosened or fallen out and set them into the walls neatly again to match the others nearby.

He turned to Ricky. 'You've worked hard today, lad. Well done. If you could just clear up any mess then put my tools in the van, I'll work out exactly what we'll need for tomorrow and measure up for the door frame.'

'All right, Mr Pollard.'

Wilf had heard the sound of a motor vehicle coming to the farm a short time ago but hadn't paid any attention to it, so when he turned round, he was surprised to see Roy Tyler standing a few paces away, arms folded, watching him.

'You've made a nice job of that wall, Wilf.'

'Thanks, Mr Tyler. There's no one whose opinion I value more.' He wondered what the builder was doing here. He must be a friend of Tidsworth, but if so, why had he come across the muddy yard to where they were working? Who stopped for a chat on a cold, wet day like this?

The older man nodded his appreciation of the compliment but didn't smile. He hadn't done much smiling since his only son had been killed while working on the roof of a house a year or so ago. He hadn't taken on as many new jobs, either, from what folk said, which was a pity because it left Higgerson as the biggest builder in the valley, with no real competition and no one to hold him to account for his shoddy ways.

Folks said Tyler had grown old overnight after the accident, but though his hair was grey and sadness had added new creases to his weather-beaten face, he still seemed a sturdy figure of a man to Wilf. He couldn't be more than fifty or so.

Wilf turned to Ricky, jerked his head towards the van, then waited. Tyler wasn't known for being free with words and would say what he wanted when he was ready.

'Have you time for a chat before you go home tonight, Wilf lad? About business.'

'I've always got time for you, Mr Tyler. Do you want to talk here or somewhere else?'

'How about you follow me back to my home in Birch End? It'll be warmer there. It's going to freeze tonight or I'm a Dutchman. Besides, what I have to say is private and I don't want anyone else listening in.'

'I have to drop Ricky off first, but it's on the way. He's a good worker, that lad is, if you ever have any little jobs.'

'I could see that. I'll bear him in mind from now on.'

'All right. I know where you live so I'll meet you there as soon as I can. You'd better get yourself out of the cold. Eh, I don't know when we've had a November like it.'

With a nod, Roy walked back to his van – a much bigger and newer one than Wilf's, but it looked rather neglected. The older man's shoulders were bowed as if he was carrying a heavy burden.

Hard to lose your only son, Wilf thought. His own children might be adopted, but he didn't know what he'd do if anything happened to either of them. They'd quickly become part of his life and he loved them dearly.

After he'd paid Ricky and dropped him in Ellindale, Wilf headed back down the valley towards Birch End. Roy Tyler lived in the better part of the village. It was a modest house, considering its owner was a builder, but detached with a large garden. It was pleasant to look at, especially now with lights showing at the windows against the dark sky, spilling out a welcome trail for visitors to walk along.

Roy opened the door before Wilf got there, hung his visitor's coat on the hallstand and took him into the front room to one side.

Wilf stopped just inside the door and looked down at his clothes. 'Nay, I'm still mucky from work, Mr Tyler. I can't sit on those nice chairs of yours.'

'I'll ask the missus for an old sheet to put over one of them. I don't want us to be disturbed. If we sat in the kitchen we'd be in Ethel's way, not to mention getting interrupted by neighbours coming to the kitchen door. She's friends with everyone around here, my lass is.'

He left the room and came back with a paint-stained dust sheet, followed by his wife with a tray containing a platter of small cakes and two big mugs of steaming tea.

She nodded to Wilf. 'Nice to see you, lad. I've got one of your carved animals sitting on my kitchen windowsill. A squirrel it is. You've a rare talent there.' She put the tray down and left Wilf with cheeks warm from embarrassment. He never knew what to say to compliments about his hobby of wood carving.

Roy flung the sheet over a chair and passed Wilf one of the mugs. 'Help yourself to sugar and put a cake or two on your plate.'

He then sat staring into the fire, hands cradling his mug, and once again Wilf waited for him to speak. The delay and the serious expression on his companion's face only made him more curious.

After a couple of minutes Roy sighed and looked across at him. 'Well, I'll come straight to the point. Now that our Trevor's dead, I'm trying to work out what to do about the business, him being our only child and all the cousins being girls. It was Charlie Willcox who thought of me taking on a partner and teaching him what I'd have taught my son. He suggested you.'

Wilf could only gape at him.

'I didn't rush into anything. I asked about you and had a look at what you'd worked on. Charlie was right. You're an excellent workman, meticulous. I couldn't have done those jobs better myself.'

'Oh. Well, thank you.'

'My wife saw that studio you built for Charlie Willcox's wife, so she asked Marion about you as well. And Marion could only say good things, not just about your work but about your ideas for designing her studio.'

Wilf didn't know what to say to that. Compliments always flustered him.

'So, my Ethel and I looked into what was involved in making someone a junior partner and that's what I'm offering you, a junior partnership. Would you be interested in coming to work with us?'

'I'd love to work with you, Mr Tyler, absolutely love it, but don't partners buy into businesses? I don't have any money to do that with. And I'm not a trained builder, just good with my hands.'

'I'd say you're *very* good with your hands and have a rare instinct for putting the pieces of a building together in your head. I always feel building is like doing jigsaw puzzles in three dimensions. Not many people can do that, you know. I believe, and so did my father before me, that you're either born with the skill or not.'

He leaned forward to pat Wilf's arm. 'And Charlie is a shrewd fellow. I trust his judgement. If *he* vouches for you, you're all right.'

'Oh. Well, thank you for your kind words.'

'If your family had been able to afford it, you should have been apprenticed to a carpenter or to any trade in the building industry. You still seem to have picked up a lot of skills and you're able to do the basic work in most trades, not just the one. I always say there's no keeping a good man down.'

Wilf didn't often get such glowing compliments, and for these to come from a man he admired greatly made them even more precious.

'How did you learn so much, lad?'

'I took on all sorts of odd jobs when I was on the tramp

and I learned whichever way I could. I don't do electrics, mind, though I understand a fair bit about that side of things.'

'It's just as important to know what you can't do as what you can. If it wasn't for the money, would you like to be my partner, Wilf?'

'Of course I would. But I've not got much saved, Mr Tyler, only enough to see my family over a bad patch.'

'Well, I don't want money from you. What use is money to me now that I've no one to leave it to? No, what I want from you is, well . . .' It was his turn to pause and look embarrassed. 'Best way I can say it is that I want the chance to pass on my skills and leave some worthwhile buildings behind when I die. I'd like to put up a few more good ones that'll outlast you and me, not rubbish like that Higgerson's rat-holes in Backshaw Moss. Does that make sense to you?'

Wilf nodded. 'Aye. You want to leave the world a better place because you've been here.'

'Exactly. So what I want to do is *give* you a minor share in my building company and the first chance to buy a bigger share of it later. If you show promise at *running* a business, I'll arrange for more of it to come to you without payment. Me and Ethel have talked about it, worked it all out. She's got a rare clever brain, my lass has.'

Wilf couldn't believe what he was hearing. '*Give me?* You'd give me a partnership?'

'Yes. But we'll do it legally, mind. Charlie Willcox is buying in as a sleeping partner at the same time, because I've let things run down financially more than I like, but I'd be obliged if you'd keep that to yourself.'

'Of course I will.' Wilf struggled to find words to express his delight. 'Eh, I don't know what to say, Mr Tyler. I've never had such a gift offered to me, not in my whole life.'

That drew a slow smile from his companion. 'Just say thank you very much and come with me to my lawyer tomorrow afternoon to sort it all out. He's prepared the papers already.'

'You were that sure I'd agree?'

'I'm that sure you're not stupid. And Charlie agreed with me.'

Wilf drew in a long, slow breath, fighting for control of his voice and his thoughts. 'Does Mrs Tyler really approve of this?'

'Oh, yes. It was partly her idea and I never do anything major without discussing it with her. She runs the office side of my business, always has done. She's not one for sitting at home and fiddling around with embroidery.' He waited, then prompted gently, 'Well? You haven't actually said yes.'

Wilf was hard put not to cry for sheer joy. 'Yes please. Eh, I can't get over it. No one has ever given me anything so wonderful, Mr Tyler. Not just the money side, but the chance to learn more and do things that matter. People's homes are so important to them.'

The older man reached across to offer his hand and as they shook on the bargain, he kept Wilf's hand in his for longer than usual, patting it with his free hand.

Eventually, he let go and said quietly, 'That's settled and I'm very pleased. You'd better call me Roy from now on.'

'Thank you, Roy.'

When he went back to his van, Wilf sat there for a few moments in the darkness, trying to come to terms with his new role in life. Sometimes good news could be harder to take in than bad, because it was harder to believe in. Eventually he realised how cold he was and set off back home.

As he passed Mrs Morton's house, which was the end one in Croft Street, just before the lane that connected Birch End with the main road, his headlights shone on her as she opened her front gate. The street lights were on by now and she recognised his van so turned to wave.

Not wanting to seem rude, he stopped and leaned across to wind down the window of the passenger seat and call a greeting. 'How are things, Mrs Morton?'

'Fine, thanks. Would you have time for a cup of tea, Wilf?'

He heard the hope in her voice, knew how lonely she was, so said yes. Half an hour wouldn't make much difference and he could maybe ask her advice about Enid.

'I'd love one!' he yelled, wound up the window and parked his van near her gate.

She asked her maid to bring them some tea, gestured to him to hang up his overcoat and cap, and took him into the small parlour she usually sat in, where a cheerful fire was burning.

Once again he had to ask for something to sit on.

'Just a minute and I'll fetch a dust cover from the kitchen.' Mrs Morton was back in a couple of minutes.

He sat down, as he had several times before when doing jobs for her. 'Been out visiting, have you, Mrs Morton?'

'Oh, just an old chap who's sick in Backshaw Moss.'

'You shouldn't be going there. It's getting worse every year, that slum is. The council ought to knock it down, they really ought.'

'I agree, but I can't desert Ben. He used to work for my father so I took him something for his tea and a loaf to keep him going tomorrow. What are you doing in Birch End at this time of day, Wilf? I thought you'd have been home from work by now. It's been dark for a while.'

'I've been visiting Mr Tyler.' He paused. Should he tell her or not? But he couldn't keep his news to himself and after asking her not to mention it to anyone until he'd had time to tell his wife, it all came out in a happy rush of words.

The maid interrupted them with the tea before he'd finished and he stopped talking till she'd gone. Luckily, he could always fit in another cup of tea.

When he'd told her everything, Mrs Morton clapped her hands. 'Oh, Wilf, my dear boy, I'm so *pleased* for you! It couldn't happen to a nicer chap. And if Mr Willcox is involved things will go well. He's such a clever man. Your Enid will be thrilled when you tell her, I'm sure.'

'Eh, well, I'm a lucky chap, that's for sure. I'm still finding it all hard to believe.'

'It's not luck that this has happened, Wilf. I know how hard you work and yet you still find time to help others, not to mention cheering up lonely old ladies like me. You well deserve what Mr Tyler's offering and he'll be the lucky one to get you as a partner.'

She patted a lace handkerchief to her eyes, shedding the tears of joy that men weren't supposed to give way to, though Wilf felt very close to it today.

Then he remembered Enid and told Mrs Morton about his worries.

Her smile vanished. 'I was going to ask you about her because I saw her in town the other day and was shocked. She's lost a lot of weight lately, hasn't she?'

He could only nod because he didn't know what to say.

'You should take her to see the new doctor.'

'Do you know what he's like?'

'Folk speak well of him. He's Scottish and is rather blunt, but apparently he hasn't turned anyone away, even if they can't pay, *and* he's started a free surgery twice a week for those in need. So he must have a good heart.'

'That's good to hear.'

'Get Enid to go and see him. Old Dr Mitchell's never been any good with women's troubles. He always treats me like an idiot child, even though I'm older than him. If I ever need a doctor, I'll go to the new one.'

'I'll try to get her to see him, but she's a rare stubborn woman and she's got it into her head that it's "women's troubles" and she just has to put up with it until it passes.'

'If you can't get her to go and seek proper help, maybe I can. I'll call and see her tomorrow, if you like.'

He nodded, but he doubted she'd be able to change Enid's mind.

When he looked at the clock, he was shocked at how quickly half an hour had passed in such pleasant company. 'I'd better get going now, Mrs Morton. I'm looking forward to telling my wife about Mr Tyler's offer. That news will cheer her up if anything will.'

3

The following Wednesday, Stella could see Lena looking at her with a strange expression on her face, but as they were at work, she couldn't ask what the matter was. At lunch time Lena waited for Stella outside the cloakroom.

'Get your coat and come with me. We'll go and sit in the park to eat our lunch.'

'It's freezing cold outside.'

Lena looked at another woman who was standing openly listening to them and said in a low voice, 'Just do what I say! This is important.'

Stella got her lunch and followed her friend outside, shivering as the cold air hit her.

The park was only a couple of minutes away and when they got there, Lena sat down on the most sheltered bench they could find. She didn't even attempt to open her packet of sandwiches and as soon as Stella was seated, said, 'The payment details are out for the football pools. You didn't give them a phone number, so they couldn't let you know directly, but they'll write to you, I suppose.'

She hesitated and took a deep breath. 'You won't want anyone at work to find out, but how I kept it to myself this morning, I don't know.'

'How much have I won?'

Lena swallowed. 'Nine hundred and fifty-eight pounds.'

The world seemed to blur around them and Stella found

it hard to breathe let alone say anything for a moment or two, then asked in a whisper, 'Are you sure?'

'Yes. My Alistair nipped out to buy a paper early this morning so he could check for his payment, because he's won something too. But six pounds ten is nothing compared to over nine hundred pounds, is it?'

'I can't believe it.'

'I'm really glad for you, love.'

Stella could only shake her head, then say, 'It's a shock, even if it is good news. You won't tell anyone, will you?'

'I didn't tick the box that says to keep your name secret, I was in such a hurry. I'm sorry, love, but your name will be in all the papers tomorrow in the list of winners.'

Stella's heart sank. 'Isn't there any way of stopping them from doing that?'

'Not that I know of.' Lena took out a sandwich and had a big bite. After she'd swallowed that mouthful, she added, 'You'd better go to the newsagent after work and show them your coupon, so that you can register as a winner.'

'Right. Yes.'

Stella couldn't eat a thing. She felt numb with shock.

It seemed a long time till the working day ended and she had to wait in line at the newsagent's. To her relief, Mrs Ball was busy and barely looked at her coupon, just ticked her name off on a list and signed the coupon.

Stella was ravenously hungry now, so bought fish and chips from the shop two streets away and hurried home before her food got cold. But she didn't really taste her meal and kept stopping to think about how much she'd won. She felt faintly surprised when she found her plate empty.

What was she going to do tomorrow? The people at work would find out and expect her to have a celebration, only she wasn't going to buy cakes for the whole laundry. There were too many people working there and she'd never even spoken to some of them. She didn't have much to do with the other typists, either, except for Lena.

As for the money itself, the only thing she was certain of was that she wasn't going to do anything silly with it. She'd put it in her savings bank account while she worked out what was best. And she'd try again to persuade Lena to accept a share.

When she went into work the next day, her heart sank because everyone she passed turned to stare at her.

The people in the office chorused 'Congratulations!' as she walked in.

Mavis in the corner called, 'How does it feel to be rich?'

'I'm not rich.'

'Nearly a thousand pounds seems rich to me,' one woman said.

'I haven't got used to the idea of it yet and anyway, I won't get the money for a few days.'

'I'd give up work straight away if I'd won that much,' another woman said.

The young office girl sighed loudly. 'I would too an' then I'd go to the pictures every single day, dressed in my best.'

'What *are* you going to do to celebrate, Stella?' Mavis asked.

'Nothing.'

They all gaped at her.

'You're not going to do *anything*?'

'No. I'll probably save the money for my old age.' She took the cover off her typewriter and got ready to start work.

She could feel their disappointment at her response hovering like a dark cloud in the room. They wanted to live vicariously through her, she knew, wanted to share her excitement. Only she was still half numb and trying to come to terms with it all.

When she looked up, Lena winked at her from across the

room, then Miss Marlow came in and the usual noise of typewriters started up. She'd not miss the constant tapping sound, Stella realised, not at all.

The supervisor came to stand beside her desk and said sourly, 'The work still needs doing, you know.'

Lena stuck her tongue out at Miss Marlow from across the room and Stella was hard put not to laugh.

During the day she overheard various comments when the supervisor was out of the office, some of them intended to be heard.

'She's not even going to celebrate her win.'

'Can you believe it? All that money and she's just going to put it in the bank.'

'Mean, I call that,' another girl said. 'She could at least have bought a cake.'

At one stage Lena said loudly, 'Will you lot stop going on about it. This is her money, so it's her choice what she does with it. Mind your own business.'

The supervisor came back just then and there were no more comments for a while.

But there were lots more remarks tossed around as everyone got their coats and left for home at the end of the day.

Stella walked slowly back home on her own because Lena had gone to the shops. What a horrible day this had been! How long would it take for the fuss and jealousy to die down? She hated to be the centre of attention. If they continued to treat her differently, she'd have to move away. She couldn't live like this. One day of it had upset her.

Inevitably her thoughts turned again to the idea of finding a job in a country town, away from the smoke and crowded streets, somewhere she wouldn't have to live so close to other people.

That might actually be possible now. If she could find a job. And she'd have enough money to buy a little house.

Her breath caught in her throat. Could she do it? Find a new home and way of life?

And was she brave enough to do it on her own?

When she got home the next day she found a letter waiting for her: the cheque. And only then did she admit to herself that she was definitely going to buy a cottage in the country and live in more peaceful surroundings.

She nipped out to the corner shop and bought the big box of chocolates that stood on the top shelf. From time to time someone bought it to celebrate a special birthday or a win on the horses, and it got replaced. But the shopkeeper couldn't afford to stock more than one, so you had no choice.

When she took it around to Lena's house as a thank you, she refused to go in for a chat because she knew her friend was in the middle of preparing tea, and afterwards Alistair liked to spend his evenings quietly reading his newspaper.

Lena gave her a hug. 'Thanks for these. They're my favourites. I'll see you at the weekend.'

Stella woke in the middle of the night after a lovely dream that had given her an idea. She could buy herself a little car, nothing expensive, not a new one, a little Austin perhaps or a Morris. She'd have to get help with that. She had a vague idea that it'd cost about thirty or forty pounds for a second-hand vehicle, from what she'd seen advertised in the newspapers.

It would make life so much easier and more pleasant. She'd always fancied learning to drive, but as they didn't own a car neither she nor her husband had bothered to try. Even if they'd had a car, Derrick didn't think women made safe drivers. She'd not argued when he said that because what did it matter? People like them could rarely afford cars. She always saved her disagreements for things that mattered and mostly got her own way then.

Now . . . well, Derrick wasn't here any longer and she

didn't see why she wouldn't be able to drive as well as a man. She had two eyes, two hands, two feet, just like they did.

It was as if a genie had escaped from a bottle and she didn't get any more sleep that night. The money and the independence that came with it seemed to have brought something in her to life again. For the last three years she'd been marking time. Now, she was going to do something different and live a more interesting life, if she could.

The next day she asked if she could take an early dinner break, explaining to the supervisor about the need to put her winner's cheque in the bank.

Miss Marlow stared at her. 'You're carrying it around with you? Oh, my goodness! I shan't feel safe with that in the office. Go and put it in the bank straight away. You're never late, never take time off, so it's not as if you ever take advantage as others sometimes do. Go on! Get it done now!'

At the bank, the manager himself came out to congratulate her. He'd never so much as spoken to her before.

'If you need advice about what to do with your money, that's what banks are for, my dear lady.'

'Thank you. But I'm going to have a good long think before I do anything. I will take out twenty pounds now, though.'

'Very wise. And in the meantime, we'll keep your money safe.'

That evening she was so worried about carrying twenty pounds with her to the library, which she was going to visit on her way home from work, she stuffed it into the top of her knickers. She had trouble finding books that interested her and was later leaving than usual, so took a shortcut home.

Suddenly, two men came at her. One knocked her down and the other tore her handbag away from her. She tried to scream for help, but one put his hand across her mouth.

There was enough light from a nearby house to see the

other fumbling in the bag and bringing out her purse. He opened it and said, 'The bitch has only got a couple of shillings. They said she'd won a lot of money.'

The grasp on her slackened and she managed to roll out of the way, yelling for help as loudly as she could.

One man tried to kick her feet from under her but missed, and the other threw the handbag at her head, keeping her purse. A man came running out of the nearest house, followed by a screeching woman brandishing a rolling pin. He chased her attackers, but only enough to send them on their way. He didn't really try to catch them.

The woman stayed with Stella and when her husband came puffing back, they took her into their house and sent their son for the police.

Stella couldn't stop shaking at first, but a police constable arrived and she managed to pull herself together. She gave him her particulars and details of the attack.

'Oh, you're the lady who won all that money!' he said at once. 'Well, you'd better not walk about on your own at night from now on.'

'But I don't carry that money around with me.' She wasn't going to tell anyone where she'd had it hidden, it would be so embarrassing. The main thing was, it was still safe.

'They won't know that, will they? I'll walk home with you now and mind you take care where you go after dark.'

All that trouble for two shillings and the cost of a new purse, she thought as she lay sleepless in bed.

That settled it. She was definitely going to move away, and sooner rather than later. And when she settled somewhere else, she'd not tell anyone about the money.

The next day, she and Lena went out to get a breath of fresh air at their midday break. As usual, they wound up in the small park.

Stella pulled the envelope out of her handbag. 'This is for you.'

Lena started to look stubborn.

'It's only twenty pounds. Please take it.'

For a moment all hung in the balance then her friend took the envelope. 'I didn't need paying.'

'It's a present from a friend, that's all. Because you've made my dream come true.'

She explained what she was intending to do and Lena gave her a big hug.

'I'm so glad for you, love. After losing your husband like that you deserve some luck. But you'll write to me, won't you?'

'Yes. But not till I'm settled.'

Lena stuffed the envelope down the front of her dress, winking at Stella. 'Can't be too careful, can you?'

Stella felt better about the money, then.

During the next two weeks, Stella grew more and more frustrated. She went to the library after work every day and checked the jobs advertised in the *Manchester Guardian*, taking care to stay on the main road. But there was nothing that seemed any better than what she was doing now, let alone a job in the country that might suit her long-term plans.

She didn't intend to find herself another boring job because she felt as if her mind was starting to wake up after a long sleep. She began to wonder about buying a business instead of a cottage. Only, she didn't want to run a lodging house or split up her home into rooms like the one she lived in currently. And shopkeepers worked long hours on their feet. Mrs Ball had terrible varicose veins.

No, Stella still wanted a peaceful life, and a home to which she could retreat after work and enjoy her own company, maybe with a cat or dog.

The idea of owning a car and learning to drive had really taken hold, though, and she'd begun to gather information about that already, because it stood to reason it was no use buying a car if you didn't know how to drive it.

She bought a copy of the Highway Code first. It cost only a penny, and she read its eighteen pages several times till she knew all the rules by heart. Next, she paid for a driving licence, which cost five shillings. It amused her when the clerk at the post office told her you had to sign it with your usual signature or you could be fined up to five pounds. What other signature did he think she had?

She also found out that the government was going to introduce a compulsory driving test next year for those wishing to drive vehicles. From March 1935 you'd be able to take a driving test voluntarily to get your certificate, and from the first of June it would be compulsory to take a test before being allowed to drive a car on your own. That seemed a good idea to her.

Even though she wouldn't need to take a driving test this year, she wasn't going to start driving until she'd had a few lessons and felt she knew what all the levers and knobs in a car were for. At the moment, she'd ridden in private cars so rarely she only had a vague idea of what to do in order to make a vehicle move around.

Finding out about all this gave her something to do in the evenings.

Her next step, she decided, would be to learn more about cars. She'd started looking at those that passed her in the street and wondering which would be a good one to buy. Goodness, where did you learn about that sort of thing? No one she knew round here even owned a motor car.

One evening after work, she went to the library to change her books and found a small local paper lying on a chair. It was from Rivenshaw, a town she knew slightly from occasional walks in the Pennines with Derrick. The paper must have been left there by someone using the reading tables, because it was rather untidily folded and didn't have the library stamp marking it.

She asked the librarian if she could take the paper home, thinking she might use the information in it to place an advert seeking employment in the area.

The librarian had pulled a face as if about to refuse when Stella surprised herself with a glib lie. 'I'm trying to find a job near Rivenshaw, you see, because I have an elderly relative living there and I want to be nearby in case she needs help.'

'Oh well, it's not one of our usual papers, someone must have left it. And it's quite crumpled now as well, being three days old, so I wouldn't like to see it on my newspaper shelves. Why not?'

Stella walked home with two new books to read and the paper folded carefully under them in her shopping basket. She didn't take any shortcuts and she kept her eyes open in case anyone was following her.

She decided to do a boiled egg and toast for tea, with an apple to follow. Easy to prepare, easy to clear up afterwards.

The occupant of the room next to hers had left her dirty cooking things in the sink – again! So Stella piled them up and left them on the floor in a corner while she used the gas ring to boil her egg and the grill under it to make her toast. She smiled as she bent to watch the piece of bread turn brown. Who knew she had it in her to tell lies like that?

As soon as the food was ready, she collected her cooking things and went back into her room to eat the meal. It was raining outside, so she drew the curtains and settled down afterwards to read the newspaper in her armchair.

Unfortunately it was missing its middle double page but the adverts and notices were still there near the back, so she looked down the 'Jobs Vacant' column to see what sort of work they were advertising. Then she gasped as she started checking the second column.

One advert jumped out at her immediately. *Secretary wanted by doctor. Must be able to do accounts as well as all the usual office jobs, and be eager to learn new skills.*

She pressed one hand to her mouth. That sounded so interesting. Oh, please, let her get a job like that, which would take her away from the boring work typing invoices and entering small shillings and pennies amounts into neat columns in the ledgers.

She knew the newspaper was three days old, but she wasn't giving up. Surely, if she sent away a letter immediately, she'd stand a chance of being considered?

She ought to type the letter, because that'd look more professional, but she didn't own a typewriter. She didn't dare ask to use one at work, either, because they'd want to know why and she might lose her job if they thought she was trying to leave.

Then she remembered a postcard in the window of the newsagent's where you could put things for sale for twopence a week. It had said someone would type letters for a small fee. She peered out of the window at the street. Yes, the shop light was on, so Mrs Ball must still be open.

Heedless of the weather and the possible danger of being attacked again, she put on her mackintosh without buttoning it, pulled up the hood and hurried across the street, clutching her notebook.

When she went inside she bought some fruit gums, knowing Mrs Ball didn't like people coming in without buying something.

'There's a card in your window offering typing. I'd like to contact the person doing that. I need some typing doing urgently, tonight if possible.'

Mrs Ball brightened. 'That's my daughter-in-law's card. She had to give up her job when she got married but she still brings in money by doing typing at home.' She looked up at the clock. 'I was just about to close, so I'll take you round to her house now. She's always glad to earn a bit extra and she does lovely work.'

Amy Ball was indeed pleased at the prospect of paid work. She left her mother-in-law telling her little grandson a bedtime story and took Stella into the front room, where she had a table set up with a typewriter on it.

'I need a letter of application for a job – and I don't want anyone to know about it or I might lose the job I have at present.'

Amy gave her a very direct look. 'You can trust me, Mrs Newby. I never talk about my clients' private affairs.'

'I can dictate the letter now if you've time. I've lain awake a few nights thinking about how I would apply for a job and making notes.' She got out her little notebook. People laughed at her for carrying it around in her handbag, but it often came in useful, and so did her lists.

'I can ask my mother-in-law to stay and look after my son. I'd have to charge you five shillings to do a job like this. I'm sorry, but only a payment to her as well will ensure she keeps quiet about it. I'll throw in an envelope free. You'll need a bigger one than usual. And I can put the carbon copies I make for you in a used envelope to keep them dry. I never waste a thing that comes into the house.'

'Thank you. I'm happy to pay what you ask. This is really important.'

An hour later, they went back into the kitchen where they found Mrs Ball, who had put her grandson to bed and was sitting listening to the radio with her son.

'I'd appreciate it if you escorted me home via the post box so I can catch the last evening collection, Mr Ball,' Stella said. 'I'll add a shilling to your wife's payment if you do that. I was attacked a few nights ago because people had heard about me winning some money and thought I'd carry it round with me. I'm not that stupid.'

'Mrs Newby is paying me extra for us all to keep it secret.' Amy gave her mother-in-law a stern look. 'And I said of course we will. If any of you tell about that, I'll have to give her the payment back. Thanks for your help tonight with Tommy, Ma.'

Her husband stood up, smiling. 'That's fine by me, Mrs Newby. I can take Ma home at the same time.'

Stella walked through the streets with Mrs Ball and her son in silence. Once she'd posted the letter, she sighed in relief, feeling even more relieved when she reached home safely. She nodded goodbye to her two escorts and hurried inside.

The only thing she could do now was wait – and apply for any other jobs that were advertised. But oh, this one sounded so much more interesting than any other job she'd ever seen in the papers.

She hadn't let herself dream of a proper home of her own when there seemed no hope of getting one with women not getting paid as much as men. She didn't expect to remarry. She was only thirty, but there was still a shortage of eligible men because most men were married by that age, and those who needed a second wife seemed to go for the younger and prettier women. She might not be able to have the children she'd longed for, but she'd at least be able to buy a home of her own and look forward to a pleasant, comfortable life.

If she'd had a brother or sister, she might have had nieces and nephews to spoil, but she was an only child and her relatives didn't seem to produce large families, so she'd be on her own.

Just be thankful for what you have got, she told herself firmly. And she was, definitely. She'd been very lucky indeed.

4

Wilf stretched wearily as he went through the front door of their small house and along the narrow hall. He'd intended to go straight into the scullery to have a wash and change out of his work clothes. But though someone had switched on the light, there was no one in the kitchen and the fire was almost out.

He stopped in surprise and called out, 'Enid! Are you there?'

Hearing feet pattering down the stairs, he turned round to see the children run in, looking upset.

Peggy reached him first, tugging at his hand. 'Dad! Come quick. Mum's asleep an' she won't wake up, even though her eyes are open.'

Startled, he pushed past them and ran up the stairs into the front bedroom, which only Enid was using now.

She was lying on the bed, eyes staring sightlessly at the ceiling, one arm trailing over the edge. He stopped in shock. He'd seen death too many times not to recognise it now. 'Ah, Enid, no!'

How could this have happened?

For a few moments he stood frozen in the doorway, too shocked to move, then he went across to check the pulse in her throat, just to be sure.

Behind him Peggy said in a wobbly voice, 'Dad?' She was looking up at him and what she saw made her press both hands against her mouth.

When he didn't reply, she whispered, 'Mum's dead, isn't she?' as if afraid to say the words too loudly.

He looked at her for a moment, also finding it hard to say the words. *She knew*, he thought. Young as she was, only just turned seven, Peggy had had a hard life before coming to live with them and had probably seen death a few times. No use trying to pretend about this.

'Yes. I'm afraid that your mother *is* dead. There's nothing we can do to help her now.'

'She was like this when we got home from school. I didn't know what to do.'

He turned the child round, keeping his hand on her shoulder as he moved with her to the bedroom door. Ronnie was waiting there, peeping in at them, his eyes big and fearful, his thumb in his mouth.

'Look, it'll be a big help to me if you two go next door and fetch Mrs Harper. Tell her why I need her, Peggy. When you come back, send her upstairs but you and your brother wait for me in the kitchen. You can put some more coal on the fire, but be careful.'

He caressed her cheek briefly and she nodded, then took her little brother's hand.

After watching them go downstairs Wilf went back to bend over the bed and feel Enid's forehead. Her skin was already cooling, so this couldn't only just have happened.

A couple of minutes later footsteps came pounding up the stairs and Mrs Harper burst into the room. 'Your Peggy says – oh no, it's true!'

He could only manage a gruff 'Yes'.

She came to stand beside him, squeezing his shoulder with one hand.

He reached up to hold on to that warm, work-worn hand for a moment, appreciating the unspoken comfort.

Her voice was gentle. 'Do you know what happened?'

'No. The children found her like this when they came home from school. She's not been well for a while, but she said it was just, you know, women's problems.'

She went across to close Enid's eyes gently. 'You never know when it's your time, do you?' She stood looking down for a few moments, then said more briskly, 'There's nothing more you can do for her now, Wilf lad. Your job is to look after the children. Go next door and send my Vic to the shop to phone for the doctor. He'll have to see her.'

'We have our own phone here for my business.' Another thing Enid had protested about, though it had more than paid for itself.

'Eh, I keep forgetting. You phone him. Call the new Scottish chap who's took over from Dr Blain. He's more likely to come quickly than Dr Mitchell will be. It's the same phone number as Dr Blain had.'

As Wilf got to the foot of the stairs, the two children ran out of the kitchen to cling to him.

'I told Ronnie that Mam's dead, but he just keeps crying for her,' Peggy said. 'He's too little to remember, but I seen it before. They stare an' stare but they don't move.'

She waited and when he didn't say anything, asked, 'Will me an' Ronnie have to go into the orphanage now?'

This was something he hadn't expected. He didn't have to think about his answer, though, not for one second. He knelt and put his arms around them both. They were more important than the phone call. 'No, of course you won't, Peggy love. This is your home and that hasn't changed. I'm still here and I'm still your father. Eh, what would I do without you two?'

She flung her arms around his waist at one side and Ronnie held on to him at the other side. 'I don't want to leave you, Dad. I'll be good as gold, I promise. An' so will Ronnie. Won't you?'

The little boy nodded vigorously. 'Don't send us away, Dad.'

'I'd never do that. Never, ever.' Wilf waited a moment or two, letting them hold on to him, drawing comfort himself from holding them. Then he bent to kiss them both. 'I have to phone the doctor now. You can come and stand near me in the front room as I do it, but you have to keep quiet.'

They both nodded and did that, but Ronnie had his thumb in his mouth again, something he'd grown out of, and was clutching his big sister with the other hand. Eh, what a little mother she was, such a dear brave child.

The new doctor answered the phone himself and Wilf explained what had happened.

'Give me your address and tell me how to get there, Mr Pollard. Don't move the body. I need to see how you found her. I'll be there as soon as I can.'

'Thank you.' As he put the phone down, Wilf again put an arm round each child and walked with them back into the kitchen, taking them across to sit at the table. 'I want you to wait for me here. I've got to tell Mrs Harper what the doctor said.'

Upstairs his neighbour was standing by the bed, dabbing her eyes. She turned to him.

'The doctor said not to move her.'

'I haven't done. I know about that.'

'He's coming straight away but I reckon it'll take him about twenty minutes to drive up here from Rivenshaw. I forgot to ask his name. Do you know what he's called, Mrs Harper?'

'Dr McDevitt. He's Scottish and very blunt spoken but he's all right, doesn't look down his nose at you.'

He shivered, suddenly feeling chilled. 'I'd better go down and make sure the fire's all right.'

'I'll see to the fire and keep an eye on the children, Wilf.

You stay with Enid and say your goodbyes before all the fuss starts.'

Before he could reply, she'd gone clumping down the stairs and he was left staring down at his wife's body. She didn't look like Enid any more. She looked like a poor waxwork copy of his wife, without all the life and determination in her eyes.

Guilt speared through him. He wished desperately that they hadn't quarrelled so much in the past few months. 'Eh, my poor lass. How brave you were.'

He felt even more guilty that he wouldn't miss Enid's company these days, because they'd been living fairly separate lives – well, as separate as you could be in such a small house.

How was he going to manage the house and children without her now, though? He'd heard other men who'd lost wives worry about that, seen them re-marry quickly out of sheer need for someone to run their homes. Only he wasn't going to do that. Living with someone you disagreed with was not a good thing.

He suddenly realised that he'd have more money coming in if he was a partner with Roy Tyler, so perhaps he'd be able to afford to hire a housekeeper. Then he felt even more guilty about thinking of that at such a time.

The only thing he knew for certain was that those children weren't going into the orphanage. He hadn't realised Peggy still worried about that. He'd have thought her too young to remember many details of her previous life, like what a dead person looked like.

Apparently not.

He didn't go downstairs. It seemed wrong to leave Enid on her own and he could hear Mrs Harper speaking gently to the children and making up the fire.

Anyway, he needed a quiet minute or two to try to get used to this.

★

It seemed a long time before Wilf heard a car stop outside. When someone knocked at the front door, he let his neighbour answer it.

'Mr Pollard is upstairs, doctor, with his wife. I'm Mrs Harper from next door, keeping an eye on the children for him.'

Wilf went to stand at the top of the stairs and was surprised when the doctor shook his hand, saying with a slight Scottish accent, 'I'm McDevitt. Sorry to meet you at a sad time like this, Mr Pollard.'

'Thank you for coming so quickly.' Wilf indicated the bedroom. 'She's in there. I think she must have gone for a lie-down and . . . it just happened. She hasn't been feeling well for quite a while.'

The doctor went into the bedroom. 'Do you want to wait outside while I examine her?'

'No. I'd rather stay with you in case you have questions to ask. I won't get in your way.'

He watched the doctor examine Enid, lifting her clothes gently in a way that showed respect.

He was a strange-looking chap, not young, but not old either. He was short, scrawny and starting to go bald, with gold-rimmed spectacles hanging from a chain round his neck when he wasn't using them for close work. His clothes were shabby but clean, his instruments and medical bag were clean and shiny, looking well cared for.

'How long has she had this growth, Mr Pollard?'

'Growth? What growth?'

The doctor looked surprised. 'She didn't tell you? You can't have been having marital relations with her or you'd have noticed it.' He indicated Enid's swollen stomach.

'All she told me was that she was going through the change, that it was women's problems and she'd be better sleeping on her own for a while.'

'She must have been in a lot of pain. Had she not seen a doctor about it?'

'She said she'd seen Dr Mitchell and he'd told her to rest more and take a tonic until she was past the change.'

'Ah.' He didn't comment but his expression was angry.

'I suggested to her only this morning she should come and see you, because the old doctor doesn't always, er, take much care of his poorer patients.'

Dr McDevitt didn't comment but he didn't look surprised at this.

Wilf shook his head, baffled. 'She kept saying she'd be all right, only needed time to get better.'

'No doctor could have failed to see what the problem really was, so she might not have seen anyone or she might not have told you what he really said.'

'I don't think she went back to see him again. We've had some hard years and she didn't like to spend money on doctors or anything else she could do without, even though things are much better for us now.'

'She must have been in great pain at times.'

'Would it have made a difference if she'd gone to see him?'

'To her dying from it? No. These growths are hard to treat. But he could have prescribed something for the pain.'

Wilf went across to take his wife's hand and pat it. 'Eh, lass. Why didn't you *tell* me?'

But of course she couldn't answer that now, so he'd never know whether she'd really understood what was wrong with her.

He looked across her at the doctor. 'She could be very stubborn when she fixed her mind on something.'

'What about your children? What's going to happen to them now?'

'I'll look after them, of course. They're adopted but I'm not giving them up! They're mine now and I love them dearly.'

The doctor's expression softened. 'Good man. I'll get Dr Mitchell to come and confirm my diagnosis, then write you a death certificate. It's so obvious what killed her, I don't see the need for a post-mortem and inquest.'

'Can you do that?'

'Yes. Now, where's the nearest phone? I'll call him now.'

'There's a phone here in the house. I use it for my business.'

'Well, that will make things easier for you, at least.'

'It's in the front room. I'll show you.'

Wilf left the doctor to make the phone call and went into the kitchen. 'He's asking Dr Mitchell to come and see her. Can you take the children back to your house and give them some tea, Mrs Harper, while we deal with . . . with all this?'

When she nodded, he gave her a half crown piece, knowing it was more than would be needed to buy extra food but hoping it'd buy her ongoing help. 'Here. Keep the change.'

Her face brightened and she nodded. 'Your Enid didn't encourage neighbours popping in, so the children don't know me very well, but I'll look after them for you an' they can sleep at my house, if you like. My children have all left home now, so we've got a spare bed.'

He smiled at the children who were looking from one adult to the other rather anxiously. 'No. Thanks for offering but I'd rather they slept here. It's still their home.'

He looked across to the door as Dr McDevitt came back from making the phone call.

'Dr Mitchell is coming straight away. Says he has a dinner party to attend tonight so we'll need to be quick.'

'Thank you.' Wilf turned to the children. 'You two go with Mrs Harper for now, but you'll be coming home later to sleep in your own beds.'

'Promise?' Peggy asked.

'I promise faithfully.' He made the cross-your-heart sign and that seemed to reassure her and Ronnie.

The two of them were still holding hands, clinging to one another as they always did if they were upset about anything. 'No one's going to take you away from me,' he repeated. 'You're mine now, I'm your father and this is your home.'

When they'd gone the doctor said, 'Good man. Those children will need you.'

'I'll need them, too.'

'They can be a big comfort.'

'Are you married?'

The doctor shook his head. 'I was engaged once but she died. Now, I'm married to my work.'

As the two men waited for Dr Mitchell, the topic of building led to a discussion about the shameful state of Backshaw Moss.

Dr McDevitt scowled at the mere name. 'They should knock that disgusting slum down. It's a disgrace to the valley.'

'I agree.'

When the old doctor arrived, he was not happy that Wilf wanted to be present. He gave Enid's body a very cursory examination and ignored the husband completely.

'You were right, McDevitt. I checked my records and I did see her a few months ago. There was no sign of a tumour then, just a small weight gain in the belly, which is common in middle-aged women.'

Middle-aged! Wilf thought. She was only thirty-three.

'I'll sign the death certificate tomorrow and send it to you to deal with.' He nodded to his colleague and said to Wilf, 'I'll send you my bill, Mr Pollard. Make sure you pay it within the week.'

When he'd gone, Dr McDevitt said with a bitter edge to his voice, 'You'll get a half guinea bill for those few minutes of his time, I'm afraid.'

Then his tone changed as he asked gently, 'I presume a man with his own phone can afford a proper funeral?'

'Yes, I can. Not a fancy one, but a decent one. I've had plenty of work lately.' His voice broke and it took him a minute to pull himself together. 'I was coming home to tell her that Roy Tyler, the builder, had just offered me a partnership.'

'Congratulations. I've met Tyler. He did some repair work on my surgery and it was very well done, too. I've heard nothing but good of him. He must think highly of you to offer you the partnership.'

'He's a skilled builder, best in the valley.'

'Far better than that Higgerson chap!'

'Yes. I was so happy that Roy wanted me to work with him.' His voice broke. 'I didn't even get the chance to share my news with her.'

For a moment the doctor's hand rested on his shoulder. 'You can still tell her, though. In some religions they insist you talk to the dead.'

That surprised Wilf, but he liked the idea of doing it.

Dr McDevitt picked up his bag. 'Shall I call at the undertaker's on the way back into Rivenshaw and tell him he's needed? I'm assuming you'll want Jeavons.'

'Thank you, but I'll phone Owen myself. I know him, did some work for him a few months ago.'

'I'll send you the death certificate tomorrow.'

And then Wilf was left alone. He felt numb, disoriented, shocked. How could this have happened so suddenly?

He should be weeping for Enid. Or for himself. Or for the children, who had just lost a second mother. But all he could remember were his recent disagreements with his wife, how far apart they'd moved, and a little relief crept in as well. To his shame.

Anyway, there was too much to do and only him to do it.

He couldn't give in to any weakness or guilt, just had to get on with things.

He took a few deep breaths and made a start. First, he needed to call the undertaker, Owen, who said he'd come straight away.

His brother didn't have a phone, so Wilf would have to send the lad next door to tell Daniel what had happened. He'd do that when he picked up the children.

Moving slowly, feeling like an old man, he had a quick wash and changed his clothes then went up and told Enid his good news, standing by the bed, feeling strange about this need. His voice came out thickly and in little spurts, because the tears he still couldn't seem to shed were clogging his throat.

Why wasn't he crying?

When he finished telling her, he took a step backwards. 'Goodbye, lass. You can be sure I'll look after them two children.'

There seemed nothing else to say so he went back downstairs to warm himself by the kitchen fire.

He definitely wasn't going to fetch the children back until Owen had taken Enid's body away. He'd let them see their mother to say goodbye at the funeral parlour, after Owen's wife had made her look nice. Other people would want to have a final look at her, too, he supposed. It was what people usually did. She'd have hated the thought of that.

Wilf didn't want to see her again, though.

And once the funeral was over . . . what then?

He studied the kitchen, which was already looking untidy, and took his mucky clothes into the back scullery, hanging them on the ceiling airer to dry. He probably wouldn't need them for a few days. Ought he to wash them? It wasn't something he knew much about, but you didn't usually send your muddy work clothes to the laundry. Or did you?

He'd need to find help to look after his house and children, and as soon as possible. He couldn't let Roy Tyler down. On that thought he went to phone Roy, spoke to Mrs Tyler and told her what had happened.

Her voice was warmly understanding. 'You must take as long as you need to deal with it all, Wilf.'

'I'll try to get back to work as soon as I can.' He put the phone down. Another job done.

He'd start asking around in the morning about a house-keeper, some motherly person who'd be kind to the children. Maybe Mrs Harper would know some suitable woman who needed a job.

It was a relief when Owen arrived, an even bigger relief when the undertaker finished upstairs and Wilf helped him carry out the temporary coffin.

He watched Owen drive her away.

Yes, that was definitely a relief.

When he went back into the house, Wilf looked round the kitchen and shook his head. He didn't want to sit in here because it had been Enid's domain, and it still felt as if she'd come bustling in.

He lit a fire in the front room, which she'd never wanted to use and which was sparsely furnished, then went to fetch the children home. The Harpers sent one of their sons to tell Wilf's brother Daniel about Enid.

Mrs Harper put one hand across the doorway to stop him leaving. 'Have you had any tea?'

He had to think for a minute before he could answer. 'Er . . . no. But I'm not hungry.'

'You need to keep up your strength.' She brought out a package wrapped in white butcher paper and handed it to him. 'Here. I bought you a loaf for breakfast tomorrow.'

'Thank you.'

She turned to the children. 'Peggy love, you make your dad a jam butty when you get back, and see that he eats it.'

The little girl nodded. She was always solemn and responsible. Once this was over, he vowed to find a way for her to play outside and come in dishevelled like other children.

When Wilf took the children into the front room instead of the kitchen, they looked round it warily, because Enid hadn't let any of them use it except on rare occasions like Christmas.

'I thought we could sit in here so that we'd all fit on the sofa together.' He was pleased to see their expressions brighten at that.

'That's a good idea, Dad,' Peggy said. 'But I'll get you a jam butty first.'

'I'll have that later, love. I stopped at Mrs Morton's on the way home and she gave me a cup of tea and a biscuit.' He'd have to let the kind old lady know about Enid as well. He'd phone her tomorrow. In fact, he ought to start making a list of people to contact. But not now. He was feeling weary.

'All right, Dad. But don't forget to eat something. Ronnie, you sit on that side of the sofa and I'll sit on this. Dad, you can sit between us.'

He did as she'd ordered, touched by the way she'd taken charge. As he put his arms round them, he wondered what to say. But they didn't seem to want to talk, just burrowed close to him.

It was Peggy who broke the silence a few minutes later. 'Who will look after the house an' get our meals an' do the washing?'

He decided on the simple truth, now and in the future. 'I don't know yet, love. It's happened so suddenly I haven't had time to think. We'll work something out. Perhaps Mrs Harper will help for a day or two.'

'Mam didn't like her coming in, said she was nosy, but I like Mrs Harper. She smiles a lot.'

'She's been very kind to us today, that's for sure. What did she give you for tea?'

'She got a loaf an' some fresh butter an' a jar of jam. We both had two big slices and a drink of milk as well.'

'You're not hungry now?'

'I wasn't hungry then but Mrs Harper said we had to eat everything on our plates, so that you'd not worry about us.'

'She was right.'

He'd only lit a small fire in the room, but their body warmth made that enough and it was good just to sit peacefully. When the fire began to burn low, he said, 'It's getting late. You two had better get off to bed now. You'll have to tell me what to do to help you.'

'Me an' Ronnie go across the backyard to the lavvy an' get ourselves undressed, but Mam used to tuck us in an' kiss us.' She gulped and blinked her eyes.

'I can do that from now on. And Peggy? Thank you for being such a big help to me. You're a good girl. I don't know what Ronnie and I would do without you. You'll have to show me what to do in the morning as well as tonight.'

That brought a nod and an almost-smile from her.

Before the children could start getting ready for bed, there was a knock on the front door and Wilf's brother Daniel came in without waiting to be asked.

'Is it true what young Ollie Harper just told me? Your Enid's dropped dead?'

Wilf nodded. 'Mmm.'

'Bloody hell! What happened?'

'She had a growth in her belly an' never told anyone. She said it was the change. I don't know if she thought that or was just making the best of things. The doctor said that's what killed her, anyway.'

'Eh, the poor lass. What can I do to help?'

'Wait here for me while I get these two to bed, then we'll talk. Say goodnight to your uncle Daniel and don't forget to go across the yard before you go upstairs.'

They went out quietly.

'How are they taking it?' Daniel asked.

'They're worried that I'll put them in the orphanage.'

'No!'

'As if I ever would.'

'I'd not put a dog in one of them places.'

When the children came back, Peggy was holding her brother's hand. She turned to Wilf, speaking as if she were another adult. 'We'll shout for you to come up an' tuck us in when we're ready, Dad. I'll make sure Ronnie buttons up his pyjamas properly.'

The little boy had hardly said a word and was clinging to his sister. He kept giving his father worried glances, so Wilf said it once more. 'I'm right glad I've got you two. I'd not like to be on my own.'

They both seemed relieved at that. How insecure they must feel, poor little loves.

He'd meant what he'd said. He did need them as much as they needed him. And if he had to tell them so a thousand times to get them to believe it, he would. 'I'll come up as soon as you shout.'

As they clattered up the stairs, Wilf turned to his brother and gestured to a kitchen chair. 'I'm still a bit shocked.'

'Aye. You would be. If me and Mary can do anything to help, you've only to say.'

'Your Mary's expecting and she's not got long to go now, has she? You two will have enough on your plates. I think Mrs Harper next door will help me for a while and I can afford to pay her.'

He hesitated, then added. 'Roy Tyler asked me today to

go into partnership with him. I'll tell you the details another time, but I thought you should know. I wish I'd been able to tell Enid. It'd have maybe made her a bit happier. She always worried about money.'

There was a shout from upstairs.

'I'll be up in a minute,' he called, turning to his brother. 'You go home now, lad. If you can tell folk in the village about Enid for me, that'll be the most help. You and I can talk tomorrow after you finish work. I'll maybe have more idea of what's happening by then, and about the funeral. Owen's got her body now.'

'He'll do you a good funeral.'

As they walked to the door in silence, Wilf said, 'Eh, I'm still all of a muddle about how we'll live afterwards.'

'If anyone can figure everything out, it's you. You're the cleverest chap I've ever known, allus have been, even when we were children.'

Then Daniel did something most unusual for him: he hugged Wilf, hugged him long and hard, rocking to and fro but not saying a word.

And Wilf clung to him for a few moments, glad of the hug.

As Daniel hurried away, Wilf saw him brush one hand across his eyes.

He locked the door, feeling exhausted. It was a relief to be left on his own with the children safe in bed, a relief not to have to pretend about anything.

He went up and kissed them good night. They were in the same bed, but he didn't tell Ronnie to get back into his own bed. If they could comfort one another, he'd not stop them.

When he went into the bedroom he'd previously shared with Enid, he realised he'd have to put clean sheets on and as he did that, the tears came. Pouring down his cheeks. Dripping on to the clean sheets.

He flung himself on the half-made bed and wept, trying desperately not to make a noise and upset the children. He wept as much for the bright new love he and Enid had once had and then lost, as for anything.

Then he lay thinking about how his life would change. What was he going to do without a wife? How was he going to look after those children properly and still go out to earn money? And in a new job, too! He didn't want to let Roy Tyler down.

He shivered and realised how cold it was, so got off the bed and finished making it up with clean sheets. Putting on his pyjamas, he crawled under the covers, which felt icy. He couldn't be bothered to go down and fill a hot-water bottle.

He didn't expect to fall asleep but was woken abruptly by the sound of the milk being delivered to the village shop just across the open space in front of his home. He jerked awake and saw the lights on over there. It was just starting to get light.

For a few seconds he looked around for Enid, thinking she must have got up early and let him sleep on. Then he remembered what had happened. His mind had slipped back to the past, when they'd shared this room. Oh, hell! How was he to face the day?

He lay curled up for a while, then grew angry at himself and got up. He'd had his weak moment last night, weeping like a baby.

From now on he had to be strong, for the children's sake as much as anything.

There would be a lot to do.

It saved his sanity, being busy did. That and the children. He didn't send them to school, but kept them at home, giving them little jobs to do, cuddling them sometimes. Eh, they were a loving little pair.

5

A week passed and Stella didn't hear back about her application to the doctor in Rivenshaw, so she gave up hope of that job. She continued to search the newspapers at the public library for other positions, but there was very little on offer for women except for the most tedious office and shop jobs, or else working as domestic servants.

She'd have appreciated knowing why she'd failed to get an interview for the doctor's job, so that she could do better in future applications, but didn't like to write again to ask that.

On yet another rainy day, she opened the door when she got home after her daily search through the newspapers at the library and felt something crackle beneath her feet. When she looked down, she saw a white envelope – with a partial footprint from her shoe on it – and snatched it up.

Why hadn't her landlady put it on the shelf in the hall out of the way of people coming in? There weren't many letters delivered here, which was a good thing, because the woman was lazy about things like that, just wanted the money from renting out the rooms upstairs.

The door to the downstairs sitting room opened just then and her landlady came out. 'Oh, was there a letter? I must have missed it.'

'Yes. I can't stay to chat because I want to get these wet things off.'

'Just a moment. I need to tell you something.' She hesitated, saying in a rush, 'I'm afraid I'm going to have to give you notice to leave.'

Stella stared at her in dismay. 'Why? What have I done?'

'You haven't done anything wrong, dear. My cousin's husband has died and she's invited me to go and live with her in Fleetwood. Imagine, living at the seaside. I'm that pleased to be going. Eh, I don't know whether I'm on my head or my heels. I'm not getting any younger, so it'll be ideal.'

'Oh. Well, I hope you'll be happy there.'

'I'm sure I will. Look, I'll write you a reference, if it's any help, because you've been an excellent tenant, clean and conscientious. Not like some.' She scowled up in the direction of the back bedroom as she said that.

'Thank you. I'd appreciate you doing that – with your new address on it, if you don't mind, in case someone wants to contact you.'

'Of course.' She gestured towards the envelope, incurably nosy as always. 'I hope it isn't bad news, Mrs Newby?'

'I haven't opened it yet. I'd better go and find out.'

Stella climbed the stairs slowly and wearily. The last thing she needed was to hunt for a new place to live at the same time as she was trying to find a job so she could move away from Rochdale.

She dumped her shopping basket on the table and flung off her mackintosh, draping it on the back of her only upright chair to dry.

When she opened the envelope, she found a polite note saying the doctor thanked her for her application but as it had arrived late and he'd needed to find someone quickly, he'd already given the job to someone else. He wished her well in her search and had found the application very impressive.

She went to sit on the bed, feeling upset. Two pieces of

bad news in one day, even though this one, at least, had been expected. Lena would say a third one was due before the run of bad luck ended, but Stella disliked such superstitions.

Oh dear, it was going to make her life difficult to have to find somewhere else to live without knowing where she was going to work and whether she might want to move away from Rochdale soon.

She suddenly realised she didn't know exactly when she had to move out, so went downstairs and knocked on her landlady's door. 'Could you please tell me when I have to move out by?'

'I'm not sure. Two weeks, perhaps. I haven't set an exact date yet. I'll let you know as soon as I've arranged it. In the meantime, you can stay or go as you please and pay rent daily.'

'Thank you. I'll, um, start making plans.'

She went back upstairs and made herself some cheese on toast on the little gas cooker on the landing. Then she let it go cold and congeal as she stared out of the window, wondering what her next view of the outside world would be like. Nicer than this one, she hoped.

What on earth was she going to do?

The most sensible thing would be to find temporary lodgings and continue to search for a job.

She was suddenly very tired of being sensible.

If only she knew how to drive, she'd buy a car, load everything into it and go searching for her future in the country.

No, she should be more careful than that. First find a job, second move to the new place.

She got out the *Manchester Guardian* newspaper, which she'd bought to look for a job. Nothing.

Suddenly, rebellion seized her and she screwed up the jobs page, tossing it across the room. She was fed up to the teeth of being sensible. What good had it done Derrick? He'd never done anything exciting with his life and been dead before thirty.

Could she . . . ? Did she dare . . . ? She couldn't even let herself finish those thoughts, then she looked round and her resentment burned even more brightly. This was where sensible had got her. Widowed at twenty-seven, living in a dingy room with hardly room to swing a cat – if she'd had a cat, that was. Only you weren't allowed pets in places like this.

But if she did something risky, she'd have only herself to rely on and – no, that wasn't right. Her breath caught in her throat. She had over nine hundred pounds in the bank to rely on as well. That was a very comforting thought. You could live for a good long time on that, years if you were careful, even if you didn't have a job.

Did she dare go out into the world and look for a new life?

She nodded a couple of times. Yes, she did dare. What had she to lose, after all? She was being forced to leave this place and good riddance to it. She'd take that as a sign.

Time to move on, Stella Newby. More than time.

She got up and went to stare at her reflection in the fly-specked mirror on the chimney breast. She used to look nicer than this when Derrick was alive. When had she stopped caring about her appearance?

Slowly she lifted one hand and pulled out the hairpins holding her bun in place. She ran her hands through her hair, letting it tumble down to her shoulders. It felt good. She fluffed up her hair and decided it looked much nicer like that than in a bun. She might get it cut a bit shorter, wear it loose. There was no law against looking your best and sometimes that raised your spirits.

Taking a deep breath, she nodded to the younger-looking woman staring back at her from the mirror and said the words aloud, 'Don't be such a coward, Stella Newby. You won't starve with all that money in the bank.'

Did she really have the courage to move on?

Yes. She nodded at her reflection. She would hand in her notice tomorrow at the laundry and ask if she could be released straight away. And then she'd go out into the country and search for a place to live and a more interesting job. Whatever she found surely couldn't be worse than this place and the boring lists of pennies and shillings to be filled into regular customers' accounts day after day after day, till she felt like screaming at the mere sight of a ledger.

But where to go? She'd have to study the atlas at the library and work something out, or even simply stick a pin in it to find a starting point.

She picked up the crumpled envelope and letter from where she'd thrown them into the hearth and stared down at the envelope. It was postmarked 'Rivenshaw' and that seemed like a sign.

Why not start her search there? It was a nice little town, if she remembered correctly. She'd been there two or three times with Derrick and they'd both liked that area. She still remembered the way the town nestled at the foot of a valley that led up to the moors. The air had tasted so fresh there.

After she'd first applied for the job, the librarian had found her a book about the Pennines with a couple of photos of Rivenshaw to jog her memory and a few views of the Ellin Valley. There were two villages higher up the valley. If she went to live there, she was bound to find another job eventually, even if it was only another boring one.

Excitement slowly gathered inside her until it was overflowing. She spun round and round on the spot, laughing out loud when she accidentally knocked the chair sideways so that it leaned on the bed.

She'd do it, pack all her things and go to Rivenshaw by

train. You could send your luggage to a station to be picked up later, and it could be stored in left luggage for a small payment. It'd only take a trunk to hold everything she owned. And she could take the battered suitcase she'd bought from a second-hand stall at the market with enough clothes to manage on for a few days.

She looked across at her books. They were like old friends and she didn't intend to lose them. She'd get a box to pack them in.

There must be a hotel or lodging house in Rivenshaw. She'd find a taxi at the station and ask about it. She'd take a room for a week or so to start with and if she still liked the town, she'd look for a small cottage to buy.

Oh, the thought of that! She spun round again, beaming happily as she took her small notebook out of her handbag and began making a list of jobs.

She'd give notice at the laundry and refuse to stay on. It'd only take a day or two to get ready to leave. After that she'd just go.

She made herself a cup of cocoa and tried to read, but couldn't settle. The book would have to go back to the library. She added that to the list, then got ready for bed.

Smiling, she snuggled down, thinking that she ought to be worried about the future. Only she wasn't. She'd had enough of being fearful.

Stella remembered a poster she often looked at on the wall at the library of a young woman striding forward across the moors, head held high as if heading for an adventure. She'd always liked that poster.

To her amazement she slept soundly that night.

In the morning, Stella got up early and before work she went to ask Mrs Ball at the newsagent's if she had any cardboard boxes. Thank goodness the shop opened early.

'What for?'

She hesitated but there was no need to keep these plans secret. She wouldn't be around to listen to the gossip. 'I'm going to look for somewhere to live in the country. I need a change and my landlady is closing down, so I have to move anyway.'

The older woman looked at her sympathetically. 'Well, if you can't afford it now, you never will be able to. And yes, I do have some boxes. Wait here and I'll get them.'

She came back with two sturdy cardboard boxes and as she passed them over, she studied Stella, head on one side. 'I've never seen you look so pretty before. You should wear your hair loose all the time. It's got just the right amount of curl to it. Some girls would die for hair like yours.'

'Thank you.'

Stella carried the boxes back across the street to her room, then hurried off to work. She was late for the first time ever and instead of going to her desk, she went across to the supervisor. 'I wonder if I could have a word with you in private, please, Miss Marlow?'

When they were alone in the staffroom where everyone sat during their breaks or to eat their lunch, Stella said it straight out. 'I wish to give in my notice.'

'Give in your notice? Why?'

'I'm moving to the country. I'd be grateful if you'd let me go without working my two weeks because my landlady is closing down the rented rooms and going to live with her cousin, so I'll have nowhere to live.'

'This is rather sudden, isn't it? You haven't let that money go to your head, have you? You need to think before you spend it.'

'I don't think I *could* be careless with money. But since I have to move soon anyway, it seems silly to try to find somewhere else to live, just for a week or two.'

The supervisor stared at her in the same way Mrs Ball had. 'You look different today with your hair like that. Full of energy. Younger.'

'I'm excited about the move. Um, I'd be really grateful if you could see fit to give me a reference as well. I shall of course be looking for another job after I find somewhere else to live.'

'Yes, of course I will, and a good one, too. It's a pity you're leaving, though.'

'Why is it a pity?'

'We were going to offer you the job of deputy supervisor and timekeeper because Miss Lawson is leaving. You can still have the job, if you want to stay on.'

Stella wasn't even tempted and shook her head. 'Thank you, but I need a change.'

The supervisor looked round as if to check that no one was nearby and said in a low voice, 'I understand how you feel. I'd do something more exciting with my life, too, if I'd won all that money.'

This was the second person to envy her for that. 'Thank you for understanding how I feel. I really appreciate that. And may I finish straight away?'

'Yes, why not? I have a list of young women desperate for a job in an office. They won't be as good as you, but they'll be good enough to keep up with the typing and accounts.'

She could only say it again. 'Thank you so much. You've been wonderful about it all.'

'Better go and clear your desk, then say goodbye. We'll pay you until yesterday. I'll go and get the money now and I'll send the reference to your home later today.'

Stella felt strange walking through the streets on a weekday morning, swinging a carrier bag containing the few personal possessions she'd kept at work.

A man coming out of the newsagent's eyed her cheekily from across the road and winked, as if he liked what he saw. How long was it since that had happened? Did she really look so different?

She left the carrier bag in her room and strolled to the station to ask about trains to Rivenshaw. Before she could think twice, she'd used up her wages to purchase a ticket for the following day and arranged for her luggage to be stored at the station there for up to a week.

Next she visited the bank and took some more money out. Enough to put some in her Post Office Savings Bank so that she could take money out from any other branch.

The teller had the cheek to ask if she was sure she wanted to take out so much all at once. That made her furious. Some of the males working in banks didn't seem to think their women customers knew how to handle money.

Back in her room, she caught sight of herself in the mirror and went closer to study her face. Her cheeks were flushed, her eyes bright and she really did look younger.

For the rest of the day as she packed and cleaned her room, she alternated between sheer terror at what she was doing and happy excitement at the prospect of a new life.

There was a knock on her door around teatime and, as she'd expected, it was Lena with the reference from Miss Marlow.

'Why didn't you tell me you were planning to leave so soon?' her friend demanded.

'I didn't make up my mind until yesterday evening.' She explained about the landlady selling the house and going to live with her sister in Fleetwood.

Lena sat looking at her with tears in her eyes. 'Oh dear! I'm going to miss you so much.'

'I'll miss you, too. You're the only person I shall miss, though. You've been such a good friend to me. And it's all because of you that I've got the money to do this. I shall always be grateful to you for that.'

'You won't forget me?'

'Of course I won't. I'll write once I'm settled somewhere, but it'll probably be a few days before you hear from me.'

'When exactly are you leaving?'

'Tomorrow morning. I've bought a train ticket and booked a taxi to pick me and my luggage up at eight o'clock.'

'You should have waited another day. We could have organised a farewell party.'

'I don't dare wait, in case I lose my nerve.'

Which made Lena cry some more, and Stella couldn't help crying with her, for all her new resolution to face the world bravely.

'Do you want to take my book shelves?'

'Alistair will want the wood, though not to make bookshelves with. He's no reader. I'll send him across to collect them.'

When her friend had gone and Alistair had taken away the shelves, Stella took the bricks that had held them into the backyard, then sat on the bed and looked around. The place was bare except for the trunk, the two cardboard boxes and the suitcase.

Was she doing the right thing? Who knew?

Would Derrick have approved?

It took her a while to admit to herself that he definitely wouldn't have approved of what she was doing. He'd always been a very careful man. And yet he'd lost his life because of an impulsive act of heroism.

She didn't let herself dwell on that. Blind chance could be so cruel.

Her husband had gradually faded from the forefront of her mind over the years. She couldn't remember the last time she'd looked at the slightly charred wedding photo. Both people on it seemed like strangers.

The younger woman she'd once been had loved him dearly. The woman she was now had moved forward, was too different to marry a quiet, careful man like him again.

Her old life was about to end and the future was beckoning. Whether that new life was successful or not would be in her own hands.

Where would she be this time tomorrow?

Who knew? But she'd cope with whatever turned up. Like the girl on that poster, she'd stride forward into life. That image would stay with her forever, she was sure. It seemed to have pointed the way.

6

There was a knock on the door the following morning about half past eight and Wilf opened it to see Mrs Morton and her maid Mona standing there. A taxi with its engine ticking quietly was waiting in the narrow dirt road that ran around the edge of the open space.

'I've only just found out about Enid,' Mrs Morton said. 'Mona heard the news at the shops and came straight back to tell me. Oh, Wilf, I'm so sorry for your loss.'

'Thank you.' He assumed she'd come to offer her condolences, as others no doubt would, but what she said surprised him.

'We've come to help and we're not taking no for an answer. There's a lot to attend to when someone dies and I've gone through it a few times so I know what to do. You helped me when I needed it and I'm helping you now.'

She gestured to the taxi to go away, then turned back to him, so Wilf automatically stepped aside to let her and Mona in. He was feeling lost and bewildered, couldn't seem to make sense of anything today, let alone make any decisions. The two women's presence was an immediate comfort, which was strange because he usually coped with whatever life threw at him.

'I, um, didn't send the children to school today. They were too upset.'

'Quite right.' She stopped in the kitchen doorway. 'Oh, the little dear! Isn't she wonderful, trying to take her mother's place?'

Peggy was washing the dishes, standing on a footstool by the sink with one of Enid's aprons tied round her, reaching to her feet. She'd obviously been crying.

Ronnie was sitting on a little stool to one side, his eyes red and puffy. He was hugging the stripy teddy bear Enid had knitted for him from scraps of wool.

'Poor little lambs,' Mrs Morton went on in a low voice. 'Is it all right if Mona keeps an eye on them while you and I have a chat in the front room, Wilf?'

He nodded, following her into the other room, waiting for her to speak. Instead she looked at him, head on one side and pulled him into her arms, like the mother he'd lost when he was barely seventeen used to do. He clung to her, fighting the urge to weep.

'I can't think straight,' he admitted.

She smoothed the tangle of hair from his forehead. 'It's the shock. I doubt you'll see things clearly for a while. No one could have expected poor Enid to die so suddenly.'

'No, but I can't *afford* to be stupid about it, can I? There's too much to do and only me to look after those children. I feel I'm being . . . weak.' And he despised himself for that.

'Of course you're not. Losing someone makes a big change to your life and it takes a lot of getting used to.'

He gestured to the sofa. 'I'm forgetting my manners on top of everything else. Do please sit down, Mrs Morton.'

'I will, but may I suggest you light the fire before we start making plans? It's cold in here and if people come to offer you their condolences, it'll be more suitable to see them in here than in the kitchen.'

That seemed sensible. He bent to clear the ashes away and found himself staring at the kindling in the little box to one side of the fireplace as if he'd never seen it before, making no move to put it in the hearth.

'Let me do that.' Mrs Morton moved him gently to one side and quickly proved she was good at lighting fires.

'I'm a poor host.'

'Think of us as friends, not guests. I do hope I count as a friend nowadays?'

He was sure of that, at least. 'Oh yes. And a good friend, too. Even before this. You're more like family, if you don't mind me saying so.'

She flicked the coal dust off her hands with a handkerchief then patted the sofa beside her and took his hand. 'I'm honoured that you feel like that. And since I'm now going to count as family, it makes my suggestion even more suitable. How about you and the children coming to stay with me for a while? You know I have several empty bedrooms.'

'We can't impose on you like that!' But oh, he wanted to.

She gave him a sad smile. 'It wouldn't be imposing. I have a lot of empty hours to fill each week, Wilf, because there's none of my own family left. Mona and I would be really happy to help with the children and keep an eye on them after school. That way you'll be able to start working with Mr Tyler after the funeral without having to worry about them.'

'I couldn't ask you to do that.'

'You didn't ask. I offered.'

Peggy came into the room just then. 'Mona says to ask if you and Mrs Morton would like a cup of tea, Dad?'

'Um, yes.'

Mrs Morton took over. 'Where's your brother?'

'Ronnie's sitting on Mona's knee an' she's playing Incy Wincy Spider with him till the kettle boils. I like Mona. She helped me finish washing the dishes.'

'I like her too. Please tell her your father and I would love a cup of tea.'

Wilf waited till his daughter had left the room to say, 'That's the first time Ronnie has let his sister out of his sight since it happened.'

'Mona's always been good with children. She'll enjoy having them around and so will I.' Mrs Morton waited, head on one side. 'Say yes, Wilf. Say you'll come to me. You can't do everything here and you'll need ongoing help. You don't want to let Mr Tyler down. Or yourself. He's offered you a wonderful opportunity.'

He felt like a child as he knuckled away a few tears that had escaped his control. 'I don't know what I've done to deserve such help, but yes, we will come and stay at your house until I can see my way clear. This place isn't what I want for them and it needs a lot doing to it, which the landlord won't pay for. I can't thank you enough.'

He suddenly remembered how short of money she was and added quickly, 'But only if you'll let me pay for our food and other expenses.'

'I shall have to let you do that, dear boy. I don't have a lot of money coming in, as you know, even though I still have quite a lot of family possessions.'

'You have a generous heart, which is the most important thing.' He reached out and took her hand again, sitting holding it like a child. And she didn't disturb the peace of this moment by speaking.

He only let go when Mona brought in a tray containing tea and biscuits, with Peggy following behind her carrying the milk jug and finally Ronnie carrying both his teddy and the sugar bowl, which was tipping dangerously close to spilling its contents.

He watched Mona look at her mistress, a question in her eyes and when Mrs Morton nodded, the maid beamed at him.

'Will you tell the children what we're going to do, Wilf dear?'

So he held out his arms to them and they moved to stand close to him.

'You asked me last night how we'd manage, Peggy love, and I hadn't worked it out. But now I have.' He gestured to the two visitors. 'Mrs Morton has invited us to stay at her house for a while. She and Mona will help me look after you two. We'll all be together still, but not here. What do you think of that?'

She clapped her hands together. 'I like it there.'

Ronnie didn't say anything but he nodded his head several times, then made his teddy bear nod its head as well.

Peggy looked across at Mrs Morton. 'We'll both be very good, I promise.'

'I'm sure you will, dear.'

Mona sniffed loudly and blew her nose a couple of times at that.

Someone knocked on the front door and she stuffed her handkerchief into her pocket. 'I'll answer that.'

She came back two minutes later. 'Mr and Mrs Tyler to see you, sir.'

'Um . . . show them in.'

What next? Wilf wondered, astonished by this visit.

As Roy Tyler and his wife paused inside the doorway of the front room, Mrs Morton poked Wilf surreptitiously in the ribs and he stood up to greet the newcomers. The two children, who hadn't met the Tylers, went across to stand near her armchair, as if for protection.

Roy came to stand beside him. 'Ethel told me about your wife. We're so sorry, lad. What a shock that must have been. Is there anything we can do to help?'

'Yes, it was a shock. Do you know Mrs Morton?'

'Oh, yes. Beryl and I have met a few times.' Mrs Tyler smiled across at the other lady. 'And I'd guess we're probably here on the same errand.'

'To help Wilf and the children? Yes.' She looked across at

Mona. 'Perhaps the children could give you a hand in the kitchen while we talk?'

Mona held out her hand to them and Ronnie ran to take hold of it and Peggy followed them out.

Once they'd left the room, Wilf remembered his manners and gestured to the sofa. 'Won't you please sit down?' When they squeezed on to it with Mrs Morton, he pulled forward the only other chair, a wooden one, and sat down with them, not sure what to say.

'We'll not stay long but there must be something we can do to help you,' Roy said.

'Ah. Well, Mrs Morton has kindly offered to let us stay at her house for a few days.'

'Longer than that, I hope. For as long as it takes to sort out new permanent arrangements,' she corrected.

'What a good idea!' Mrs Tyler gave Wilf a warm smile. 'Perhaps I can help with something else? For instance, what are you doing about clothes for the funeral, Mr Pollard? For yourself *and* the children?'

He stared at her blankly. He hadn't even thought of that. People round here couldn't usually afford to buy new clothes to show they were in mourning. Most just tied a black rag or ribbon around one arm. Only, he was going to be a partner with Mr Tyler, so if his new partner's wife thought it necessary to wear mourning, he'd have to do something about it. He'd already realised he'd need to buy better clothes for work than the ones which Enid found on the second-hand stall for him to wear. He'd need sturdy ones, but not so ragged and stained.

Yes, he really ought to do something about clothes for the funeral. But what?

'How about you let us ladies deal with that, Wilf?' Mrs Tyler suggested. 'You see, I help out at the church and people give us clothes for those in need and to sell at jumble sales.

There won't be time for you to have a new suit made specially, but we can get some suitable things for you and the children from the church boxes.'

He frowned, bringing a picture of the children into his mind. 'Enid said the children's clothes would last a while yet, but now I come to think of it, they do look to be growing out of them.'

'Children always do, dear. It's hard to keep up with them. I'm sure I can help you find something.'

Eh, the kindness of these people! Wilf thought. He couldn't remember the last time someone else had offered to help with his personal needs. Enid had attended to the house but like many women from poorer homes, she couldn't sew beyond mending and darning, so she'd gone to second-hand stalls mostly or to pawnshops when he needed something to wear and got whatever would be hardest wearing. She'd done the same for herself and the children, though she never acted until their clothes were in a desperately bad state.

Like most of the people he knew, he'd never had any brand new clothes in his whole life, not even when he got married, let alone had a suit made especially for him.

He pulled himself together. 'I'd be very grateful for your help, Mrs Tyler. I must admit, I've never dealt with clothes for the children before and wouldn't know where to start.'

'Few men have, whether they're poor or rich.'

Mr Tyler stood up. 'If that's settled, I'll get back to work and leave the ladies to help you here. Ethel, you can phone for the car when you need it to go anywhere and I'll send Robson up with it. You've got a phone here, haven't you, Wilf?'

'Yes, Mr Tyler.'

'Roy now, remember.'

'Sorry. I forgot. Roy it is.' Wilf walked with him to the front door, where the older man stopped and laid one hand on his shoulder. 'Don't even think of coming to work until you've done everything you need, Wilf lad. We'll sort out what your first jobs will be then and arrange a new appointment with my lawyer. I'm sure you've got other small jobs you'd already arranged to do as well, and we must honour those too. I can see to that if you'll let me know what they are.'

'That'll be a help. Look, there's the barn still to finish for Farmer Tidsworth. It's nearly finished, as you saw, and I don't want to leave him in the lurch.'

'Leave that to me.'

'Ricky could find someone to help him and get on with the work. You can trust that lad. But he'd need himself and the tools taking to and fro each day, and someone to deliver the materials he needs. He doesn't have the skills to cut new tiles accurately but he's helped me retile parts of roofs a few times now. There are enough extra tiles from the one he's working on and another ruined shed lying around at the farm. Those bad storms last winter did a lot of damage.'

'I'll deal with all that. It'll give me a chance to see how your Ricky works. Will he find someone else to help him or shall I?'

'Eh, I can think of a dozen men in our village who'd queue up for any job going. I'll send word to Ricky. He knows who the best workers are.'

'Tell them to wait near the village shop at half past seven tomorrow morning and I'll send someone to pick him and whoever it is up. It'll still be dark then but it'll be light by the time they get to Farmer Tidsworth's.'

'Thank you.'

'Sad, isn't it, how many chaps round here are still seeking work? Let's hope things pick up a bit, as they're already doing in the south and midlands.'

'Ah, but they've got new industries like car making, lucky devils.'

'Well, even in bad times, buildings need repairing, so I still find work here and there.'

After Mr Tyler had gone, Wilf let the three women order him around and help make arrangements, relieved not to have to think, just do as he was told.

He hadn't realised until now how many of life's small decisions had been in Enid's hands. Like most men, he'd concentrated on finding work and putting bread on the table.

Even now, it was women who were rescuing him and his children. They called women the weaker sex, but he didn't think they were. No, definitely not.

What it came down to was, they all needed one another just to survive. It could be a hard world.

That afternoon Ricky saved Wilf the need to visit him by turning up to offer his condolences. His relief at finding he still had work showed in his face.

'Can you find someone to help you, someone who does good work?'

'I can find half a dozen. Who do you prefer?'

'You decide that. You'll have to work with them. I just want the job doing properly.'

'Leave it to me. We won't let you down, Mr Pollard.'

'Think on, if Tyler is pleased with your work, there will be the chance of other jobs with him. Do your very, very best.'

'I always try to do that.'

Relieved to have one thing sorted out, Wilf sat down on the sofa just for a moment or two and leaned back in the corner of it. He woke with a start when the telephone rang but while he was still struggling to stand up on a leg that had gone to sleep, Mrs Tyler nipped into the room and took the call.

When she'd finished, she put the phone down, which surprised him – he was expecting her to pass it over to him.

'Sorry. I was sound asleep and then my leg had pins and needles.'

'That's all right. You must have needed a rest. Lie down properly next time. Um, look, that was Mr Jeavons. He needs some clothes for Enid, something nice for her to wear for the viewing, before they close up the coffin.'

'That never even occurred to me!'

'I don't suppose it would. How many funerals have you organised?'

'None. It was my brother and his wife who saw to Mum and Dad's send-offs. I was away for one of them, on the tramp, picking up work where I could, so I didn't even know Dad had died. I never went on the dole, you see. I'd have rather starved, and Enid felt the same.' It was one thing they'd never argued about.

'Well, there you are. I've done that sad duty many times and Mrs Morton has too, so you can rely on us to help you. Why don't you come upstairs now and we'll sort out some clothes for Enid together? We could clear out all her other clothing while we're at it, and that would be one more sad task completed.'

Mrs Morton was standing in the kitchen doorway as they came out of the front room and had obviously been listening. 'Mona and I will look after the children while you do that. They can walk across to the shop with me to buy some food. They could do with some fresh air.'

He fumbled in his pocket and pulled out a ten-shilling note. 'Here. Use this. Keep the rest for buying us food when we come to your house, and we'll work out a weekly amount.'

She hesitated and he pressed the money gently into her hand, then looked from one to the other. 'Eh, what have I ever done to deserve such kind friends as you ladies and Mona?'

'Helped people when you could, lived a decent life, been

a good neighbour. It all mounts up over the years,' Mrs Morton said at once. 'Even people who don't live in this village think well of you and your work, Wilf Pollard.'

He didn't know what to say to that, had never been good at handling compliments, so changed the subject hastily. 'There will be the rest of the house to sort out as well.'

'We'll come back and do that tomorrow,' Mrs Morton said. 'And later tomorrow, in the afternoon, we can go to the church and find you and the children some suitable clothes for the funeral from among the donated goods stored there.'

Of course, there were regular interruptions and apparently had been others while he was sleeping. People came to knock on the door, offering condolences and help if needed. One or two had even brought small dishes of food for Wilf and the children. He left it to Mrs Morton to tactfully refuse the gifts and explain that they were going to stay with her.

Everyone wanted to know when the funeral was, and he realised he hadn't fixed the date yet, so asked Mrs Tyler's advice on whether he should do that today.

'We can sort that out tomorrow when we take the clothes to Mr Jeavons. It'll be getting dark soon and I think we should go home when the light fails. Those children will need you with them for the move to Birch End, even though they've been to Mrs Morton's house before. They're turning to you regularly for reassurance at the moment, and rightly so. You're clearly a loving father.'

He was beginning to wonder if he'd been a better father than husband. He ought to have realised something was seriously wrong with Enid. But they'd been at odds about a few things.

When he and Mrs Tyler went upstairs, he was embarrassed at how poor his wife's clothes were and how few of them she had. When he thought of her, he thought of her wearing a big pinafore that covered all her clothes, as many women did.

There was no choice about which garments to give to Owen for Enid to be dressed in on her last journey, because she only had one set of clothes for best, the unflattering brown ones she'd always worn to church. Her underclothes were mere rags.

He could feel himself flushing as he tried to explain this state of affairs to Mrs Tyler, who was setting aside things to give to the undertaker. 'We were short of money for a few years and when I started to bring in more my wife couldn't get out of being a miser. We quarrelled about it a few times over the past year. Eh, I'm sorry about that now.'

'Hard times have a continuing effect on everyone. I'm sure both you and Enid did the best you could. We all have regrets about things we've done or not done, but you can't change the past, just try to make the future better. Now, I think we've finished in here, so let's go into the children's bedroom and find out what clothes they have. I'll put these underclothes in the sack you brought up, shall I? They can still be used as rags.'

Once again, it was a sorry collection of frayed and torn garments in the children's room; and once again he felt embarrassed – until Mrs Tyler gave him a sudden hug.

'Oh, Wilf. It's all right, really it is.'

So, he hugged her back. He was beginning to realise how short he'd been of such gestures in the past few years. He and Enid had worked well together, but she hadn't been demonstrative in the small ways that could brighten up your day.

As dusk started to fall, Mrs Tyler phoned for her chauffeur to come and collect her.

Wilf waited for her in the hall. 'Could you take Mrs Morton and Mona back with you, if you don't mind? It's nearly on your way. I want to let the children say goodbye to their life here. I'm not going to bring them back tomorrow to see their home pulled apart and our possessions thrown away.'

'Of course, I can take the ladies home. Good idea.'

Mrs Morton came out of the kitchen to join them. 'I couldn't help overhearing. This is a small house. Mona's already said that the children can stay with her tomorrow. She'll enjoy looking after them and letting them help her in our house. I can come back here with Mrs Tyler to help you clear things out completely.'

He nodded gratefully. It was going to be a hard enough job for him emotionally, he knew.

'I'll pick you up about nine o'clock, then, Beryl,' Mrs Tyler said.

Wilf realised Mrs Tyler was still talking and tried to pay better attention.

'I like to have breakfast with Roy, but after that I'm free to help here. Will you be able to fit everything into your van tomorrow, Wilf?'

He nodded. 'I shan't want to take much stuff with us, mainly my tools and my carving things.' He scowled around. 'This place is a disgrace but Enid liked it for the cheap rent and closeness to the shop.'

When Mrs Tyler's car arrived the three ladies left and he took the children to sit on the old sofa again.

'Are we going to be taking this with us?' Peggy fingered the frayed material on the edge of the seat.

'No, love. I don't want to take any of our old furniture. Where would we put it? Mrs Morton has a house full of much better stuff. Mrs Harper next door says she'll take anything we leave behind.'

She nodded.

'Another thing I've decided is that we won't be coming back to live in this house.'

'Not ever?'

'No. We'll stay with Mrs Morton in Birch End for a while and then who knows? But wherever we end up, the three of us will be staying together, I promise you that.'

'We'll still be seeing Mrs Morton once we leave her house, though?' Peggy asked anxiously. 'She's such a kind lady.'

'And Mona,' Ronnie added. 'Teddy loves her.'

'Of course. They'll always be our friends from now on.'

Peggy smiled. 'It'll be nice to live with them. It's a lovely house.'

'Mona says we can play with those toys in the box every day,' Ronnie put in. 'I'll be really careful with them.'

'There you are. We'll be just fine living there for a while.'

'Good. Um, Dad, I'm getting a bit hungry now,' Ronnie said.

'You can have tea at Mrs Morton's. We'd better leave now. I've put everything in the van. You two can squash into the front seat.'

Peggy took her brother's hand. 'I'll help you put your coat on.'

How quickly they were adapting, Wilf thought as he led the way outside. As long as they were sure of staying with him, they seemed able to cope with all the other changes.

And he was starting to cope better too, thanks to three kind ladies.

Mrs Morton might be short of money, she made no secret of that, which was why he'd done some necessary repairs for her a couple of times. But she was from a better background than he was and he hoped she would teach the children a politer way of living – and teach him the way things were done in such families as well.

When he drew up outside her house, it was fully dark. The lights were on inside and in the porch, and were shining through the stained glass of the front door. It felt as if the whole place was offering them a welcome.

He loved this tall, elegant terraced house, which was so very different from the cramped dwelling they'd just left, not only because of its size, with three storeys, but also the pretty brickwork and neat garden wall at the front. He was going to own a place like this one day, however hard he had to work to achieve it. It was one of his secret dreams, one he'd never shared with anyone else.

He realised he was sitting staring at the house and the children were waiting for him to take them inside. 'Come on, my little loves. Let's get you out of the cold. I'll unload the van later.'

'It's pretty here, isn't it?' Peggy said. 'Look at the colours from the glass.' She did a hop, skip and jump across the multi-coloured reflections thrown along the path.

'You can hop about tomorrow. Let's get inside out of the cold.' Since the door was slightly open, he gave it a push and they ran happily ahead of him, shouting, 'We're here, Mona. We're here, Mrs Morton.'

It did his heart good to hear them.

Wilf carried in their small bundles of clothes and left them at the foot of the stairs, watching Mona show them where to hang up their outer garments, after which she took them into the kitchen at the rear of the house.

He hung up his own clothes on the hallstand as well. He'd unload the other bits and pieces from the van later. There was a shed round the back, if he remembered correctly from the previous visits to help Mrs Morton. Perhaps she'd let him put his tools, pieces of special wood and carvings there.

And, he thought wistfully, perhaps once things settled down he'd have time to do some carving again.

He paused in the hall to say a silent thank you to whatever fate had brought him here, then he went to join the others.

7

In the morning Wilf woke up in a bed so comfortable all he wanted to do was snuggle down and go back to sleep. Then someone knocked on the door and he remembered where he was . . . and why.

Mona came in with a cup of tea and a big towel folded over one arm. 'There's a bathroom at the end of the landing, as you know, Mr Pollard. We're early risers and I think you are too, usually, so you won't disturb anyone if you use the bathroom when you need to.'

An indoor bathroom with plumbing! What a luxury! He vaguely remembered using it the previous night but his mind had been blurred with exhaustion. 'Thank you. Have you seen the children today? Are they awake yet?'

'Bless them, they woke when I did over an hour ago. I got them up and washed their hands and faces, but I'll give them a proper bath after everyone else has left, sir. We'll all have a bit of fun because I've found a little boat and a rubber duck for them to play with.'

'Thank you so much. They'll love that.'

'So will I. Anyway, they're sitting in the kitchen at the moment, good as gold, eating a slice of the new loaf the baker delivered. Mrs Morton is with them doing the same. She does love the new crusts.'

'Good. Thank you for keeping an eye on the kids for me.' He suddenly realised that she'd called him 'Mr Pollard' instead of Wilf. Other people had started doing that, as well. It made him feel strange, not himself, not sure of anything. It was even more unnerving when she called him 'sir'. But he supposed as a partner in Mr Tyler's business he'd have to get used to both ways of being addressed.

His world had changed in more ways than one in the past few days.

'We let you sleep in a bit this morning but we thought you'd want to wake up now, sir. There's a lot to be done today.'

'Yes. Thank you. You were right.'

'The children are going to help me make toast when we all have our proper breakfast. I'll keep them occupied today, don't you worry.'

'I shan't worry at all if they're with you, Mona.'

'It's very kind of you to say so, sir.'

He didn't like to get out of the bed while she was there because his clothes were as bad as those of the rest of the family and he'd had to sleep in his underwear. As soon as she'd gone, he got up and grabbed the towel. After peeping out of his door to make sure no one was around, he hurried along to the bathroom. It was wonderful just to turn the tap and get as much hot water as you wanted. He managed to shave before giving himself the pleasure of a quick all-over wash, standing in the bath. No time for a proper bath today.

When he was done, he wrapped the towel around himself and peeped out again to make sure no one was around before rushing along to his room to get dressed. He couldn't run around half naked with two ladies in the house, and would have to buy some pyjamas and a dressing gown. As for the working clothes he was putting on, they were nearly falling to pieces they were so shabby and frayed.

Was there no end to the decisions that needed making, big and small? And how much was all this going to cost? He had some money saved but didn't want to use it all up. The funeral would be quite a big expense.

The kitchen was warm and welcoming, and the children looked rosy and relaxed, which immediately made Wilf feel good.

They all five ate together, a simple but satisfying breakfast of boiled eggs and slices of toast that Mrs Morton and Mona called 'soldiers', followed by strawberry jam on toast. Neither of the women brought up any sad topics while they ate, but discussed the weather and what they might have for tea.

When Wilf hesitated about taking another piece of toast, Mona noticed and urged him to do it. 'Take as many as you want, sir. We've always got plenty of bread in the house and today we ordered extra. The children are going to help me make some scones this morning so that'll be a treat for us all later.'

Once they'd finished eating, Mrs Morton suggested he go up to Ellindale and make a start. She'd wait for Mrs Tyler to pick her up in the car and follow later.

He was feeling positively cherished as he went outside. Yes, that was the word: cherished. What with a cup of tea in bed, a proper bathroom and a delicious breakfast made for him. Eh, he hadn't felt like that for a long time.

The first thing Wilf did when he arrived in Ellindale was walk around what he was already thinking of as his old home. The daylight was particularly cruel to its contents after the comforts of Mrs Morton's house. But at least that confirmed he'd been right in one of his decisions last night: there was very little he wanted to take with him, apart from the rest of his clothing, tools and carving equipment that he'd already put into the van.

A friend still sold the odd carving for him at the market. It made him feel good to give people pleasure as well as earn a little extra money. Why, even Mrs Tyler had one.

He stood in the kitchen and it looked so shabby, he vowed never to allow his children to live like beggars again. They'd been using the same cracked pieces of crockery and mended saucepans for as long as he could remember. The ragged, dress-like overall his wife had worn most of the time was still hanging limply on the hook behind the door.

The words were out before he could stop himself. 'There was no need to live like this, Enid. We could have afforded better for those children, yes, and for ourselves too.' Then, of course, he felt guilty at speaking ill of the dead.

When the two ladies arrived, just after nine o'clock, he let Mrs Tyler take the lead and plan their day's activities. Mr Tyler had once told him she organised his office and was very capable, and now he was experiencing that efficiency for himself.

'This morning should see us finished here, Wilf. You and I can go through the things in the church box this afternoon.'

That stung all over again! 'I don't need charity, Mrs Tyler! I can *buy* some clothes for us. There's a second-hand stall at the market which sells decent stuff.'

'I'm not offering you charity. Believe me, I shall charge you for the items we choose, the same amount as the church would have received for them in a jumble sale, neither more nor less. That way we shall all benefit.'

'Oh. Well, yes. That's all right then.'

As they worked their way around the house, he continued to feel ashamed, though he tried to hide that.

'Don't,' Mrs Tyler said to him at one stage.

'Don't what?'

'Don't feel ashamed of what your life has been like in the past. People have been experiencing hard times all over

Lancashire since the Great War ended, and it's no different here in Ellin Valley. Yet in spite of that, you've started to make a name for yourself and you've managed to acquire many skills. That is a huge achievement, Wilf, make no mistake about it.'

She let that sink in then went on, 'My husband thinks you'll have a good future as a builder and so does our friend Charlie Willcox. There's only you being hard on yourself.'

That made him feel better, as did the brief touch of her hand on his.

There was a shelf of Enid's personal possessions and when Mrs Tyler picked up the Bible on it, she exclaimed, 'Look at this, Wilf!'

The book was far too heavy and the cover opened to show that the interior pages had been sliced out and the hollow now contained some small pouches, which clinked as he lifted them out.

The two of them exchanged glances.

'Her savings, I presume,' Mrs Tyler said. 'They'll be yours now.'

Had Enid even felt it necessary to hide her savings from him? He opened one of the pouches and found it contained mainly half crowns. 'She wasn't feeding the children properly, but she'd got all this money saved.'

'She must have felt very insecure.'

He bit back further angry words – this was wrong, so very wrong.

By noon they had worked their way back to the kitchen, which was now full of neat piles of things from upstairs, where only the bed frames were now left.

Mrs Tyler stood gazing around. 'I think that's it. You're still sure you'll not be coming back to live here? Because if so, you'll need to have the telephone taken out here and put in at Mrs Morton's.'

'I'm definitely not coming back. This house is owned by

Higgerson and his rent agent refuses to spend any money on maintenance.'

'That man is a disgrace as a landlord, and as a builder, too.'

He nodded. Everyone knew Higgerson's houses were built as cheaply as possible, especially the ones for poorer folk. 'I'd have moved before now but Enid refused to leave.' He hesitated then said, 'I don't want to be a burden on Mrs Morton, though.'

'You'll be far from that, I promise. Beryl has had some lonely times in the past few years because she couldn't afford to entertain other ladies to tea and so on. I don't know what she'd have done without Mona, who's more a friend than a maid. And as for her son, who'd lost nearly all her money, he was a thief as well as stupid. But it was still sad that he died so young.'

Wilf must have still looked unconvinced, because she added, 'I'm sorry about the circumstances behind your move but trust me, Mrs Morton and Mona will both be much happier with you and the children living there. And the longer you stay, the happier they'll be.'

She wouldn't lie to him, or to anyone, he was sure. 'That's good to hear.'

'And don't forget, Wilf, you'll be able to do all sorts of small maintenance jobs for her while you're living there. So, you'll be more than paying her back for her help.'

'I'll do that. And I'll definitely bring her house up to scratch in every way. There are a few things I've noticed already that need sorting out.' That thought cheered him up considerably. But he wouldn't be able to do anything until after the funeral. How he was dreading that!

Just before noon, Mr Jeavons telephoned and they arranged to hold the funeral in two days' time, at nine o'clock in the morning.

Wilf had asked the undertaker to provide the simplest and cheapest sort of coffin for Enid, knowing she wouldn't have wanted him spending money on anything fancier, and besides, she didn't really have any close friends or family to care about such things.

'Mr Tyler's chauffeur has brought in your wife's clothes,' Mr Jeavons went on, 'so we'll have her looking her best for the viewing, which we'll hold in the church just before the ceremony.'

'Will that be all right with the vicar?'

'Um, it'll be the curate who holds the service in the small church at Birch End, Mr Pollard.'

'Yes, of course, what was I thinking of?' The vicar only officiated for the better class of parishioners and had a large, fine church near the Rivenshaw town centre to do that in. The small church in Birch End was modern and very plain, built at the end of the nineteenth century. It was mainly run by his curate, with the vicar only holding services there on special occasions.

Wilf doubted there would be many people attending. He wasn't a regular church attender himself, either, after all the years of wandering around Lancashire hunting for work. It was Enid who'd gone to the morning service regularly on Sundays, but she'd not joined in other activities held there as many women did.

At midday he said, 'I'd like to provide something to eat for you two ladies as a thank you for your help. I could go and buy us something at the local shop. It's very clean and Lily does really nice sandwiches. We can eat them there, if you like. They have tables for hikers and get quite a lot of custom from people going walking on the moors in fine weather.'

'Not for me, thank you,' Mrs Tyler said. 'I need to get some things done at home now and I can drop Beryl off on the way back. But you might like to buy yourself something and take the time to say goodbye to your neighbours. I don't think they'd feel as comfortable doing that if we were with you. Come to my house after you've finished here and we'll go to choose some clothes from the church stores.'

She was right, he knew that. People would be much more comfortable with just him.

Once the ladies had been driven away, he went across to the shop and asked Lily for a couple of sandwiches, one with ham and one with the sharp, crumbly Lancashire cheese she sometimes stocked. Before he left he explained to her where he'd be living from now on and asked her to tell people where to find him.

'I'll do that. And Wilf – I hope things will go well for you. We'll miss you in the village.'

'Oh, I'll be working round here sometimes, I'm sure, so I'll no doubt be popping in for sandwiches and cups of tea.'

A few people he knew came in while he was waiting and he told them about his plans.

He ate the sandwiches quickly at home, standing looking out across the village green, and had a drink of water in a chipped glass before going to see Mrs Harper next door.

'I wanted to say goodbye to you and to thank you for your help with Enid and the children. I don't know how I'd have managed without you.' He slipped a ten-shilling note into her hand. 'I know you're short of money so please don't refuse this. I've got good, regular work now. And what's more, if you're ever in need, don't hesitate to come to me.'

She folded the note carefully and put it into her apron pocket. 'You'll end up a master yourself, if you stick with your kind new friends, Wilf.'

'Maybe. But I'll not forget kind old friends like you. Don't think I don't know that you occasionally used to slip extra food to the children. Ronnie let it out the other night.'

'Oh, well. I don't like to see little 'uns looking hungry.'

'Can I ask a further favour of you?'

'Aye, of course.'

'Will you let my brother know where I am when he gets back from work tonight?'

'Happy to.'

'Now, there are a few bits and pieces of food left in the kitchen next door. Take them or they'll go to waste. There's the rest of the furniture as well as that sofa you've got your eye on. You and Daniel should go through everything together, take what you need then give the rest away. Or sell it, if it's worth anything.'

She gaped at him. 'Are you sure?'

'Yes. I need to make a completely new start.' He was surprised at how desperately he needed that.

'I'll sell the things your brother doesn't want at the market, if you don't mind, Wilf. I've been collecting stuff for a while, ever since my youngest son left school. I'm thinking of starting a second-hand stall, you see. Do you think that's a silly idea?'

She was flushed and anxious now. But he knew older women did sometimes start up small businesses after their children had left home. It was usually the time of life when they had the most money and time at their disposal. Eh, life was too short by far for all you wanted to fit into it.

He took her hand in his and looked at her earnestly. 'I think it's a very good idea. Use my old possessions for that with my blessing.' He pulled out another note. 'Here. Give yourself something to buy stock with.'

'I can't keep taking money from you.'

'It's not much, but it'll help.'

She blinked hard, then gave him a smacking kiss on each cheek.

He wouldn't be surprised if she made a success of a market stall. She was a hard worker and shrewd with it. Everyone liked her because though she was a bit of a gossip, she was never malicious. She'd be good at chatting to customers.

Then at last it was over. Everything he wanted to keep was in the van and he didn't even look back at his former home as he left and drove slowly down the hill towards Birch End.

As he passed the houses of friends and former workmates in Ellindale, he slowed down but didn't see anyone he knew well, so contented himself with waving back to anyone who noticed him and carrying on.

I'm driving into the future, he thought, as he passed the railway carriage Harry Makepeace had turned into a home, and went on down past the few small fields that separated Birch End from Ellindale. *Yes, that's what I'm doing now, driving into the future.*

What would the new life in Birch End hold for him and his children? Something very different from what he'd experienced already, that was for sure, and different too from what he'd been expecting a few days ago before Roy Tyler had made his offer of a partnership.

If hard work continued to pay dividends, he should at least manage to give his children a better start in life. In spite of the sad circumstances, the first seeds of hope had already crept into his heart, put down roots and begun to grow. He patted his chest as if to encourage them, then smiled at his own foolishness.

Living with Mrs Morton would be a big improvement, too. He and his children would learn a lot from her.

He admitted to himself that he didn't just want a decent life; he wanted to be a respected builder in his own right one day. You had to have dreams or what would you aim for next? Well, that was his view of the world, anyway.

He was going to press forward towards that goal with all the courage he had, and it would take courage at times, he was sure. People from the poorer parts of the valley didn't usually succeed in anything but the very smallest of businesses. And some people resented seeing them even achieve that.

He turned left into the lane that led to Birch End. It was one thing to dream but first he needed to give Enid a proper send-off, something the children would share with him and remember. It was she who'd wanted to adopt them, she who'd kept the home together all through the hard years. He'd never stop being grateful for that, even if they'd differed about how to live towards the end.

From now on, though, he'd not forget to *show* Peggy and Ronnie how much he loved them, by word and deed. He'd never forget that after seeing how the ladies treated them, and how much the children loved being touched and praised and cuddled.

You could learn something, big or small, from everything you encountered in life. He'd teach his children that.

Those two were not only a vital part of his life and future, they were a grand pair of kids.

8

Stella woke early and was ready to leave her lodgings long before the taxi arrived to take her to the station. After some consideration, she'd decided to wear her best clothes to travel in because her work clothes might be decent, but they were a bit shabby.

She needed some new clothes, really, as these were also old-fashioned. From what she'd seen in the women's magazines at the library, her skirt was too full and her hat too small, though it looked better with her hair in a more loose style than all dragged back into a bun.

She'd been making do with those clothes for best because she didn't linger after church and none of the congregation would have cared what she looked like anyway. She only attended that place of worship occasionally on Sunday mornings because it was the closest to her home and the owner of the laundry had insisted that all his employees should be 'regular churchgoers'.

Today she had to force herself to eat the food she'd kept for breakfast and only did that because she didn't want to risk feeling weak later in the day.

A few minutes before the taxi was due, she carried all her boxes down to the hall, though she had to go backwards with the heavy box of books, lifting it down one step at a time. She heaved a loud sigh of relief when she got it to the bottom. She'd been terrified it'd fall and split apart, then how would she get them to Rivenshaw?

Her landlady popped her head out to say goodbye but didn't linger. She'd already been up to check that the room was in good order, which it was, of course it was, but she hadn't offered to help carry anything down. The other tenant had gone out to work at the usual time without a word of farewell.

Stella waited on the doorstep, glad when the taxi arrived on time. The driver was happy to help her with the trunk and had no trouble lifting her boxes and suitcase into his boot, after which she settled down to enjoy the ride.

They went by way of the town centre, which pleased her because the library and town hall were such beautiful buildings, and up the hill past the shops on Drake Street to the station. The journey felt like a chance to say farewell to Rochdale. The centre was far prettier than the part she'd lived in and she'd come there for walks occasionally at weekends or taken a detour on the way home from work to change her library books.

She found a fatherly porter to carry her things into the station on his trolley. He chuckled when she warned him that the box of books was heavy, and patted her shoulder when she said they had to go in the luggage van.

'Don't worry, love. Just settle down and enjoy your journey. I've carried far heavier luggage than yours and the other porter will help me with your trunk as soon as the train arrives. I'll make sure your boxes are placed safely in the luggage wagon.'

She slipped him a sixpenny tip, guessing she must be looking anxious.

They both waited for the train to arrive and another porter found her a compartment, hurrying her into it before helping with her luggage.

But she couldn't settle till she was certain the boxes got on to the train with her. So she opened her carriage door again, just a little, and peered out to make sure that the porter did as promised. After that she closed the door properly, collapsed on to her seat and leaned back.

First stage done!

The whistle blew and slowly, slowly the train pulled away. 'Goodbye, Rochdale,' she said aloud, then felt silly and was thankful no one else was in the compartment to hear her talking to herself.

She had to change trains at Manchester and again found an obliging porter to make sure all her boxes went with her across the busy station.

After that, since it was a slow train, it took well over an hour of tedious stopping and starting, doors banging and whistles blowing as the train chugged its way towards the Pennine Hills and Rivenshaw. It halted at all the small stations en route. They might look pretty in summer with flowers in the corner beds, but now they looked bare and winter grey. The paved areas of the early stations were still wet from a recent shower.

At last they arrived in Rivenshaw and she heaved a sigh of relief. She oversaw her luggage being taken off the train and placed in the long-term storage area behind the left-luggage office, then put the ticket for it safely into her purse.

Second stage done!

She took a deep breath, picked up her shabby suitcase and went to find a taxi.

As she'd remembered, Rivenshaw station occupied one side of a large square. The other sides were surrounded by shops and buildings that were too large to be homes. The sun had come out now and everything looked more cheerful. It felt like a sign that she was doing the right thing.

She paused, smiling at her own silliness, and stood taking it all in for a few moments before beckoning a waiting taxi and asking the driver if he knew somewhere respectable where she could put up for a few nights.

Head on one side, he studied her, nodding slowly, as if she'd passed some sort of test. 'Mrs Tucker's will suit you, I think, miss. She only takes lady lodgers and has a good reputation. And her place is within easy walking distance of the town centre, which is always useful if you're new to an area.'

'That sounds just right. Let's hope she has a vacancy.'

'She usually does, because she takes a few short-term visitors, says there's more profit in them.'

Half an hour later Stella had a pleasant room looking on to the street at the front of the house.

Third stage done! The final of today's plans.

She arranged to have tea with the other lodgers at six o'clock, then asked directions for finding her way around the town centre.

'You'll have plenty of time for a nice stroll before it gets dark,' her new landlady said. 'And do call me Mrs T. Everyone else does.'

Stella set out to explore the town centre, strolling along feeling tired but happy. She'd done it, taken the biggest step of her whole life, moving herself lock, stock and barrel to a small country town.

Could she now find a job, learn to drive and buy a car? They would be quite big steps too, so if she didn't achieve them straight away, she'd simply let herself enjoy a restful few days, or even weeks. She'd never had that luxury before in her whole life.

As she had many times in the past few days, she murmured 'Thank you, Lena.'

Oh dear, she was talking to herself again. She really must stop doing that.

Maybe she should start by taking driving lessons then buy a car. It would make life so much easier if she had a vehicle of her own.

As she was walking along, she saw a young woman walking just ahead of her stumble and put one hand to her forehead. It all seemed to happen very quickly, but she guessed what was about to happen. As the woman began to crumple, she fell towards the road, where a car was driving towards them far too quickly.

Without even thinking about it, Stella jumped forward and grabbed the woman by the back of her coat, hauling her unceremoniously back on to the pavement.

She was barely in time!

The car's brakes screeched and then the driver carried on again, driving just as quickly. He'd probably have managed to stop in time to miss the fainting woman, but he hadn't bothered to find out if she was all right.

An older woman, who hadn't been close enough to do anything to prevent the accident, ran forward to help Stella lower the unconscious woman on to the bench of a nearby bus stop. Stella sat beside her, holding her in place, and the stranger sat on the other side, staring down the street indignantly.

'Did you see that? He just drove off without stopping.'

Their conversation was interrupted because the woman began to regain full consciousness.

The older woman said to Stella, 'You know, I reckon you saved Mrs Howarth's life just now and—' She broke off to call to another passer-by. 'Go and tell Mr Howarth his wife's had a bad turn, Don.'

The man gaped at them and hurried back the way he'd come.

The woman who'd fainted opened her eyes and frowned. 'What happened? I feel dizzy.'

How strange! That was the first thing people said in books after they'd fainted, Stella thought, then told herself not to be silly. Books weren't real life, however important they were to her.

The older woman seemed rather excited, almost as if she was enjoying herself. 'You fainted, Mrs Howarth, and would have fallen in front of a passing car if this lady hadn't grabbed you and pulled you back. She probably saved your life.'

'Oh, no. I never faint.'

'Well, you did today.'

A man rushed around the corner and pounded along the street to kneel in front of the young woman. 'What happened?'

This must be Mr Howarth and he'd said the same words as his wife, Stella thought. The books were clearly right.

'I can't remember properly,' his wife muttered, rubbing her forehead.

The other woman explained again exactly how quickly Stella had reacted and she could feel herself blushing.

Still holding his wife steady, Mr Howarth turned to her. 'I can't thank you enough.'

'Er ... I'm glad I was there.'

'Hello! That's my bus coming. Will you be all right if I leave now, Mr Howarth? Only there isn't another bus for an hour.' The woman stood up and waved at the bus to stop. She was gone within a minute.

The crowd of gaping passers-by had also dispersed, much to Stella's relief.

'I wonder if I could trouble you to carry my wife's shopping bag so that I can carry her?' Mr Howarth asked. 'We're only just around the corner.'

'Yes, of course.' Stella picked it up and followed him along the street and around the corner.

He was strong enough to carry his wife, though she was quite a tall woman, but he was panting by the time he stopped in front of a business with a sign saying *Willcox and Selby Motors*. He set her down so that she could lean against the nearest of several motor cars.

Mrs Howarth had a bit more colour in her cheeks now, Stella thought, and as she waited she took the opportunity to study her surroundings.

This was a business that sold used cars. What luck! She'd been keeping her eyes open for one so that she could find out what prices were like. Several vehicles were parked in front of a house on an expanse of tarmac, which had probably once been the garden of a large family home. The cars were at an angle to the street.

'I can walk into the house from here, Nick,' Mrs Howarth said crossly. 'If you'd given me a minute to recover, I could perfectly well have walked back.'

'You'd fainted, Jo. You might have done it again and hurt yourself badly this time. I wasn't risking it.'

Stella listened in amusement as they continued to bicker about whether Mrs Howarth could walk across to the house. My goodness, she sounded angry. And she spoke differently, with some sort of accent. She certainly didn't come from this part of the world. Yet underneath the arguing, anyone could sense that they loved one another.

While she waited for them to calm down, she continued to look round. To the right was what looked like a workshop, in which a car was standing with its bonnet raised. A man had been leaning over it fiddling with something in the engine, but he'd looked up when they arrived. Once he realised that Mr Howarth was supporting his wife, he put down his tools, wiped his oily hands on a rag and came across to join them.

'Open the front door for me, will you, Todd? She's not easy to carry.'

Mrs Howarth batted away her husband's hands as he tried

to pick her up. 'Just let me hold your arm, you idiot. I've still got legs.'

Scowling, he did so.

Hiding a smile, Stella followed them inside with the wife's bag of shopping, passing two offices, one on either side of the entrance hall, with smaller rooms behind them. At the rear was a large kitchen.

Only after Mrs Howarth had grudgingly agreed to sit down at the table and not move without someone to steady her did Mr Howarth turn to Stella. 'I can't thank you enough for preventing my wife from falling in front of a car.'

Stella shrugged. 'Anyone close enough would have done the same, and it'd probably have been able to stop in time. I just didn't want to risk it. I've seen people faint before. You can't mistake that look.'

'From what that other woman said, you were very quick to take action.'

'I'm glad I was there. And no one's hurt, that's the main thing. Now, here's your shopping bag. I'll leave you to recover in peace now, Mrs Howarth. I'm glad you weren't hurt.'

The woman took it from her. 'Call me Jo. After all, you just saved my life. And this grumpy fellow is my husband, Nick.'

'He was worried about you. I should be going.'

'No, wait! What's your name? I'd like to know who saved me.'

'Stella Newby.'

'Miss?'

'No, Mrs. I'm a widow.'

'Oh, I'm sorry. How about staying and having a cup of tea with us? Nick will have to make it since I'm not allowed to move around till he gives me permission.' She grinned cheekily at her husband, who shook his head in mock anger and picked up the kettle.

'Do you want a cup, too, Todd?'

'Do I ever say no?' He turned to Stella. 'So, Mrs Newby? Are you new to town?'

'Yes. And, actually, I'd appreciate some help from you, if you have time. I'm thinking of buying a car, you see, but first I have to learn to drive. Only since this is a car yard, I thought I'd take a preliminary look at cars and find out about prices, before I find a driving school.'

They all started chuckling, though not in a nasty way.

'What did I say?' she asked in bewilderment.

It was Jo who replied. 'This is Todd's car yard, yes, and you may not have noticed our sign, which is much smaller. My husband and I run a driving school from one of those offices at the front of the building. You've certainly rescued someone from the right place.'

'Oh. I see.' She smiled at that coincidence. What a bit of luck!'

'We can have a quick look at cars after we've finished our tea,' Todd said. 'Just to give you an idea of what you can get for your money. That's probably all you need at the moment, if you're just starting to look for a car. Am I right?'

'Yes, you are.' She turned to Nick. 'And perhaps I can book a driving lesson for tomorrow.'

'You'll need to buy a Highway Code and study it first.'

'Oh, I've done that already. I've read it so many times I think I know it by heart.'

'Jo will book you in for a lesson after you've looked at the cars. As long as she doesn't faint on us again.'

His wife punched him in the arm and he pretended to be in agony.

Stella looked at the clock on the mantelpiece. 'Will there be time to look at them before dusk?'

They all stared towards the clock and out of the window. 'The days are so short in winter, the darkness takes you by surprise sometimes. We'd better not delay.' Todd picked up his cup and drained it rapidly. 'I'll give you a quick tour of what cars I've got at the moment, then I'll go home to my wife. You can come back tomorrow and have a better look, and I'll take you for a ride in anything you're interested in. But a quick look now will give you an idea of the sort of thing that's available – and give me an idea of what you might need.'

'And I can book you in a lesson for ten o'clock in the morning,' Jo said. 'I happen to know Nick has nothing booked at all for tomorrow morning.'

So Stella followed Todd's example, drank her cup of tea quickly and went out with him to look at the cars.

This must be her lucky day.

9

When the other two had left, Nick looked at his wife in puzzlement. 'Have you picked up the influenza or something, darling? I've never known you faint before.'

Jo flushed. 'Well, it's your fault I fainted just as much as mine.'

He looked at her in surprise, then his expression changed slowly to understanding.

She took a deep breath and said it. 'I've never been expecting a baby before, have I? I went to see Dr McDevitt early this morning before I called at the greengrocer's and he agreed with me that I was expecting.'

'Oh, my darling! That's the most wonderful news.'

'It's what we wanted but not completely wonderful if it makes me faint. I never realised before what a horrible, helpless feeling it is.'

'Is this the first time you've done it?'

'First time in my whole life, as far as I remember.' She looked at him anxiously. 'You don't think there's something wrong with me, do you, Nick?'

'We'd better go back and check that with the doctor. Why McDevitt? I thought you were going to see Dr Mitchell, as most of the other ladies seem to.'

'I've met Mitchell and I didn't like him. He's arrogant and patronising towards women. He treated me as if I hadn't got a brain and needed talking to slowly in words of one syllable. Some men are like that and I don't put up with it, whoever they are. I wish we had a woman doctor in the valley. If we had, I'd go to her.'

'You are a fiery creature sometimes. Must be your Aussie upbringing.'

'Well, what would you do if someone treated you like that, Nick?'

'I'd do the same as you, not have anything to do with them.' He grinned and added, 'Or punch them good and hard. Go on.'

'So when I heard about the new doctor, I went to see him instead. And I liked him. He'd go down well in Australia. Tells you the truth and looks you in the eye as he does it. Talked normally to me and didn't dress everything up in fancy words to show off, either.'

'I love your independent Aussie spirit.'

She shrugged. 'I think women in the country towns down under have to do so much to help run their families' farms, they don't have time to be meek with doctors, or with anyone else for that matter. At least, that's what Dad always said. Oh, I do wish he were still alive. He'd be so happy to be a grandfather.'

'I'm sure he would.' Nick let out a sudden cackle of laughter. 'But I bet your stepmother won't be happy!'

She lost the anxious look and laughed with him. 'Edna will absolutely hate it. It'd almost be worth going to visit her and tell her, to see her face when I call her grandma.' She grimaced. 'No. Not quite worth it. She is as silly as ever and has no morals. I haven't forgiven her for conspiring against me with that horrible cousin of hers to try to get hold of the money I'd inherited from Dad. I was glad when Rathley died.'

'You and half the town.'

'I wish Edna would find another husband. She's the sort of woman who needs one to think for her and look after her. And preferably a husband who lives in a different town, well away from the valley, then I wouldn't need to see her again.'

'I bet Gertrude Rathley wishes Edna would find a husband even more than you do. I've heard she's regretting the day she invited your stepmother to live with her, even if the woman is a cousin-in-law.'

He paused and gave Jo a very loving look. 'Never mind that fool. Well done, my darling. I can't wait to see our child.'

She slipped her hand in his, her face lit up by the softest of smiles. 'I can't wait, either.'

He frowned again. 'I'd have said you were the last woman in this whole valley who'd ever faint. Look, promise me you'll take care what you do until we find out what's making you lose consciousness so suddenly.'

'Of course I will. But what about the office? We're going to need someone else to work there now, anyway. Your driving school is starting to keep you busier.'

'And the person will presumably be working for Todd part-time too, as you have. We'll have to put an advert in the newspaper.'

She stretched up to kiss him and watched him go with another fond smile.

What sort of questions did you ask when you wanted to buy a car? Stella wondered as she followed Todd Selby outside. She usually planned what to do well in advance but this had happened unexpectedly. She would no doubt find out a lot simply by talking to him.

'Let's look at the cars.' Todd stopped at the first car in the row of eight.

Stella studied it with a frown. 'One thing I do know, Mr Selby, is I don't want a big car like this one. There's only myself to think about, after all.'

'It's also more difficult to manoeuvre a larger car in busy towns and as you haven't learned to drive yet, I'd not have recommended one like this for you.'

She decided it was no use pretending. 'I'm not really sure what to look for when choosing a car, Mr Selby. Perhaps you can tell me something about these vehicles and what I should take into account?'

'Happy to. Let me start by saying that there are only two that I'd recommend for you as a beginner, and, er, not very tall. There's a small but important point: you have to consider whether people's legs can reach the pedals easily.'

She stared down at her own legs and sideways at him, so tall and pleasant-looking. It wasn't something she'd have thought about in relation to cars, but it made sense.

He moved straight to the fourth car in the row. 'This one is more your sort. The Ford Seven is a very reliable vehicle. They've been making them for years and they're made in Coventry now, you know.' He went on to the sixth car. 'And this one would be all right as well. It's a Morris. Both are good makes of car.'

She nodded again.

'These days modern cars have electric starters, lights and windscreen wipers, which makes life a lot easier for drivers. The old cars were often based on horse-drawn carriages and it took a while to change to modern equipment. You should get as modern a car as you can afford.

'In addition, you'll note that these two are saloon models so there will be no problems with putting up a hood on them, which I think wouldn't be easy for someone of your height, either.'

She looked at the cars he'd pointed out, walking round each one, and they did indeed look as if they'd be more manageable than the bigger ones or those with hoods. She couldn't imagine raising and lowering a hood on her own.

'Try sitting in the driver's seat of each one in turn and see how comfortable you feel.'

She did that, feeling excited because it was the first time she'd ever sat behind the steering wheel of any vehicle.

When she got out of the second car, he hesitated then said, 'Please believe me that I'm not telling lies or trying to push you into buying a car too quickly, but this Ford would be far better value. It belonged to an elderly gentleman who used it only to drive around Rivenshaw and the valley to visit his relatives or to go to church. He died last month and his son has sold it to me for a very fair price because he already has a car. I can let you have it for forty-five pounds.'

She looked at him instead of the car, more concerned at this stage with whether she trusted him than whether the vehicle was worth what he was asking. Well . . . she liked his face, the way he looked you straight in the eyes. And as he owned a business here in town, she doubted he'd be selling a vehicle that was faulty to anyone, not if he wanted to continue in business. But how could she find out for sure whether to take his advice?

One thing occurred to her. 'I wonder if you could reserve the Ford for me for a few days, Mr Selby, until I've had a try at driving? It'd be no use buying a car if I proved a failure at that.'

'Yes, of course I could. Good idea. Ah!' He raised one arm to wave to a gentleman coming towards them along the street. 'This is my partner, Mr Willcox. Charlie, this is Mrs Newby, who has just come to live in Rivenshaw and is interested in buying a car.'

The new arrival nodded. He was probably about forty with a cheerful open face and was wearing spectacles which made him look like a rather plump owl.

'Welcome to Rivenshaw, Mrs Newby. Is your husband not with you to help choose a car?'

Todd hurriedly interrupted. 'Mrs Newby is a widow.'

'Ah. Sorry.'

'It's all right. You weren't to know. My husband died three years ago.'

Todd took over again. 'Just to show that we're respectable businessmen, I'll tell you that Mr Willcox owns two pawnshops, one electrical goods shop and has an interest in several businesses including this one. He's also on the town council.'

'So is Todd. On the town council, I mean. And his wife is as well.'

Stella liked the idea that Mrs Selby was also a councillor. That spoke well for her husband. Some men wouldn't have allowed their wives such independence. Well, Derrick wouldn't have liked her to stand for council, come to that. She'd been too meek in those days, letting him make most of the important decisions. If he hadn't been so kind and loving, she might have stood up for herself more often. Oh well, water under the bridge now. She wasn't going to be meek again, not with anyone.

'Mrs Newby has made a wonderful first impression on me by saving Jo from an accident,' Mr Selby went on.

Stella could feel herself flushing and muttered, 'Anyone would have done the same.'

'They might not have been quick enough to grab her.'

She decided that both men had honest faces and she liked them, and she liked Jo Howarth too. She doubted they'd be in business together if one of them was a cheat. Taking a deep breath, she decided to risk it.

'If you can keep that Ford for me for a few days, Mr Selby, I'll arrange for some driving lessons and be able to sit in it and have a little drive along a straight stretch of road, perhaps, before I buy it.'

'Good idea. You can also make enquiries about us and find out whether we're trustworthy.'

She felt another blush stealing up her face and both men smiled at her.

'No need to be embarrassed. It's what any sensible person would do,' Mr Willcox said.

'Right. That's agreed, then. It's getting late, so I'd better make my way back to my lodgings or I'll be late for tea.'

As she turned to walk away, she heard Mr Willcox say, 'Now, Todd, how's that car of mine coming on?'

'The repairs are almost finished. I do wish you'd stop driving it into gateposts. You've scraped the paintwork on the left wing again. I don't have time to attend to that today.'

'They make gateways too narrow for modern cars.'

Stella was about to head back to Mrs T's when a cold breeze made her shiver and realise she'd left her coat on her chair in the kitchen. She went back into the house, calling out from just inside the open front door. 'Anyone there?'

'I'm still in the kitchen,' Jo called. 'I saw you'd left your coat and thought you'd come back for it. Nick has nipped out to the shops for me.'

'I didn't ask about the cost of lessons but I just saw the notice on the wall outside as I was coming in.' She gestured towards the entrance where a sign said *Driving Lessons 10/- an hour.*

Jo looked at her shrewdly. 'Does ten shillings seem expensive?'

'It's not exactly cheap, but I suppose the person giving the lessons has to buy a car and pay for all the running costs before they can even start earning money.'

'Not many people have the sense to see that.'

'It must be an interesting job, meeting lots of different people. I've been working in an office until recently, doing very simple accounts and mostly entering figures in ledgers. It was really boring.'

'Do you have a job waiting for you in Rivenshaw?'

'Not yet. I'll need to find one.'

'Family here?'

'No. I don't know anyone.'

'You know us now. They say if you save someone's life you're connected from then onwards. If you don't mind me asking, why did you come here if you don't know anyone and don't have a job?'

'I'd visited it with my husband a few years ago and remembered how much we liked the area. Where I've been living since my husband died was too industrial, smuts in the air, lots of smoke. I wanted to live in a country town and breathe fresh air.'

Stella hesitated, then thought: in for a penny, in for a pound, so added, 'And I, um, came into a little money, not a lot but enough to buy a car and perhaps a small cottage. I hope to have enough to tide me over until I can make a more interesting life. So I just . . . well, came here. I'm staying at Mrs T's.'

'I stayed there when I first arrived. I'm from Australia, as you may have guessed.'

'I've been trying to place your accent, but I've never met an Australian before.'

Jo laughed. 'We have one head, two arms and two legs, just like anyone else.' She studied Stella. 'You're looking for a job, you say?'

'Yes.'

'I've been acting as part-time secretary, clerk, receptionist and general factotum to my husband's driving school, as well as working for Todd part-time, since they share these premises. That's not been boring. But I shall soon have to stop.' She smiled down at her stomach in the way women expecting a child often did, though hers showed no signs of the baby, so it must be early days.

'A baby? Oh, congratulations!'

'Thank you. We've been living upstairs but we've just bought a house in Birch End, so we'll have to move in and sort all the furniture out before I get too unwieldy.' She gave Stella a questioning look. 'Does the job here sound more interesting than your previous one?'

'Oh, yes. Though almost anything would be more interesting than that one.' Stella looked at her and guessed why Jo had asked that question. 'Are you encouraging me to apply for it?'

'I was hoping you might. It's not just because you saved my life, but because you talk like a sensible woman. I'm a little bit younger than you, I think, but old enough to have met a fair number of people on both sides of the world, and I'm conceited enough to count myself a good judge of character.'

Stella felt the same but didn't say it, just waited, hoping, oh definitely hoping.

'How about working with me for a few days, so we can both see whether it'll suit?'

'I'd love to.' Was she asleep and dreaming? This couldn't be happening to her. She'd never been particularly lucky. She immediately contradicted herself mentally. *Until recently!* She'd been very lucky indeed recently, but hadn't expected any further pieces of luck to come her way after winning the money.

She glanced towards the window and realised it had grown dark outside. 'I'd better get back to my lodgings. What time shall I come here tomorrow morning?'

'Eight thirty. The first lesson is usually at nine, you see, so we have to open the office before that to get ready for it. It's been easy while Nick and I have been living here, but our new home is further away. There isn't an early lesson tomorrow, you're having the first one at ten o'clock, so I can make a start on showing you the office arrangements.'

'Sounds like a good idea. I'll see you then.'

Stella walked home feeling as if she was floating along in a dream. It was a good thing the way lay along well-lit main streets so she had no trouble finding her way back.

What a good start it had been to living in Rivenshaw.

10

The following morning Stella had breakfast with the other lodgers, after which they all scattered to go to work. She walked down the gently sloping streets to the car sales business, and had to admit to herself that she was feeling rather nervous about both the try-out for the office job and the driving lesson.

She kept telling herself that she could do a job like that, yes, and enjoy it, too. Well, of course she could. But that didn't stop her feeling nervous, so she fell back on something her grandma had always told her when she was little: put on an imaginary 'brave hat' then you can do anything you like. That thought usually made her smile at least, which never hurt.

She'd read the Highway Code again last night in her room, but though she'd gone through it slowly and carefully, she'd found nothing in it that she hadn't already learned by heart. So she could be sure that she at least knew the rules of the road. Was that enough? She didn't want to seem a fool.

Yes, of course, it would be enough. Nick must know how to give a nervous beginner her very first lesson.

Here it was. Taking a deep breath, she walked across the tarmac, pausing for a moment to study the car that might become hers soon. She found the front door slightly open and when she pushed it, she heard the sound of someone being sick upstairs.

'Are you all right, Jo?' she called.

A croaky voice said, 'Could you bring me up a mug of hot water, please?'

'Yes, of course.' She found the kettle on the top of the gas cooker. It had boiled recently so she opened cupboard doors till she found a mug, poured some water in and carried it up the stairs.

When she stopped at the top, not sure which way to go, Jo called, 'I'm here. In the bathroom.'

She found the other woman sitting on the rim of the bath, looking wan, and held out the mug. 'Here you are.'

'Thank you.' Jo took a sip, clasping the mug to one cheek then the other, shivering and holding it with both hands. 'I feel so cold!' After another sip she added, 'I didn't expect this. It's the first time I've had morning sickness. Nick got up first and went out to buy some fresh bread. When I got out of bed, nausea hit me and I had to run in here. Ugh.'

Stella leaned against the door frame. 'Anything else I can get you, or shall I help you back to bed?'

'I don't know whether I dare move yet. This is ghastly. Have you ever had it?'

'I've been a widow for three years and nothing happened in the years before that even though we'd have loved a child. I've never stopped regretting the lack of one.'

Sick as she was, Jo put out a hand to clasp Stella's comfortingly and they stayed there till the door banged downstairs.

'Jo?'

'I'm up here, Nick. I've been sick.'

'What's wrong?' He came pounding up the stairs two at a time.

'Just morning sickness,' Jo said.

'*Just?* Darling, you're as white as a sheet.'

'Do you want me to leave you two together?' Stella asked.

'No. Nick, go away and leave me to recover. You'll have to get your own breakfast.' Jo shuddered as if the mere thought of food upset her. 'Why don't you go and poke around the office, Stella?'

She went downstairs with Nick, who whispered, 'Does this sickness go on happening?'

'I think it depends on the woman. I've known some have it only at the beginning, but one neighbour had it every day she was carrying the child. A few don't get it at all. You'll have to wait and see.'

'Well, that settles one thing. I'm not having her dragging herself to work if she's feeling rotten. It's a good thing you turned up.'

'I'll go and poke about in the office.'

Stella peered out of the office when she heard footsteps coming down the stairs about ten minutes later. 'You look a little better, Jo.'

'Yes. I think it's passing.'

Nick came rushing out of the kitchen. 'Are you all right? Don't you want to go back to bed? Shall I call the doctor?'

Jo rolled her eyes at him. 'Stop fussing. I'm all right.'

'Yes, but—'

Stella could see that his fretting was annoying Jo. 'Why don't you sit down in the kitchen and I'll make you a cup of tea?'

'That'd be lovely. Thanks. And you go and check the car, Nick.' She held up one hand to stop him protesting. 'Go!'

By half past nine, you'd not think Jo had been ill at all and she insisted on giving Stella a quick tour of the office cupboards and drawers before glancing at the clock. 'Time for you to get ready for your driving lesson.'

'I can postpone it if you need help here.'

'No. I'm feeling perfectly normal now. Isn't that strange?'

As they got into the car Nick used for giving driving lessons, a neat little Morris, he said glumly, 'I don't know how women stand it. It nearly killed me to see Jo looking so bad this morning.'

'We don't have much choice about how our bodies make babies. And I think your child will be very much wanted, from what Jo's said, whether it makes her sick for a few months or not.'

'I suppose you're right. Well, you're not paying me to chat about babies, so let's turn to the driving. You said you'd read the Highway Code?'

'I think I know it by heart.'

He grinned at her. 'That doesn't surprise me. Now, I'm going to drive and I'll explain what I'm doing and why as we go. Never mind looking at the scenery today. You should watch me as I drive, more carefully than you've ever watched anyone driving before. That way you'll be able to connect what I'm doing with what the car does.'

He was right about that, at least. His actions fascinated her and his explanations of what he was doing and why were clear and helpful.

When he turned off the main road and stopped on a quiet little lane that led to the village of Birch End, he said, 'Like to try driving now? You seem to be one of the people who understand what to do quickly from your reactions and questions. We'll just go up and down this lane today.'

For a moment Stella froze in near terror, but took a deep breath and said, 'If *you* think I can manage, I'll have a go.'

He switched off the engine. 'All right. We're about to find out how much you've taken in during our drive today. And stop looking so worried. Since you're not likely to meet any other vehicles or pedestrians around here, people will be perfectly safe from your actions, whatever mistakes you make.'

She knew he was making a joke, but she couldn't smile. Heart pounding, she mentally put on her brave hat, moved round the car and got into the driving seat. Following his instructions, she started the car and managed to put it into first gear and then second. She didn't dare go fast and the car crawled to the end of the lane at a snail's pace.

He pointed to one side. 'There's enough room to turn the car round on that piece of spare land, and there's a wide gateway at the other end.'

She managed that, thankful that she didn't have to cope with going backwards yet.

They went up and down the lane several times, after which Nick took over again. She watched what he did with considerably more understanding as he drove them back.

'You did well today,' he said casually.

'I did?'

'Yes. Truly.' He chuckled. 'We'll go to another place tomorrow and you can try getting up to a speed of more than ten miles an hour.'

When they got back she returned to the office and Jo joined her again, this time showing her how the paperwork for Todd's business was organised.

The rest of the day passed amazingly quickly and Stella couldn't believe it when the daylight started to fade.

'Nick said you did well with the driving. You're good in the office too,' Jo said quietly. 'See you tomorrow? Or have I put you off with my performance this morning?'

'Not at all. I just hope you'll feel better tomorrow.'

'So do I. But I doubt it. I'm trying not to think of that. Sufficient unto the day . . . '

Stella walked home feeling exhausted but happy. How lucky that she'd come to Rivenshaw. Even more lucky that she'd met Jo and Nick.

Sergeant Deemer stopped to ring the doorbell of the three-storey building that had once been an elegant home in the town centre. A sign to one side of the entrance said *G. Higgerson, Esq, Builder* in gold letters.

It ought to say builder of future slums, he thought to himself. Even Higgerson's better quality houses were skimped in the details unless the person buying them kept a very sharp eye on what was being done. He knew Charlie Willcox had had to complain about several things when he moved into his home a few years ago and if anything, Higgerson had gone from bad to worse since then.

When no one bothered to answer the door, Sergeant Deemer walked straight in.

A clerk got hurriedly to his feet. 'Excuse me, what are you doing— Oh, it's you, sergeant.'

'I'd like to speak to your employer.'

'Mr Higgerson's busy I'm afraid. Perhaps I can help you?'

'It's not about his building business, it's something personal. I won't keep him long. I'm definitely *not* going until I've seen him.'

The clerk frowned but when Deemer folded his arms and waited, foot tapping impatiently, he vanished through a door at the back, coming out a minute or two later to say, 'My employer can spare you five minutes.'

Deemer walked in, not surprised at how luxurious the office was. Higgerson was known for treating himself to anything he fancied, sometimes even young women.

The man didn't rise from behind his desk. 'How can I help you, sergeant?'

Rude devil! Deemer thought. 'Two days ago you drove through the town centre and almost knocked down a lady.'

Higgerson frowned then snapped his finger. 'Oh, I remember. She stepped out in front of my car.'

'She fainted. And *you* were driving too fast for safety, witnesses said. If a bystander hadn't managed to pull her out of the way, you might have killed her – and her unborn child.

What's more, you didn't even stop to check that she was all right.'

'It was obvious that she was. I hadn't touched her. Is that all?'

'Not quite, sir.' He produced a piece of paper and plonked it down on the desk behind which Higgerson was still sitting. 'This is an official warning about unsafe driving, which is against the local by-laws. If it happens again, you'll be fined.'

Higgerson turned so red and angry, Deemer was afraid for a moment that he was going to have a seizure.

'And any magistrate will refuse to apply a fine to *me*. I repeat: the near accident was caused by the young woman and I didn't touch her. Who was she by the way?'

Unfortunately, Deemer wasn't allowed to deny him this information. 'Mrs Howarth.'

'Never heard of her. Who's Mr Howarth when he's at home?'

'A businessman in the town.'

Higgerson scribbled something down, presumably the name. Deemer wished he wasn't obliged to supply this infor-mation. People who crossed Higgerson could find themselves in trouble. He'd better warn Nick Howarth to take care how he went.

Higgerson began tapping his pencil on the blotter. 'Is that all? I have real work to do, unlike you.'

'That's all for the moment . . . sir.' Deemer turned his back and walked out of the office, sickened by the way Gareth Higgerson had behaved today. Well, the fellow always acted as if he considered himself superior to other folk. He came from a decent family who had lost their money through inept business practices. He had made their fortune back and more before he was thirty, and Deemer considered him a greedy sod.

No one knew how Higgerson had made his first chunks

of money, because he'd gone 'down south', but after he'd
come back, he'd bought a few tumbledown houses. From
then on a lot of his income had come from renting out houses
in slum areas, and still did.

First he'd bought a few houses in Backshaw Moss and
stopped renting them as whole houses, instead using the
building company he'd started to divide them into single
rooms, which he'd crammed full of poor souls who could
only afford one room per family. He'd done the minimum
maintenance to keep the houses standing upright and gradually bought other dwellings there. He probably owned half
of that slum now.

Nowadays Backshaw Moss was not only an eyesore on the
outskirts of Birch End, but a shameful blot on the whole
valley and dangerous to people's health, due to its inadequate
sanitation arrangements. The new doctor had already made
a complaint about it to the town council.

If Deemer wanted to catch a petty criminal 'the Moss' was
the first place he looked.

Higgerson hadn't become a real builder for a few years,
then suddenly he'd bought out another builder and changed
the company's name. One or two other smaller building
companies had gone out of business in the next few years.
Roy Tyler and his son had been the only big one left, though
it had been touch and go when the son died. And there were
one or two very small builders still clinging on.

Maybe now, working with Wilf, Roy Tyler would be able
to give Higgerson a run for his money. Deemer hoped so.

He'd been gathering information gradually over the years
and knew one or two things about Higgerson's past that he'd
not scruple to bring up if necessary when the time was ripe.
He wasn't having innocent people mowed down by such
reckless driving or little children killed by disease from
sewage-borne illness.

But he was saving his ammunition for use with a magistrate who wasn't in Higgerson's pay. Dear heaven, what they desperately needed in this town was an impartial judge. There was a new one returned to the area, Miss Peters' brother, Dennison Peters. From what the sergeant had heard the man was highly thought of and was in legal circles tipped to be about to climb rapidly. If he proved more honest than the current chap, it might be possible to act.

For the moment, Deemer would content himself with warning Higgerson and keeping a more careful eye on what he did. Unlike some officials, he couldn't be bought, whatever anyone offered him or threatened. He believed in law and order, and had spent most of his life upholding it.

He hoped he was right about Judge Peters' honesty.

II

Wilf got up on the morning of the funeral with a leaden sense of dread weighing down his whole body. He took a bath, not lingering because he knew the others would want to have their turn. He'd forgotten to bring his clean clothes into the bathroom and they were still lying on the bed, so had to put on his new pyjamas again – well, new to him since yesterday and not badly worn, either.

When he passed the children's room, he saw them sitting up together in the same narrow bed, cuddling close.

'Do you want to use the bathroom?' He knew they'd never lived in a place with an indoor bathroom, so he added, 'It's all right to do that any time you need, but please leave everything clean and tidy after you've finished.'

Peggy nodded and hurried off. Ronnie stayed where he was, staring at his father.

Wilf tried to think of something to say that wouldn't upset the poor, bewildered child. 'Do you like my new pyjamas?'

Ronnie nodded and pointed to his own nightwear. Mrs Tyler obviously hadn't forgotten anything or anyone.

Wilf patted his son's shoulder. 'You've got nice new pyjamas too.' That won him a half-smile.

When Peggy came back she sent Ronnie along to the bathroom and turned to her father. 'You'd better go and get dressed now, Dad. Mrs Morton says we're only having a light breakfast and eating properly after the funeral.' She lowered her voice and whispered, 'She says there will be cake after-wards – for everyone!'

His kids hadn't had many cakes in their lives and that upset him. Sometimes small things could upset you as much as big ones. 'How nice that'll be. You'd better get dressed now, love.'

He jumped in shock as Mona spoke behind him.

'I'll see to them, sir.'

'Thank you. And my name's Wilf.'

She smiled. 'Wilf, when there's just the family, now I'm sure it's what you want. The rest of the time you'll have to put up with being called Mr Pollard.'

Back in his bedroom he put on the nearly new suit Mrs Tyler had found for him in the church box, a dark grey three-piece, hardly worn. After slipping the black, elasticated band Mrs Morton had provided around his upper arm, he stared solemnly at himself in the mirror. He looked smart, almost like a gentleman, which surprised him. Even his shirt had been well ironed, the collar nicely starched. He hadn't realised clothes could make such a difference, even to a man from a poor background like him.

He fingered the hair at his temples, which was starting to get streaks of grey in it now. Life passed so quickly! You shouldn't waste a second.

Funerals were held later in the day for the better-off people who used the big church in Rivenshaw. Enid's would be the first of several to be held this morning at the small church in Birch End. He didn't know much about the curate who'd be conducting it because he'd rarely attended church, in spite of his wife's nagging about it. Maybe the man would remember Enid, and if he didn't, Mrs Tyler would probably have told him what to say about her.

How terrible to think of not being remembered after you died! He would never forget Enid but when he looked back, he realised they'd spent more time apart than together during the hard years when he'd been on the tramp, chasing work.

His thoughts turned to his brother. Daniel had sent a lad with a message yesterday evening to say he'd be coming down from Ellindale to attend but his wife wasn't up to the walk, being too close to having the baby. She sent her apologies.

Food was laid out as usual for breakfast, but Wilf didn't feel hungry and only ate one piece of toast. Neither of the ladies urged him to have more today. He had never lived with such thoughtful people.

The two women spoke in hushed voices and after they'd cleared away, Mrs Morton said, 'A lad came round earlier to say that Mrs Tyler has arranged for a van from their yard to be sent up to Ellindale to pick up your brother and Mrs Harper.'

'I never thought about picking them up. I could easily have nipped up there in my own van.'

'It's far more important for you to be with your children today.'

She was right. He wasn't thinking very clearly, and was that any wonder on a day like this?

He drove the children to church and saw Daniel already outside the door waiting for him. Mrs Harper and two other women from Ellindale were standing to one side of him and he guessed they'd been driven down as well.

He left his van to one side and took the children across to stand near their uncle. They were too shy to talk and clung to Wilf's hands.

'Do you and the kids want to say a last farewell to her?' Daniel asked in a low voice.

He hesitated, then told the truth. 'No, I don't want to see Enid like that again, and I don't think they should, either. I'd rather remember her full of energy. But you go in and view her, if you like, Daniel lad. Jeavons said the open coffin would be over at the side for that, as usual.'

'I will, if you don't mind, Wilf. I'm still finding it hard to believe she's dead. And anyway, it seems only right to pay my respects.'

His brother and the women from Ellindale went into the church and turned to where Jeavons was standing next to the coffin, ready to screw the lid down.

Wilf followed them inside the church, holding a child's hand at either side. He stopped in shock because the place was almost full. There were men he'd worked with, neighbours, even Charlie Willcox and Todd Selby. Mr Tyler was standing up at the front and beckoned to them to join him and his wife in the pew.

It took a while to get there, however, because Wilf's friends and workmates kept standing up to offer him their condolences as he passed each row of mourners. He had to let go of the children's hands to do that and whispered to them to walk behind him.

'I'll take them to the front, Wilf.' He turned to see Mrs Morton so he moved to let her pass him with the children. He continued to shake people's hands and listen to their murmured regrets about his loss.

He was touched to the core that so many had come to be with him and it brought a big lump to his throat, so that his voice came out husky.

Once they were all sitting at the front of the church, Mrs Tyler said firmly, 'You're not to try to carry the coffin across that last unpaved bit to the grave, Wilf. Daniel's arranged for himself and some of your friends to do that. You should hold the children's hands as you all walk behind it. They need you.'

He nodded. No one needed to remind him of that because Ronnie and Peggy had clung to his hands every minute they could. They'd done that again as soon as he joined them in the pew.

Once the coffin was trundled to the front on its wheeled frame, the curate came out and looked questioningly at Mrs Tyler, who nodded.

The service was short. Words like 'good mother', 'loyal wife' floated out among the usual trite phrases. It could have been the funeral of any decent woman, Wilf thought. Nothing about it seemed special to poor Enid.

And then that part of the ceremony was over, thank goodness.

It was only about fifty yards from the church door to the rear of the graveyard where Jeavons had found a plot for Wilf to buy. The rear area wasn't paved, so Daniel and five others stepped forward to hoist the coffin on their shoulders and carry it to its final resting place. It felt like a long walk to Wilf because though Peggy could keep up, they had to go more slowly with Ronnie, who kept stopping to stare around and would have tripped and fallen a couple of times had his father not been holding his hand.

After the committal ceremony was over, Wilf threw some dirt into his wife's grave and gestured to the children to follow suit. He'd heard Mona telling them about doing that earlier.

Ronnie's handful missed the hole completely and someone in the crowd murmured, 'Ah, bless him.'

Wilf gave his son another handful of earth and helped him aim it better this time. Mrs Tyler took his arm to walk out of the churchyard, and Mrs Morton and Mona followed with the children.

'We've arranged for refreshments to be provided at our house,' Mrs Tyler said.

He looked at her in dismay. All he wanted now was to get away from people and be on his own in a quiet place.

'Not long now,' she said, as if she understood how he was feeling.

The refreshments were simple: a big urn held enough to pour cups of tea quickly, and there were also plates of scones and cake being passed to people. He saw Mrs Morton make sure the children got their cake and Mona slip them another piece each later.

He endured it all with numb patience, summoning up every last dreg of courtesy he possessed to respond politely to people's kind remarks.

At last, just as he was feeling he couldn't cope with much more, Mrs Morton came across to him. 'Mona and I can take the children home now, if you like, Wilf. They're getting tired. Mr Tyler arranged to send us back in his car when he took us to church earlier on. You'll need to stay here till the end, I'm afraid, but that should only be another few minutes, a quarter of an hour at most.'

A sigh escaped him. 'Thank you.'

One quick pat of the hand said she understood.

'Later on, I think you should go for a walk on the moors, Wilf. You'll find some of the peace and quiet that you're craving up there, I'm sure. I always have done, anyway. And it looks as if the weather will stay fine for you.'

He glanced up at the sky and nodded. 'Thank you for all you and Mona have done for me today. I don't know how I'd have managed without you.'

'We were glad to help.'

Just after midday, Nick gave the only driving lesson that had been booked for the afternoon, then came into the office. 'We've decided to close up for the rest of the day, Stella. Jo needs to buy some new, looser clothes and I don't want her driving on her own till she's stopped being so dizzy.'

He cocked one eye at her. 'She had another dizzy turn this morning, didn't she?'

'How did you know?'

'Todd overheard you two talking when he came back from the funeral. At least she didn't faint this time.'

You couldn't breathe around here without someone noticing, Stella thought. But that had its good side as well. She'd been too much on her own over the past few years.

He echoed her thoughts. 'If you stay in the valley, people will get to know you and notice what you do. That's something you'll have to get used to if you live in a small town, though I think you'd rather live outside Rivenshaw in one of the villages, from what you've said, and it'll be even worse there.'

'Yes. But nice not to be alone. Todd told me how many people went to support Mr Pollard at his wife's funeral today. The man must be very well thought of in the valley.'

'He is. His wife didn't mix much with the other women in the village, though, especially in the last year or two, but he's helped many people over the years and has given some of the men an occasional day or two's work when he could. So a lot of people attended her funeral out of respect for him, Leah and Todd included. Did a lot of people attend when your husband died, Stella?'

She shook her head. 'No. Derrick was a rather quiet person. There were just a few friends and his family.' And she'd quarrelled with them because she had refused to spend all her remaining money on a fancier funeral.

'So you were left on your own.'

'Yes. We hadn't had any children, you see, so there was no reason for his family to stay in touch with me after that.' They'd nodded as they passed her in the street but never really spoken to her again.

The first few weeks on her own had been the worst time of her life until she got used to the utter loneliness and learned to escape into her library books.

'It was very courageous of you to come to Rivenshaw on your own.'

A few of her doubts escaped. 'Who knows? It could turn out to have been stupid to leave everything I knew, including one particularly good woman friend, to whom I owe a lot. Only time will tell.'

'I believe it was courageous,' Nick insisted. 'Anyway, we thought, since you came here to get some fresh country air and it's a nice, sunny afternoon, Jo and I would start our outing by driving you up to the top of the valley and then showing you a nice walk that'll bring you back down by a country route to Rivenshaw. If you don't mind walking a few miles, that is?'

'I love walking. I'm stronger than I look.' She looked down at her feet. 'I'll need my other shoes, though.'

'That's all right. We'll leave in five minutes and stop at Mrs T's on the way for you to change into some walking shoes. I'll just get the *Closed* sign ready.'

She smiled when he'd gone. Walking shoes, he'd said! She had the shoes she was wearing, the sturdy winter shoes she would wear this afternoon and a pair of slippers, and that was all her footwear. And she'd had to manage her money carefully to get those.

It still seemed incredible to think she'd be able to buy any clothing or shoes she needed without economising on other things. Once she was settled somewhere, she might buy one or two items of clothing. She frowned as she looked down at herself. Something prettier than this, for a start, even if it wasn't as practical and hard-wearing.

Stella enjoyed the drive up the valley. Nick took his time and stopped at a couple of places to show her things he and Jo considered of interest.

One man had made a home in a railway carriage which had cost him only £10 to buy. Fancy that! When someone he'd quarrelled with had spitefully destroyed part of the upper road to try and stop him getting his 'house' up there, people from the valley had got together to mend the damaged retaining wall and push the carriage up the last stretch of hill.

She was amazed at how neat and pretty the carriage looked now, surrounded by a garden and with a kitchen in a sort of shed to one side at the rear. It was as big as many houses.

On the upper side of the village there was Heythorpe House, nestling in a hollow to the left of the road. A friend of Nick's lived there, a rather shy philanthropist, who had apparently helped a lot of people in these difficult times. The gardens were quite large, looking neat and well cared for.

Finally, at the head of the valley, they came to Spring Cottage with the fizzy drink factory and youth hostel next to it, both of them started and run by Todd's enterprising wife while she was married to her first husband.

Nick introduced Stella to Leah, whom she liked on sight, and they all walked with her to the start of a rough but clearly marked track that led across the moors. There Leah explained exactly where to turn off it to get back on to the main road at Birch End, and then they left her to it.

Once she'd gone a hundred yards, Stella could hear nothing but the occasional faint sound of humming insects and birds. She felt as if she'd arrived in paradise. It was cold, yes, but she was walking fast enough to keep warm, given that she was wearing her winter coat, together with a woollen scarf, knitted hat and gloves.

And the space! Ah, the moors seemed to stretch for ever, as if inviting you to explore them with more than your eyes.

She didn't walk too quickly so that she could appreciate the scenery, moving along the clearly marked path steadily, stopping every here and there to look at the view. She was really enjoying getting to know her new neighbourhood.

When her path met another one, she turned to the right, following Leah's instructions. This should lead her towards Birch End, a village she had yet to explore apart from driving around the quiet lanes on its outskirts.

Then, at the top of a small slope, where the path vanished round a stone outcrop, she heard something and paused to try and work out what it was. Surely that was – yes, it was! – the sound of someone sobbing. She was unsure whether to make herself known or not. Sometimes people sought privacy to purge themselves of sorrow. She'd done that herself after Derrick died.

She took a couple of steps forward to a bend and could see a man lying face down on the ground further along, weeping as if his heart was broken. She had good eyesight and could also see the black band around one arm, just above the elbow. Someone in mourning.

Could this be the man Jo had mentioned, whose wife had just died? What was his name? Oh yes, Wilf Pollard.

It wasn't possible to continue without passing close to him, so she went back about a hundred yards, started singing and she moved on again. That was a bit embarrassing because she had rather a weak voice, but it was the only way she could think of to give him warning of her approach. She definitely couldn't whistle a tune, had never even tried because girls weren't encouraged to whistle.

There was even a stupid saying: *A whistling woman and a crowing hen are neither fit for God nor men.* She hadn't dared go against that tradition as a girl, for fear of being ridiculed. Her parents hadn't wanted her to be different from others, and her mother had even warned her not to appear too clever or she'd put men off and never get married. She'd had to bite her tongue a good few times during her marriage, even to a kind man.

When she came to the bend for a second time, she could

see that the man was now standing beside the path, staring back at her across the moor.

She moved forward and since he said nothing, she spoke first. 'Oh, sorry! I didn't realise there was anyone around or I'd have kept quiet.'

'You have a pleasant voice. It was nice to hear someone sounding cheerful.' He studied her. 'You don't see many women walking across the moors on their own.'

'Nick Howarth and his wife dropped me off in Ellindale. Do you know them?'

He nodded.

'I'm heading towards Birch End – at least, I hope I am. I'm new to the valley and this is my first walk on the tops for many years. It seems to clear your head, somehow, being out here, don't you think?'

At another nod, she said, 'Shall we move on? It's a bit cold to stand still in this breeze.'

When she continued on her way, he fell into place next to her, not too close and anyway, she didn't feel at all nervous of him. His face was too honest, somehow.

They walked in silence for a while, then he said suddenly, 'I buried my wife this morning and I'm just . . . clearing my head, too. You must have heard me giving in to my grief.'

Her heart went out to the poor man. 'Yes. But I understand how difficult it can be at first when you lose someone. My husband died three years ago and I found it very hard going at first.'

He relaxed visibly as she said that.

'You must have loved your wife very much,' she ventured.

He stared at her as if surprised, then shook his head. 'No. That's partly why I was so upset. We'd drifted apart because I've had to spend a lot of time away during the past few years, looking for work wherever I could find it.'

'A lot of men have had to do that.'

'Enid and I weren't at odds or anything, just . . . not close. I was loyal to her and she was a good, hard-working woman, mind.'

'How you felt about her must make it even harder for you now.'

He stopped to stare at her, so she stopped too, waiting patiently for him to speak. If he needed someone to listen to him, she was happy to fill that role.

'I think you understand my feelings better than anyone I've spoken to.'

'I've lived through quite a few difficulties myself in the past few years and hope I've learned from it. Besides, if we can't help one another in times of trouble, what sort of human beings are we?'

'Poor ones. But I doubt anyone will ever say that of you.'

'Thank you.' That was the sort of compliment which pleased her, not silly remarks about how 'neat and small' she was. She particularly hated being told that. 'We'd better carry on. I don't want to be out at dusk so far away from other people.'

'You don't mind if I continue walking with you? I'm ready to face the world and my children again. I live in Birch End but I'll fall behind and let you move ahead if you prefer to walk alone. Only this is the only path that leads directly there.'

'I don't mind your company at all.' He hadn't made the slightest attempt to flirt with her, which would have made her wary.

'May I ask what you're going to do in the valley?'

'First I have to find somewhere more permanent to live than Mrs T's lodging house. I'm working for Nick and Jo Howarth in their office and I'm learning how to drive because—' She took a deep breath and said it firmly, 'I'm going to buy a car. Won't that be wonderful?'

That won a smile from him. She hoped she hadn't sounded

too silly. 'I came into a little money, you see, not a fortune but enough to change my life.' She waved one hand at the beautiful rolling uplands. 'I don't know where living here will lead me, but I was stuck in a dead end before and bored silly by my work entering figures in ledgers, so I doubt it's likely to be any worse.'

'I wish you well. Oh, sorry. I don't know your name.'

'Stella Newby. And you're Wilf Pollard.'

'Yes.'

They continued walking for a while, mostly in a comfortable silence. She didn't know when she'd felt at ease with a stranger so quickly.

All the people she'd met in Rivenshaw so far had been kind to her.

She'd made such a good choice coming here.

12

As they got closer to Birch End, Wilf said quietly, 'Thank you for your company. I'm ready to go back to my children again. I just needed some quiet time. It all happened so abruptly.'

'Ah, you have children.'

It was a sigh as much as a word and he looked at her, wondering what had brought that sadness to her face.

She surprised herself by telling him more about herself. 'I've always been sorry that Derrick and I never managed to have any children. How old are yours?'

'Peggy is seven and Ronnie is five. They're dear, brave little creatures. Enid and I didn't manage to have any children, either. We adopted these two when they were orphaned and I'm so glad we did.'

'Who's looking after them for you now?'

'Mrs Morton and her maid Mona. We're going to live with the two of them in Birch End. They're older ladies and we've all been friends for a while, ever since I did some repairs on their house. They don't have any close family and are lonely in that big house, so they've offered us a home. Our old place wasn't suitable and I shall be glad to have someone to look after the children when I start work again. They'll have to go to the Birch End infants' school now, but I might wait till after Christmas to send them there.'

'That sounds a sensible arrangement.'

'Who knows what's sensible or not? When I went through

Enid's things, I found out that she had more money saved than I realised, and yet she'd been skimping on food and clothes for the children.'

She quoted another old saying: '"There's nowt so queer as folk"!'

'Yes. I certainly didn't know Enid nearly as well as I thought.' He let out a huff of embarrassed near-laughter. 'And I don't know why I'm telling you this.'

'Because you need to talk. I wish I'd had someone to talk to after Derrick died because in some ways I found life easier without him. It took me a while to realise that he'd only seen me as a housewife.' She chuckled. 'He even worried that I read too many books and would addle my brain.'

'You don't sound at all addled to me.'

When Wilf stopped walking, she did too, seeming glad of a breather.

He studied her. 'You're looking tired.'

'I am a bit. I thought I was stronger than this, but I'm out of practice at long walks in the countryside.'

'I know a shortcut, if you're interested. It'll save us more than half a mile, but it'll mean pushing through a hedge and climbing over a gate. This path has to take a detour nowadays around some new houses that have been built at this side of Birch End in the past few years.' He couldn't help grimacing as he said that and she noticed, of course. She didn't miss much.

'Is there something wrong with the houses? You looked rather . . . um, scornful as you mentioned them.'

'Quite a lot wrong in my opinion. For a start, the builder, Higgerson, ignored a right of way that had been there for as long as anyone can remember, which is why people have to go round it. And although the people who live nearby protested, nothing was done to stop him by the council. Worst of all, he skimps on materials whenever he can, so whatever you do, don't buy a house that he's built unless you're prepared to do a lot of small repairs after the first year or two.'

She could hear the disgust in his voice. 'I'll remember that. And you're right. I am tired, so I'd be very interested in a shortcut. I'm not afraid of climbing over gates. I was quite a tomboy as a child.'

She'd be sorry to part company with him, because though he didn't say much, what he did say was worth listening to. He'd pointed out a few birds and small features of the landscape that she'd have missed otherwise. It had been nice simply to have a companion.

She'd done a lot of walking on her own during the past few years, watching people but not with them. But walking in towns wasn't nearly as enjoyable as in the countryside.

Wilf stopped and pointed. 'The shortcut starts here. We have to push our way through a gap in this hedge. Here you go.' He held back the branches for her and moved ahead to lead the way along the side of a small field where a ramshackle gate was held in place by a rusting padlock. 'We'll need to climb over this. Can you manage?'

'I think so. If you could just stand nearby in case I need you to lend me a hand, I'd be grateful.' But she managed just fine, hadn't lost her childhood skills, even if she was a little slower at getting over the gate than she used to be.

On the other side of it, she found herself in a garden filled with tangles of winter-dead plants. The place had clearly been left to run wild for years. They walked past a wall and a couple of huge evergreen shrubs that almost blocked their way, then they came to a house. She stopped in surprise, because it had been so well hidden by vegetation she hadn't expected it.

It was more of a country cottage than a town house, with

dormer windows set in the roof. 'I thought this was just the remains of a garden. Does anyone live here now?'

'No. It's been deserted for several years that I know of but someone has done repairs and kept it weatherproof. I don't know what it's like inside because as you can see, the curtains are drawn. It could be pretty, couldn't it?'

'I think it is pretty. Who does it belong to?'

'I've lived in the valley all my life yet I don't know. No one else seems to know, either. The former owner was old when I was a lad, so he's surely dead by now. Whoever inherited it hasn't been seen visiting, or folk would have talked.'

'What a pity. I'd love and care for it if I owned a cottage like this. It's such a nicely balanced building, even if it is old-fashioned, exactly the sort of place I've dreamed of owning. I have just enough money to buy a small house, you see, but I couldn't afford one with all this land.' She gestured to the side, beyond the garden. 'Does it all belong to the cottage's owner?'

'Again, I don't know the present situation, though everyone assumes it does.' He led the way round the side of the house, then along a path that wound past a shed and various bushes, some of them evergreen and some of them with many years' growth showing in wild, leafless tangles of branches and twigs.

There was further dead vegetation to the front of the house and the garden sloped down quite steeply from the road, so she could see why the place was nearly invisible to passers-by.

'That cottage makes me think of the fairy tale about Sleeping Beauty.' She stopped to ease her shoulders and shake her arms about. She was probably going to be very stiff tomorrow.

He watched her. 'I think you've had enough walking for one day. Look, I could drive you down to Rivenshaw in my van, if you like. It would only take us a few minutes to get there. It's a couple of miles further for you to walk otherwise.'

She'd have loved to accept but hesitated. 'Are you sure you don't mind? On a day like you've had, I don't want to impose.'

'I vowed up there,' he gestured back towards the moors, 'that now I've buried my wife, I'll look forward not back. The tears were a sort of farewell to Enid and to the hopes we shared for raising our family together.' He stared blindly into the distance for a moment or two, then turned back to her. 'It wouldn't take me long to drive you into Rivenshaw and we can call at the house and pick up the children to go with us. An outing will probably do them good as well.'

And make her feel more secure about being alone with a stranger. How perceptive of him! The more he said and did, the more she liked him.

He gave her a quick smile as if realising she understood what he was doing and went on, 'They love going out in my van. They were so subdued and bewildered this morning at the funeral, poor little dears. A treat will cheer them up a bit, I hope.'

'Will the two ladies mind you taking me to their house?'

'Not at all. Come and meet them. They'll probably offer you a cup of tea – and don't say you wouldn't enjoy one. I'm thirsty now and you must be too. I shall probably drink at least three big cups. I usually do and they don't seem to mind.'

He led the way across the road to where six large, comfortable-looking houses stood in a rather incongruous row, opposite this patch of what appeared from here to be merely abandoned land and with a field at the end of the street, between them and the main road down the hill.

At the front door Wilf stopped, wondering whether it'd be rude just to walk in. He wiped his feet vigorously on the outside doormat and his dilemma was solved by Mona opening the door.

'Peggy was watching for you and came running to say she'd seen you coming to the door. We haven't given you a key yet, have we, Mr Pollard?'

'No. I'd appreciate some keys. I'll come in the back way after work, though, so as not to mess up the hall carpet.'

He gestured to his companion. 'This is Mrs Newby. I met her on the moors. She's new to the town and is going to work for the Howarths. She's found the walk down from Ellindale more tiring than she expected, so I thought we could give her a nice cup of tea, and afterwards I'll drive her back to Mrs T's lodging house. The children can come with us for a little outing.'

He saw Stella hide a smile as he made it clear to Mona that she was a respectable person. She'd already found out that Mrs T was very fussy about what sort of ladies she let stay in her lodging house.

Shouts from the kitchen and running footsteps heralded the approach of two children, who burst into the hall and flung themselves at their father. He picked up each of them in turn and plonked kisses on their rosy cheeks, seeing Stella smile at that.

When he put them down, he said, 'Children, this is Mrs Newby, who's been walking on the moors. Say hello to her. I'm going to drive her home after she's had a cup of tea and if you're very good, she'll let you come with us in the van.'

They smiled at her shyly and he noticed that when Ronnie's thumb crept towards his mouth, Peggy gently pulled it away. He was hoping that Mrs Morton would lift that burden of responsibility from her and let the poor girl enjoy being a child.

Mona soon brought in afternoon tea on a trolley and he heard Peggy whisper in awed tones, 'More cakes!'

As he was finishing his second iced bun, Wilf asked suddenly, 'By the way, Mrs Morton, do you know whose house that is across the road, the one that's hidden by foliage? Mrs Newby and I took a shortcut through the garden, which hasn't been touched for years. I don't remember anyone living there, but it must belong to someone.'

She flushed and glanced at Mona, who said abruptly, 'You'll have to tell him, ma'am, now it's started up again.'

Mrs Morton sat with her head bowed, nodded. 'Perhaps the children would like to go and play with their toys till you're ready to leave.'

'You won't go without us, will you, Dad?' Peggy asked, looking anxious again.

'No, I promise I won't.'

When they'd left he turned to Mrs Morton. 'You look upset. What is it that's started up again?'

She hesitated, looking at Stella.

'I can wait in the hall, if you'd prefer to talk in private, but I promise you I won't tell anyone what you say.'

'No, you're part of it now you've seen that cottage, so you might as well stay.' Mrs Morton took a deep breath, got up and fumbled in one of the kitchen drawers. 'This was waiting for us when we got back today and I've had other letters from this man, Wilf.'

After another deep breath, she said jerkily, 'You see, I'm the person who owns the cottage and land you were asking about. I inherited them from a distant relative, oh, several years ago. It's what's been keeping me so poor, having to pay the rates and other expenses.'

'*You* own it! Good heavens!'

'I haven't told anyone so please keep it to yourself. I've continued to deal with it through my relative's lawyer in Manchester, but that horrible Higgerson man somehow found out who the owner was and has been pestering me for . . . oh, about two years now, wouldn't it be, Mona? Yes, at least that long. He wants me to sell it to him.'

She paused, looking even more distressed. 'He was polite at first, then started making threats.'

Wilf was startled. 'He threatened you! Why didn't you go to the police?'

'He didn't exactly threaten me himself, just talked about what might happen if someone unscrupulous was determined to get hold of the land. He kept saying he could take it off my hands and save me all the trouble and worry. He stopped for a while after I told him that in case anything happened to me, I'd made a will and left it to a distant relative on condition they didn't sell it to him.'

She mopped her eyes. 'I thought he'd given up but this letter arrived today. He says now is the time for me to sell so that the children will be safe. Read it.'

'He must be very arrogant to do this openly.' Wilf scanned the single page quickly, shaking his head and muttering something under his breath. 'How much is he offering? He just says the same as before.'

'Not much at all: one hundred and fifty pounds.'

'*What?* For a house and all that land? He's definitely trying to cheat you. It must be worth three or four times that much, at the very least. He could cram a lot of cheap houses on it, though they'd soon turn into another slum, given how poorly he builds if he can get away with it.'

'I know. I definitely don't want to sell to him, Wilf.'

'It'd be worth even more if the house were in a better condition. And if he so much as lays a fingertip on one of my children, or on either of you two ladies, I'll make sure he finds that *he* is the one in trouble.'

Stella had been shocked at what she heard. It was like something you saw at the cinema or read about in a whodunit, a greedy villain trying to cheat an old widow.

She could see the other women staring at Wilf's face in

surprise because suddenly his gentleness had disappeared and he was looking distinctly menacing. She didn't blame him. Any decent father would protect his children, whatever it took.

Mrs Morton continued. 'I'm right, aren't I, Wilf? That cottage alone is worth more than a hundred and fifty pounds, even without the land, and there's more land than you realise when you really look at it. The cottage may be old-fashioned and in need of painting but the roof doesn't leak. If it had needed repairs, I'd have sold some more of my mother's jewellery and had the place made good again. But it's sound enough, though everything inside is very . . . well, shabby and run down. It's just as it was when that cousin of mine went to end his days by the seaside in Lytham St Anne's over twenty years ago, even to the furniture. He simply locked the door and left.'

She blew her nose quickly, as people do when trying to stop themselves crying. 'I didn't tell my son I'd inherited it. He was acting foolishly, spending my money as well as his own. I covered the furniture up and left it there, thinking he might need the cottage one day, if he married and settled down. Only he died suddenly. You don't expect your children to die before yourself. I haven't been back into the cottage since.'

Mona went to stand near her, putting one arm round her as she paused again, fighting tears.

'But that latest letter makes me afraid for the children's safety, so I'll have to do *something* now. I can't bear to think of anything happening to them. But what am I to do? I definitely don't want to sell it to Higgerson. That's the only thing I'm sure of. And how did he find out so quickly that you were coming to live here? That worries me too.'

'There are ways of finding things out,' Wilf said grimly. 'Some people will do anything for money and Higgerson could be – in fact he *must be* – paying someone in Birch End to keep watch on you and your house.'

She shuddered. 'I hate the thought of that. If I end up having to sell the cottage, Wilf, I'll ask for more money than that, and I'd rather not sell it to him, with all the land it's got. Everyone knows what he's like, building shoddy houses and bullying people. I don't want to put any of you at risk though – or for my dear Mona to be in danger either.'

His voice was firm. 'Please don't do anything without giving me a chance to sort things out. I have some very good friends who'll help me to protect you and my children, if he starts causing trouble.'

Stella was reminded of something in a detective story she'd once read. 'If you don't mind me saying so, Mrs Morton, you should put that letter, and any others of his you have, in a safe hiding place. Just in case you have to prove that he's been threatening you.'

'I'm afraid I burnt the others. They felt . . . well, unclean!'

'Keep that one. Hide it somewhere. You may need it as evidence.'

'I don't feel as if anywhere in this house would be safe if someone paid by him broke in and started looking for it while we were out. Or worse, forced their way in while one of us was at home on her own. In fact, I'm wondering if you ought to find somewhere else to live, Wilf dear, much as I'd miss you and the children.'

'I'm not letting him drive us out as long as *you* want us here.'

'Of course I do!'

'Look, if you give the letter to me, Mrs Morton, I can keep it safe for you,' Stella offered. 'He won't have the faintest idea where it is then.'

Wilf turned to her. 'Are you sure you want to risk getting involved?'

'I don't think the risk would be all that great. I can't bear people who cheat and lie and I have no dependants or close relatives, so he can't threaten me through anyone else.'

Wilf folded the letter, put it into the envelope, waited for Mrs Morton to nod and held it out to Stella.

She put it in the well-worn leather satchel whose strap crossed her shoulder when she was out walking. 'I'd be happy to keep any other evidence safe for you as well, Mrs Morton, believe me.'

'You're very kind.'

'You've been a true friend to us all today, Mrs Newby,' Wilf said. 'I'll get the children now and we'll drive you back to Mrs T's.'

That compliment made her feel good.

Stella noticed with approval that he'd strapped a big flat cushion to the side of the van with straps for the children to hold on to in case they went along bumpy roads. A clever, ingenious man, Wilf, as well as a kind one.

The children alternated between peering out of the front and back windows of the van and chatting to one another excitedly about what they were passing, so Stella and Wilf were able to have a quick few words as they drove into Rivenshaw.

'Are you really worried about Mrs Morton's safety, Wilf? Surely a businessman won't hurt her.'

'Yes, I am worried. Higgerson is totally unscrupulous and a woman of her age can be rather vulnerable. He could make it seem like an accident, a fall. She'd be easy to overcome physically.'

'It's a pity she can't sell that cottage to someone else instead of Higgerson, someone who would pay a fair price and then be able to stand up to him. That'd stop him pursuing her.'

'Good idea, but who would want it? It's not in a very good condition.'

'Aren't there any other builders in the valley?'

'Not as big as Higgersons. They've nearly all gone bust.'

It was out before she could stop herself. 'I'd want the cottage if I could afford it, but not the land.'

He shot a quick, surprised glance at her. 'But you haven't even been inside it!'

'I know. I'm probably being silly, but I fell in love with the outside and you can make the inside of a house pretty with a little effort. I shall probably dream about that cottage for days now. My husband used to say that I had an over-vivid imagination.'

They drew up outside Mrs T's just then, so Stella thanked him and turned to the children.

He was out of the van quickly and had opened her door before she had finished saying goodbye. He waited till she had been admitted to the house before getting into his vehicle again.

He had such good manners, Stella thought as she took off her coat and answered a couple of questions about how poor Mr Pollard and his children were. Her landlady certainly liked to keep up with gossip.

Stella didn't mention the cottage at all, just said how pretty the moors were, even in winter.

She was glad to have met Wilf, hoped to further her acquaintance with him, as well as with his delightful children and the two older ladies who had taken him into their home.

She wasn't surprised when she dreamed about the cottage that night. The strange thing was, she dreamed she was walking about inside it. Why, she hadn't even peeped through the windows! How could it seem so real?

13

Wilf spent a restless night worrying about Mrs Morton and Higgerson, and as sometimes happened, he came up with an idea of how to help her that might work and still keep the land out of Higgerson's hands.

The following day was Saturday and he'd arranged to not go into work until Monday so that he could help the children settle into their new home. He thoroughly enjoyed eating a leisurely breakfast with everyone, because Mona usually ate with them. It felt as if they were a real family.

Mrs Morton must have been thinking the same because she looked at him across the breakfast table and asked, 'Do you think the children could all call me Auntie Beryl from now on?'

'Auntie Beryl!' Ronnie repeated loudly. 'Auntie Beryl. I like it.' He drummed his heels against his chair in excitement.

Wilf was about to scold his son for bad manners when his kind hostess laughed.

'There you are. One person convinced.'

'Are you sure you don't mind the familiarity?'

'Oh, I'll relish it. If you decide that they can adopt me permanently as an auntie, you could call me by my first name too.'

'Auntie Beryl is a nice name,' Peggy said. 'We haven't got any aunties.'

'And I'd like to be Auntie Mona to them, Wilf. If you don't mind.'

Wilf nodded to the maid. 'That would be lovely too. Thank you, Beryl and Mona.'

Both elderly ladies beamed at them. They'd been together for many years, he knew, and seemed more like sisters than maid and mistress.

After breakfast he lingered to ask Beryl if he could have a word with her privately, marvelling at how right it seemed to use her first name.

'Yes, of course, dear. Shall we go into my sitting room?'

'Please. It's not that I want to keep you out of this, Mona, but I don't want the children to know so perhaps you can make sure they stay out of hearing. You never know when they might let something slip, otherwise. Beryl can tell you what I'm thinking about doing later.'

She nodded and followed the two little ones into the room where their toys were kept.

'What did you want to talk to me about?' Beryl asked as soon as they were alone.

'Your cottage.' Wilf gestured across the street to the scrubby wasteland where the building lay hidden. It still surprised him how well concealed it was. 'I wonder if I could go and have a look round inside? There may be something that needs repairing and it'd be easy for me to sort out that sort of thing. And I have to admit that I'm curious to see what it's like.'

'Oh, would you do that, dear? I do worry about the place deteriorating. I'll get you a key of your own for it.'

'Thank you. I think I'll tell the children I have to go out and meet someone, and I'll make sure no one from the village sees me going into the cottage. Luckily we're not in a direct route to the village shop. Do many people know about that shortcut through the garden to the moors, do you think?'

'I doubt it. I've never seen anyone coming from the back of the garden anyway. Most of the people around here who live in the new houses Higgerson built have another way up to the moors, and even that's not much used. Those who live in Backshaw Moss can get to the tops more easily from the other side of their area, and anyway the other residents of this street don't encourage them to hang about here.'

She grimaced because as everyone knew there were some rogues living in the nearby slums as well as decent people who were scratching for every penny.

A few minutes later Wilf checked that no one was in sight before strolling down their street heading towards the main road not the village. He paid careful attention to what was going on around him and quickly became aware of muffled footsteps behind him.

Stopping as if to re-fasten his shoelace, he took a quick glance behind him. Yes, there was definitely someone nearby. He couldn't see the follower, who was hiding in a gateway, but a man's shadow lay across the street, betraying his presence. The person must be stupid not to have noticed that himself.

Wilf abandoned any thought of going straight to the cottage, snapped his fingers as if he'd forgotten something, said, 'Bother!' loudly and hurried back home.

There he explained what was happening to the ladies, then got into his van and drove away, leaving Beryl to keep watch for anyone following in case she could recognise them another time. She stood behind the net curtains across her front windows, seeming delighted to be involved.

Wilf drove the van to the Tylers' house, a couple of streets away. He could have walked but didn't want whoever it was to keep following him.

Mrs Tyler opened the door when he knocked, looking at his expression as if she could tell something was wrong. 'Wilf. Do come in.'

When Roy joined them, Wilf quickly explained what was going on, ending with, 'I wondered if I could get across to that piece of unused land from your back garden.'

Roy shook his head. 'No. But I bet you could get there from Charlie Willcox's garden. Let's go and see him.'

Wilf hesitated. 'I don't want to tell any more people about this than I need to.'

'Charlie can keep a secret as well as any man I know. And he loves to be in on things that other people aren't aware of. Let's give him a treat and include him. He often has good ideas. I'll phone him and see if he's at home.'

Two minutes later, as Wilf walked along the street to Charlie's house with Roy, he looked around enviously. This part of Birch End was certainly pretty, thanks to the residents putting a lot of effort into their gardens, though to his mind the houses let that down somewhat when you studied them closely. They could have been built to a more balanced design, with slightly larger windows and a higher roof. It wouldn't have taken much more effort, or even cost much more, but it'd have been *right*.

He didn't understand how he knew such things, he just did, quite instinctively and always had done. These days he was starting to have confidence in his own judgement. The job doing renovations at Heythorpe House a while ago had been a turning point for him.

Charlie opened the door to them and took them inside. When they explained what they wanted, he said at once, 'Come out into the back garden and we'll look over the rear wall.'

They did that and he nodded. 'I thought so. If you climb over this part of the fence, you're straight on to that piece of land without anyone being able to see you. Looks a mess, doesn't it? Fancy Mrs Morton owning it. And how the hell did Higgerson find that out?'

Wilf scowled. 'I'd be interested in discovering that myself. She thought only the lawyer in Manchester knew and she hasn't dealt with anyone here.'

Charlie tilted his head to one side, as Wilf had seen him do before when thinking about a problem. 'It can only be someone who works at the council and deals with rates and so on. I'll try to nose around there. The mayor's secretary usually knows what's going on. I might get old Reg to ask her if she can help me.'

'Will she keep it quiet?'

'I trust her absolutely and so does he, or he'd not have kept her on as secretary when he took over as mayor.' Charlie eyed the wall. 'You know, if we get my stepladders, we can climb across quite easily. You won't leave me out of the fun, will you?'

Wilf didn't say anything and left it to Roy to say, 'Of course you can join us', but he was feeling somewhat frustrated. He had wanted to have a quiet look around on his own. But there you were. You didn't always get what you wanted. At least this way no one would see him go into the cottage.

What's more, he realised suddenly, he'd have allies in dealing with the situation, respected men able to testify in court about any problems they encountered, if necessary. So it was probably a good thing to do it this way.

Wilf put one finger to his lips before he helped the other two get over the wall and into the garden of the cottage. They nodded and grinned at him, two middle-aged men enjoying themselves.

The key turned easily in the front door, which opened so smoothly as they let themselves in, that Wilf wondered if someone had oiled it recently. He looked for a key nearby on the inside to let people out with, but there wasn't one. That was strange.

The house was in semi-darkness because the curtains were drawn but there was enough light coming through them or around the edges to see their way round the interior without altering the position of anything that would show from outside.

In the kitchen, Wilf stopped with an exclamation of annoyance. 'Look at that! Someone's broken in, damn them!'

A pane of glass had been smashed near the handle that opened one whole side of the multi-paned, old-fashioned hinged window, and the fragments of glass knocked out of it. A piece of wood had been inserted in the gap, presumably to keep the weather out, but in such a way that it could be pulled out again from outside. The hole was easily big enough for someone to put a hand inside and undo the lock, then swing open that half of the window.

'They left it like this so that they could get back in if they needed to.'

Roy looked at the mess in annoyance. 'I don't like the idea of people breaking into a house so close to mine.'

Charlie scowled at it. 'Nor do I.'

'I'll come back later and nail a piece of solid wood across the inside of that gap so that it can't be removed from outside, and I'll put bolts inside as well across the top and bottom to make it harder to get in,' Wilf said grimly. 'And what's more I'll change the lock on the front door, because if I'm guessing correctly, they now have a key to it.'

Roy looked at him in mild surprise. 'Is there any job you can't do?'

'I can do a lot of the simpler jobs, but some of the more complex tasks are far beyond me.'

'Well, it'd be good to have a new lock, and if you can get a couple of spare keys, Charlie and I will keep them handy as well. Just in case.'

'All right. I know a locksmith in Rivenshaw who won't tell

anyone what I buy from him. I wonder what the intruders were after. Let's walk round and see what's been taken.'

Only there were no obvious signs of pilfering, which was even more puzzling.

'They must just have been looking round,' Charlie said. 'Look at the thick layer of dust everywhere. No one's dusted for years. There would be marks in it if they'd taken ornaments or anything else from the shelves. If they'd been sleeping here, that would show, too, but the sheets protecting the beds are smooth and covered with dust. You're not telling me they'd sleep on the floor when there are several beds available. So what did they want?'

'To look round?' Roy said. 'As we're doing.'

'You're probably right.'

When they were back downstairs, Wilf examined the front-door lock more carefully. 'The dust has definitely been disturbed on this.'

Roy peered at it. 'Yes. You're right.'

'I've seen enough for now,' Wilf said.

'Let's have a proper look at the land that goes with the house,' Roy suggested. 'What I'd really like is to walk across it and pace out the distances.'

Wilf shook his head. 'Better not. I can't see any way of doing that without being seen from the street. And that fellow will still be watching Mrs Morton's house, I reckon, so he'd be bound to see us walking about in the field. Unlike them, we should do this carefully. The best we can manage at the moment is to find a vantage point and have a good look at it. You and I can make a pretty good estimate of its size between us, eh, Roy?'

His new partner nodded. 'By rack o' th'ee.'

Charlie looked at him in puzzlement. 'What does that mean?'

Roy grinned. 'It's a common way of describing how you can estimate something by using your eyes. You hear it all the time from Lancashire men working in the building or carpentry trades.'

The three of them found a vantage point in the cottage garden where they were fairly certain they couldn't be seen from the road and had a good look over the fence.

'I hadn't realised there was this much land involved,' Roy said thoughtfully. 'No wonder Higgerson wants to get his hands on it. I could make a nice terrace or two of neat little houses for working folk here, decent places, not like those in that damned slum up the road. But he'd cram people in like sardines. You don't often get pieces of land this size becoming available in the valley.'

He shook his head as if in disapproval, then explained. 'I've heard that the council is supposed to do something about slum clearance now the government has made the 1930 Housing Act compulsory. They've delayed as long as they dare, I should think. It stands to reason if they clear people out of Backshaw Moss, they'll need to put them somewhere else and that'll cost them money.'

Charlie nodded. 'Reg has already applied for funding. Even that lot who were on the council before didn't dare try to stop him completely but they've certainly slowed him down. I reckon they didn't think we'd get any funding for the valley. We'll know by the next council meeting if our proposal has been accepted, Reg says, and if it happens as he plans, he wants us all to support him in making a real start on dealing with Backshaw Moss.'

'It won't be easy. Even if decent houses were built, how would people pay to rent them when they can barely afford one room? It's a problem everywhere that slums have been cleared. I read somewhere that folk are living longer, and not as many children are dying, so they're crying out for somewhere to live.'

Roy was still scowling. 'Well, I bet Higgerson is expecting

to get the contract for building any new housing and he'll find some way to profit from the grant money himself. He's got rid of most of his competitors in the building industry in our valley, so who's to challenge him?'

'You. You've managed to stay around.'

'I reckon he's only left me alone because he considers me a spent force. I've not been doing much since my lad died, so I'm a bit short of ready money, but with the help of Wilf here, I'll get more active again. Higgerson won't find it easy to push *me* out of business, that at least I can guarantee.'

'Good to hear. But it'll be hard to stop Higgerson getting contracts unfairly, because numbers on the council are almost even. It'll only take one person being ill to give him a chance,' Charlie said.

Wilf looked from one to the other. 'Or someone being put out of action deliberately.'

They were all silent for a few moments, then Charlie shrugged. 'Well, we're not here to talk about council business. That's for another time.' He turned round to look at the cottage again. 'What would you do with this place, Roy?'

'Either sell it or knock it down.'

Wilf had kept fairly quiet and let the other two do most of the talking, but the rest of the idea he had during the night seemed so right that he took a chance. 'I might know someone who'd buy the cottage off you, then you could keep the rest of the land and build on it. What would be a fair price? She's a widow with a small inheritance and is looking to buy herself a home.'

Charlie gave him a sharp look but didn't say anything.

Roy thought for a moment, head on one side. 'Two hundred pounds. No, if she's a widow, I'd make it a hundred and ninety pounds. That's a very good price as long as we find the cottage is still sound. I'd not sell it if it wasn't, I'd rather knock it down. But we're getting ahead of ourselves. This land plus cottage belongs to Mrs Morton at the moment, and my friend who's interested in the cottage won't want the land, even if she could afford it.'

'Yes, but I'm certain Mrs Morton would sell the whole to you if you offered her a fair price for land plus cottage. She's afraid of what Higgerson might do to her and those she cares about, you see. And anyway, it's costing her too much to pay for council rates and so on. How much would you give her for the lot?'

Roy looked at Charlie. 'I'd need a partner for a project this big, because there'd be the costs of building on it afterwards.'

Charlie grinned at them both. 'I'd be in that. My electrical appliances shop is turning a nice profit now, not as much as it will when times really improve, but nice enough. This is thanks to Harry Makepeace's skills on selling modern items to housewives and teaching them how to use them, as well as repairing things when they stop working.'

He added with a grin, 'I'm thinking of letting him buy a share of the shop, so that he doesn't get tempted to move away. Men with his understanding of electrical gadgets are as rare as hens' teeth.'

'He's a decent fellow,' Roy said. 'Wouldn't hurt to give him a hand up. Is he still living in that railway carriage up in Ellindale?'

'Yes. Says he's saving to build a proper house there, but he's got the place set up just as nicely as any house of the same size, so I don't know why he'd bother till he's got more money behind him.' Charlie rubbed his hands together. 'I'm getting cold now. Let's go home and have a cup of tea and discuss what a fair price might be in a bit more comfort. Who's Mrs Morton's lawyer, Wilf?'

'Someone in Manchester. I don't know his name, but I can ask her.'

'Sound her out and if she's interested, get back to me. And ask that other woman if she's interested in buying the cottage while you're at it. Never hurts to get your skittles in a row, if you want to knock them all down with your first ball.'

Wilf stood up. 'All right. I won't bother with a cup of tea, if you don't mind. I'll go and see both the ladies straight away. To tell you the truth, the sooner we do this, the happier I'll be. I think Mrs Morton has good reason to be scared. I might hire someone to act as nightwatchman at both her house and the cottage for a while.'

Charlie looked at him in surprise. 'You think Higgerson's going to do things so openly, that he'd actually hurt an older lady who's well respected?'

Wilf hesitated, then said slowly, 'Yes, I do. The thing is, you see and hear a lot when you're doing various odd jobs, and I've worked nearly everywhere in the valley during the past few years. A wise man doesn't talk about what he's seen or he'd not get any other work, but some bosses don't seem to think the men working for them are clever enough to notice what's going on.'

'Never underestimate a tradesman,' Roy said quietly.

'Exactly. But even if you don't talk about it, you don't forget what you've seen and heard. You never forget those who play nasty tricks on others, if only to make sure they don't try to do the same to you. And you watch out for the people you care about, too.'

He stood for a while, then nodded as if coming to a decision. 'I'll go straight down to Rivenshaw to speak to the lady who may want to buy the cottage. I can ask Mrs Morton about selling her property after I come back. Give me some idea of your best price for Mrs Morton, will you? I don't want to waste time haggling.'

They debated for a while but couldn't come to any firm decision, because it was hard to guess without having studied the land more carefully for boggy parts or other problems they might encounter.

'We'll leave it to you, Wilf, to find out a price that would suit Mrs Morton. I'm sure you'll be fair to both sides.'

'What about the woman who may buy the cottage?' Charlie asked. 'Come on, who is it?'

'Can't you guess?' He saw the moment when the penny dropped for both men.

'The one I heard about who's working for Nick and Jo!' Roy exclaimed. 'Has she got that much money?'

'I think so, just a small inheritance so it's no use putting up the price from the one you've already suggested. From what she told me, she has only just enough to buy a house, but she'll need a job to cover the expense of running it afterwards.' And if that was a bit of an exaggeration, well, he was sure these two men were not short of a pound or two.

'Good thing for a woman in that position to invest in a home of her own,' Charlie agreed.

'She hasn't seen the inside of the cottage, though, so I'll have to show her round first. She might not like it. Can I use your phone to ask Mrs T if Stella is there at the moment, Roy? They're going to put me a phone in at Mrs Morton's, but not till Monday.'

'Feel free. It's in the hall.'

Wilf picked it up and found out that Mrs Newby was in the lodgers' sitting room so asked to speak to her.'

After a brief conversation he returned to the other men. 'I'll drive down to Rivenshaw straight away and talk to Mrs Newby. If she's interested in the cottage, I'll bring her back to look round it. All right if we climb over your wall again, Charlie?'

His host chuckled. 'Be my guest.'

'I think Mrs Morton would accept the amount we've discussed. It sounds reasonable to me in the circumstances.

Presumably you'd buy the land and cottage as one from Mrs
Morton, then sell the dwelling to Mrs Newby – as long as
it's on a separate land title. We might be in trouble there
otherwise. Though of course the council could allow us to
change the land title.'

'Not if Higgerson is involved, they won't.'

Charlie gave a tight little smile. 'I'll make sure people on
our side know they've got to attend meetings even if they're
on their deathbeds. And I'll get Reg to warn the clerk in the
land section that if word gets out about anything, he'll be
sacked. I think Reg will be happy to do that. He's intending
to tighten up a few things now he has more support from
the members of the new council.'

'Higgerson won't like anything being tightened up.'

'So what? A lot of people don't like the way he's been
behaving. He seems to think no one dare touch him, but he's
getting over-confident and over-ambitious too. What do they
call it? There's a fancy word for it that I read somewhere.'

'Hubris,' Roy said quietly. 'It's a Greek word.'

'That's it. And it seems to describe the way he's behaving.'
He hesitated. 'There's something else you ought to know. Just
between the three of us, Deemer is keeping an eye on
Higgerson too, waiting for an opportune moment to pounce.'

'Ah.' Roy beamed at that. 'I'm glad Deemer is sergeant
here. We're lucky to have him supervising the police in the
valley. He's as shrewd as they come. I still remember how
annoyed I used to get at the last chap, who was just serving
out time until he could retire.'

'I'll get off now,' Wilf said.

Roy walked to the door with him. 'You're going to be a
busy fellow, aren't you, lad? You haven't even spent a day
working with me at the office and yet you've found me a deal
that I find very interesting indeed. My wife was right. I do
need someone like you to work with. You're a man of ideas.'

Wilf saw sadness briefly cross his companion's face and knew he was thinking of his son. He was sorry for Roy and his wife. Life gave and it took away, as he knew only too well himself.

'I'll get back to you both quickly. I'm hoping I'll be able to show Mrs Newby around this afternoon.'

14

Wilf arranged for Beryl and Mona to look after the children, something which seemed to please both the ladies and the youngsters, before setting off for Rivenshaw.

He'd arranged to see Stella Newby but refused to tell her why exactly on the phone, in case someone at the exchange was listening in. You couldn't be too careful, because Higgerson had to be getting his information from more than one source. The only hint he gave her was that it had to do with something they'd seen yesterday and that she might need to wear sturdy clothes.

'Ah. I'll be ready when you arrive.'

Had she really guessed what he meant so quickly? He liked dealing with people who were quick on the uptake. Well, he liked her.

As he drove down into Rivenshaw, he whistled 'Sweet Georgia Brown', one of his favourite tunes, then was filled with guilt for feeling cheerful with his wife only just buried. But he couldn't help it; he was looking forward to working with Roy and, he had to admit, to seeing Stella again as well.

She was ready when he knocked at Mrs T's, calling a cheerful goodbye to someone inside the house and following him out to the van. And, of course, she was wearing her sturdy shoes again.

He didn't start up the engine straight away, but asked, 'Did you guess where we were going?'

'To see inside the cottage? It's rough ground near it so I thought these shoes would be best.'

'Right first time.' He started the motor and set off.

'Have you been inside it already?'

'Yes. But I had to do it sneakily.' He told her about the watcher. 'I'm taking you to Charlie Willcox's house and we'll need to climb over his back fence to get to the cottage without being seen.'

She chuckled. 'I'm certainly doing lots more active things since I've met you.'

'And that pleases you?'

'Oh, yes. I sometimes felt like screaming at work when I had to sit still for hours on end. They used to frown if you fidgeted at all. It'll be much better working at the driving school, I'm sure, because there are a variety of tasks involved in the job and I'll have to get up and down from the chair regularly. And I'll have my driving lessons to look forward to as well.'

Her attitude didn't surprise him. She was small and on the scrawny side but looked rosy with health, and today she seemed to be absolutely bursting with energy. 'Did you sleep well after your long stroll over the tops?'

'Well enough, but I had the strangest dreams. I seemed to be walking round the inside of that cottage. It's surprised me how much it's been on my mind since we saw it yesterday.'

'What did it look like in your dream?'

'Three bedrooms and a box room upstairs, two rooms downstairs and a large kitchen with scullery and some outbuildings off one side of the rear. Everything was very dusty and there was something wrong with one of the kitchen windows. It was the old-fashioned sort with a lot of panes and one had been broken and a piece of wood put into the gap.'

He was glad she was looking out of the side window just

then, because that remark made him gape at her in shock. He was positive she hadn't been inside the cottage and though she could have been guessing at the number of rooms upstairs, they hadn't gone round the outside near the kitchen, so how could she possibly know about the broken window pane?

She'd been very specific about the interior details and correct about all of them!

By the time she turned back to him, he'd hidden his surprise, or at least he hoped he had. 'It'll be interesting to see whether your dreams coincide with the reality.'

'Oh, they surely won't do that. It'd be far too much of a coincidence.'

It was already enough of a coincidence to make him feel uneasy.

They turned off the main road and were outside Charlie's house within a couple of minutes.

She looked at the building and her brow wrinkled as if something was puzzling her. 'This seems to be a nice house from a distance, but—'

'But what?'

'It looks as if it were meant to be bigger, the roof should be a little higher and the windows on the ground floor wider.'

He stared at her in surprise for the second time since she'd got into his van. 'That's exactly what I think, too. It's one of Higgerson's houses and he always skimps on the details if he can get away with it. I doubt that fellow could lie straight in bed.'

'I despise people who don't do their jobs properly, whatever the jobs are.'

'Me too. Every task is worthy of respect. Come on.' He took a workman's bag out of the back of the van and led the way to the front door, which Charlie opened before they had time to knock.

He took them straight out to the back. 'Did Wilf warn you there's a wall to climb over, Mrs Newby?'

'Yes. But he said there would be a ladder.'

'I was thinking—'

'We'll talk later, if you don't mind,' Wilf told him firmly. Charlie might be able to keep a secret when necessary but he could also talk the hind leg off a donkey, and anyway, he didn't want him to warn her about anything, wanted to see her reaction to the cottage's interior. 'Stella and I want to look round straight away.'

'Oh, all right.'

Wilf dropped his tool bag over the top of the wall and it made a soft clunking sound as it hit the ground on the other side.

Charlie started to move forward. 'Here, let me help you, Mrs Newby.'

But she didn't need help to get over the wall, so he stayed where he was, admiring her surprisingly elegant legs and neat ankles, more of which showed as she climbed over the top of the wall.

As she vanished down into the other garden, Charlie's wife grabbed him from behind and dragged him back towards his own house, saying in a low voice, 'Shame on you, Charlie Willcox. You shouldn't stare at women's legs in that odious way.'

'Well, you have to admit, Mrs Newby has beautiful ones.'

'And how would you be an expert on that? Don't let me catch you again, staring at any part of a woman's body like a silly young lad! I thought you had better manners.'

He wriggled uncomfortably. 'I don't usually stare, but she looked so meek and colourless, it was a surprise to see those legs.'

'I'll surprise you if you gawp at her again, my lad.'

'Yes, ma'am.' He gave his wife a quick hug. 'I'll gawp at you instead.'

'And only me, if you please.' She returned the hug, giving him the soft, loving smile only he and their son could win from her, so he knew she wasn't really angry with him.

Stella climbed up the first stepladder and down the other so quickly that Wilf was also surprised that she didn't need a hand.

'You're very nimble.'

'I like being active but once girls grow up no one wants them to climb trees or run around like hooligans. You're supposed to be *ladylike* and move everywhere at a snail's pace.'

'My Peggy is turning into a tomboy. She's full of energy now she's getting better food. I shan't stop her climbing trees or running about.'

'She's going to be pretty too.'

He paused to consider that. 'You think so? I wondered if it was just me being a fond dad.'

'No. She's got a lovely little face.'

Pleased at the compliment, he opened the front door and led the way in.

She stopped in the hall and gasped. 'It can't be!'

'What's the matter?'

'It looks just like my dream.'

'Ah. That's strange. But these old cottages often resemble one another. We'll go through to the kitchen and I'll leave my tools there. I'm going to make a couple of changes before I leave here today, so that the place is more secure.'

He stepped back to let her go first but she was slow to move, looking round as if upset. He began to worry what she would say when she saw the broken window in the kitchen. Before he could think how to prepare her for it, she'd gone ahead.

She stopped again just inside the doorway, turning to him and grabbing his arm. 'How could I possibly have known what it was like, Wilf?'

He put his hand over hers for reassurance. 'Who knows? I don't usually believe in that sort of um, spooky stuff, but you described it very accurately.'

'I don't normally believe in it, either, only I walked round this house in my dreams and it was definitely *this* cottage, even to the same pieces of dusty furniture. I can tell you what furniture is in the bedrooms upstairs, to test it.'

'Go on. Tell me about the biggest bedroom.'

She did that, even describing the elegant inlay work on the wardrobe and dressing table there.

He could only shake his head in bafflement. 'That's it exactly.' It was such a pretty bedroom suite, he remembered it clearly.

'Phew! It's a good thing I like the cottage so much or that would bother me.'

'It doesn't?'

'Only a little.' She turned back to point at the kitchen window. 'Why is it broken? The damage to the wood shows that it's happened recently.'

'That's what we thought. Someone has broken into the house that way, which is why I've brought my tools and a few bits and pieces, to stop them doing it again.'

'I'm glad you have. Will you be able to make everything fully secure?'

'Fairly secure. Nothing can stop someone smashing windows or doors with a sledge hammer, but they'll make so much noise doing it that people will come running, and as our street is near the slum the neighbours are always ready to help one another. I'm going to change the lock on the front door as well. We couldn't find a key to it anywhere in the house, so we think the intruders took it away with them.'

She frowned, shaking her head as if mystified. Well, who wouldn't be?

'If what you dreamed has put you off the cottage, I'll make the repairs quickly and take you home again.'

She gave him a long, thoughtful look before replying. 'No. I still love this place. It shocked me at first that I'd dreamed about it so accurately, but now I'm mainly angry that someone broke in. It might sound stupid, but I really think this is meant to be mine, Wilf. I felt an affinity with it as soon as I saw it from outside, as if . . . well, I'd come home. I feel it even more strongly now I'm inside.'

'I like the feel of it, too.'

'Can we walk round the rest?'

'As long as you can face the dust.'

There were two other rooms as well as the kitchen on the ground floor, with a scullery and coal store leading off the kitchen. Beyond them there was an old door, which was locked. He felt along the lintel for the key, the usual hiding place. 'Sorry. There doesn't seem to be a key.'

She went into the scullery and fumbled along the lintel inside, taking down a rusty old key. 'Here. Try this.'

How had she known to look there?

The key opened the door, though the lock was stiff as if it hadn't been used for years. When they looked inside they found a dark room with shutters bolted across the only window, a door in one of the side walls and another door at the far end.

Unlike the rest of the house, this part contained no furniture and from the signs of dampness at one corner, there was a leak in the roof.

He went to check on that. 'Can't be a big leak or there'd be much more damage. Easily repaired, I should think. Where does this lead?' He tried to open the far door but it seemed stuck. He gave it a stray kick out of sheer annoyance and it moved slightly so he threw his body weight against it and it burst open.

It led into the set of outhouses he'd noticed from the road, but they were bigger inside than he'd expected. The floor was covered in flagstones and was dusty. Since there were no footprints in the dust, it must have been years since anyone had been in here. There was a narrow window with shutters on it and when he tugged at them, one of the shutters came away and hung drunkenly on its lower hinge.

'Who'd have thought there'd be all this under cover!' he marvelled. 'Let's go and see what's behind the other door.'

When he got it open, they both stood gaping at the narrow stone stairs leading down.

'There's another cellar here,' Wilf said. 'Stay up here while I check that it's safe.'

He made his way carefully down a flight of stone steps and found himself in a cellar that was smaller than the main one. It seemed dry and safe so he called up, 'You can come down.' He shone his torch on the steps to guide her down safely.

'It's not damp. But why would they need a separate cellar?' she asked.

'Who knows? What do you think that's for?' He pointed up to what looked like a sheet of dirty glass with a grating over it on the other side. One end looked as if it'd open like a window only it was covered in what seemed to be garden soil. 'Who knows? I'll uncover that another time. It's quite big. Gratings for letting in air are usually smaller.'

'Maybe it's to let in light as well.'

Back in the end room upstairs, he looked round. 'What do you think this place was used for?'

She considered it for a moment. 'Maid's room? Storeroom? I didn't dream about this part of the cottage. Could be a workshop, perhaps.'

'Let's go and look for that grating in the garden.'

Outside he kicked away the soil until he uncovered part of it.

She looked down at it, head on one side, then said thoughtfully, 'I think it *is* a workshop, one from quite early on, before factories were invented, perhaps. I've read about those home workshops. People fitted them in wherever they could.'

He studied it too and nodded. 'Possibly. It wasn't for weaving, though. They built weavers' rooms on the top floor usually with bigger windows to let in plenty of light. Let's cover it up again. I think the grating was designed to keep people out and we don't want anyone seeing it and trying to get in. They'd make a right old mess inside if they broke that glass and let the loose earth fall down.'

When they went back inside they locked the door that led into the end room from the kitchen and he put the key back on the scullery lintel. 'Upstairs now?'

She led the way up. 'We'll go into the biggest bedroom first, shall we?'

They looked at the suite of furniture, which was exactly as she'd described from her dreams. It made him feel distinctly uneasy. He didn't believe in the supernatural, of course he didn't. But how did you explain this?

Stella went across to the window to look out across the street. 'I can see Mrs Morton's house from here.'

The other bedrooms were smaller and more plainly furnished.

He stood in the doorway of the small box room. 'This could be made into a bathroom. You'd have to modernise the plumbing, so you might as well do it properly if you buy the cottage. Everything's so old-fashioned.'

'As long as it's not too expensive.'

When they went downstairs, he hesitated, looking at the final door just off the back of the hall. 'That only goes down to the cellar. There's nothing there.'

'I'd still like to see it.'

'Lucky I brought my torch.'

'Not lucky. I should think you're very good at practical preparations like that.'

'You seem to understand me.'

'That's mutual.'

They stared at one another for a moment or two and he didn't know what to think about how comfortable he felt with her, so broke the silence hastily. 'Before we go down, do you know what the cellar is like? Did you dream about that too?'

'Yes, I did. Two rooms, empty except for some very old jars of preserves on two of the shelves to the left of the far part. No patches of damp anywhere.'

He nodded but couldn't summon up a smile because she was again accurate. The cellar was dry and in good condition, which in an old cottage was a sign that it had been properly built in the first place.

He shook his head in bafflement as he moved forward into the second cellar, shining his torch to the left.

'Oh, look! There are the jars.' She picked one up. 'You can only guess what's in them because it's turned into dark mush. This one looks like some sort of fruit, pears perhaps from the shape. They must be very old, but I expect they could be cleaned and re-used if you bought new rubber seals.'

He didn't comment but she looked at him in the shadowed space as if he had. 'I shouldn't be making plans, should I? I'm a long way from buying the cottage yet. Only I feel so at home here. That's strange, isn't it?'

'Yes. But as long as you're still feeling comfortable, we might as well discuss buying it. Let's go up into the daylight, though. You go first.'

As he followed her up the stairs, he admitted to himself that he felt comfortable here too.

15

Once they were in the kitchen standing looking out at the garden, Wilf started the discussion.

'I've found out the price Mr Tyler would charge you for this cottage and its garden if he bought all the land from Mrs Morton.'

'How much?'

'A hundred and ninety pounds.'

'Hmm.'

'Is that more than you can afford?'

'No, but it's a large amount of money to spend.' She didn't want to let him or anyone else know how much she'd won.

'It's a good price for a house with three bedrooms and a decent-sized garden.'

'How much garden is there?'

'I think you'd go by the line of that broken-down fence. You'd have to discuss the exact details with Roy. But the cottage would definitely need modernising and electricity putting in before you moved in, as well as the leak at the corner fixing. The interiors of houses have changed a lot over the past two decades, but Mr Tyler could do the various improvements for you, and do them well, too, at a reasonable price. I've seen and admired his work for years.'

'Is there anyone you don't know in the building industry in this valley?'

'Oh, quite a few. Some of Higgerson's workers I don't

even want to know, but others are decent blokes, doing what's necessary to earn a living, even if it means working for him and skimping on jobs. And there are one or two minor builders who do mainly renovations and improvements, like Redfern's, for instance. They've been going for over a hundred years according to the sign on their workshop. Higgerson has left them alone because he's not interested in renovating anything.'

He was surprised by a sudden urge to touch Stella's shining hair – eh, what had got into him? – and hastily carried on speaking. 'Now, back to the cottage: the sewage line and services like electricity run along the street because of the houses on the other side, so if you buy it you won't need to spend a fortune on getting connections put in.'

She nodded, not seeming worried about the prospect of needing to pay for having work done on the cottage. He guessed she must have enough left to deal with that, which was quite a lot of money by his standards.

On that thought he said, 'Don't tell Roy or me how much money you have if you intend to buy the house off him. Pretend you can barely afford to buy it and bring its amenities up to scratch.'

She chuckled.

He liked her gurgle of laughter. It was infectious.

He was still smiling as he led the way back to the living room.

She looked round. 'If the furniture goes with the cottage, that'd be a big help, though I'd want to get new mattresses.'

'You're that certain you want it? Already!'

'Yes.'

'Well, there are a few other things to tell you. We don't know whether the cottage is on a separate land title. The information about that is held by Mrs Morton's lawyer and she's not sure about such details. I don't think she's very good at the business side of life. If it isn't separate Roy, as the person buying the whole piece of land from Mrs Morton, will have to apply to the council for a change of land title so that he can sell the cottage to you as a whole, though he could maybe rent the ground to you in the interim.'

'And would the council be likely to agree to a change of title?'

'We don't know. There have been difficulties in the past with council employees not working honestly – and nowadays that can mean Higgerson.'

'He sounds to be a dreadful person.'

'He is. I'm worried that since he hasn't managed to buy the land from Mrs Morton – he's already tried to do that several times and she refused – he'll try to change her mind with more threats and dirty tricks. So don't count on anything, or tell others about wanting to buy the cottage, until the sale has gone through. Unless that makes you change your mind.'

He watched the stubborn look return to her face and knew she'd not change her mind.

'I still feel it's going to be my home.'

'Then we'll do our best to get it for you. At least there will be no difficulty in Roy Tyler buying the land from Mrs Morton. She's eager to sell as long as it's to someone other than Higgerson and who'll give her a fair price, which Roy will. But even if that happens, there will still be the land title to be sorted out.'

He smiled. 'Anyway, that's for the future. I wanted to put you in the picture and if you're still eager to buy the cottage, I can tell Roy to include the money from selling to you in his financial considerations. He hasn't got unlimited funds.'

She nodded, her face intent.

'Now, before we leave, I'd better repair that kitchen window and make it harder for whoever it is to break in again. And I'll see if I can change the front-door lock. I have a few lock fittings that might slot in. It's only a standard old-fashioned lock.'

'While you do that, I'll have another walk round and take a closer look at what furniture there is.'

He found himself whistling again as he worked. Damned if he too didn't feel comfortable in this cottage. She was right. It could be made into a lovely home.

What the hell was going on here, though? How could she possibly have dreamed in such detail about the interior of a cottage she'd never been inside before?

Upstairs, Stella took her little notebook and pencil out of her satchel and started making a list of all the furniture, excitement rising in her. If it was included in the price, there would be more than enough for her main needs. The cottage felt cosy, as if people had once been happy here.

Having a home of her own would make her happy, too, because it would make her dearest dream come true.

She heard Wilf mutter under his breath as he fiddled with the front-door lock and suddenly say 'Aah!' There were clicking sounds as the door was opened, shut and locked a couple of times, then he must have picked up his tools because they clinked as they were put back into his bag.

He appeared in the doorway, beaming. 'I did it. Changed the lock. I'll just need to get a couple of extra keys made, which I can do at the locksmith's in Rivenshaw. Have you finished looking round?'

'Nearly.' She took a deep breath. 'Do you think I should try to knock Mr Tyler down a bit in price?'

'It's up to you but I wouldn't. It's a fair price and he already came down ten pounds when he heard you were a widow. That's the sort of man he is. I doubt he'll go any lower. But remember, this is still dependent on him being able to buy it all from Mrs Morton.'

'I know. I do understand a fair amount about local councils and their rules as well. I've been reading newspapers and
books for the past few years. It didn't matter what they were,
it was just something to fill the evenings. I've learned about
how the parliament of our country is run, too. I enjoy finding
new things out.'

'I do, too. I especially like to learn about other countries.
I may never be able to visit them in person, but there's a
wider world out there and Britain can't help being influenced
by what's going on in those countries.'

'Like the things happening in Germany at the moment?'
she asked.

'Yes. Exactly. There are some disturbing signs, aren't there?
I pray we don't tumble into another war.' He fell silent, shook
away those dark thoughts and looked at her enquiringly. 'So?
What do you want to do?'

'Will you please tell Mr Tyler I'd definitely like to buy the
cottage?' She held up one hand to stop him as he opened
his mouth to caution her again. 'And I'm prepared to give
him a deposit to prove I'm serious.'

'I have no doubt you're serious. I knew you'd want to buy
it. I'd do the same if I had any spare money. There's something about this place that I like too.'

'Am I taking it away from you?'

'No, no. I don't have the money to buy a house, and I
won't have for a long time. That's just a very long-term dream
for me. I've only recently started as Mr Tyler's partner.'

Before they clambered back across Charlie Willcox's wall,
Wilf stopped. 'There's something else. I wonder if you'd
come with me to Mrs Morton's now, so that it'll look as if
you and I are walking out together?' He could feel himself
flushing as he said that, so added quickly, 'We need to be
careful what we're doing, you see, and that would mask

our real purpose here. But if you'd rather not be gossiped about . . . ?'

'I'd like us to become friends, but I'm not expecting anything more if that worries you.'

'No. I never even thought of that. I just meant we should act as if we're courting. It's to protect you, as much as anything.'

'You're seriously worried about this Higgerson man, aren't you?'

'With reason.'

'Pretending to be courting will seem rather strange. I hardly know you. And your wife has just died.'

'Enid and I hadn't been getting on for a while, and I think anyone who knows me was aware of that. But I was sorry when she died and I'm not ready to court anyone seriously. It's just that this is a ticklish situation and I want to keep you safe. I'll treat you with the utmost respect, I promise you. There won't be any . . . you know, funny business.'

'I wasn't thinking you'd misbehave, Wilf. You haven't got that sort of face and I've seen how you treat women.'

'An expert at judging men's behaviour, are you?' he teased.

But she didn't smile back at him. 'After I was widowed, I had some difficult moments. I grew to recognise the signs of a man who thought he'd . . . you know, be able to treat me disrespectfully. It was one of the reasons I pretended not to have ever been married when I moved to Rochdale. Men are less likely to make advances to spinsters who dress plainly and go to church than they are to widows.'

'I'm sorry you had to face that.'

'Actually, people assuming that we're courting might help protect me here because I've told Nick and Jo that I'm a widow – I didn't want to lie to them – so no doubt word will get around. And I'd be happy to spend more time with your two little 'uns. I really enjoy children's company.'

He suddenly saw with blinding clarity how lonely Stella must have been and how vulnerable she'd felt at times. It must have taken a lot of courage to make a new life for herself like this.

'Well, I promise never to treat you in any way that upsets you, if I can help it, and actually, I think you and I could easily become genuine friends. We never have any trouble chatting or sharing ideas, do we?'

'No. Very well. We'll do it.'

'Good. It'll look more realistic if you call me Wilf from now on.'

She gave him another of her thoughtful looks. 'Yes. All right. And you'll call me Stella, of course.'

As they clambered back across the wall, Charlie came out of his house to greet them. Wilf told him only that Stella was interested in the cottage.

Charlie beamed at them. 'That's good. We'll be neighbours, then.'

They drove the short distance to his new home and it felt good too to walk in and call, 'I'm back. And I've brought Mrs Newby to visit us again.'

Beryl came out to join them, putting one finger to her lips. 'Shh. The children are just having a little nap in their bedroom. I think yesterday exhausted them and they didn't even try to protest when I suggested they lie down for a few minutes. How nice to see you again, my dear. Do come and sit down.'

'You'd better call her Stella from now on,' Wilf said. 'We're going to pretend to be, um, getting rather friendly, to give us an excuse for any business meetings we need to have. It'll be safer from you know who.'

Her smile faded. 'Oh yes, it will. Unfortunately, we haven't solved that problem yet. I'd better be Beryl to you in return, my dear.'

'Thank you. I hope you don't mind.'

'Of course I don't. So how did you like the cottage . . . Stella?'

'I loved it . . . Beryl.'

'There! I had a feeling you would. Personally, I've never felt quite comfortable in it, I don't know why.'

When they were seated, Wilf got straight to the point. 'I have some good news for you, Beryl – at least, I think it's good. Mr Tyler and Charlie Willcox are interested in buying your cottage and land.'

Her voice was little more than a gasp. 'They are? Really?'

'Yes, and for a reasonable price, too. But we need to act quickly so that Higgerson can't interfere. Can you give me the name of your lawyer in Manchester?'

'Yes. I have one of his business cards.' She went to a small bureau and opened a drawer, fumbling inside it, then looked at him in puzzlement. 'I know I put it away here. I always keep business cards on top of these papers in this pretty box lid, because I don't get many, and that one was right on top. Only it doesn't seem to be here now.' She sorted through the others again, as if doubting herself. 'No, it's definitely not here. You check, Wilf.'

There was dead silence as he looked through the cards and shook his head. 'Check the drawer, in case it's fallen out.'

'There are only these pencils and boxes of odds and ends like paper clips. I never throw anything like that away.'

He watched her getting more agitated and went to put his arm round her. 'Come and sit down again.'

'I don't understand, Wilf. It's definitely not anywhere in the drawer and I know Mona would never touch anything in it.'

He knew it would upset her even more, but he had to ask. 'Is it possible someone could have got into your house and had a quick look round when you were out?'

She looked at him for a moment, eyes wide in horror. 'I suppose so. We don't always lock the doors when we're nipping to the shop in the village. No one here does. But oh, Wilf, I don't like the idea of someone doing that, I don't like it at all.'

'I don't either. I'll change all the locks here, as well as those in the cottage, and you'd better keep the outer doors locked even when you're at home, and be especially careful until the sale of your land has gone through. Shall I ask Roy to telephone your lawyer and arrange a meeting? I don't think we should even wait for the phone to be put in here on Monday to do that. It might not be installed and connected till late afternoon. Or even the following day.'

'Will you do that for me?'

'Yes, of course. Can you remember your lawyer's details?'

'They're on the headings of the letters from him. I have some here.'

But when she went to the next drawer down, in which she kept the letters from her lawyer, they were missing, too.

'Someone has definitely been in here and taken my folder of letters connected with my inheritance.' She pressed one hand to her mouth, then continued, 'My lawyer's name is Barrenby and his rooms are in Durrakin Street, near the centre of Manchester. I'm certain of that because I've had to write the address on envelopes but I don't remember his phone number.'

'What's he like?'

'I haven't met him, because I dealt with his father originally when I inherited, but he died. I've only exchanged letters with his son since, because there wasn't much that needed doing.' She hesitated then scribbled down the lawyer's name and address. 'I think his first name is Lewis.'

'I'll phone him from Roy's first thing on Monday.'

Wilf looked at the bureau again. 'It must be Higgerson

who arranged to have the letters stolen. Who else would bother?'

'I agree. Only what I don't understand is why he would do it. They were only a few letters, to do with paying the rates mainly, nothing of importance. I left all the deeds and official papers with the lawyer. I've owned the place for years and never told anyone.'

'How did Higgerson find out you were the owner? Did he say?'

'No.'

He saw Stella frown and look as if she wanted to say something. 'Go on,' he said encouragingly.

'There's another question we need to ask ourselves: why do this now? What does he intend to do with the information, do you think? Or is he just gathering it in case he needs it?'

'Whichever it is, since we don't even know when they were taken, I think we should act as quickly as we can. It's a pity everywhere will be closed for the weekend now. If the lawyer were living in Rivenshaw, I'd know where he was and be able to call on him at home, but who knows where he lives in Manchester?'

'Oh dear.' Beryl dabbed at her eyes with a lace-edged handkerchief.

Wilf exchanged glances with Stella. He didn't like to see Beryl so upset. 'I don't want to wait until Monday now to tell the lawyer there might be trouble brewing. I suspect some trick is being planned. But how can Higgerson get hold of your land without you selling it to him?'

He watched Stella move to put her arm round the older woman. Poor Beryl. He was glad he was living here now and would be able to help her.

'Stella and I were going to discuss her buying the cottage with Roy Tyler and his wife after we'd seen you, Beryl. I think, in view of what we've found, you should come with us. They know a lot of people. They may have a suggestion about what to do.'

Beryl nodded, but was still looking upset as she put on her hat and coat to go out and asked Mona to keep an eye on things here.

And her voice sounded old and quavery as she said, 'I'm ready.'

16

Roy's wife opened the door, studied their faces and immediately asked, 'What's happened now?'

Wilf blinked in surprise. 'Are you a mind reader?'

'I'm good at guessing how people are feeling. And you all look rather down in the mouth. Do come in. I presume you want to talk to Roy.'

Wilf couldn't help envying them their cosy house and what was obviously a very happy marriage. You could tell that from the way people looked at one another, not always needing words to communicate. Most of all he envied Roy his intelligent wife. It was well known among people involved in the building industry that although she usually stayed quietly in the background, Ethel Tyler was an asset to her husband and his business, and oversaw the office and all their finances.

Then he realised he was making uncomplimentary comparisons with his late wife and told himself to stop doing that. Enid had managed through hard times as best she could and who could do more? His travelling in search of work had changed him, taught him so much, and it was as much his fault as hers that they'd grown apart.

He told the Tylers all that had happened, ending, 'I thought you ought to know about this, but the trouble is, we can't do anything about Mrs Morton's lawyer till Monday. I wish we could catch him at home, just to make sure nothing's gone wrong already. You don't happen to know where he lives, do you?' He sat back to wait for their comments without much hope.

He didn't know why, but he felt a sense of urgency about this. Never give Higgerson a chance to meddle with your affairs, people said, and the fellow had been trying to get Beryl's land off her for a while now. This finding could only be connected to that.

'What's the lawyer like?' Roy looked at Beryl.

'I've never met young Mr Barrenby in person, I'm afraid. It was his father I dealt with when I first inherited and he was a very kind man, but he's been dead for a few years now, died very suddenly, poor chap. If I remember correctly, the son lived in Rivenshaw for a while, working with a local lawyer to broaden his experience beyond the sort of cases his father usually handled. But he moved away to take over the family business when his father died.'

Wilf sighed. 'I think we're going to have to wait till Monday to speak to him.'

The lawyer's name sounded familiar to Ethel Tyler and she suddenly remembered why. 'Just a minute! I may be able to help. I met a woman called Barrenby at my cousin's house, then this lady and her husband moved away from the valley suddenly. It was a few years ago, mind. She was a nice young woman and I think – no I'm sure – she said her husband was a lawyer, though I never knew his first name. It must be the same man, mustn't it? Barrenby isn't a common name.'

'Do you have her address or telephone number?'

'No, but I could phone my cousin if you like. Hilda may have kept in touch with them and know where they went.'

Her husband shrugged, clearly not expecting much from this. 'It's worth a try, I suppose.'

She went to find her address book, crossed the hall into

their home office and left the door open. Everyone fell silent, trying not to look as if they were listening.

Ethel put a call through to her cousin, nodding to Roy, who had come across the hall to listen. Then there was the faint squawky sound of someone answering and she turned her attention to the person at the other end of the line.

'Yes, please do.' She looked up. 'Hilda's gone to find her address book. She's not sure whether she got their new address or not.'

When Hilda came back on the telephone, Ethel listened to her and sagged in disappointment. 'Oh dear. What a pity. Well, thanks for trying. What? Yes, it was rather important.'

She put her hand across the receiver and whispered to her husband, 'She doesn't know exactly where they moved to.'

'What a pity.'

'But she might know someone who does. She isn't sure. Shhh.'

Ethel removed her hand and listened intently. 'Yes, that's very kind of you, Hilda. Goodbye.' She put the phone down and turned to Roy. 'I'm sorry I couldn't help you today, dear. She's just going out for the evening, but she'll phone her friend tomorrow before church.'

'Thank you for trying. We'll have to wait till Monday morning and go to his place of business early.'

They went back to tell their visitors what had happened.

'Wilf and I will go into Manchester on Monday,' Roy said. 'I'll let you know what time we should leave after I've spoken to my driver. He may know the area better than I do.'

Wilf stood up and Beryl followed suit. 'Thank you. We'll leave the two of you in peace now.'

On Sunday morning the telephone rang at the Tylers' house just as they were about to set out for church in Rivenshaw. Roy answered it then passed it to his wife, left her in his home office and began to pace up and down the hall, muttering to himself about thoughtless people who rang at inconvenient times.

'Roy! Come here quickly!'

He hurried to join her, worried that Ethel might have received some bad news. 'What's wrong?'

But she had already put the phone down and was smiling so he relaxed again.

'Nothing wrong, love. I told you yesterday that my cousin thought she knew someone who might have the new address of the Barrenbys. And this person did have it, but she doesn't have their phone number because she didn't have a telephone herself in those days. I've scribbled down their address on the back of this envelope. She says it's on this side of Manchester, at least an hour's drive away from here, which is why she lost touch socially with Mrs Barrenby because she doesn't drive herself.' She frowned and murmured, 'I really must learn to drive, you know. It's so useful.'

The idea of her getting behind the wheel upset him, because he was nervous about women driving. He didn't say that, of course, because if he objected, she'd only get more stubborn about it. 'I wonder if I should go and see them today. What do you think? Wilf is really worried about Mrs Morton's safety, and probably with reason.'

'You know, I think that's a good idea, dear. We all know that Higgerson can cause a lot of trouble for people who've upset him, and we don't want anything happening to that nice old lady. The quicker we do something about it the better we can be sure of keeping her safe.'

'Do you think one day will make a difference? It's my driver's day off.'

'It could be important. We don't know when those thefts occurred.' She hesitated. 'I've got one of my feelings about it, so I'm coming with you.'

'Oh. In that case we'll go straight away.'

Did every woman have 'feelings' like that, he wondered as he started the car. Sometimes the things females came up with were beyond a plain man's comprehension. But his wife really did have an instinct for the best thing to do, and was rarely wrong, so instead of going to church he drove round to see Wilf.

He didn't need to persuade them to come and visit Mr Barrenby immediately. Indeed, Wilf brightened visibly on hearing the news.

'We'll leave Mona here with the children and tell her to keep all the outer doors locked,' he said. 'I can't see Higgerson causing any trouble today, because there's no way he can be aware of what we're doing.'

When they all went out to the car, Roy hesitated, then turned to Wilf. 'Look, lad, my driver doesn't like to work on a Sunday because he sings in the church choir, and my eyes aren't as good as they used to be. Could you drive us today? Younger eyes see better than older ones and we'll be needing to watch the signposts carefully and ask directions. I don't know that part of Manchester at all well.'

'I don't know it either, but I enjoy driving. And what your driver doesn't know, he can't gossip about. Not that I think he would let anything slip on purpose. He's always seemed a nice chap. But we can't be too careful at the moment.'

'Should we invite your friend Stella to join us, do you think, Wilf?'

He considered this, head on one side. 'No, I don't think so. I can tell her what happens – *if* anything happens. This is a long shot, after all, just a precaution and she won't be directly involved until after you've bought the land and can sell the cottage to her.'

'I do hope this Mr Barrenby is as kind as his father and

won't be angry at us for disturbing him,' Mrs Morton worried from the back seat. 'I don't like to trouble people about business matters on the Sabbath.'

Ethel turned sideways to smile at her and say soothingly, 'It's worth a try. If there's nothing to be concerned about, we'll only take a little of his time. It's always best to make sure when you're concerned about a legal situation.'

Roy let out a snort of disgust. 'Especially when it's Higgerson who's involved. The only thing you can trust him to do is something bad.'

They found the street where the Barrenbys now lived quite easily, thanks to the clear directions of a man they stopped to ask. Mr Tyler opened his car door. 'I'll go and find out whether he's in and if so, whether he'll see us. Better if we don't all descend on him at once.'

'I'll come with you, dear,' Ethel said. 'It'll look much more respectable for you to have a wife on your arm.'

Wilf couldn't help smiling as he watched them walk up to the front door. In his opinion her mere appearance, so pleasantly plump and tidy, would instantly establish their respectability and she had the sort of smile that won people over.

Roy came back on his own a short time later and beckoned to them. 'He'll see us for a few minutes.'

'Here we go, Beryl. Chin up!' Wilf spoke encouragingly because he could see how nervous she was.

They were taken into a plainly furnished room, set up as a sort of office with a desk and a couple of hard chairs for visitors in front of it. Mr Barrenby pulled forward another couple of chairs for them from a row against the wall, then gestured to them all to sit down. 'How exactly can I help you?'

'I think my partner can explain best,' Roy said. 'He knows everyone involved.'

'First, we're sorry to disturb you on a Sunday and are

grateful for your time,' Wilf began and proceeded to give as concise a summary as he could manage.

The lawyer asked a couple of questions, but mostly left him to it. When he'd finished his tale they all waited, watching their host, trying to gauge his reaction.

'Hmm.' Barrenby studied them one by one. 'I don't usually see people on Sundays but when I heard that one of the visitors was a Mrs Morton from Birch End, I was puzzled. As it happens, I have an appointment to see a Mrs Morton from Birch End tomorrow afternoon.'

'I don't understand,' Beryl said at once. 'It's not me and I don't know anyone else of that name living in our village.'

'Could you please give me your address there?'

'Number Six, Croft Street.'

'Goodness. That's apparently where the lady coming to see me lives.'

'But that's not possible. I've lived at that address for over twenty years.'

'Clearly something isn't right.'

'Who made the appointment?' Roy asked. 'Was it Higgerson himself?'

'No. The appointment was made by a lawyer from just outside Rivenshaw, a Mr Gorton. Do you know him?'

Roy Tyler pursed his lips. 'I know *of* him. He, um, doesn't deal with our sort of people. Takes small cases mostly and does work for Higgerson from time to time.'

'Ah. Well, Gorton did say he was acting on behalf of a Mr Higgerson, who will be attending together with this Mrs Morton.' He studied Beryl. 'I'm sorry to have to ask you this, but do you have any proof that you are the genuine Mrs Morton of that address?'

She looked bewildered. 'What sort of proof?'

'Letters addressed to you at that address, bills paid from there.'

When they all made involuntary noises of shock, he looked at them in surprise.

'Mrs Morton's house has been burgled recently and some of her papers and bills were taken. We couldn't understand why anyone would steal such things, but now, well, perhaps . . . ' Roy let his words trail away.

Wilf finished it for him. 'Perhaps someone else is planning to use these papers to prove their identity. Do you know why they're coming to see you?'

'Higgerson wishes to buy some land this so-called Mrs Morton owns.' He glanced at Beryl again. 'My father dealt with a lady of that name when she inherited and we still pay the rates and deal with any other matters arising for her. My new partner deals with that side of our business. It says in her file that she doesn't want it known by people in Birch End that she's the owner.'

There was silence, then Wilf had a sudden idea. 'You know what? We could get the local sergeant of police to bear witness to this lady's identity, and to ours too. Indeed, you could telephone him right now and ask him, if you wish, Mr Barrenby. He's known me and Roy for years and will easily recognise us by our voices.'

'And I met your wife a few times some years ago, Mr Barrenby,' Ethel said. 'She should be able to vouch for who I am. I doubt I've changed that much.'

Mr Barrenby pushed his chair back. '"Curiouser and curiouser", to quote my youngest daughter's favourite storybook. We'll start with my wife. I won't be long.' He left the room and returned almost immediately with a lady and another gentleman.

He held up one hand to prevent his visitors from speaking and turned to his wife. 'Do you know anyone in this room, my dear?'

It took only a glance for her to say, 'Yes. I know Mrs Tyler.

We met a few times at a friend's house, though we've not seen one another since you and I moved here.'

'And I know for certain that you've not spoken to each other today, because you've been at home with me.' He turned to the gentleman who'd also joined them. 'You'll bear witness to this, if necessary, Atfield old chap?'

'Certainly.'

Barrenby smiled at his wife. 'Would you mind leaving us now, dear, and please don't mention this to anyone. I'll explain what's going on later.'

Once she'd left, he sat on the top of his desk and indicated that Mr Atfield should take his chair. 'I presume you've no objection to my colleague joining us? Atfield is my junior partner in the practice and is bound to be involved in sorting it all out. What a good thing he's here having lunch with us today!'

Roy looked at the others, who nodded. 'We've no objection to his presence at all.'

'Let's see if we can contact this sergeant of police next. Will someone be working at the police station on a Sunday?'

'Rivenshaw is a small town. There is one telephone shared between the police station and Sergeant Deemer's home next door, so someone nearly always answers it promptly, whatever the day or time. I dare say it'll be the sergeant himself, given that it's a Sunday and the police station will be closed. I know the number by heart but you can check it with the operator, if you like.' He recited it.

Barrenby nodded. 'I will check it, if you don't mind.'

He did this. 'I'll call them now. Atfield, will you listen to my conversation?'

His partner moved to stand beside him, looking eager and alert.

When the call was connected Barrenby said, 'Is it possible to speak to Sergeant Deemer?'

A deep voice said, 'Speaking.'

'Ah, good.' He introduced himself. 'Look, sergeant, I have some people with me who said you might be able to identify them by their voices. Would you mind doing that for me? I need to be sure they're who they say they are before I take further action.'

When he handed the phone to each of his male visitors in turn, his partner leaned closer to listen to each of the conversations. These were very brief because Deemer identified each man almost as soon as they spoke to him.

'Thank you so much. That's very helpful.'

'They're both honest and respected citizens, I can assure you,' Deemer volunteered.

'Do you also know a Mrs Morton, sergeant?'

'From Birch End? Yes, I do.'

'Would you recognise her voice if I put her on the phone as well? She's not sure whether you would or not.'

'Probably. We've only met a couple of times but I've a good memory for voices and names. Comes in very useful in my line of work, that does.'

'Perhaps you could describe her appearance as well?' He listened, nodding and holding out the phone to Beryl.

She spoke to the sergeant, answered a couple of questions, then laughed as he asked her if she remembered an incident with her cat. 'Oh, dear me, yes. And your nice constable rescued her from up in the tree. His hair colour? Red.'

She held the hand piece out to Barrenby, who took over again, thanked the sergeant for his help and put the phone down. He looked at his partner first. 'Well, the sergeant vouched for them without hesitation.'

'Which makes this quite an interesting situation,' Atfield said.

'I've certainly never had a case like it.'

Barrenby stood thinking for a moment or two. 'Could you all attend the meeting tomorrow afternoon at my office, do you think? I'd like to confront these people and I'll ask the local police to send an officer to be present, just in case there's any trouble. I don't think I've met this Gorton chappie. He and I obviously don't move in the same legal circles.'

'Dour sort of fellow. You always feel he's working out how much your clothes cost.' Roy's grimace showed what he thought of Higgerson's lawyer.

'Well, they're coming here at two, so perhaps you could arrive at about half past one and park round the back of the building in case they recognise your car. We have a meeting room on the ground floor, with a partitioned extension area from which you can listen to what they say.'

Beryl looked at Wilf, who nodded encouragingly to her, so she said in a voice which trembled, 'I'll do that, I can see it's necessary, but I have to admit I'm a little afraid of confronting Higgerson, Mr Barrenby. The way he looks at you when you don't do what he wants is so . . . threatening.'

'This Higgerson knows you by sight?'

'Yes, of course. He's visited my house a few times to try to get me to sell that piece of land to him. Only I refused. I didn't want him cramming his horrible little houses right across the road from me. The area would quickly go downhill.'

'That makes it even more interesting. So he won't be able to claim mistaken identity if he brings someone impersonating you along. But you'll be quite safe, my dear lady. You'll be in the next room for most of the time, listening to what they say. And when we unmask this imposter, there will be enough of us there to protect you. Believe me, he won't dare do anything violent with a pair of lawyers and probably a police constable as well watching him.'

'No, but I have to go home afterwards and I shan't feel safe there. He might set one of his men on me.'

Wilf interrupted. 'I'll be there, Beryl.'

'You can't be there all the time, Wilf, dear. You have to go to work.'

'Hmm. How quickly can you push the genuine sale of that land through, Mr Barrenby? It'll take one reason for him troubling her away, at least.'

The two lawyers exchanged surprised looks and Atfield shrugged. 'I usually handle that sort of thing, Mr Pollard. A week maybe, if we push hard and the people at the council cooperate. We can draw up an interim contract to sell that you can sign on Monday before he comes to our office, then we can say with truth that contracts to sell have already been exchanged.'

Wilf asked whether the cottage was on a separate land title, disappointed when Atfield shook his head. 'No. It isn't. But I can look into changing that when I deal with the council.'

'I doubt the land department at the town hall will allow it to be changed.'

The young lawyer looked at him in surprise. 'Why would council officials object? It's a simple enough transaction if there are no objections likely, happens all the time. And you said the cottage had been there for years. It's not a new building.'

'Higgerson has people at the council in his pay. I'd guess he'll tell them to find a reason to refuse.'

'Are you sure? This all sounds, well, rather incredible.'

'Unfortunately, I am sure that's likely to happen.'

Roy joined in. 'So am I. You should take a witness with you when you go to see whoever's dealing with this sort of thing at the council offices now, Mr Atfield. There have been some changes recently and one or two dishonest clerks have been thrown out of their jobs. But there are still some others around who would claim black was white if they thought they could get away with it and be paid extra on the side.'

'It'll be a nuisance getting the title changed if we have to take it to appeal. There really sounds to be no reason to refuse.'

Roy shrugged. 'It takes time to reorganise a whole local council and clear out the pockets of corruption. The new councillors were only voted in recently. As a builder, I've had to deal with some difficult situations there, I can tell you. Maybe the new mayor can help, though. I'll speak to him.'

He pushed himself to his feet. 'Anyway, if that's all for today, we'll leave you in peace. Thank you for seeing us.'

17

Everyone was silent as Wilf drove them home. Then suddenly Roy wondered aloud, 'How did things get into such a mess in our town?'

'Who knows?'

'Well, I know one thing: since our Trevor died I've not been paying attention to what's going on at the council as I should have done,' Roy said. 'I used to know exactly who was doing what, even if I couldn't always stop them. And I'd been here for longer than Higgerson. People knew and trusted my work so that mostly kept him away from me and my jobs.'

A short time later, he asked, 'How did he think he could get away with it, though? Mrs Morton had only to complain afterwards.'

Wilf didn't like the thought of how Higgerson would do that, but he put it into words, because Mrs Morton needed to be on her guard.

'If Mrs Morton died, and no one had known she owned the land, there would be no objections.'

Apart from a gasp, Mrs Morton didn't say anything.

It was left to Roy to put another thought into words. 'He's getting worse, getting over-confident and greedy. I hope Deemer catches him out before he does anything worse.'

As they were driving through Rivenshaw, he slapped one hand down on his knee. 'I'll make up for my inattention from now on. Maybe I should stand for council myself next time. I'm not having my town ruined by that grasping sod and his minions. The more he gets away with, the more he wants. He'll be stealing the moon out of the sky next.'

When Wilf stopped the car at the Tylers' house, he and Beryl said goodbye and walked slowly along to Croft Street. As they drew near her house, he stopped and said abruptly, 'I'll check that everything is all right and say hello to the kids, after which I have to go out for a while. We won't tell them there might be trouble brewing, but you'd better let Mona know on the quiet.'

'Will you be out for long?'

She was worrying about their safety already, he could tell.

'Not long. I'm going to hire some men I know and trust to keep watch on this house day and night until this mess is sorted out.'

'But that'll cost a fortune.'

'I have some money. What better way to spend it than on protecting you and my children? It'll only be for a short time, I'm sure. I presume you won't mind the men staying at your house overnight?'

She relaxed visibly. 'I'll be glad to have them around and so will Mona, I'm sure.'

After playing with his children and having a belated luncheon, as he was now learning to call the midday meal instead of 'dinner', Wilf left the ladies to look after Peggy and Ronnie. He drove up to Ellindale, where he knew several decent men who were either out of work or only working intermittently.

He called in at the job club first and was lucky enough to catch his first choice, Silas Johnson, working in the kitchen area. 'How do, lad. Got a minute?'

'I've got too many minutes.'

'Carry on with what you're doing while we talk.' Wilf watched Silas continue cutting slices of bread, taking great care to make them all the same size because this would probably be the only meal some of the men at the job club got today. He guessed Finn Carlisle would have paid for the food. Finn did a lot of good work in the district without broadcasting the fact.

'Want a few days' work, Silas?'

The bread knife quivered in mid-air and his companion looked at him eagerly. 'Of course I do.'

'You didn't ask what sort of work.'

'I'll do anything honest to earn money, as you well know, Wilf Pollard. One day, when times get better, I'll get work driving or even teaching driving. As for this job you're talking about, I didn't ask because I'm sure *you* wouldn't offer me anything dishonest.'

'I need two men to guard Mrs Morton's house in Birch End day and night. They'd have to sleep there as well. I'm going to be out and about so I need to be sure the ladies and my children are safe at all times.'

Silas was frowning now. 'Guard them against what? She doesn't live in the Backshaw Moss end of the village.'

'Higgerson.'

'Ah. Then I'm definitely your man. One day that sod will get what he deserves and I'll be the first one to cheer as they lock him away. Who else will be keeping watch?'

'You can choose someone you get on well with. You'll know better than I do who's most in need of money at the moment.'

'All right.'

'You know where Mrs Morton lives?'

'Croft Street?'

'Yes. And I'd be grateful if you'd keep an eye on the cottage across the street as much as you can, the unoccupied one that's nearly hidden from view, though the people you're guarding at number six are more important than it is, of course. You should be able to see the cottage from one of the bedrooms or you could even take the odd walk round its garden when no one's nearby to see you coming and going.'

'What in particular do I need to keep watch for at the cottage?'

'Mostly whether anyone's been prowling around it. Look for footprints or broken windows. Someone got in through the back recently and took away the front-door key, so we've changed the locks. And I must measure up for a new pane of glass. I'll give you a spare key when I've had some more made.'

'Higgerson's work again?'

'Must be. He's been trying to buy that cottage and land from Mrs Morton at a knock-down price, you see.'

Wilf hesitated but he'd trust Silas with his life, so he added, 'Roy Tyler is in the middle of buying it from her instead and we're hoping she'll be safer once that goes through.'

'I didn't know she owned it. Higgerson will be furious, of course. You're right to get someone to keep an eye on her. I'll be very careful, believe me. She's a nice lady.'

'Deemer's determined to catch that sod out and long term, my money's on him succeeding.'

'He's a good bloke. Best policeman we've ever had in the valley, I reckon. Higgerson's been getting away with things for years, even so. He's a cunning devil and he'll be hard to pin down.'

'That's why Deemer is treading softly. Oh, and they're going to install a telephone at Mrs Morton's some time tomorrow. I need one for my new job.'

'I heard Tyler had made you a partner. Well deserved, that. Gives a chap hope when he sees someone else get on.'

'Thanks. Now, back to this job. Keep an eye on the workmen who put the phone in tomorrow. She's had things stolen from inside her house recently. Not valuable things, paperwork.'

Silas let out a low whistle of surprise. 'Higgerson's getting worse, isn't he? Thinks he can get away with anything. But his greed will be his undoing, I bet you anything.'

'I hope you're right. Times are hard enough without villains like him adding to people's troubles.'

They both sighed and shook their heads sadly.

'Can you start work early tomorrow, Silas lad? Mrs Morton and I will be going out in the late morning, leaving Mona and the children on their own. Maybe if you and the other man could get there early, about seven say, and slip around the back quietly, there wouldn't be anyone around to see you arrive. What do you think?'

'We'll be there.'

'Good. Breakfast will be waiting for you. Any idea who you might bring?'

'I thought of Jericho Harte, if that's all right with you. He's a good fellow to have beside you in a fight and he lives in Backshaw Moss so he knows Birch End well. And he's got two brothers, both only working intermittently, if we need anyone else. Good set of lads, they are, look after their widowed mother. None of them are married. Like a lot of chaps, they say they won't get wed until there's more chance of getting a permanent job and putting bread on the table. So – is Jericho all right?'

'Yes, he's fine by me. See you both tomorrow early.'

On the Monday morning, Wilf introduced Silas and Jericho to Mrs Morton and Mona, and showed them round the house, pointing out the bedroom with the best view of the cottage opposite.

When Wilf and Beryl left for the Tylers' house later in the morning, Jericho moved towards the kitchen door. 'I'll go out the back way and make sure no one else is following them and spying on where they go.'

'Good thinking, lad.'

Jericho came back ten minutes later with a bruise on his cheekbone, grazed knuckles and a broad grin on his face.

Mona let out a shriek at the sight of him, which brought Silas running to ask, 'What the hell happened to you? You've only been gone a couple of minutes.'

'There was a chap following them, sneaking in and out of gateways. But he'll not come near this house again, at least not in daylight.'

'Hell, who was it? Someone from Backshaw Moss?'

'Aye. Jack Livings.'

'I might have known. He's done a few nasty little jobs for Higgerson, that one has. Enjoys hurting people. Did he give you the black eye?'

'Yes. He's quick, I'll grant him that. But I'm quicker. I knocked him out cold and he didn't come to until after the Tylers' car had driven away, so I don't think he'll even know which way Wilf and Mrs Morton went after they left Croft Street.'

He looked across at Mona, who was still looking anxious. 'It's all right, love. We'll keep you safe. This is only a love tap.'

'You'd better let me bathe it and that graze on your hand. Best to keep cuts clean.'

'I'd rather have a nice cup of tea.'

'You can have them both.' She lit the gas under the kettle and added, 'I know Jack's wife. She'd be horrified to know he was spying on Mrs Morton, who's given her a helping hand a few times.'

'Hunger can drive anyone to desperation,' Silas said.

Jericho shook his head. 'There are some things I'd not do, however hungry I got or whatever anyone paid me. And putting my neighbours in danger with Higgerson is one of them.'

'You're right there, lad.'

Mona sat Jericho down with a strong cup of tea and made sure there was no dirt in the scrapes on his knuckles. 'How are your brothers?'

'In and out of work. Lucas copes well with it, but Gabriel gets angry and goes off on his own every now and then.

'And your sister?'

He shrugged. 'She's just joined her husband in Coventry. He wrote to her saying he's found them a place to live. He said to tell me I could get a job there as well, making cars. Only I don't want to go. I'm a Lancashire lad, born and bred. Lucas feels the same and Gabriel doesn't know what he wants, except not to be stuck indoors in a factory. As for Mam, she'll never leave here. She'll not go away from my aunt Mariah. They're twins, you see, closer than most sisters.'

'Families are important,' Mona agreed.

After the two men had accepted a hearty snack, the sight of which made their eyes light up, they settled down to keep watch. The house was mostly quiet because even the children seemed to have picked up on the worries of the adults and were speaking in hushed voices – well, most of the time anyway.

All three adults were wondering how things were going at the lawyer's, because they knew how ruthless Higgerson could be.

Wilf stopped Roy's car at the rear of the lawyers' rooms, leaving it next to two other large vehicles. He opened the rear door for Mrs Morton. 'Cheer up, Beryl, love. You look as if you're going to your own funeral. There are three of us here with you as well as the lawyers, so you're not facing him alone.'

She tried to smile but when he offered her his arm and they followed the others towards the building, he could feel her trembling and she was very pale. Higgerson did this to people, picking on those weaker than himself and making them afraid to fight back.

Beryl had done well to hold out this long against Higgerson, but now she had friends who were going to help her end his demands once and for all.

Mr Atfield opened the back door before they reached it. 'I hope you don't mind coming in this way.'

'We'll do whatever you think best,' Roy said.

They passed through a kitchen, which was clean but had an unused air except for the utensils needed to make cups of tea sitting neatly on one half of the table, together with a biscuit tin. From there they followed Mr Atfield into a narrow corridor and through a door to their immediate left. There were a few hard chairs in the room and one wall consisted of a hinged wooden partition.

Atfield gestured towards it. 'On the other side of this is our main meeting room. We can make that room bigger by folding back the partition but we don't often need to do that and it saves on heating to keep it closed. At a suitable moment I'll pull the partition back and invite you to join us. You'll need to keep absolutely silent until then. Now, why don't you sit down and make yourselves comfortable till they arrive? We'll sign your bill of sale agreement afterwards because we don't want to be caught out if they arrive early.'

They did as he'd suggested, but Wilf could see that Beryl's knuckles formed a white line across her tightly clasped hands.

Mr Atfield continued to talk. 'I've got the office boy keeping an eye out for Gorton and his client arriving, and he'll call out when he sees them. Oh, and Mr Barrenby has asked for a policeman to be sent here, just in case there's any trouble. The constable is waiting in my office at the other side of the building.'

'Good idea,' Roy said.

'He's not much more than a lad, unfortunately. I wish they'd sent one of the more experienced, older policemen, but the sight of the uniform usually helps calm people down, even topped by a young face.'

Mr Atfield looked at Beryl, clearly the weak link in the group, and his voice softened, 'We'll look after you, Mrs Morton. It'll be worth it. You don't want strangers going about impersonating you, do you? Let alone selling your property out from under you.'

'No. Of course not. I'm sorry to be a coward. It's just that I do so hate violence.'

Wilf put his arm round her shoulders for a moment. 'A lot of people are afraid of Higgerson, but you're not facing him alone and we're going to keep watch over you at home as well until he's been stopped once and for all, however long that takes.'

She relaxed only a little. 'You're always so kind, Wilf. I feel lucky to have you to help me.'

'And I feel lucky to have your friendship and a home for my children.'

As they settled down in the small room, Wilf said, 'I wonder what the false Mrs Morton will look like. How can Higgerson think he's going to get away with bringing in an imposter?' He hoped he was wrong about the drastic crime that might be part of the plot.

Atfield shook his head, looking grim. 'Well, we'll soon find out.'

Ten minutes ticked away slowly by the plain, old-fashioned clock on the wall. Suddenly a young man's voice called from the hall, 'A big car has just stopped outside at the front, Mr Atfield. I think it's them.'

Beryl jerked in shock. 'Oh, dear!'

The lawyer glanced at her anxiously. 'I'll leave you now. Remember, no noise, whatever they say or do.'

18

L ewis Barrenby had arranged for Atfield to greet the second group of visitors. He intended to keep them waiting for him, hoping that a delay would make them a little more anxious about what they were doing.

He heard his partner greet them and say that Mr Barrenby would be with them shortly, then winced as Higgerson's loud voice boomed out. Was the man going deaf or did he speak this way in order to dominate any situation?

'I'm not used to being kept waiting,' Higgerson declared.

Lewis smiled, delighted to have irritated the fellow so soon.

Atfield spoke even more softly. 'Please come this way and take a seat, everyone. You must be Mrs Morton, madam. Perhaps you'd like to sit by the window?'

Lewis had to strain to hear the woman's response.

'Thank you. I'd prefer this other chair, if you don't mind. I'm very sensitive to light.'

She spoke slowly, almost as if she was speaking a foreign language. And was that a hint of a Welsh lilt in her voice or some other accent? Lewis wondered. She certainly sounded nothing like the real Mrs Morton. He was hoping she would be the key to stopping this trick.

He delayed for several more minutes before joining the newcomers. As he left his office and began to walk towards the meeting room, he heard Higgerson say, 'Our appointment was for two o'clock, Atfield. It's nearly quarter past now. What the hell is your partner playing at? This is no way to treat clients.'

Lewis opened the door, taking a few seconds to study the group as they gradually became aware of his presence. 'Good afternoon, everyone. I'm sorry to have kept you waiting. I had an unexpected phone call that was rather important.'

It was obvious which man was the lawyer, because he was dressed in a dark suit, though rather a cheap one from its bad fit. His shirt collar was an old-fashioned rounded type. 'Mr Gorton? I don't think we've met before.'

'No, we haven't. And this is—'

The client took over without waiting for Gorton to introduce his female companion, as would have been polite. 'I'm Higgerson and I'm a busy man, so can we please get on with this? It ought to be a simple enough transaction.'

'Certainly, but I'd prefer to be introduced to the lady first.'

Gorton said hastily, 'This is Mrs Morton, who wishes to sell Mr Higgerson some land she owns.'

'It's a long time since we met, Mrs Morton,' Lewis said. 'I was just starting out as a lawyer and I remember my earliest cases particularly clearly.'

She shot a quick, anxious glance at Gorton.

'That's . . . um, nice. I didn't think you'd have met before,' he said. 'Wasn't it your father who dealt with Mrs Morton when she inherited?'

'Oh, I sat in on a meeting or two. I'm surprised you didn't come straight to me about this sale, Mrs Morton.'

To Lewis's surprise, she did look a little like the real owner of the land and was even wearing similar clothes. But there was something in the way she held herself that suggested she was younger, though it was hard to tell that from her face because she was deliberately keeping it turned away from the light and kept dabbing at her nose with a handkerchief, as if she had a cold.

He sat down behind the table and stared at her with deliberate rudeness, waiting a further moment or two before continuing. 'Shall we get down to business? Mr Gorton, will you please explain the details of this proposed transaction?'

'It's very straightforward. As I said to Mr Atfield when I telephoned, your client, Mrs Morton, has agreed to sell her land and cottage to Mr Higgerson for one hundred pounds. We're here to sign the sale documents and take back the deeds from you, then hand over the payment to the lady. I took the liberty of drawing up a simple bill of sale to save the need for another meeting. I can submit the necessary paperwork to the Rivenshaw Council myself to complete the transfer.'

'May I see the bill of sale?'

There was silence, broken only by the rustling of paper as Lewis turned the pages, passing them to Mr Atfield. It amused him to see Higgerson tapping his fingers on the arm of his chair with increasing impatience.

When they'd both finished reading them, he turned back to his alleged client. 'I shall need proof of your identity, Mrs Morton, given how many years it is since we met.'

It was Gorton who answered. 'I have a selection of letters and bills, all addressed to Mrs Morton at her home in Birch End. I think those should do the trick.'

'May I see them? Yes. These are the papers I was told about.'

Gorton looked surprised. 'Told about? I don't understand what you mean.'

'I was told that some papers had been stolen from the real Mrs Morton.' He raised his voice, 'Would you like to join us now, everyone?'

The group behind the partition all stood up. But as Wilf began to fold the wooden panels back, he heard a shrill exclamation of 'What's going on here?' from the other room and the sound of a chair falling over.

Barrenby said firmly, 'Please sit down again, madam, and—'

As the partition folded back Wilf saw a woman who did indeed bear a faint resemblance to Beryl take everyone by surprise by running to the outer door of the meeting room. She yanked it open and vanished through it.

And, was it his imagination, or had Gorton deliberately got in Atfield's way as the young lawyer moved to stop her?

'Halt!' a man's voice ordered from the hall. There was a cry of pain and a clattering sound as if something had been knocked over.

From where he stood, Wilf could see out of the window and watched in amazement as the woman ran outside into the street, moving like a much younger woman than the real Mrs Morton. The office boy was chasing her, but there was no sign of the policeman.

Barrenby joined him at the window and they saw the lad lunge and grab the woman by her hair.

As the hair came off in his hands, showing a head of auburn hair, he slowed down in shock, still clutching the grey wig and staring at it in utter horror. She sped up and vanished down a side alley.

It was a few seconds before the office lad pulled himself together and ran after her, but he was markedly slower than she was and stumbled as he turned into it.

Barrenby said in a mild voice, 'It's a long time since I've seen someone run that fast. She's definitely not an older woman. I doubt he'll catch her.'

Wilf turned and nearly bumped into Higgerson, who had joined them at the window.

Barrenby ignored him and looked across the room. 'You'd better have a good explanation for this, Gorton.'

'I want an explanation too,' Higgerson said. 'You told me you'd met Mrs Morton and she'd agreed to sell to me.'

'That wasn't Mrs Morton,' Barrenby said, 'and you've seen the real owner enough times over the past year to have realised that when you first met her surely, Mr Higgerson.'

He laughed and flapped one hand as if brushing away an annoying insect. 'One grey-haired old woman looks much the same as another to me, I'm afraid.' He scowled at Beryl and took a couple of steps towards her, jabbing his finger into the air in front of her and only just missing poking her with it. 'Look at her. Very similar to the one who just ran out, don't you think?'

She gasped and stepped hastily back.

The young policeman who'd been meant to keep order came in to join them, walking slowly and awkwardly as if it hurt him to move.

Wilf was suddenly hard put not to smile as he realised the imposter must have kicked the constable in a rather delicate place. What with the grey wig coming off in the office boy's hand, this was turning into a comedy of errors.

'Well, that was a waste of time.' Higgerson turned as if to leave. 'You'd better not try to charge me for your time, Gorton. You've made an appalling mess of things.'

Barrenby moved quickly to bar the doorway. 'Stay where you are, Higgerson! The police will need to take a statement from everyone. Atfield, can you phone them and explain that we need a more senior officer here?'

The constable started to move, winced and abandoned the attempt, hunching over and leaning against the wall with a low groan.

Higgerson shrugged and sat down. 'Tell the police to hurry. I've got better things to do than waste my time on this farce. However, I must admit that I too would like an explanation.'

He glared at Beryl again. 'You look upset, Mrs Morton, but it's your own fault. You might find life easier if you did

sell me that land. Who knows what other criminals will try
to cheat you out of it? Or how you might get hurt trying to
stop them?'

'That sounds suspiciously like a threat to me,' Barrenby
said sharply.

'No such thing. I'm merely talking common sense. Apart
from anything else, that land can be put to much better use.
There's a desperate shortage of housing for the lower classes
in the valley. *She* just leaves that field doing nothing. I could
fit a hundred new homes on that piece of land.'

He turned to address his lawyer again. 'That woman you
brought along clearly wasn't Mrs Morton, Gorton. How did
an imposter get involved?'

Gorton ran one finger around his collar as if it had suddenly
grown too tight. 'How could I have known, Mr Higgerson?
I sent my clerk to call on her and he said she'd agreed to
sell. When this woman turned up at my office today she had
all the correct paperwork and she matched the description
you'd given me, so naturally it never occurred to me that she
wasn't the real owner.'

Wilf lost all desire to smile and exchanged disgusted glances
with Barrenby. They all knew Higgerson was lying but there
was no proof that he'd been involved in a deception – not
proof that would stand up in a court of law anyway. It made
him feel furious that the fellow was going to get away with
this and probably his lawyer would too.

The only casualty would be the lawyer's clerk, who would
presumably have vanished into thin air by the time the police
went to find him at Gorton's office.

If he had ever existed at all.

It was a few minutes before a more senior policeman arrived
and the details of the situation had to be explained to him.
The look the sergeant gave the young constable said the latter

would be in trouble later for letting himself be caught out like that.

'I shall require statements from everyone. Is there a room where I can conduct the interviews privately, Mr Barrenby?'

'Yes, of course. And I have a clerk who can assist you.'

'No, thank you. The constable can do that. I prefer to use our own people when it comes to gathering evidence. *If* you can hold a pen without dropping it, that is,' he added sarcastically to the young fellow.

'It seems we've all been taken in by an imposter,' Higgerson said. 'Anything we can do to help you catch her, sergeant, you have only to ask.'

But there was a near smirk on his face as he looked across the room at Barrenby.

And that changed to a chill, subtly threatening stare as he turned towards Beryl, who shrank away visibly, even though he was nowhere near her.

As soon as the interviews were over, Higgerson and Gorton left, escorted to the door by the sergeant. He watched them get into a big car then turned to Barrenby, who had followed him out into the hall. 'Do you believe them?'

'No.'

'Neither do I, Mr Barrenby. But unless we can find better proof that they arranged to use an imposter, they'll get away with it. And how were they expecting to keep the land afterwards?'

'By threatening her, I suppose. Or worse. A dead woman couldn't have challenged the sale.'

The sergeant looked startled. 'You think him that bad?'

'Those who know him better than I do feel he's ruthless.'

'Well, he won't get what he wanted from her, at least.'

'He might try again but he still won't get it. Just between you and me, sergeant, Mrs Morton will be signing a bill of sale for the piece of land in question before she leaves this office today. She really does wish to sell it but to Mr Tyler, whom you've just met, not Higgerson. And for a fair payment, not the risible sum he offered.'

'Good to hear. If you find out anything else, Mr Barrenby, could you please let me know, whether formally or informally? I shall keep my eyes open for that fellow and he'd better not try anything on my patch again.'

'Happy to do that and I'd be grateful if you'd do the same for me. You may like to contact Sergeant Deemer in Rivenshaw, as well. He's got Higgerson in his sights. Who knows? The pair of you may be able to help one another.'

'I'll do that. I've met Deemer a few times. Good chap.'

As the two men shook hands, Barrenby sighed. 'I'd better go and get the bill of sale signed, sealed and delivered. That poor woman is in a terrible state of anxiety. Luckily, Mr Pollard lives with her and he's arranged for two men to keep an eye on her.'

'I'll bear all that in mind and I will get in touch with Deemer.'

The police sergeant walked off down the street and Barrenby went back to finalise a very simple agreement for selling Mrs Morton's land.

19

Stella passed a quiet Sunday, the morning broken only by going out to purchase a *Manchester Guardian* and bring the newspaper back to read at her leisure.

By the time she'd eaten a couple of the sandwiches provided for the simple luncheon of full-board lodgers, she was feeling twitchy so ignored the grey skies and went out for a brisk walk in the park.

When she bumped into one of her fellow lodgers on her way back, she couldn't get out of returning to Mrs T's with her. However, she refused an invitation to join the others in the living room for a 'pleasant chatty afternoon' on the mendacious excuse of having some letters to write.

She didn't feel like chatting to a group of strangers, and anyway, she was half-expecting Wilf to turn up with news of the cottage, maybe bringing the children with him.

As for writing a letter, she didn't have anyone except Lena to write to and intended to wait to do that until she had something to report, even if it was only starting her new job officially and taking more driving lessons. If she waited another couple of weeks she could send a Christmas card at the same time.

After catching up with her diary and wondering why she bothered with it, she took out one of her favourite novels, which she'd planned to read again till she could join the local library. Only, she couldn't settle into it. She knew the tale well and usually enjoyed the author's witty comments on life but today her mind was too full of her own problems.

She'd have to join the library as soon as she was allowed and borrow some new books to occupy her time. Would they let her join before she had a permanent home in the town, though? If not, she'd buy a second-hand book or two. There was usually some shop or market stall selling the more tattered ones cheaply.

That thought made her smile. She kept forgetting that she didn't have to watch every halfpenny now, but she didn't think she could ever be extravagant, however much money she had.

She stared out of her window at the street, which was very quiet at this time on Sundays. Nothing to watch from this dreary little room. No sign even of bird life because there were no trees near her window.

'Oh, come on, Stella Newby,' she said aloud. 'Stop wallowing in self pity.'

Should she look for somewhere else to rent or continue to lodge here at Mrs T's till she could move into the cottage? Although the food provided here was more than adequate and the bed linen was apparently changed regularly, there was little privacy. It might be a long time until she could buy the cottage and it would need modernising, so perhaps she should find out what was available to rent.

She spent a lot of the afternoon gazing into space, and for at least part of it she was trying *not* to think about Wilf. He was recently widowed, so she shouldn't have been thinking about him at all in that way. But there you were. You couldn't choose who you'd be attracted to. It just happened.

This was the first time she'd been interested in a man since she'd lost Derrick, and it had taken her by surprise. She not only liked Wilf, she even liked his children.

If the weather hadn't been so chancy this afternoon, she might have gone out for another walk up the hill. She wanted to explore the centre of Birch End. She'd asked one of the other women whose brother lived there about the village.

Apparently, there were a couple of shops, an infant school and a small church.

When the gong rang to signal that the evening meal was about to be served, she was relieved to go down and join the others.

As she walked back into her room after the meal, she looked at the darkness outside and sighed. What a pity the days were so short at this time of year. There would be no chance of going for a walk after work during the week, even if the weather was fine.

She might go to the cinema, though. She could afford to go every week now, if she wanted. Perhaps they'd show her favourite film again at some point, *Flying Down to Rio*. She'd enjoyed it as a birthday treat she'd given herself earlier in the year and it had left her feeling happy. The people starring in it were new to her. The man wasn't all that good looking – Astaire, his name was – but he was a brilliant dancer, as was his pretty companion.

Before she went to bed, Stella made sure she had everything ready for going to the office the next morning. She hoped Nick had meant it when he said he'd give her another driving lesson if he had free time. He'd offered her an employee discount, too.

She'd have to plan her Sundays better than this in future. Today had seemed to pass so slowly, and pleasant as most of her fellow lodgers were, they seemed to have settled down into dull, repetitive lives.

As she had done after becoming a widow.

Well, she wasn't going back to that. Having even a modest amount of money had shaken her right out of her rut, given her the courage to do something different.

On the Monday morning Stella decided to walk to work and managed to get out of the house without someone else joining her, thank goodness. It wasn't worth waiting for the bus with only a few streets to go, but as it was cloudy and looked as if it might rain again, she took her umbrella.

Most people smiled or said 'Good morning' as she passed them in the street, but there were a few loitering on corners who didn't. They looked hungry and were poorly clad. Out of work, probably, poor things. There had been similar folk standing around in Rochdale, mostly men. Some of them preferred to stay out on the streets all day, out of their wives' way. She supposed it gave them the chance to chat to others like themselves, something to watch and the occasional opportunity to earn a copper or two for helping someone with a small job.

Before she went into the building, she stopped at the line of cars to smile again at the one she was going to buy. Oh, she did hope she'd prove to be a good driver. The cost of lessons was well worth it because it would make such a difference to her life to be free to go wherever she wanted.

A few spots of rain fell and she hurried into the building, finding the front door slightly open. She called out as she entered to let them know she'd arrived.

Jo came out of the kitchen to greet her as she was hanging up her hat and coat. 'Hello. Hope your lodgings are all right.'

Stella couldn't help grimacing. 'They're clean and the food is good, but there are a lot of women crammed into a warren of small bedrooms.'

'Not fond of living in herds?'

'Not really. More importantly, how are you this morning?'

'I've finished being sick for the day, I think.' She pulled a face. 'It does take the edge off the joy of expecting a baby.'

'Worth it, though.'

Jo changed the subject. 'I can lend you a book or two, if that helps.'

'Yes, please. I like to keep busy and a lot of things like my embroidery are still packed in my trunk, which is now in a storeroom Mrs T keeps for her tenants' overflow of possessions. There's nowhere to put it in such a small bedroom, anyway.'

'I know what you mean. I sometimes miss the wide spaces of Australia.' She looked out as rain pattered against the window and added, 'I miss the sunshine, too.'

'Imagine living somewhere that's always sunny.'

Jo laughed. 'Not always. A lot of people think that but winter in Western Australia is intermittently rainy and quite cold, though we don't get snow in Perth. In summer it hardly ever rains.'

'That must be lovely.'

She shrugged. 'I miss some things about it, but people are more important and I have my Nick now. Shall we get started?'

Picking up her satchel from the hallstand, Stella followed her into the office at the front of the building. 'What do you want me to do today?'

'Mainly stay around here to answer the phone. Oh, and could you get those papers filed? Nick has a habit of just dumping letters and invoices on the nearest surface. I made a start on sorting out the files, but we've been so busy since we got married I've let things slip, too. You can reorganise the drawers and cupboards in both offices in any way you like. Neither of the men will care and I'm going to be busy setting up our new home, I hope.'

She hesitated, then added, 'Look, talking of homes, if you think you'll be all right on your own today, Nick and I would like to go out and take another look at the house we're buying.'

Did that mean they were leaving her to hold the fort on her first day? Stella tried not to show her surprise.

As if she'd read her thoughts, Jo said, 'It's always quiet on a Monday. There aren't even any lessons booked till this afternoon. Nick and I desperately want to move into that house as quickly as we can, you see, so we need to be sure of what to buy to start us off.'

'What's it like?'

'It's quite old, stone built and to the east of Rivenshaw, looking out over some fields.' She smiled and added quite unnecessarily, 'We're a bit excited about it, actually. Just think of us owning our own home, and one with an acre of land as well! We'll really be able to put down roots.'

Stella felt exactly the same. She was quite desperate to put down roots. But she didn't say anything to spoil the other woman's pleasure.

'I grew up on a farm in Australia, but I don't want us to be farmers. It'd be nice to have our own chickens and a big garden for the children to play in, though – once we have children, that is.' She smiled down at her body.

Nick came out of the kitchen to join them, looking as excited as his wife. 'If no one else books any driving lessons for this afternoon, Stella, I can fit another one in for you after Mr Spurling before it gets dark. Otherwise, we'll make a definite booking for you to have one first thing tomorrow morning. In fact, let's book one then as well as today. If you practise every day, you'll soon build up your driving skills.'

He'd brought his wife's coat from the hallstand and held it out for her with a loving smile. 'Here you are, madam.'

Stella was rather surprised that they would leave her on her own so early in her employment, not to mention trust her to run things. At her last two places of employment, the supervisors had hardly trusted the clerks to breathe in and out properly.

As they reached the door, Jo slowed down to call over her shoulder, 'I nearly forgot. Do help yourself to a cup of tea and a biscuit whenever you fancy one.'

'Come on, woman.' She let out a gurgle of laughter as Nick took her hand and tugged her across to his car.

Once they'd gone, Stella walked round the ground floor, savouring the silence after the noisy breakfast at Mrs T's. It was lovely to watch people walking past in the street outside, too.

She'd enjoy her day, she was sure.

A few minutes later Stella saw Todd arrive and was on her way out to talk to him about starting work on his office when a man turned up and started speaking to him, pointing to what she now thought of as *her* car.

Oh, no! Surely Todd wouldn't sell it! She'd better put a deposit on it to make sure of that.

To her relief he shook his head and took the customer to look at a couple of other smaller vehicles instead.

Only after the man had left did Todd come into the building. 'He'll be back. He's a fusser and such people rarely buy the first time, or even the second time of looking.' He studied her face. 'Don't look so worried. I won't sell your car.'

'Let me give you a deposit to show I'm serious.'

'No need. I know you're going to buy it as soon as you can drive properly. I'll get all the paperwork in order, and you'd better look into insurance. Is Nick out on a driving lesson already?'

'No. He and Jo have gone to have another look at their house.'

'Ah. That doesn't surprise me. They can't stop talking about it. It sounds a nice place but it's further out of town than I'd like to live. At least in Ellindale we're on a bus route into town. But I think Jo is a country lass at heart.'

'Will you be using your office today or can I make a start on catching up with the paperwork and filing?'

He grinned and flourished one hand towards its door. 'Be my guest. Jo had made a start on it but she got caught up in some trouble with a young relative of hers, then she fell in love with Nick and now they're setting up home together. All of which are much more important than doing the paperwork. I'm afraid I've let things slide again, for which I apologise in advance.'

She chuckled. 'Don't worry. That's what you're paying me for.'

'Yes. And you're going to well and truly earn it. Now, I have a car that needs repairing and I'll have my head under the bonnet, so if you see someone looking for help buying a car and I don't seem to have noticed, please come and get me.'

As the day turned into afternoon, she half-expected Wilf to pop in to see her to let her know how things were going about her buying the cottage, but he didn't. She admitted to herself that she was disappointed.

Jo and Nick didn't return until well past midday and by then Stella had caught up on the basic paperwork in Todd's office and booked in a couple of driving lessons for later in the week.

'Any new lessons booked for this afternoon?' Nick asked at once.

'Sorry, no. Just those two for Thursday and Friday.'

'Come on, then, Stella! I'll take you for another driving lesson. And this time we're going right up the valley to Ellindale.'

They did that and she found her nervousness fading as she started to change gear more smoothly. This time she was easily able to keep the car on the left side of the road. It had surprised her how hard that was the first time she took the wheel.

She was glad there weren't a lot of other cars on the road up at the top end of the valley, however, because she still felt a bit tense when she had to pass vehicles going the other way. Which was silly really, because it wasn't a busy road and they all kept to their side of the road.

She felt even more nervous when they encountered a horse and cart.

'You're more frightened of it than it is of you,' Nick teased.

And he was right, the horse just clopped on down the road, completely ignoring the car.

When Nick said, 'Pull over to the side and stop,' she did that, wondering if she'd done something wrong.

'I want you to try a hill start now. This isn't flat country-side so it's important to be able to do that well.' He explained exactly what to do, but it seemed rather daunting.

'I'm not sure I can do that yet. What if I let the car run backwards?'

He chuckled. 'You'll put your feet on the brake and clutch at the same time and it'll stop, then you'll put the handbrake on and try again. You'll be just fine, trust me. It's only taken a few goes for you to get the hang of how to do the other things, and this will be the same. After that, practice will make each action instinctive. Now, take a deep breath and try it. *Courage!*' He pronounced it the French way.

She repeated the word inside her head and after a few attempts was able to manage hill starts without any problem at all. He was right. You had to listen to the sound of the engine changing slightly, and get the feel of it. It was almost as if the car was a live thing sometimes, eager to move on.

'We'll have a go at driving your own car around next week if we can manage a lesson a day this week, and by the week after that, I'll probably be able to turn you loose to drive about on your own. That's when you'll really start to learn how to manage on the roads.'

Drive her own car! That thought both terrified and delighted her. She took a deep, shaky breath. She could do it. Couldn't she?

By the time the lesson was over, she was exhausted from the tension of remembering what to do when, and was glad to let Nick take over again for the last stretch into the town.

'I can teach you all the correct moves and rules,' he said as he pulled up outside the car sales area, 'but only practice will make it instinctive. Don't forget that by next year you and many other people will have to take a driving test, unless you do that voluntarily before the date the government has set for it becoming obligatory. I think there will be a lot of people who leave it to the last minute to book a test, so I'd advise you to do it earlier.'

'Yes. I see. I'm still a bit worried about driving in Rivenshaw, though. There's so much more traffic in a town. And I don't think I'll ever dare drive in a big city like Manchester.'

He chuckled aloud at that. 'Oh, I think you will. But not yet. You can have your first go at driving in Rivenshaw tomorrow, but we'll do it at a quiet time of day. Trust me, and remember my golden rule.'

They chanted it together with him waving his arm around like a man conducting an orchestra. 'If in doubt, hang about.'

That made her smile, but it was comforting to have such a rule nonetheless.

'Between eight and ten lessons is usually enough for our better pupils like you, you know,' he added.

She felt a glow of pride that he thought her a quick learner.

But as she walked back to her lodgings afterwards, she wondered once again what Wilf and Mrs Morton had been doing today and whether they'd managed to arrange the sale of the cottage and land to Mr Tyler.

Was she being unreasonable expecting to hear from them? She couldn't really do anything about where she lived, couldn't make any real plans until she knew about the cottage.

20

Wilf had intended to go and see Stella when he got home from the visit to the lawyer, but realised he'd forgotten about picking up Ricky and his helper from the farm.

Roy had arranged for one of the men who worked for him to do that while Wilf was sorting out a new life without Enid. But Roy's man had told him this would be the final day's work there, and Wilf wanted to check it for himself. He could bring back Ricky and Pete, as well as the tools and equipment he'd left there for them to use.

It was the first time he'd left Ricky in charge of another worker and that was another thing he wanted to check – that his protégé could handle other men. He was pretty sure the work would have been completed in a satisfactory manner because Ricky was good with his hands. If all had gone as he expected, he had his eye on that young chap for future steady work.

When he got to the farm, the two young men were clearing up and doing a thorough job of it. He was pleased to see Ricky giving the other youngster instructions or pointing out things he'd missed. That boded well for the future.

'Hello, lads. You carry on.'

He climbed the ladder to inspect the roof, checking everything he could think of, satisfied that all the details had been finished properly. He looked down from the roof and saw Ricky watching him a little anxiously, so nodded and saw him relax.

When he got down again, he left the two of them to fasten the ladder on to the van's roof because Farmer Tidsworth had come out to join him. 'Good pair of lads you've got there, Wilf.'

'I'm pleased with how Ricky's shaping up, but the other lad is new to working for me.'

'I kept an eye on them, like I do anyone working here. They both made a thorough job of it.' He paused and shot a quick glance at Wilf. 'What about you? I was sorry about your wife. How are things going in the new home? The kids coping all right? Hard for them to lose their mother at such a young age. And for you to lose a wife.'

Wilf nodded as his loss hit him again. It did that every now and then, striking suddenly for no reason he could see. It was more sadness for Enid and guilt about not longing desperately for her company, though.

'The kids have settled in well at their new home, Mr Tidsworth, and they're getting plenty of loving and attention from Mrs Morton and her maid. That's helping them a lot.'

'And you?'

'I keep busy.'

'Well, you'll have to be father and mother to them now. Remember, you need to give them a good dose of love, but fair and firm discipline as well. Spoiling a kid is nearly as bad as ill-treating one.'

'I agree.' Wilf accepted the final payment for the work, paid mostly in grubby one-pound notes, and said goodbye. Many people were offering him advice, and he'd found it best to listen, nod and go his own way.

The two young men were waiting for him near the van and he paid them before driving them back to Birch End. This time they unloaded his tools into Roy's building yard, not into the rough shed at the back of his former home, putting them where the older man employed by Roy indicated.

It was good to have somewhere more secure to leave his equipment, though he'd suggest making a few changes to the door locks tomorrow. And to the gates. They looked to be getting a bit old and loose. Things had changed in the valley as Higgerson became the biggest builder, and thefts of tools were more common these days. Was that a coincidence? He didn't know, but he wasn't risking his possessions.

It was fully dark now and he was late for tea. He ate his in the kitchen and afterwards helped put the kids to bed, telling them a silly story about a happy worm called Wiggly-Woo, one where they all had to make wiggling gestures with their hands.

When that was done, he intended to use the new phone to call Stella. She must be wondering what had happened today. He wondered if she still felt the same about the cottage or whether her enthusiasm had waned.

No – somehow, he doubted that would have happened.

Mrs T sent the young maid up to tell Stella she was wanted on the telephone and waited in the hall to pass it to her, hand across the receiver. 'It's Wilf Pollard. Early days for him to be looking around for another wife. You be careful how you go, my dear. There are some men who can't do without a bit of bed play and they don't always wait for marriage, especially when they know someone's a widow.'

'I know the whole family, Mrs Morton, and the children as well as Wilf. I'm *not* looking for another husband any more than Wilf is looking for a wife. I'm just trying to make a few friends.'

Mrs T's expression said she wasn't sure whether to believe that, which surprised Stella.

'Well, it never hurts to be careful, Mrs Newby.'

'I will.' It was none of her landlady's business, though. Mrs T was pleasant enough and set a good table, but was proving to be a bit of a gossip.

Stella picked up the phone and waited till the older woman had gone back into the kitchen before she spoke. 'Hello. Stella Newby here.'

'It's Wilf. I wanted to come and see you this afternoon to tell you what happened today, but I had something else I couldn't avoid doing. I won't go into details about our visit now but I'll maybe bring the children down to visit you at the car yard later tomorrow afternoon. As long as you don't think Jo and Nick will mind.'

'I'm sure they won't. I'm having another driving lesson first thing in the morning.'

'How's it going?'

'It's going well. At least Nick says so. But there's a lot to learn. What time shall I expect you?'

'About three o'clock. But don't worry if I'm a bit late. Sometimes jobs take longer than you think they're going to.'

'I'll look forward to seeing you all.'

She guessed he didn't want to risk the telephone operator listening in to whatever had happened today, but it was annoying to have to wait to find out more about the sale of the cottage.

She noticed that the door from the hall to the lodgers' sitting room was slightly open, and it moved a little. Had someone opened it to listen to her call?

There were too many nosy parkers here.

Wilf woke a couple of times during the night, wondering if everything was all right at the building yard. But Roy had high fences topped with barbed spikes, so he didn't think anyone would find it easy to break in.

Today he'd be settling in properly, meeting some of the men who worked for Roy and now worked for him as well. Mrs Tyler ran the office. He'd never worked closely with a woman before, but everyone said how efficient she was. She was very shrewd and would keep an eye on everything that he did, Wilf was sure.

As he got ready for work, he admitted to himself that he was a little nervous about today. This was a step up in the world for him, and his first time of going into work as the junior partner.

He wasn't sure what to wear, but in the end he settled for his usual working clothes, with his overcoat on top. If he remembered correctly, Roy didn't dress in fancy suits for work. Well, you couldn't, could you? Not if you were going to get your hands dirty, and Wilf wasn't the sort of person to sit in the office and simply give orders, any more than Roy was.

When he went downstairs, he found Silas watching the street in front of the house and went to stand beside him. Not that there was anything to see because not many people passed along it.

'Did you see anything?'

'Jericho kept watch during the night and he said everything was mostly quiet. Since I've been here this morning one or two people have walked along Croft Street on their way to work but no one looked twice at the house. Jericho says he saw something at the back just after midnight, though.'

'I'll go and check. You stay here.'

It was fully light now, a grey sort of day, and Wilf found Jericho outside the back gate crouching to study the ground.

'Something wrong?'

'I thought I heard someone prowling around during the night, so I switched the kitchen light on and pretended to be getting myself a drink of water. Best that prowlers know there's someone here who wakes easily. It's easier to avoid trouble when you can.'

'I agree. Who are they, do you think?'

'Whoever Higgerson has hired to keep an eye on us. You can be sure he'll have done that.'

'Which is why I hired you and Silas. What exactly happened?'

'I thought I saw someone moving along the back fence and I was right. Look!' He pointed to the ground, still soft after some rain early in the evening.

Wilf stared down at the footprints, which had been made by someone with very worn boots, particularly along one side, as if the person wearing them favoured one leg slightly. 'You're sure no damage has been done?'

'Not that I've found. And they didn't come into the yard. Maybe they're checking out the place for future reference.'

'Or for Higgerson. We should get an electric wall light fitted outside the back door, then you'll be able to switch it on from inside if you think you hear a prowler.'

Jericho nodded. 'Good idea.'

'Well done.'

'It'll be well done when we stop them sods, not until.'

'You've made a good start, though. Did you hear anything over at the cottage?'

'No. I went across to stand on the footpath outside it a couple of times but I didn't like to let this house out of my sight.'

'If you get a minute today, go over and have a poke about, see if there are any recent footprints there. I'll have a new door key cut for you and Silas by teatime.'

'All right.'

He clapped Jericho on the shoulder. 'Go and get your breakfast now. They've made a bed for you in that little room next to the kitchen.'

'Thanks.'

He watched Jericho smile at Mona and positively beam at the big plate of food she served him.

Full bellies won you specially good help when you hired a man these days, Wilf thought. He'd been in Jericho's position many a time: hungry, willing to work at anything. Some men grew sharp-tempered under the strain. Jericho seemed quiet and watchful, but there was a strength to him that Wilf liked.

Eh, there were some good men going to waste. If he could help Roy set up jobs for a few, as well as providing for his own children, he'd consider his time well spent.

When Wilf got to the builder's yard, which was on the outskirts of Rivenshaw, he stopped his van outside it and looked up at the sign. It hadn't been changed since Roy's son died and still said *Tyler & Son, Builders*. How sad for Roy to see that reminder every morning as he arrived at work.

It suddenly occurred to him that if things went well, that sign might one day say *Tyler & Pollard, Builders*. That made him feel strange as he went through the gate, as if he was stepping into another world.

He found Roy sitting in the office, looking thoughtful.

'Everything all right here overnight?'

'Yes. How were things at your place, Wilf?'

'Jericho heard someone prowling around at the back of the house. We had a look this morning when it got light and found fresh footprints.'

'Damn that man! Can he not leave that poor woman in peace? Did you phone Deemer and tell him you'd had a prowler?'

'No. What's the point? We've no idea who it was, there was no damage done and they didn't try to get into the yard, let alone the house.'

Roy waved towards a telephone. 'Do it now. There's no reason for anyone to be walking along the back lane behind those six houses in the middle of the night. The lane's only there for people to empty the dustbins and deliver coal. It doesn't lead anywhere and it's only a dirt track, not a made-up road. Deemer wants every scrap of evidence he can get.'

'What evidence can anyone get from footprints in the mud? They'll be gone in the next shower of rain.'

'Don't underestimate him. He's got all sorts of tricks up his sleeve. I've seen him use plaster of Paris to get a copy of a footprint: you pour it in, let it set and out comes a copy of the print. If he isn't busy, I bet he'll come and do that.'

'Well, it's a good, clear print, someone who walks with a limp maybe.'

Roy frowned and sat tapping his fingers on the desk for a few seconds. 'What about that cottage? Have you checked it today? I reckon Higgerson will go after that.'

'I reminded Jericho to have a walk around there, but we can't keep watch on everything.'

'We need to keep that cottage safe if I'm to sell it to Mrs Newby. People think I'm rich but I'm not, never have been, and I've eaten into my savings this past year. Her money will help pay for the houses I build. No, we must keep watch.'

Wilf sighed. 'We'll need a damned army to keep peace in the valley at this rate.'

'We've got a damned army.'

'What do you mean?'

Roy stopped tapping and pointed his finger in the air emphatically, a mannerism he had, as he thought out loud. 'We can't afford to pay every man and his dog wages to keep guard, but we can supply food to people who'll agree to come out once or twice in the middle of the night and have a walk around, or we could pay a nightwatchman in food. I'll have to think how best to do that.'

'Jericho's got two brothers.'

'Yes. Eh, I know a dozen men who'd snap up even a half-job like that.'

'If the brothers are like Jericho, they'd be good value.'

'All right. You obviously want them, so hire one of them for food.' He flapped one hand at Wilf. 'We need to look after that cottage. Eh, I used to have a dozen or more men working for me full-time – and I will again one day. Go on, phone Deemer.'

Wilf picked up the office phone and dialled the number for Rivenshaw police station, explaining to the sergeant why he was calling.

Deemer listened carefully, asking a couple of questions. 'Thanks. Let me know if anything else happens.'

'Even if we're not sure about it? I don't want to waste your time.'

'You don't always know what will help, Wilf. But part of my job is to put the pieces together. Sometimes information builds up gradually till you see a pattern and you find a way to get a bit ahead of the villains. I'll come and have a look at the footprints as soon as I can. Don't touch them.'

'Do you need me to meet you there?'

'No. Jericho will show them to me. Just phone Mrs Morton and tell her to expect me.'

After that, Wilf was taken by Roy on a tour of the building yard. He was introduced properly to the chap who ran the stores and whom he'd met briefly last night. 'Let Paddy know about anything you're getting short of or if you want to hire extra help. He's the one who really runs the yard.'

Paddy grinned. 'Don't you be listening to him. He has eyes in the back of his head, this one does. An' so does the missus.'

As they walked away, Roy sighed. 'Won't be much that needs stocking up on for a while. There are more supplies than work at the moment. I've let things slip, I know. But trade would have slowed down whatever I did. I've got one or two feelers out for smaller bread-and-butter jobs, and I've been tipped the wink that there's a big job coming up for the council if they get some of the government funding for clearing slums and building new houses. It's more than time they did something about Backshaw Moss, don't you think?'

'Oh, yes. It's a disgrace, that place is.'

'In the meantime, we can make a start today on planning some nice houses to put on that land of Mrs Morton's, places for working folk who do have jobs and can pay rent. We'll get Ethel in on designing the kitchens and bathrooms. She knows what women want. But I can't afford to provide housing for the poorer folk from places like Backshaw Moss, who're going to be moved sooner or later. The poor sods haven't worked for years and are scrabbling to feed themselves and their families. I'd never get my money back from re-housing them. It has to be government or council money that does it for them.'

'What about that cottage? What are we going to do about that? It'll need modernising if Stella is going to live in it.'

'It'll take a while to get it put on a separate title, but how about I sign a commitment to sell it to your young lady and let her move in and pay a ground rent till we can sort it all out? We'll put some men to work and she can move in within a few weeks, maybe even before Christmas.'

Wilf could feel his cheeks growing warm. 'She's not really my young lady, you know. I've only just lost my wife and Stella's a widow. And we're neither of us all that young, either. We're just letting people think that so that no one will come after her for wanting to buy the cottage.'

Roy laughed gently. 'You seem young to me. You're not even forty yet and she's a few years younger, I'd guess. Any road, that's beside the point. How about you have a chat to her and see what she thinks about the cottage? She might have changed her mind, given the trouble there's been.'

'I almost hope she has. I worry that living there on her own might put her in danger.' He didn't like the thought of her getting hurt, didn't like it at all. She was a nice person, lovely with his kids, with a really warm smile, and so easy to talk to.

'We'll have to think about that as well, see if we can work out a way of keeping her safe. And keeping you safe as well, my lad. Backshaw Moss is only just down the road from your new home, think on.'

'I'll be all right. I'm keeping Silas and Jericho on to guard Mrs Morton's house. I've arranged to see Stella this afternoon and tell her what happened at the lawyer's, so I can check that she still wants the cottage.' He'd bet his life she did.

'Right. Now, about your changeover. Do you have any jobs of your own outstanding?'

'One or two small ones. Tylers can take them over.'

'You sure?'

'Yes. If they bring in a bit of money, we can count it as a small contribution from me towards the partnership.'

'It's a deal. I'm glad to have you as my partner.' Roy stuck his hand out and the two men shook on that.

'Right. Get those jobs of yours organised, but hire someone else to do the labouring – ask Danny if you need to find someone. You won't be wasting your skills on that sort of thing from now on.'

Things were definitely changing, Wilf thought.

'After you've sorted the jobs out, we can maybe spend an hour or two looking through my collection of house plans. My wife's getting them out for us and she'll answer the phone while we do it. We need to start working out what sort of houses we could put on that land, how many and what style of outside we want. I'm not cramming them together like Higgerson does, but it stands to reason we'll want to make a profit, so we need to make the most of the land we've got.'

He stared into space for a moment, then exclaimed suddenly, 'Eh, I'm looking forward to getting my teeth into a proper building job again.'

He sounded surprised at that, Wilf thought. He didn't say it, but he reckoned Roy was like a plant coming to life again in the spring, showing signs of the man who'd been known for hard work and who could think of surprisingly different ways to do some things. But best of all to Wilf, Roy was known as honest and he built sound houses – unlike a certain other person.

21

Wilf picked up the children and drove into Rivenshaw. He enjoyed going out with them, seeing their wide-eyed wonder as they took in new sights.

They'd all have to go and put flowers on Enid's grave soon. It was what you did; it was supposed to give comfort. He wasn't sure it did, wondered if time was the only thing that truly did that. Sometimes life could be cruel.

He arrived at the car yard in time to see Stella return from a driving lesson and he was cheered up by the expression of glowing pleasure on her face. She got out of the car and was about to go towards the office when she noticed his van.

After a quick word with Nick she hurried across to him, still smiling but in a different and gentler way, now.

'I'm so glad to see you, Wilf. I've been wondering how things were going. Have you found out about the—'

'We'll talk about that later, if you don't mind,' he interrupted, 'so that Beryl can join us. It's only fair to include her. She's sent me to invite you to tea.' He lowered his voice. 'We can have a little chat at her house without any risk of being overheard.' He gestured with his head towards the two children. 'I'll drive you back to Mrs T's later.'

'I'd love to come. I'm not supposed to finish work for another hour yet but I'll ask Nick if I can make it up tomorrow. There's nothing urgent happening at this time of day. Oh, and I'd better let Mrs T know I won't be in for tea.'

'You can telephone her from my house.'

'You got the phone installed, then? That'll be so useful.'

Nick and Jo were chatting in the kitchen when she went in to ask if they minded her leaving with Wilf. They fell silent when they saw her, so she assumed they were discussing something private, perhaps their plans for the new house.

'Oh, yes, you go,' Jo said at once. 'And there's no need to make up the time. I doubt anyone will turn up now. It's going to pour down soon and that'll prevent people even thinking about driving lessons or anything else except getting home before the storm breaks. You enjoy your tea party.'

'I shall.' Stella dashed out again.

The children were both sitting in the back of the van now, and she leaned round her seat to shake hands with each of them in turn, which made them giggle.

'They look well,' she said to Wilf. 'Rosier.'

'They're eating properly now.' That slipped out before he could stop himself.

She looked puzzled. 'Didn't they eat properly before?'

'My wife was . . . um, a bit parsimonious after all the years of struggling to put enough food on the table. She didn't starve us, but she wasn't over-generous with food and children sometimes get hungrier spells when their bodies are growing.'

He clicked his tongue as if annoyed. 'Sorry. I shouldn't go on about that now. Enid always did her best.'

'I feel the same way about Derrick sometimes. He was very set in his ways, wanted only a quiet life. It used to drive me mad sometimes, just sitting around the house every evening and weekends too, once the work was done, except for going to church.'

'And you wanted more out of life?'

'Oh, yes. Much more. He was a good man, mind. Just . . . well, old-fashioned about some things, like a woman's place in the world. And his own place, come to that. He wasn't ambitious to better himself.'

She looked out of the window next to her seat and he guessed she was signalling that she didn't wish to pursue this conversation. They both had regrets about their marriages, it seemed.

As he set off, he tried to imagine this woman with her lively expression and eyes sparkling with intelligence married to a quiet, old-fashioned man. It would have been such a waste of her potential.

As they set off up the hill, he tried for a lighter topic of conversation, 'How are the driving lessons going? You looked so happy as you got out of the car.'

She beamed at him. 'I'm thoroughly enjoying them and Nick says I'm making good progress. I'm going to have another lesson tomorrow morning. And as soon as I can drive it, I'm going to take possession of that car Todd is saving for me.'

Her blissful sigh made him smile.

'So everything's going well since your move to Rivenshaw?'

She didn't respond and he shot a quick glance sideways to see that she was frowning slightly, couldn't resist asking, 'What isn't going well?'

'Um. Well, it's living at the lodging house. It's clean, the food is good and the other lodgers are friendly, but it's a bit crowded. I might try to find a room to rent somewhere quiet, where I have more privacy and can cook for myself.' She lowered her voice. 'It'll be a while before I can buy the other place, from the sound of things.'

'It'd not be wise to move into it alone at the moment, anyway. I'll explain later about an idea Mr T's had about it.'

When they arrived, she phoned Mrs Tyler, then they had the pleasure of chatting to Beryl and Mona, and enjoyed a delicious tea in a spacious room.

Silas joined them and Wilf introduced him. 'Silas is helping me keep watch on this house and the people in it. Jericho's doing that as well. You'll probably meet him later, but he does nights so he'll still be asleep.'

Once again, they couldn't continue the discussion while the children were there.

When they'd finished their tea, Wilf said, 'We'll leave these rascals to help Mona clear up. You'll help her, won't you, my loves?'

They both nodded vigorously.

He looked at Beryl. 'Shall we have our little chat now?'

Mrs Morton stood up. 'Yes. Come into my sitting room. We can be private there and I lit a fire so it's nice and warm.'

Once they were comfortable, Wilf explained Roy's suggestion about Stella renting the cottage from him.

'That'd be wonderful.'

He shook his head. 'The trouble is, it's not safe to be there on your own at the moment. There have been prowlers in this part of Birch End, footprints found near the back of this house. And don't forget that the cottage has already been broken into.'

'Oh dear. Yes. And yet it feels so welcoming inside. But why would anyone be interested in attacking me?'

'Not you so much as the cottage. Higgerson will be furious about Beryl selling it to Roy. I wouldn't put it past him to burn it down, even.'

She stared at him open-mouthed. 'You can't mean that!'

'Sadly, I do. He won't want you or anyone else living in it, let alone modernising it, because he'd rather knock it down and cram half a dozen shoddy houses in its place.'

'But Mr Tyler owns it now.'

'With Higgerson's contacts at the town hall, it'll be hard even to get the title changed so that you can buy the land as well as the cottage. He uses a mixture of bribery or threats or even violence to make people do what he wants, and he seems good at finding people's weak spots. However . . . '

She looked at him. 'Go on.'

'If you were to offer free housing to a family with some strong young men in it, you might be safe there. Sergeant Deemer is working on the problem of Higgerson and the fellow can't get away with his villainy for ever.'

'Some people seem to.'

'Well, we'll make sure *he* doesn't. A few of us are keeping our eyes open and we'll catch him out one day. Our mayor is particularly keen to stop him. He couldn't prevent Higgerson getting re-elected to the council, but he's determined to clear up the corruption at the town hall. Unfortunately, all the hard years have meant that some people are more willing to take chances and break the law in order to put bread on the table, so Higgerson has no trouble finding people to cause trouble at his bidding.'

He waited a moment or two and when she didn't respond, prompted, 'What are you thinking?'

'I don't really want to share my home with a lot of other people. I like living quietly.'

'I've thought of that. With a few modifications to that end room, we could make two separate areas to live in and you get to it from the kitchen, so it'd leave your living space quite private.'

She nodded, listening intently.

'The cellar at that end of the house could be made into a sleeping area if we uncover the window again to let air in. And we could put in a sink and a small electric cooker in the end room. I know where we can get a second-hand one cheap because it got dented.'

'You've thought of everything.'

He smiled. 'Not everything. There isn't room for all possible modern conveniences in two rooms, but a family used to living in one room would consider two a step up in the world. And if they were rent free, even better. They'd be happy to stay out of your way and live quietly, I'm sure.'

'It sounds as if you have a family in mind?'

'I do. But before any of you move in, we'd put a bathroom and proper plumbing into the main part of the cottage, as well as connecting electricity to it. And if you're going to let them live there for a while, perhaps even a separate lavatory and washbasin in the other area while we're at it.'

She couldn't help smiling at that. 'Some houses don't even have one indoor lavatory and several families have to share an outdoor one, yet you're thinking of putting two into the cottage.'

'I'm thinking of keeping you safe and as private as possible. Anyway, life is changing, getting easier with the new modern conveniences like electric kettles and irons. Why should you or anyone live without them?'

'It's very kind of you to help me.'

'I enjoy helping people. I've had a few good turns done to me during the past few years.' He hesitated, before adding, 'Let's face it, you and I are already good friends and my kids like you as well. They'd love to have an extra auntie living across the road from them.'

Was that how he saw her? As an auntie? That sounded as if he was considering her in a sisterly role, which definitely wasn't how she was starting to see him. Stella pushed that thought away and concentrated on the house, annoyed with herself for being so foolish. She was a thirty-year-old widow, should be past all that sort of girlish silliness now.

'I'd have to meet the people who might share the house with me, see if we got on.'

'Why don't you two go and look around the cottage again, and discuss exactly how you could make somewhere for other people to live?' Beryl suggested.

Wilf glanced towards the window. 'It's almost dark now and there's no electric light there yet. We'd not see enough by fumbling around with a torch. Could you get away from work early again tomorrow, Stella? If so, we could have a thorough look at that area of the cottage and perhaps meet Roy there. He's bound to have some good ideas about how to bring the place up to scratch. Eh, I'm looking forward to learning from him.'

'I'm sure they'll let me leave early. They're very kind and the office isn't busy yet because the driving school is still getting known. Nick's going to place some adverts in the local paper. That should help bring in customers.'

They went to play with the children for a while, then Wilf left the two ladies to put them to bed and drove Stella back to her lodgings.

When he came back, he went to find Jericho, who had taken over from Silas to keep watch. 'Got a minute?'

'As many minutes as you like, since you're paying me.'

'How's your family getting on?'

Jericho shrugged. 'We manage.'

'Still in one of those horrible rooms in Backshaw Moss?'

The younger man's voice grew sharper. 'Where else can we afford to live when we can none of us find steady work? Mam sleeps on the sofa and we lads sleep on mattresses on the floor. It's weatherproof, at least.'

Wilf couldn't resist finding out more about them, because now that he was going to be in a position to employ people, he wanted to know who to call on and trust. 'You and your brothers could have gone to work in another part of the country and found jobs. There are quite a few who've done that and are working in the car factories in the Midlands or other places down in the south. Why didn't you?'

Jericho's sigh was heartfelt. 'I belong to Lancashire, that's why. An' Mam's the same. She won't even leave the valley. She can trace our ancestors back seven generations in her family Bible and they're all good, plain Lancashire folk, mostly from hereabouts. She wouldn't leave her twin sister, either, whatever anyone offered her somewhere else.'

'How would you and your family like to have two decent rooms rent free in Birch End in return for a bit of help with this and that?'

'*What?* Rent free? Just tell me how to do that an' I'm your man.'

'You and your brothers would have to prevent Higgerson attacking a friend of mine. Mrs Newby is thinking of living in the cottage opposite once we put in a connection to the sewage system and wire it up for electricity. This is to go no further, mind.'

'I'll not tell anyone. What brought that on? I thought she was working in town.'

'She's going to buy the cottage off Roy eventually. He's just bought it from Mrs Morton but the land title has to be changed before the cottage can be sold off as a completely separate parcel. And she's buying a car as well so she'll have no trouble getting to and from work from there. Nick's teaching her to drive. So, until all the problems with titles can be sorted out, she's going to rent the cottage.'

'That still doesn't explain why she'll need guarding.'

'Higgerson's annoyed about Roy buying the place.' He stopped, watching as the meaning behind the words sank in.

'Ah. I see. But where would she find rooms for us? It isn't a huge cottage, is it?'

Wilf explained about the cellar and end room, and his idea of putting in a lavatory and washbasin down there.

His companion whistled softly. 'My brothers would work day and night to help get it ready for us, they're that fed up of where we're living now. An' Mam would think she was in heaven after Backshaw Moss. She'd be closer to her sister, too. When Dad died, she lost heart for a while. This would brighten her up, I'm sure.'

'Good. I'll tell Roy about the arrangements and we'll start work on the cottage. We'll be calling in a few favours to get it done quickly and Charlie will get Harry Makepeace to oversee putting in electricity. There's no one better in the valley than him. And Roy knows a man who'll sort the plumbing out. Jim's a quick worker.'

He paused and smiled at his companion's excited expression. 'If we get our skates on, we could maybe get you all in before Christmas.'

'That'd be grand.' Jericho frowned. 'It might be better if our Gabriel lived there while that was going on, though, so that no one damages the work before it's finished.'

'Good idea. I should have thought of that. I can't afford to pay him in money but I'll make sure he's fed. He'll keep it clean?'

Jericho laughed. 'Mam's trained us all to be clean. You could eat dinner off her floor, even in Backshaw Moss, she mops it that often. Some folk think she's mad to make such a fuss, but it's nicer to live with. So are clean clothes.'

'Do you want to go and talk to your family about it?'

'Yes. Though I know they'll agree.'

'Do it now. I'll keep watch for an hour or so. Swear them to secrecy, mind.'

'You don't think they'll tell anyone they have a chance of getting away from that place, do you? There would be a queue of folk trying to sneak into the cottage first.'

Jericho left the house and strode towards Backshaw Moss, grimacing as he got closer at the faint smell of sewage that always seemed to linger nearby.

When he went into their room, he was glad to see his

brothers waiting for their tea, a stew made mainly of potatoes which his mam often produced, saying potatoes were better for you than bread, and just as cheap. He closed the door carefully.

'Can tea wait for a few minutes, Mam? I've got a bit of good news, for a change.' He moved across to the table and waited till everyone had squeezed on to the benches at either side of it. 'This is not to go any further and keep your voices low. These walls are paper thin.'

He explained what they'd been offered and waited as they all stared at him in amazement.

Gabriel, usually the quiet one, was the first to break the silence. 'I can't believe it.'

Lucas leaned forward. 'You're certain sure they won't change their minds on us?'

'I'm certain. You can trust Wilf Pollard. It really can happen if we want it to.'

His mother gulped and began to weep softly into her apron, struggling to keep quiet.

'Mam? What's wrong? If you don't want to go, we—'

She sniffed. 'I'm crying for happy. I'd go this very minute if I could. Oh, Jericho love, is it really possible?'

So he had to give her a big hug, rocking to and fro and not letting go till she'd calmed down. Only then did Jericho turn to his brother.

'Gabriel? Will you keep watch there while the work's being done? They'll give you food for doing that.'

'Aye. Starting tonight?'

He smiled at that. His brother was a man of few words. 'I should think so. I'll tell Wilf we'll do it. I'd better get back now.'

He felt like a man reborn as he walked back. It took him a few minutes to work out what had made the difference. *Hope.* That was it. Something that had been in short supply for the past few years.

Suddenly, there was hope not only for a better home but a better future working for Wilf. Even the most menial and poorly paid work, as long as it was regular, would not only improve life for him but for his family as well.

No one decent lived in Backshaw Moss willingly. It had nearly killed his poor mam.

22

That evening at six o'clock, the council meeting was to begin. Reginald Kirby, as mayor and therefore chairman of the council, made sure he was the first person to get to the meeting chamber. He watched the councillors walk in, counting them off mentally as for, unknown or against his plans to reorganise how the valley was run.

It wouldn't be easy, though, because in voting for controversial measures, numbers would split almost equally between those who didn't scruple to act corruptly and those who, like him, wanted to manage the council's affairs honestly. Sometimes he'd have the deciding vote if there were disagreement about any matter, but he didn't think he'd often be outvoted. If he had to stagger to a meeting from his sickbed or help others to do the same, he'd do it to look after the interests of the decent citizens of his valley.

He was relieved when the last member of the council arrived and sat down: Mrs Dentry, who always took care not to sit too obviously aligned with either side. She was a bit of a dark horse, having been persuaded by her husband's friends to stand in place of him when he'd died suddenly last year.

Reg knew she'd never had a desire to become a councillor herself and had been voted for out of sympathy, because her husband had been well liked in that part of the valley. He thought she was on the side of honesty and hoped he was right.

When they were all seated, he banged his gavel and asked

his secretary, Miss Brayburn, to read the minutes of the last meeting. Since there was nothing controversial in them, they were passed quickly.

He took over and announced that he had good news to share and waited till they were all paying attention. 'We've been offered a special purpose grant to help us make a start on clearing up Backshaw Moss.'

There was dead silence until Higgerson said loudly, 'I wasn't aware we'd asked for such a grant. And if we had done, surely those of us with interests in that part of the valley ought to have had a say about what exactly we needed.'

'Local councils were *required by law* to do something about slum clearance last year when the 1930 Housing Act was amended, instead of being merely *allowed* to do it, as the law said previously. This council has been prevaricating and voting down suggestions for how to take action ever since.'

'That's because it needs to be done properly,' a man who always supported Higgerson said at once.

'It will be done properly, believe me, but first of all we have to come up with a plan and get it approved.'

'But—'

He cut Higgerson short.

'I was telephoned by someone rather important who must remain anonymous. He told me the government is concerned about our council's lack of progress in the valley and asked me to make sure we didn't waste the opportunity. With an election coming up next year, something needs to be done quickly before funding opportunities go on hold.'

Higgerson and his cronies laughed heartily at this.

'That lot of socialists won't be elected into government in this country again,' one man jeered. 'They only just got enough votes last time. We should definitely *not* waste the money from taxpayers and ratepayers on pampering those good-for-nothing idlers in Backshaw Moss. Our council can wait this government out and then act more rationally in support of the businessmen of the town who own property all around the valley.'

'We should be acting in support of business*women* as well,' Leah put in quietly but firmly. 'And *they* will care about decent housing for poorer families.'

'There are precious few business*women*,' Higgerson mocked. 'Females may work in family businesses under the direction of their menfolk, but normal women don't usually run businesses on their own, especially when they're in a certain condition.'

He studied her belly pointedly to add emphasis to an insult aimed directly at her, as a businesswoman, and she heard Todd suck in his breath sharply.

Before she could respond, he added, 'It's well known that women's brains are made differently to men's and—'

She held up one hand to stop her husband, who was opening his mouth to defend her, and Todd breathed deeply but said nothing.

She raised her voice, interrupting Higgerson. 'There are more women running businesses than people like you care to admit. You don't understand that because you're behind the times, a modern dinosaur on its way to extinction. I don't even bother to argue with you most of the time, Higgerson, because you're too predictable in what you say and are totally boring.'

As he opened his mouth again, she raised her voice and talked over him to finish what she wanted to say. 'The day for an attitude like yours passed when women played such an essential part in winning the Great War.' She folded her arms and sat back, looking calm and slightly amused.

He glared at her and was about to say something but the mayor interrupted.

'You're quite right, Mrs Selby. It is *pitifully* old-fashioned to think that way. We need more women involved in our council doings, as well.'

'And shall we elect a few tame monkeys, too?' Higgerson mocked. 'They'd do as much good.'

Mrs Dentry was now staring at him coldly as well, letting her disgusted expression speak for her, and so were some of the men.

'Mind your manners, Higgerson!' Reg snapped. 'Or I'll suspend you.'

'What the hell for?'

'There are a few old statutes designed to stop people offering gratuitous insults to others on the council. I've made it my business to check them out. They don't say insults to men only, either.'

There was dead silence and Higgerson snorted but let the matter drop.

'Now, stop wasting our time and allow me to continue. The government official who telephoned me was offering our council a special grant to help us make a start. We didn't have to apply for it. They do this occasionally to accelerate progress and I am *not* going to turn down money which will benefit our valley.'

'What exactly did he want us to do?' Todd asked.

'Name our worst slum area and make a plan to clear it. I named Backshaw Moss there and then, of course. I definitely didn't need to consult anyone about that. The place is a festering sore on our community. Why, our new doctor stopped me in the street only yesterday to warn me of the dangers of an epidemic if the council doesn't do something about improving the sewage system there and stopping the overcrowding.'

Higgerson turned red with suppressed anger. 'Lies. All that fellow is doing is trying to interfere with people earning an honest living. What does a doctor know about housing the poor? It's their bodies he takes care of, if he's stupid enough to offer his services for nothing, not their kitchens.'

Reg ignored that, determined not to get side-tracked into bickering. He looked round the room before continuing in a calmer voice, 'Everyone must surely agree that Backshaw Moss is the place to start such work?'

There were nods from most people there, even a couple of men who usually voted with Higgerson.

'Other local councils in the north have made far more progress in slum clearance than we have – Leeds is a shining example. In our valley we have done precisely nothing except talk and argue about what can't be done. It's always *can't be done*. Well this time something *can be done*. I'm going to make sure that happens, whatever it takes.'

'Personally, I wish we could knock the whole of Backshaw Moss down and start again,' Charlie Willcox said. 'It's as bad as any of the notorious parts of Manchester.'

The dark scowl Higgerson greeted this remark with didn't surprise Reg, given how much property the man owned there, but he caught the fellow's eye and watched him close his mouth.

'Is there to be compensation for those who lose properties and income if slum clearance takes place?' one of the cronies asked.

'Yes, of course. But it's not unlimited and there will also be penalties for landlords who make no effort to clean up their properties.'

The crony continued, 'May I propose that those who own property in Backshaw Moss be involved in the actual planning for this? They should know best how long it'll take and whether this offer can be taken up now or will need to wait for a better time?'

'Seconded,' a man sitting close to Higgerson called at once.

Reg smiled. 'There isn't any possibility of waiting. This is a special offer. We have thirty days to accept it or the money immediately goes elsewhere. And if we do accept it, we must make a start on improvements or clearances within a further thirty days, or the same thing applies: the money will go to some other local authority instead. You're surely not proposing that we turn down a gift of money to our valley?'

Higgerson thumped his clenched fist on the table. 'I'm proposing we don't dive in head-first and knock down people's properties, as those fools have done in Leeds. Any dwelling can be improved, after all. That's what we should focus on, small improvements to amenities, ones that don't disrupt the occupants' lives.'

'And don't stop them paying you rent.' Charlie grinned as that remark earned him another glare.

Reg took over again. 'Some buildings in Backshaw Moss are a long way beyond being improved. Have any of you walked round it lately? I have. I'm surprised some of them are still standing. They're fire traps and the sanitation system in that area is bringing danger to all the nearby inhabitants of our valley.'

He leaned forward and added emphatically, 'Quite a few of you live in Birch End, which is close enough to be affected by sewage problems or epidemics. Don't take my word for it, go and see for yourselves how bad it's getting. Or are you prepared to continue risking your own families' health?'

There was some muttering but no one answered that directly.

The mayor raised his voice. 'I will not accept any more delays. We are going to grab this money, small though the amount is compared to what's needed to complete the job, and we're going to use it for the welfare of the poorer folk in our valley *not* for the benefit of affluent business people.'

He didn't wait for comments but said, 'Those in favour?'

He raised his own hand and others did the same, including, he was glad to see, Mrs Dentry. He saw several of the people present check who'd voted which way and scribble names down, as well as Miss Brayburn doing that for the official record and minutes.

'Those against?'

Higgerson's hand was the first to be raised but one or two of those who hadn't voted yet seemed dubious and it wasn't until they'd been nudged by the people sitting next to them that they joined in against the motion.

More counting was done.

'I declare the motion carried.'

Reg watched as Higgerson leaned across to whisper to his neighbour, who smiled and nodded. What were those rapacious sods plotting now? he wondered. You could guarantee there would be some attempt to stop anything being done.

Well, this time their local member of parliament had succeeded in getting things started, at least. The fellow would claim credit for that, and would no doubt be hoping to gain more votes because of this action in the general election coming up in late 1935. And for once he'd deserve them.

Sadly, few people in political roles took action out of mere altruism.

Charlie Willcox was driven home from the council meeting by his sister-in-law and her second husband.

Leah waited till they'd driven away from the town hall to let out her anger. 'Sometimes I itch to slap the smugness from Higgerson's face. If he had his way, women wouldn't be allowed to do anything outside the home. And he talks to them as if they're all half-wits. He's prevented several initiatives being set up for poorer mothers and their children, which would have done a lot of good in the valley.'

'You didn't show your anger at the meeting,' Todd said.

'I've learned not to. It annoys him much more when I smile at him and call him old-fashioned.'

Charlie let out an annoyed grunt from the back seat. 'He enjoys trampling on people, literally or metaphorically, that one does. His wife always looks as if she wouldn't dare say boo to a goose. I feel sorry for the poor little dab of a creature.'

'I feel sorry for his sons, too. I heard from one of the workers in my fizzy drinks factory, who has a son of the same age, that the two boys were *glad* to be sent to boarding school and dreaded coming home for the school holidays.' She shook her head at the thought of this.

'The younger one is still at boarding school but the older lad must be twenty or so now, if I remember correctly,' Charlie said. 'He seems to have vanished from the face of the earth and Higgerson won't have his name mentioned. There's been a lot of talk about that. No one knows where the lad went after he left school. I reckon Vi knows, though, from the expression on her face when he's mentioned.'

'Why should your manageress know that? Or care?'

'She's distantly related to his wife so takes an interest. She hears a lot of gossip running that pawnshop of mine but she mostly keeps it to herself. She did let one thing slip when she was angry about something Higgerson had done. Apparently, there are some who whisper that Higgerson had his son killed for disobeying orders.'

'Even he wouldn't do that, surely?'

Todd slowed down to turn right into Birch End. 'I'm sure he'd not stick at anything if he got angry enough. I saw that same vicious look in some men's eyes during the war. But they were encouraged to run amok in those days, as long as it was the enemy they killed and not their fellow soldiers.'

He pulled up outside his brother-in-law's house.

'What a cheerful way to end the evening,' Charlie said. 'Let's think of happier things. Come in and have a glass of sherry, why don't you? I've just bought some rather fine amontillado from my wine merchant. He buys it by the barrel and bottles it himself.'

'Not tonight, thanks. I'm rather tired.' Leah leaned her head against the back of her seat and closed her eyes.

'You're overdoing things,' Todd said quietly. 'Considering.'

Charlie looked at them sharply and she opened her eyes again to scowl at her husband.

'Does that mean what I think Higgerson was hinting at?' Charlie asked. 'The patter of tiny feet?'

'It's early days yet, and if you say a word to anyone, Charlie Willcox, I'll personally strangle you.'

'Oh, you can trust me to keep a secret. Except from my Marion.'

'I don't mind you telling her. What I don't understand is how Higgerson knew.'

'Oh, it was probably just a wild guess. But if you won't come in, you won't. You can sample my sherry another time.'

But being Charlie, he couldn't just say a simple goodbye and added, 'Before I go, how's that new clerk of yours going, Todd? She looks efficient.'

'We're all very happy with her. She's getting on particularly well with Wilf Pollard. They look comfortable together and she's been to tea at his new home.'

Charlie laughed softly. 'That's because she's buying that old cottage off Roy. It's to be kept secret for the moment, though.'

'How do you know?'

'I'm putting a little money into Tyler's business. He's going to erect some decent houses on the wasteland next to the cottage and about time too. It's been an eyesore for decades. Roy's almost his old self again, I'm glad to say. Must have been hard losing his only son. Nice to see him back at work.

And Wilf Pollard is going to surprise a lot of people. He's a clever chap and will go far in business.'

'His wife was very much a home body,' Leah said. 'The poor woman never joined in anything in our village. It seemed as if she only wanted to be with her children and protect them from every breeze that blew. And yet they looked rather subdued for kids of that age. Why, they weren't even allowed out to chase about with other kids.'

'No one can say that about your little Jonty.' Charlie blinked his eyes rapidly. 'My brother would have been proud of him. He's never still for two minutes these days, that child isn't. Anyway, I must be going.'

He got out and stood waving as they drove off.

'It always takes him a long time to get out of the car,' Todd commented.

'He likes to find things out. I wish he hadn't guessed about the baby, though. It's early days yet.'

When they were nearly home and driving through Ellindale, Leah asked suddenly, 'Does it upset you when Charlie talks about his brother, Todd?'

'No, love. Jonah was a very nice fellow and you'd still be married to him if he hadn't been gassed during the war and died young. And I love his son like my own.'

Her voice was thick with emotion. 'I'm so lucky. I've had two wonderful husbands.'

When Higgerson slammed the front door behind him as he entered the house, his wife jerked in terror. A slammed door was always a bad sign.

He came storming into the sitting room and flung himself down in his armchair. 'Get me a glass of brandy.'

She hurried off to do as he'd ordered, saying as she put it down in front of him, 'I'm rather tired today, Gareth, so I'll go to bed early now that you're home, if you don't mind.'

'I do mind. I married you to have company in the evening as well as a nice warm body in my bed. And now that our children are neither of them at home, you can bloody well stop this going to bed early and pay attention to what I say and what I need. I'm the master here, and don't you forget it.'

Her heart sank. She loathed it when he came to share her bed, only hoped she could continue to hide her feelings about the rough way he treated her, as well as hiding the signs of his violence, though she knew the housemaid had seen some of the bruises. But Lallie knew better than to mention them.

Why was he so angry? What could have gone wrong at the council meeting this time? She'd suffer for that – she always did when he got into one of his rages.

Only when the marks could not be hidden did he let her take to her bed for a few days. That respite was almost worth the pain.

But he'd been getting worse lately.

She was afraid for her life, sometimes.

23

Work started on the cottage the very next day, because when Roy Tyler wanted something done quickly, he didn't waste time and even in better years there were always plenty of men who were happy to work for him. He was a good boss, the best in the valley, some said, and a good builder too.

Gabriel had been told to wait near the back door if he wanted work, and went to stand near the corner of the house from where he could see who came to the cottage. Another man turned up and stopped next to him.

'Waiting to see Mr Tyler?'

'Yes.'

A car stopped in the street next to the cottage and Mrs Tyler got out of it followed by her husband, which surprised Gabriel. 'Does Mrs Tyler always come with him on jobs?'

'Oh, aye. At the start, anyway. The missus is the one who keeps track of the details of a big job like this one, and she's the one who puts our wages together. She's allus on time with the money and never gets it wrong, neither.' He stared at Gabriel. 'I thought everyone knew she helped her husband.'

'I've not worked for them before, but Mr Pollard sent word by my brother Jericho that there's a part-time job for me if I'd act as nightwatchman as well.'

'Well, if you've been told to wait here, that's what you need to do. I daresay Mr Tyler will get to us soon as he can. I'm not in any rush to break my back digging this place an' he'll pay for a full day's work as long as we're here waiting.'

'What's that other chap standing near the gate doing? Why hasn't he joined us?'

'They mustn't have sent for him. He's desperate, poor chap. His little daughter's ill.'

They leaned against the wall in a patch of winter sunlight, watching what was going on in a companionable silence.

Roy saw the desperation on the face of the man waiting near the gate and stopped next to him, saying gently, 'All right, Pike. We'll find you some work for today an' see how we go.'

Ethel tugged at her husband's sleeve and when he bent towards her, whispered and gestured towards Pike.

He nodded and turned back to the man, slipping a coin into his hand. 'Here, lad. Get yourself something to eat and be back in half an hour. You'll work better on a full belly. No spending it on anything but food, mind.'

His wife added a second small coin. 'And get something nourishing for that child of yours before you go home.'

'Thank you, Mr Tyler, thank you, missus. I'll do that.' The man hurried off, wiping his sleeve across his eyes.

'I'd better do something about that child,' Ethel said as she followed her husband inside the cottage. 'I'll phone that new doctor later and ask him to pop in and see the little girl.'

He smiled. His wife could never walk past a child needing help.

They left the front door open to air the place and took a quick preliminary walk round the interior so that Ethel could get her bearings about what would be involved.

'Nice little house,' she murmured as they came downstairs again. 'Or it could be.'

He was about to answer when another man strode up to the front door and peered inside.

'Ah, there's Jim Wasthorne. I sent word to him to come and check what the plumbing needed.'

Roy went to greet him at the door and was just about to show him round when he looked down the street and saw a van approaching. 'It never rains but it pours,' he said cheerfully. 'Ethel love, can you show Jim the upstairs? Harry Makepeace has just turned up about the electrics and I need to give Gabriel and another fellow a job to do as well so they're not wasting my time and money.'

'Of course I can, love.' Ethel took Jim up to the box room, showing him where they wanted to put in a bathroom.

'Won't be a tick,' Roy called as Harry got out of the van. He went to give Gabriel his first job of the day, clearing away the soil from the covered-in basement window. 'And watch out for Pike, who'll be back shortly. He's to help you with the digging, Gabriel.'

Then he turned to the other man. 'Can you make a start on clearing up the front garden, Tim? I know how well you look after your allotment so I can trust you to leave any plant that might still be alive and will look nice come the spring. But I reckon what's there is mostly the rubbish from years of neglect, so pull any dead plants or weeds out. There should be a few days' work for you, what with the back garden to tidy up as well.'

'Happy to do that, Mr Tyler.'

Roy went to discuss the electrical connection to the house and the wiring needed inside it in general terms with Harry. 'And while you're at it, I've probably missed things out, so if you get any better ideas about what needs doing, tell me about them. It's for a widow who's using most of her money to buy the house and I want it all done properly in the modern way for her. You'll know what that means these days better than I do.'

'It's kind of you to think of her needs.'

'My needs too. I shall learn a lot from what you do here and maybe I'll find things to put into my houses when I build them. Eh, the world's changing fast, it is that. Every man and his dog want their own indoor bathroom these days. No more tin baths hanging on the wall and filled by hand in front of the fire when needed.'

When Ethel brought the plumber down, Roy said, 'Can you take Harry round next and discuss where a woman might want to put the electric points, Ethel love, not forgetting some in the end room which is to be kept separate from the main house?'

'I'll enjoy doing that.' She paused to add for his ears only, 'You're looking full of life today, love.'

'Aye. Losing our lad stopped me in my tracks for a while but life goes on. And I do like to get my teeth into a new job.'

She pressed his forearm, gave her own eyes a quick wipe and sent him another loving look before turning back to Harry. 'Shall we start upstairs and leave my husband to enjoy himself, Harry?'

Roy turned back to the plumber. 'Let's go into the kitchen first, Jim. It's very old-fashioned and there's another room beyond it. The lady who's buying the cottage wants to put someone to live in the part beyond the kitchen.'

He paused in the kitchen doorway to add, 'You'll have to work out how the cottage can best be connected to the main sewage line and how to fit in the necessary plumbing into the end room for a separate lavatory – and maybe even a full bathroom. I hope it won't give you too many problems.'

'You're lucky there, Mr Tyler. The sewage line runs along this side of the street and from what I've seen when repairing it at another house, they made a thorough job of putting it in all those years ago.'

'I'll leave you to get on with it, then.'

Jim nodded and said in a quieter voice, 'Nice to have you back, Roy.'

'Nice to be back, lad. And you'll like my new partner, too.'

His companion grinned. 'Eh, I like him already. I've known Wilf Pollard since he was a lad, and a smart little fellow he was too. You chose well there. No one has a bad word for him. Now, I'll need someone to help me with the measurements.'

'I've got a chap doing some digging outside. I'll fetch him in to help you.' Tyler looked out of the back kitchen door and yelled, 'Gabriel, can you stop that for a few minutes and help Mr Wasthorne with the measuring up? Pike, you carry on clearing the earth away.'

Gabriel was pleased to have a chance to see what was going on inside the house. He joined the plumber and started by holding the end of the wind-out tape measure. To his surprise, Mr Wasthorne explained what he was doing as he paced out the end room, the cellar and even the outhouse.

When Gabriel realised they really would be fitting a lavatory and sink into these rooms, and just for his family's private use, happiness filled him. His mam would think herself in heaven to have these necessities placed so conveniently and not shared with anyone. He couldn't wait to tell her.

He'd work his fingers to the bone for a man like Mr Tyler who treated ordinary folk this well.

Wasthorne wondered aloud if it'd be better to put a small kitchen sink and cooker in the upper room and he went to peer at the outhouses beyond it for a second time. 'You know, we could put a bathroom and kitchen in here more easily than in that other room.'

He walked to and fro, looking up at the ceiling. 'It's quite waterproof and it's already got an inner wall of wood, even if it's not double brick. They must have used it as more than just an outhouse in the past.'

He continued to pace up and down, muttering to himself, then said abruptly, 'Before I settle on anything, I'd better get their permission to do things a bit differently. It'll cost more but it'll be well worth it. Could you go and find Mrs Tyler for me, please? She's somewhere inside the house still.'

'*Mrs* Tyler?'

'Aye. She allus sorts out the details. Never met a woman so good at it, either. She'd ha' made a grand plumber if she wasn't a female.'

Gabriel found her upstairs in the front bedroom discussing modern electrical needs with Harry and her husband, from the sounds of it. When he explained that Mr Wasthorne had sent him to fetch her, she nodded. 'I'll leave you and Harry to it, Roy.'

She went to study the end room and the building beyond it, nodding as Mr Wasthorne explained his idea.

'You're right, Jim. That'd be far better than using the cellar. The new owner is already paying towards the improvements so we'll have to ask her to pay a bit more if we do this. But I think she'll agree that it'd be a big improvement and not cost all that much, considering the advantages it'll bring her. How did you think to fit in the kitchen exactly?'

After listening intently, she made a couple of suggestions and to Gabriel's surprise they were improvements on the plumber's original ideas.

When she noticed him watching, she gave him a sweet smile. 'Women use these amenities more than men, Gabriel, so sometimes we have better ideas about what would work more efficiently. It's a fool who doesn't take advice from the experts.'

He liked the way she'd remembered his name. He hadn't thought about the planning side of the various jobs at all, really, until today. But he'd found it interesting to listen to their discussions.

Roy came down to join them. 'All sorted, Ethel?'

'Yes, dear. But we've made a few changes.'

He nodded agreement when she explained. 'Good. Now, could you go and finish up with Harry in the sitting room, love? He won't settle on the details of lighting there till he's run them past you. I thought one ceiling light might do but he says two would be better.'

'He's probably right. If anyone's sewing they'll need more than one light.'

Mr Tyler turned to Gabriel. 'Carry on with your digging now, lad. I had a look out of the kitchen window at Pike and he's working hard. Make sure he takes a few rests. He's not been eating properly for a while, poor chap.'

He turned back to Wasthorne. 'I hope you're not going to charge an arm and a leg for all this.'

'Just the usual, plus cost of equipment.'

'All right. I'm sure she'll agree.'

Gabriel took a deep, happy breath as he went outside to continue digging the basement window clear. A whole new bathroom to themselves. They were going to enjoy living here, by hell they were.

They had to take the last of the soil out by hand, because they didn't want to break the glass underneath it. They'd already found a low, partly ruined wall enclosing the area round the sunken window so took care not to knock any more of that down.

He wondered if the window would still open and tried it gently. The hinges showed every sign of still working but they were stiff and probably needed oiling, so he didn't force them open more than a crack. He went to find Mr Tyler instead to ask about an oil can, adding as an afterthought, 'And if there's the stuff to make a small batch of mortar, I can re-set the stones that have come loose back in the wall. Won't take me long.'

Mr Tyler stared at him as if he'd said something unexpected, and Gabriel's heart gave a thump. Had he taken too much on himself and upset his new employer? He waited anxiously.

'Eh, lad, you've got a sensible head on your shoulders. Do you want to work on the cottage as general labourer in the afternoons from now on for a full-time wage? You'll get shorter hours than the others because you'll be keeping watch overnight as well and you'll need to sleep in the mornings, but you'll still learn a lot.'

'Really? Eh, that'd be champion.'

'You'd better sleep in the dining room at night. You can see the street from there and you won't be disturbed as much in the mornings because there's not a lot of work needs doing to that room.'

Gabriel set to work with a will. He couldn't remember the last time he'd had a job where his employer was so thoughtful, let alone appreciated suggestions being made.

He was out of condition, got tired more quickly, but he'd be eating better now, so he'd soon toughen up.

Some time later Wilf drove up in his van and a woman Gabriel hadn't seen before got out of it, a little slip of a thing with an alert, interested expression.

'Oh, good. You're still here, lad.' Wilf indicated the woman. 'This is Mrs Newby, who's going to buy the cottage from Roy once it's been done up. Stella, this is one of your future watchmen.'

Gabriel nodded politely and studied the woman he and his family had been hired to protect. She looked pleasant enough, thank goodness, had a nice smile, in fact. They'd all tower over her, though, even his mam. He hoped she wouldn't mind that.

Mrs Tyler came to the door. 'You go inside and find my husband, Wilf. I've got to go into town now.'

These people all seemed to know one another, Gabriel thought, lingering to listen unashamedly to a final few comments on what could be done first.

Mrs Tyler turned to the plumber. 'I'll send you details of the bath and other fittings I've chosen after I've been to look at the new ones they've brought out this year, Jim.'

'Good. I'll go and draw up my diagrams properly, so that I can order the pipes and taps that will be needed.'

Gabriel shook his head and went back to work. Topsy-turvy old world it was when ladies like her ran building sites. But these chaps all seemed happy to work with her and he had to admit she talked sense. It just felt . . . different.

Later, as he was taking a break, he nipped inside to have another quick look round the rooms he and his family would be living in. He couldn't wait to move in here, but he was glad he'd be sleeping in the dining room for now. It'd be a lot warmer in there. He'd bring his mattress and his football rattle to call for help from Jericho across the road, if necessary.

You underestimated Higgerson at your own peril. He'd worked for the man once and been cheated out of half his wages in so-called fines. You didn't forget that sort of thing and it still rankled that he'd been powerless to do anything about it.

Wilf stopped just inside the doorway to watch Stella study the hall again. He smiled. She sometimes reminded him of an alert sparrow, a bird he'd always loved to watch. As he waited, he saw Mrs Tyler leave in one of the company's vans with a driver he'd known for years. When Stella had finished looking round he followed her into the sitting room.

She was smiling as if she liked what she was seeing. Well,

he liked this cottage, too. Some places had a nicer feel to them than others. Was that because people had lived happily there and that feeling had become embedded in the stone? He shook his head slightly. Eh, he did have some daft thoughts at times.

Was he being daft about Stella? The more time he spent with her, the more he was attracted to her. He shouldn't be. It was too soon. But he was. He shook away these thoughts and paid attention to what she was saying about the sitting room.

At one point they collided in a doorway and for a moment they stayed where they were, pressed together and staring into one another's eyes. He was suddenly sure she was as attracted to him as he was to her, so he smiled and took his time about moving away, pleased that she didn't try to pull away as she smiled back at him.

Sometimes you didn't need words.

Shortly afterwards, Roy bustled out of the kitchen to join them. 'My wife's gone shopping for bathroom fittings, Mrs Newby. She likes putting together stylish modern bathrooms and no one does it better.'

'Your wife is an amazing woman,' Wilf said.

'Yes. She'll come back with everything we need ordered. I rely on her for that. Now, there's just one other thing I need to talk to you about, Mrs Newby.' He explained about the idea of using the outhouse as a kitchen and bathroom for her guards and later for servants' quarters perhaps, or she could rent the rooms to tenants. He ended, 'It'll cost you about thirty pounds in all to do that as well as your own bathroom, but it'll be well worth it and will add a lot of value to your house, as well as being more convenient for housing your servants.'

'Servants!'

She looked a little shocked and mouthed the word again,

silently, then took a deep breath as if pulling herself together. Wasn't used to servants, he'd guess. He waited. It didn't do to rush clients.

'It sounds a good idea to me, Mr Tyler. I'll just go and have a look at how it'd fit in before I make a final decision.'

When she'd gone to do that, Roy held Wilf back from following her and lowered his voice. 'I'm told the council will be doing some slum clearance. We'll want to bid for that.'

'Backshaw Moss?'

'Aye. Go and have a walk around it as soon as you can, see if there's anything you'd keep. If it was up to me, I'd knock the whole place down. It might only be a few streets and a couple of alleys, but most of those buildings were shoddily built in the first place and have never been maintained properly. Not a word to anyone else about it, mind.'

'I'll do that.'

Stella came back to join them. 'It's an excellent idea. How much to put in a bath as well?'

He shrugged. 'Whatever the bath itself costs, a few more pounds at most.'

'All right. Do it. I don't want to share my bathroom with anyone, or live with dirty people.'

He stuck out his hand and they shook on the bargain, then Wilf drove her back to work at the driving school.

'Happy with what he's planning to do?' he asked.

'Very happy. If I don't want to hire a servant after everything's settled down, I could rent out the two rooms, as long as they're self-contained.'

Which sounded as if she wouldn't have a lot of money to spare after buying the cottage, so was checking on how every pound was spent. That thought made him feel more comfortable with her. He'd not like to go courting a woman who had a lot of money.

Then he stopped his thoughts there. He'd be making a lot

more money himself as Roy's partner. So he had to stop thinking of himself as a poor man, because he was beginning to think that he wanted to court her. And that she'd not be averse to that.

Harry returned a couple of hours later accompanied by a man Roy had found to help him, a chap who'd been working for Tylers on and off for years and had some experience of the expanding trade of electrics.

Wilf watched Roy, helped out where he could and marvelled at the sudden change from dusty and dimly lit rooms, slumbering the years away, to bustle and what looked like chaos but was actually an experienced builder getting several things started at once. He was already enjoying working with such a skilled man, loved learning anything and everything.

At lunchtime, Roy suggested he buy food from the village shop. It didn't have nearly as good a choice as Lily's little shop in Ellindale and could have done with smartening up. The man who served him looked deep-down tired.

He was going to have a quick word with Gabriel about where he planned to spend the nights but found that Roy had already settled that.

Wilf had thought he knew how to work hard and quickly, but his new partner was leading a positive battle charge to renovate the pretty old cottage.

24

Stella had decided to continue boarding at Mrs T's in the hope that she could move into her new home before Christmas. Everyone she met seemed to have started saying those words now and hoping to do all sorts of tasks 'before Christmas'. The weather was backing up their plans because it had grown very cold, turning into 'hard winter' as she heard someone call it.

She wrote to her friend Lena, a proper letter this time, not just a postcard to say that she was all right.

As it was cold walking to work, she bought herself a new winter coat with a cape collar from the better of Charlie Willcox's two pawnshops. She didn't try to buy a new one because although the money she'd won had seemed a vast sum, she was committing whole chunks of it to buying the cottage and turning the end room into a separate dwelling. She always tried to think of providing for her old age.

Had she gone too far with the improvements? Who knew? It was done now. She might not be able to buy the land legally yet but she trusted Roy Tyler absolutely, as she trusted Wilf.

It had been Mrs Tyler who suggested she try the upper level of Willcox's pawnshop for clothes. Stella was pleasantly surprised at what good quality garments someone had gathered together there.

Vi, the manageress, served her and tempted her into buying a tweed suit in shades of black and grey. It had a single-breasted jacket with a two-button fastening, wide lapels and slightly padded shoulders. These shoulders were a recent fashion, Vi said, when she fingered them dubiously. The skirt was slightly flared with eight panels, which would make for easy walking.

Stella was delighted with her purchase. She'd only need to shorten the skirt of the suit for it to fit perfectly. She couldn't resist buying a twin-set in pale green, which would go with her best skirt. It didn't show any signs of wear and she wondered as she stroked the soft wool whether the original owner had fallen suddenly on hard times and been forced to sell it to buy food.

Finally, she bought a pair of black leather lace-up shoes with black suede trims down the sides, and a clutch bag to match. Well, she couldn't wear her old work shoes with the new suit, could she? And these fitted her perfectly, so they weren't an extravagance.

The clutch bag was an extravagance, but she couldn't resist it and decided to call it an early Christmas present to herself. How would she fit in everything she needed when she went out with such a handbag? But still . . . the soft leather was unmarked, as if it had hardly ever been used so she'd just use it on very special occasions. Nearly all of the well-dressed ladies she saw in town carried similar bags these days.

She'd wear the new clothes to church in Birch End, because Mrs Morton had asked her if she'd like to accompany them, possibly the coming Sunday. Wilf had said he and the children would pick her up in the van for that. He could show her round the cottage afterwards and she'd be able to see how much had been done there already. One good thing about times like these was that no seller of goods kept a customer waiting, if they could help it, so everything needed had been delivered almost immediately.

In the meantime, she had driving lessons booked every

day that week and was looking forward to driving the car on her own. If she only took it out alone at quiet times of day to begin with, surely she would come to no harm?

When Stella started walking home after work on the Friday of that week, she was again deep in thought about her cottage. She only became fully conscious of her surroundings when someone gave her a hard push from behind and she stumbled forward into the path of an oncoming car.

Brakes screeched and the car started to slow down, but if a lad hadn't grabbed her arm and yanked her backwards, she'd have been hit by it.

She clung to him for a minute or two, after which he and an older woman helped her to sit down on a nearby garden wall, while she took deep shuddering breaths and tried to control the waves of shock and terror still washing through her.

The car driver got out and came to join them, looking ashen. 'Are you all right, missus?'

She managed a nod because he looked as bad as she felt and added, 'Not your fault.'

Another lad came rushing along the street to join the woman who'd helped her. 'I lost him, Mam. Sorry. He ran round the corner, got into a car and they drove off quickly. There was mud on the number plate so I couldn't make anything out, but it was a Riley saloon. Sorry, missus. I'd have liked to catch him for doing that to you.'

The driver gaped at him incredulously. 'You mean someone deliberately tried to push this lady under my car?'

Shocked, she whispered, 'Deliberately?'

'Yes. Didn't you realise?'

She tried to remember and yes, she had felt a hand on her back just before she started to fall. 'I don't understand why anyone would do that? What did this person look like?'

'He had a muffler wound round his face. It slipped down while he was running but I only saw the back of his head. He had dark grey hair with a big bald patch. Sorry.'

The driver pulled out a pocket watch and consulted it. 'If you're all right now, missus, I should carry on. I have to pick up my mother from the station in another few minutes.'

The woman was still sitting with an arm round Stella's shoulder, which was very comforting. Stella looked at the driver. 'Could you give us your name and address, please? The police may want to talk to you. We need to report this to them.'

'Oh. I suppose so.' He pulled out a small notebook and wrote it down with hands that were still shaking slightly, then drove off.

The woman turned to look at Stella. 'You *are* going to report it, aren't you?'

'Yes, but I don't know where the police station is. I'm new to town.'

So the trio of good Samaritans, who proved to be a mother and her two sons also walking home from work, escorted her there. Stella told a kindly sergeant what had happened and he looked surprised.

'Have you upset someone, Mrs Newby?'

She hesitated, not sure whether to mention Wilf's worries about her living in the cottage on her own. The more she thought of it, the more it seemed the only possible reason for someone to want to harm her in a town where she was a stranger.

'I, um, might have an idea but I have no proof so I'd rather tell you in confidence.' She threw an apologetic glance at the woman who'd helped her.

'Very right, too,' her new friend approved. 'You can leave it to Sergeant Deemer to sort out whether it's worth looking into or not. Here's the driver's address, sergeant, but it wasn't his fault. You've got my address, so I'll be off now. Come along, lads. Your father will be wanting his tea.'

The sergeant nodded to them. 'You were right to bring Mrs Newby to me. And well done, lads. Your quick thinking saved this lady from being hurt and gave us a clue about who did this.'

The young fellows blushed and smiled, going even redder when their mother plonked a loud kiss on their cheeks, one after the other, and said proudly, 'They're good lads, always have been.'

When they were alone together, the sergeant took Stella into his office at the back of the main area and gestured to a chair. 'Sit down and tell me everything you can about who might want to harm you. Take your time.'

So she explained about buying the cottage and when she said the name Higgerson, the sergeant stiffened and said, 'Ah!' as if that made complete sense to him.

'I'd appreciate it if you'd keep that information to yourself from now on, Mrs Newby. You were right not to tell the people who helped you those details. Lads that age might have boasted about knowing something, then they could have been hunted down. There have been other so-called accidents where people who've upset that man got hurt, I'm afraid. But until I have absolute proof, I'm helpless to stop him.'

He scowled into the distance. 'Rich villains are always much harder to catch than poor ones. Don't tell anyone else.'

'I'll need to tell Wilf Pollard and my employers, Nick and Jo.'

'By all means tell them. They know how to keep quiet about something. Now, how are we going to get you home safely? I think I'll ask my constable to walk with you to Mrs T's tonight, just in case your attacker is still hanging about.'

'I'm about to get a car of my own so I won't be going to and fro on foot for much longer.'

'You make sure you don't walk out alone after dusk till we get this sorted out, mind.'

'I will.' She shuddered involuntarily at how close she'd come to being seriously injured – killed, even.

When she got back to her lodgings, she asked to use the telephone, paid her twopence to the landlady to do that and phoned Mrs Morton's, relieved when Wilf answered.

'Could you meet me for a few minutes after tea? Something's happened that you ought to know about.'

'Of course I can.'

Again, she saw the dining-room door move slightly as if someone was eavesdropping and added quietly, 'It's not safe for me to talk here in the hall.'

When she put the phone down, she scowled in the direction of the door. Was there an informant here? Well, if so, they were wasting their time. She was *not* giving in to threats and changing her mind about the cottage. The attack must have been intended to make her do that, even if they hadn't meant to kill her, but it had had the opposite effect. She had always hated bullies even as a child, and had needed to outface them many times because of being shorter than most of her classmates.

After she'd finished her tea, she put on her outdoor clothes and waited in the sitting room for Wilf to arrive. Mrs T preferred to open the front door herself after dark. There were too many rules here. It was driving Stella mad. She was too old to be treated like a child.

She looked down at her scuffed satchel handbag. She was going to carry something heavy in it, something to protect herself with if necessary. The pretty handbag would have to wait. Her father had taught her a few tricks to help defend herself because he too had been short and had been forced to use his wits rather than his strength sometimes.

She had never understood why some people wanted to hurt others or bully those smaller than themselves, never would. What good did it do anyone?

When the door knocker sounded, something rather unusual on a winter evening, she heard Mrs T come out of her sitting room and answer it personally.

Stella heard Wilf's voice saying, 'I've come to collect Mrs Newby. We're going out for a little driving practice.'

She went out into the hall and Mrs T said, 'A visitor for you, Mrs Newby.' She grimaced as if she didn't approve of the outing.

He winked at Stella. 'You can practise a bit more.'

Mrs T clicked her tongue to show her disapproval. 'After dark, Mr Pollard? Surely that's rather risky?'

'We all have to learn to drive after dark, and don't worry, I'll take good care of Mrs Newby, who is turning into an excellent driver, I'm told.'

Stella ignored the unspoken criticism of her behaviour and walked briskly out with him to the van.

When they were sitting in it, he hesitated. 'What do you want to do?'

'Let's get away from here before we have our talk,' she said quickly. 'I know no one could hear us in the car, but I'll feel safer.'

He nodded and drove up the hill, not asking questions till he'd stopped by the side of the road.

'What happened, Stella?'

He listened as she explained how close she had come to being injured, if not worse, grabbed her hand and exclaimed, 'I can't bear to think of you being attacked.'

She didn't pull her hand away, found his touch comforting.

'We must do more to keep you safe, and I really question whether you should move into that cottage yet, even with the Harte family to keep an eye on you.'

'I think I'll be safer there than having to walk to and from work in the dark. I'm not giving in to threats, Wilf. I never have and I never will. I'm still going to move in as soon as I can. Besides, don't forget that I'll have my car next week, which will surely be safer than walking about after dark.'

'Not necessarily. Other cars can push yours off the road, or stones can be hoyed through windscreens or cars can be tampered with.'

She could only gape at him. 'Do you think they'll keep on attacking me?'

'It's possible. Higgerson is a dangerous man. Deemer is certain he's behind various other attacks and accidents, but he somehow manages to get wicked things done without leaving a trace of his own involvement.'

'I'm going to buy a heavy spanner or something similar to carry in my handbag and believe me, I'll not hesitate to use it.' She gave him a wry near-smile as she added, 'Men do have certain vulnerable places to attack.'

A slow smile dawned on his face. 'You're an amazing woman, Stella. Brave in many ways.'

She could feel her cheeks growing warm at that whole-hearted compliment and was glad it was too dark for him to see that.

'I've got an old spanner you can have, but you will be careful how you go to and from work, won't you?'

'Yes, of course I will. Anyway, it's the weekend now and I'm only working tomorrow morning, so I won't have to walk home in the dark.'

He took hold of her hand again, clasping it in both his, delighted that she made no attempt to pull away. 'Tell Nick and Jo tomorrow about what happened.'

'I was going to do that, but surely whoever it is won't try that sort of thing again in daylight.'

'Who knows what he'll do next?' Wilf let go of her hand and set the car in motion again. 'Let's go and have a cup of tea at Mrs Morton's before I take you home again.'

She missed the warmth and comfort of his touch. She hoped she wasn't reading too much into the way he kept looking at her and touching her, because it felt . . . right. It had been so long since anyone had touched her in a fond way.

'Hey, wake up! Do you fancy a cup of tea?' he repeated, smiling.

'Sorry. I was lost in thought for a moment or two. Yes, a cup of tea is always welcome. I suppose the children will be in bed.'

'Yes. I tucked them in myself and they'll be sound asleep by now.'

When he dropped her at Mrs T's an hour later, he said, 'Why don't I pick you up tomorrow afternoon and show you what's been done at the cottage?'

'I'd love that.'

'I'll look forward to it. I enjoy your company very much, as you must realise.'

She'd look forward to it, too. 'I enjoy your company as well, Wilf.'

When she went into the house, Mrs T was just serving cocoa, so Stella went into the lodgers' sitting room to have a cup. Best to join them sometimes or they'd think her snooty.

As the group sat sipping cocoa and chatting, Miss Wolton suddenly asked, 'Is it true that you were attacked in town today, Stella, pushed in front of a car?'

They all gaped at her as if she'd suddenly turned purple. She was puzzled as to how the woman had found this out, and rather annoyed that her affairs should be tossed into a conversation, but managed to answer calmly, 'Yes, but someone pulled me out of the way so I wasn't hurt.'

'And you're still going to live on your own in that cottage?'

That surprised her again. How could anyone here know about the cottage? She'd said when she first arrived that she was looking for somewhere more permanent to live but wasn't in a hurry to move. She hadn't said a word about the cottage to these women, not one word.

The others oohed and aahed and begged her to tell them more about the cottage she'd bought.

'Nothing to tell. I'm a widow. I need my own home.'

'Tell us about the attack then. It must have been terrifying.'

'I reported the incident to the police and was advised not to discuss any of the details. Miss Wolton shouldn't have brought the matter up.'

But the foolish woman couldn't take a hint and gave an exaggerated shudder. 'If someone had attacked me, I'd never go out after dark on my own again. What if they're waiting for you round a corner?'

'Why should they be?'

'Why should they attack you in the first place? There must have been a reason. I bet you're glad you're living here and not on your own in Birch End. You're a fool to buy a place there. Can't you get out of it and buy somewhere safer?'

'No.' She changed the subject and drank her cocoa quickly. She was sure they'd gossip after she left them, but that couldn't be helped.

When she went back to her room, she was glad the maid had put a rubber hot water bottle into her bed because the room itself was very chilly. There was no way of heating it unless you put a shilling in the gas meter for the fire and she'd already been surprised how short a time the gas lasted for that. She hated being overcharged for anything.

Tonight, she just wanted to get into bed and snuggle down.

How had Miss Wolton known about the cottage, she wondered as she put on her warm flannel nightgown and added an old shawl for good measure. Was it that woman who had pushed the door open earlier in an attempt to eavesdrop?

Only, Miss Wolton couldn't have heard anything about the cottage from the phone call, so how had she found that out?

Or rather, who had told her and why?

She would call in at the police station tomorrow and tell Sergeant Deemer about this surprise question. He had stressed that no detail was too small if she remembered anything else.

She was glad there was a lock on her door. She put her chair under the door handle, for good measure.

During the night, Gabriel heard something outside the back of the cottage, so went into the kitchen and peered through the window. He thought he saw a dark shape over by the fence, so waited and sure enough, the figure came closer to the cottage, treading carefully, not making a noise.

Having a sudden idea, he aimed the torch at the window without switching it on, waiting until the would-be intruder had started fiddling with the wooden panel where the window had been broken. He edged forward, held the torch pointed right at the shadowy face and clicked the switch. As he'd hoped, it was bright enough to show the fellow's face. It wasn't someone he knew, but he'd have a good chance of recognising the intruder again.

There was a startled yelp and the man dropped something as he fled.

Gabriel stood watching and couldn't help grinning as the would-be intruder ran in such blind panic he fell over a small pile of rocks. He didn't go outside to chase the fellow, didn't want to leave the back door unlocked and if he took the time to lock it again before giving chase, even such a clumsy chap would be too far away.

Grinning at the memory of the shocked expression when he switched on the torch, he went round the ground floor, shining the torch a couple of times near windows so that it'd be visible from outside and anyone watching would see that there really was someone awake and alert here.

Always better to avoid trouble than deal with it.

Only when he felt fairly certain no one would be close to the house, did he nip out and shine the torch down on whatever the intruder had dropped.

He was shocked to find he'd picked up a rag stinking of paraffin stuffed inside an empty food can. There could only be one reason for this: setting the cottage on fire. That disgusted him. Anyone who would do something like that for money should be tossed over the nearest cliff, if you asked him. The fellow couldn't have known whether there was anyone inside the house and whether they might be killed.

As for the man who must have paid the intruder to do it, he was worse, far worse, and Gabriel could guess who it was.

One day, he thought. One day I'll see that intruder's face again and punch it good and hard for starters, before dragging whoever it is down to the police station.

Nothing further happened that night but he didn't let himself doze, even though he was a very light sleeper.

As the false dawn turned the world outside into the faintest of grey where outlines of objects were barely in focus, he lay down on the mattress Mrs Tyler had sent and pulled the nice thick quilt she'd also sent up over himself. He'd allow himself to doze lightly.

He didn't wake until three hours later as someone opened the front door, talking cheerfully to a companion. It was fully light now, must be about nine o'clock.

The voice was Mr Tyler's and he was just the person Gabriel needed to see. He got up from the mattress and straightened his clothes.

His employer would want to know about the intruder and what he'd been carrying, and so would Wilf.

Roy listened to Gabriel and let out a growl of anger. 'I never thought even he would go so far. It's a good thing you were alert, lad. Well done.'

'I think it'd be safer with a pane of glass properly fitted in that window. They could lever the wood off quietly but you'd be more likely to hear glass breaking. And the letter box in the front door should be nailed shut for the time being.'

'I agree. Good thinking. Look, can you find a lad who'd come and keep watch with you for the next few days? One of you should stay at each end of the house.'

'My youngest brother Lucas would do it like a shot.'

'Ask him then. And I'll have a pane of glass put in this very day. You'd better get some sleep now. You look tired. Oh, and here's a sandwich my wife sent. She thought you'd be hungry.'

Gabriel ate the sandwich quickly, enjoying a rare taste of ham, had a drink of water and lay down again in the dining room. Strange how things turned out. But Lucas would be glad of the money and food too. Their youngest brother was still growing and got very hungry at times. They all did but tried not to let it show to their mother, who did her best to feed them. It had been easier to afford food since they got involved with Wilf and Mr Tyler.

Just you try it again, Higgerson! he thought as he drifted quickly off to sleep. We'll stop you one way or the other.

25

O n Saturday morning, Nick had a cancellation which gave him time to fit Stella in for a driving lesson. 'Let's do it in your car today.'

'Will Todd mind? The car isn't really mine yet. I've been trying to pay him for it but he keeps saying to wait till I'm sure I'll be able to drive it myself.'

'I've already asked him and he's left the key in the ignition for us.'

When the lesson ended, Nick didn't get out of the car's passenger seat immediately, but said in his quiet way, 'I think you can be trusted to drive around on your own now, Stella. I like the thoughtful way you drive, paying attention to what's going on nearby. We'll maybe have a lesson on reversing in and out of narrow spaces sometime next week, but I don't think I can teach you much else at this stage. You'll learn a lot more from actually driving. What you need now is to practise using the controls until every move becomes instinctive.'

Her heart began to thump in excitement and she pressed one hand to her mouth to stop herself saying something silly. But it came out anyway. 'Are you sure?'

'Of course I am. You've been the quickest to pick up the necessary driving skills of any lady that I've ever taught.'

'Oh. It's really nice of you to say so.' It was a long time since anyone had given her such a big compliment. At the laundry you'd thought you were doing well if there were no complaints from the supervisor.

'I'm not being *nice*, as you call it. You have very good hand-eye coordination, which means you must have excellent eyesight.'

'I've always been good at catching, throwing and hitting balls. Better than most boys.'

'I'm not surprised.' He grinned and gave her a quick nudge. 'Go on! Speak to Todd about buying this car. He's in the workshop and he hasn't got a customer. Ask him if you can have it to use from now on.'

'I can't do that till I can withdraw the money from the bank.'

He chuckled. 'Todd will trust you till Monday. You have an extremely honest face and we not only know where you live now but where you're going to live next. In fact, why don't you stop work for the day? You could drive yourself up to Birch End and surprise Wilf.'

'I'd like that. Thank you.' She let out her breath in a whoosh, took a deep breath and pulled herself together before taking the key out of the ignition and going across to the workshop. –

Todd looked round at the sound of her footsteps. 'Someone looks happy!'

'Nick says I don't need any more lessons and can drive on my own from now on, so I wondered if I could take my car today. I promise I'll pay you for it on Monday as soon as the banks open. I have five pounds I can give you as a deposit till then.'

As she fumbled to get the money out of her satchel, he closed his hand over hers to stop her. 'No need. You can go to the bank on Monday for the money. And congratulations. You must be a very good driver to have learned so quickly because Nick always errs on the side of caution.'

Which had her beaming again.

He turned to a board with keys hanging on it, unhooked

one and gave it to her with a bow. 'The spare key to your car, madam.'

She walked back across the parking area, her smile fading and her stomach churning with nerves as she got into the car, *her car now*. She couldn't resist stroking the seat and saying aloud, 'You can do it, Stella Newby.'

Then she realised she'd forgotten the rest of her belongings and rushed back into the office to collect them. Suddenly she was bubbling with excitement, dying to drive off on her own.

When she was sitting in the car again, she whispered, 'Thank you, Lena. One day I'll find a way to repay you for giving me my freedom.'

The car started first time, so she put it into gear and drove slowly out into the street – heading towards freedom of a sort she'd never experienced in her whole life before. She could go wherever she wanted whenever she wanted, and if everything went well, would even own her own home.

Nick turned from his position by the office window and smiled at his wife. 'Do you think she'll go above ten miles an hour?'

'Oh, she might even get up to twelve.'

'Can you remember the first time you drove on your own?'

'Yes. I was fourteen and it was on our farm in Australia. This was only on rough farm tracks, not public roads, mind you. Dad taught me what to do, took me out for a few practices, and said I ought to drive around the farm on my own until I got used to it.'

'Were you afraid?'

'No. Not at all. He said I'd be safe to drive and I believed him.'

'You're a good driver and Stella will be too once she builds up her confidence. Two thoroughly modern young women, eh?' He glanced at the clock. 'I've got to give two more lessons, the first in five minutes' time. After that we'll chat about our future plans. Once we get the sale finalised legally, I'm moving into that house if I have to camp out on the floor and live off bread and jam.'

'I'll be joining you.'

He pulled her to him and gave her a big hug before going out to give his next client a driving lesson.

Wilf looked out of the window when he heard a car stop in the street outside the cottage, was about to turn away again when it didn't seem to be someone coming to work here. Then he jerked round again as what he'd seen sank in: Stella was driving her car on her own. Clever girl!

He turned to beam at Roy. 'Stella's just arrived. Nick must have judged her a good enough driver to be turned loose on the world. I have to go out and congratulate her.'

Roy waved his hand in the direction of the door and Wilf rushed out to the car calling, 'You did it! Congratulations.'

As she got out, he realised she was shaking and clutching the open car door.

'What's wrong? Aren't you well?' He put his arm round her and it seemed natural that she should turn to nestle against him.

'I'm just . . . I was worried . . . this was the first time I'd driven anywhere on my own. I got here safely and . . . fell to pieces.' She drew in a long shuddering breath. 'I'm not usually so timid and silly.'

He brushed the hair from her forehead and had planted a kiss there before he realised what he was doing.

She looked up at him trustingly and they stood for a few moments staring at one another. He realised, and she must have done too from her expression, that they'd just taken a step forward in their relationship, so he kissed her again.

'I shouldn't have done that.' He pulled away.

'Shouldn't have done what?'

'Kissed you in public. Not yet, anyway. People will talk. It's too soon.'

'Yes. I suppose so. But it felt very comforting, Wilf.'

'You're sure you want us to start courting for real, Stella? It's definitely what I want. Am I taking your wishes for granted?'

Her smile lit up her face. 'I do want us to do something, um, well, permanent and no, you're not taking me for granted. Haven't I made that clear?'

He had to place yet another kiss on her lips to seal that decision, and it wasn't a hurried one because it felt so good.

As they drew slowly apart, he looked down at her, feeling some sort of explanation was necessary. 'You must think I've recovered rather quickly from Enid dying.'

'No, you've explained it to me, and I felt much the same about Derrick. It must have been hard going on the tramp.'

'Yes. And it was hard when I came back permanently, too – hard to settle down together, I mean. She was used to being in control of the house and I didn't always agree with what she did.'

'Even after all those years of being married?'

'Yes. And things got steadily worse after we adopted our children. She didn't want anyone else having a say in their upbringing, even me. I wasn't sharing a bedroom with her for the last few months, at her request. She told me she was going through the change of life and was sleeping badly, so I should make up a bed in the loft. If I'd known it wasn't that making her ill, I'd have taken her to the doctor by force if necessary.'

'Do you think a doctor could have done anything to help her?'

Sadness washed through him. 'No, not really. Though he

could have given her something for the pain, perhaps. She was very brave about that and never stopped looking after the kids or keeping the house nice.'

'Well, you have nothing to blame yourself for, Wilf.'

'I hope not.' He fell silent for a moment or two, shrugging. Life moved on. He'd done his best at the time according to what he knew, at least. 'So, are we going to start courting?'

'Yes. Oh, yes, Wilf.'

Her smile was glorious and filled him with happiness.

'It's nice that you and I began by becoming friends so quickly. I've always felt comfortable with you and I really like your children. We don't have to scandalise everyone by rushing into . . . anything, but we don't have to act like polite strangers either.'

He felt sure enough of her to risk saying, 'You mean we shouldn't rush into marriage?'

She gave him one of her steady, questioning looks and he held his breath, hoping – oh yes, hoping.

So he said it again. 'I'm sure marriage is where we're heading, Stella – if you're sure you want to be my wife, that is?'

'Of course I do. It took me ages to decide with Derrick, but with you, well, it happened quickly.'

'Good. That's—'

They moved further apart as they heard the front door of the cottage open. Roy came out to join them and Wilf wished his partner had waited a little longer.

Roy beamed at them. 'So, this is your new car, Stella. Why don't you take Wilf for a drive in it? You two look as if you've got things to talk about.'

There was no mistaking his meaning and Wilf couldn't help asking, 'Don't you think it's too soon for that sort of talk?'

'No. It isn't, lad. If you're lucky enough to find love, you should grab it with both hands and never mind what strangers think. That's how it was with me and Ethel, we fell in love very quickly. I don't think you should waste a day, or a minute even. Life can be too short.'

The expression on his face was suddenly etched in sadness and pain and they knew he was once again thinking of how he'd lost his only child the previous year.

Before they could get into the car, however, the door of the house opposite banged open and two little figures came running out, calling, 'Auntie Stella! Come and see what we're doing. We've made some cakes.'

'They're nearly cooked now but you mustn't touch the oven door.'

She bent to give each one a hug and Wilf shot her a rueful smile as their chance to escape was lost. But it was only postponed, because Roy was right. *Carpe diem.* This was one of the few Latin phrases Wilf knew. He'd learned it from an elderly customer. And it was so right. You always ought to seize the moment when something good was possible.

He watched Stella smile at his children and felt that all four of them would be happier together.

'I'll come and join you all in a few minutes,' he called across the street. 'And Stella, after we've tried one of their cakes, we'll have our promised tour of the cottage. I think you'll be pleased with what we've done in such a short time. And perhaps we can take a little drive up to Ellindale to finish off the afternoon. There's a grand view across the tops, even if that wind is too cold to go tramping across them today.'

Her nod was accompanied by a warm smile.

He hoped his own expression said more than his words had. It felt as if he'd unlocked something inside himself today and the warmth of his love was daring to show itself.

Roy's encouragement had helped him, too. His partner was right. You had to seize the moment because life gave and it took away. He prayed it would let him keep Stella.

After they'd spent time with the children, Wilf took Stella across to look at how the work was coming on and they walked round the cottage first. It occurred to him that he'd be living here with her. How wonderful!

They found Gabriel sitting on an old kitchen chair, yawning, and he jumped to his feet when he saw them.

'Everything all right?' Wilf asked.

'Yes, Mr Pollard. Mrs Newby.' He bobbed his head towards Stella.

'We're just looking round again. There's been a lot done, eh?'

'Yes. The chaps have worked hard. So has Mr Tyler. We reckon that outhouse roof is watertight now.'

'We're just going into that part next.' He took Stella indoors again, murmuring, 'It seems as though wherever we go, we're not able to be alone.'

She shrugged. 'It doesn't matter. I was glad to see Gabriel keeping watch here. I'd hate anything to happen to the cottage.'

He hated to spoil the moment, but she had to know. 'I'm afraid there's been an attempt to burn it down.'

'*What?*' She looked around in horror. 'But there are no scorch marks anywhere.'

'Gabriel stopped the chap who was intending to do it. But taken together with what happened to you, it all shows Higgerson hasn't given up hope of getting his hands on this piece of land, don't you think? He must know that Tyler has to be a bit short of money. It's common knowledge among people who work in the trade that he let things slip for a while after his son died.'

'He'll have a bit more money once I've bought the cottage properly and Charlie is backing him too. I shall make my will, so that if anything happens to me, someone else will get the cottage, not the government. They'd sell it to someone for the highest price, probably someone like Higgerson.'

'The government? Don't you have any relatives?'

'Not really. Not now. Would you mind if I left it to your children?' She smiled. 'In theory only. I'm hoping *not* to die for a good many years.'

'Of course I'd not mind. It's kind of you to think of them. It must feel lonely not to have relatives. I've got a brother who lives in Ellindale – Daniel's a grand chap, you must meet him – and I've a sister who lives over in Scarborough. As well as those two tykes of mine.'

'Oh, Wilf, they're such darlings. I'll love helping you bring them up. It was a great sadness to Derrick and me that we never had any children.'

'And to me and Edith. Once we'd adopted those two, she hardly let them out of her sight.'

They were both silent then he said, 'Come on!' and took her into the new area, the end room and the former outhouse.

She stared round the latter, mouth dropping open. 'This is like a real room now. How wonderful to manage that so quickly.'

'It was just the walls to finish off, mainly, a bit of bricklaying outside and plastering inside. There are only a few details needing attention before they fit the bathroom and kitchen.'

'I'd have thought myself in heaven to have a place like this with three rooms after Derrick died.'

'So do the Hartes. They've all four been living in one room in Backshaw Moss.'

'They seem a nice family.'

'They are, but they've had some hard times in the past few years and they none of them want to leave this part of Lancashire to work in the south.'

'I can understand why. The people in this valley are so friendly and helpful.'

'Except for the ones who're trying to hurt you.'

'There are wicked people everywhere, Wilf love, but decent folk usually outnumber them.'

They went upstairs and saw the box room with everything stripped out ready for the bathroom to be put in. There were holes in the wall and pipes sticking out.

In every room there were marks on the walls and ceiling where the electrics would go.

When they came down again, Stella nearly tripped over a piece of timber and Wilf caught her in his arms quickly. 'Careful!' He waited till she was steady on her feet again and, conscious of Gabriel nearby, let her go with only a quick kiss on her cheek.

He gestured round them. 'You've seen it all now. Chaos, isn't it, with all the tools and equipment? We'd not be able to leave them if Gabriel wasn't here keeping watch. It'll continue to seem like chaos until just before the end and suddenly it'll all come together and you'll have your cottage. I, um, shan't have much to gift you with in return when we get together. Nothing as wonderful as owning a cottage of your own, anyway.'

She took both his hands in hers and raised them to her lips to kiss each in turn. 'Only two wonderful children, and these two hands. Think of all the hours of good honest toil they've put in and will continue to put into building a better world for your family and other people to live in.'

'What a lovely thing to say.' He stared down at his hands as if he'd never seen them before, then asked, 'Will you stay to tea?'

'If I'm invited. I don't really like living at Mrs T's now that I know Miss Wolton is spying on me.'

'It won't be long.'

'Will I be able to move in here before Christmas, do you think?'

'Probably. Roy wants it finished quickly. He was meaning to tell you that today, but I think he wanted to give us the chance of being together.'

She beamed at him. 'It'll be wonderful to own my own home.'

'Roy's going to put the money to good use: building new homes for ordinary folk, which are sorely needed. He's already planning the design of houses for the spare piece of land, and how to fit the most dwellings in without overcrowding. Unlike Higgerson, he doesn't want to build the slums of the future.'

'I've never heard of any builder working so quickly.'

'Well, Roy's almost his old self again. I'm going to learn so much from him. I'll enjoy that.'

He looked out at the sky. Anyway, let's go and have some tea and warm ourselves up. I think it's going to rain again soon. We'd better save our trip up to Ellindale for another day.'

26

That afternoon, Gwynneth Harte went to see the cottage where she was going to live, accompanied by her youngest son Lucas.

Smiling to see how happy and excited she looked, her middle son, Gabriel, watched her approach it from the dining room. He'd felt sure no one would mind them coming but he'd asked Mr Tyler anyway. Like the rest of his family, he didn't want to do anything to upset the owner and jeopardise their move here.

They came to the back door, as arranged, by which time Gabriel had walked through the house to let them in.

'This is Mrs Newby's kitchen, Mam. We won't be coming in this way normally. We'll use the other door that Mr Tyler's made in our part of the house.'

'The one that was all boarded up?'

'Yes. It's safer to keep that entrance blocked until the improvements are finished, and that's why the new windows are boarded over, too.'

He locked the outer kitchen door carefully behind them, gave her a few moments to look around, before leading the way into what would be their part of the house, leaving the door from the kitchen open to let more daylight in. 'This will be our main room, Mam. I thought you could sleep here as well. We could put a curtain or screen across the corner for you.'

She turned around on the spot, sighing happily. 'Even this room is half as big again as our present room.'

As usual, his younger brother only nodded, but Lucas looked as happy as their mother did.

They looked round the new area, their eyes quickly adjusting to the lower level of light filtering in between the planks nailed across the outside of the window. 'This is being made into a proper living space and it'll have the kitchen at this end and—' He paused, still finding it hard to believe it himself. '—a real bathroom, with a washbasin, bath and lavatory at the other. They'll be only for our use, as I told you.'

Their mother knuckled a happy tear away.

'Oh, Gabriel. It didn't seem real when you and Lucas told me about it, but suddenly—' She clasped her son's arm with one hand and stared around. 'I'm starting to believe it's possible for us to have a proper home again, a better one than ever before with a bathroom all our own.'

'Mrs Tyler has chosen the bath and everything. It won't be fancy but it'll be brand new an' we can keep it looking nice.'

'I can't wait to move in. It'll be easy to keep this place clean. I'd come now if I could.'

For once, Lucas put his thoughts into words. 'It'll be like living in paradise after that rat-infested slum.'

'There's more to see.' Gabriel led the way down to the cellar. 'This is where us lads are going to sleep.'

His mother stayed at the foot of the stairs, taking it all in. Suddenly she burst into loud sobs. He sons didn't have to ask why. Gabriel pulled her into a hug, his own eyes over bright.

It didn't take much to make people happy, he thought. Thank goodness for folk like the Tylers and Mrs Newby who understood that.

Lucas stood close by, swallowing hard.

Gabriel smiled and gave his mother a minute or two, then

stepped away from her. 'You're not dreaming it, Mam. We really are going to live here. Now, stop crying and let yourself be happy.'

She had to walk round every room again before they left, pacing them out, memorising the measurements.

Lucas walked his mother home to Daisy Lane, still chatting happily and making plans, but stopped abruptly at what they saw. She let out a little mew of anguish because two burly men were carrying their belongings out into the street and dumping them there in the muddy puddles any old how.

'What are you *doing*?' She tried to bar the door and stop them going back inside. Lucas came to stand protectively near her.

One of the strangers shoved her away. 'Mr Higgerson don't want tenants like you, so we're clearing you out.'

'But I've paid my rent till next week an' I always keep the place clean. What's wrong?'

'What's wrong is you going behind his back to those who're his enemies. So he wants you out straight away.'

The man was so big and brutal-looking, she stepped hastily away from him and kept hold of Lucas to stop him doing anything silly. As the stranger went back into the house, she whispered, 'Son, send someone to fetch our Jericho, then help me guard our pile of belongings or they'll be stolen.'

Some of the women she knew and had counted as friends were watching from a distance, but not one of them came to help her look after their belongings. She knew why, oh yes she did, and couldn't blame them. They were afraid of being thrown out of their homes as well.

She couldn't think straight. Where would they live now? The new place wasn't ready and wouldn't be for a week or two, Gabriel had said.

How could this have happened?

How could her happiness turn so suddenly into misery?

Wilf looked up from the tea table as someone hammered on the front door. 'I'll go.'

The knocking didn't stop and Jericho came out of the kitchen to see what was going on. He stood at the back of the hall waiting, in case there was trouble, and Silas joined him there.

Wilf opened the door to find a lad who was panting for breath and looking upset.

'What's the matter?'

'Lucas Harte sent me. His family has been throwed out of their room an' their things are lyin' in the street. Is Jericho here? He's needed.'

He had already come forward to join them, explaining to Wilf, 'Mike lives in the same building as we do. Tell me again quickly, lad. Who are they and what exactly are they doing?'

He listened and said, 'I have to go and help Mam, Mr Pollard, and make sure no one hurts her.'

'We'll both go in my van. You'll need something to carry your possessions in. Silas, can you keep an eye on this house?'

'Yes, Mr Pollard. What about the cottage?'

'Ask Gabriel to stay there. Nip across and tell him what's going on, but come straight back. This might be a trick to get him away and break into it.'

He turned to see Stella standing in the doorway of the room where they ate their meals. 'Did you hear that?'

'Yes.'

'I'd better go and help them. Will you be all right?'

'Of course I will.'

He went out and got into his van, followed by Jericho, gesturing to the lad who'd brought the message. 'Jump into the back. Quick now!'

Mike shook his head. 'Best for me if I'm not seen coming back with you, Mr Pollard, or they might throw my family out as well. They've brung strangers in to do this, big men, never seen 'em afore. They've already thumped a chap as tried to stop 'em doing anything till Mrs Harte got home. I'm not going back till it's all over. I was taking a risk even coming here.'

'I'm grateful you did,' Jericho said. 'I won't forget that.'

Wilf drove off quickly, muttering, 'This is bad.'

As he turned the corner he looked in his rear-view mirror and saw the lad running along Croft Street, heading towards the main valley road.

After that, he concentrated on getting to Daisy Lane as quickly as possible.

Stella watched the van drive away, worried at the thought of Wilf going into what sounded like a dangerous situation with only Jericho to stand by him. As this had to be Higgerson's doing, it took her only a moment to decide to phone the police station in Rivenshaw, and Mrs Morton agreed. After all, the sergeant had said no detail of what that man did was too small to pass on to him.

As usual at weekends, Deemer answered the phone himself and she told him what was happening.

'You were right to let me know. I'll go there with my constable straight away and make sure there's no fighting. If anyone defies me they'll see the inside of a cell before they're an hour older.'

Stella put the phone down, feeling reassured until she went to look out at the street and saw two strangers moving furtively along it, staying close to the garden walls, looking around as they went as if trying to keep out of sight.

When they stopped just before they got to the front of the cottage, she guessed they were there to do some damage.

She felt anger run through her like the stream of molten lava that she'd seen once on a newsreel at the cinema.

That horrible man was still trying to steal her lovely home from her and ruin Mr Tyler's new business. Well, she wasn't having it. Muttering, 'Oh, no, you don't!' she went to find Silas and tell him what was happening, but she bumped into him in the hall because he, too, had seen the strangers acting suspiciously.

'I'm going across there, and don't try to stop me,' she said firmly. 'I'm not letting them burn down my cottage *or* hurt Gabriel.'

'I agree. I'll come with you.'

She ran to tell Mrs Morton and Mona what was going on and ask them to keep the children inside the house, then followed Silas out.

At that moment, a young man who lived two houses away walked along Croft Street and Silas called out to him. 'There are some burglars trying to get into the cottage across the road. We just saw them go round the back. Is there anyone here who'd help me chuck them out? There's only one man keeping watch over there.'

The young man's face brightened. 'I'll come with you. They'll be from Backshaw Moss and I'm not having those villains thinking they can break into homes in my street. Everyone around here keeps an eye open for problems and we all help one another. As it happens, I learned to box at school so I'm pretty good with my fists. If I come with you, that'll make it three against two, which should do the trick.'

'Four against two.' Stella brandished a walking stick with a big, knobbly handle that she'd just picked out from the coat stand in the hall. 'I'm not letting anyone damage my new home.'

There was a shout and the sound of breaking glass from

the far side of the cottage and Silas grabbed the walking stick from Stella.

'There are other sticks in the hallstand,' he told their unexpected helper. 'Get one and follow me. You stay here, Mrs Newby. A fight is no place for a woman.'

She didn't argue with him but gave the young man another walking stick from the hallstand, waited till he'd left the house and looked for something to defend herself with. She was left with only a choice of umbrellas for weapons. Selecting a large man's umbrella with a brass ferule, she picked it up and followed them across the road, brandishing it about to get the feel of it. Nice and heavy, it was.

She didn't know when she'd felt so furiously angry. She was *not* letting these villains spoil her lovely new life.

It'd be stupid to rush into the middle of a fight, however, because she was far too small to win against brute force. Maybe she could trip someone up or throw a stone at one of the villains, though. And she could use the umbrella to defend herself if they attacked her.

At the very least she'd be a witness to what happened.

What she'd like most of all would be to hit one of the intruders good and hard with her umbrella! How dare they do this?

Silas ran round to the back of the cottage to find the window broken and the door smashed in. Gabriel was struggling in the doorway with two big men, and getting the worst of it.

'Let him go!' he roared.

One of the men turned in surprise, then moved towards Silas. 'Go away, little man.'

Silas smiled as he twisted sideways to avoid the first punch. Not being a big man had taught him how to defend himself by cunning. 'Reinforcements are on their way,' he yelled at his assailant.

'Well, they're not here yet.' He swung a fist again, missing his target.

The young neighbour came running round the corner brandishing the walking stick. But he stopped in dismay when he saw the size of the two intruders and the brutality on their faces.

Luckily his sudden arrival distracted the nearest man's attention long enough for Silas to thump him good and hard with the knob of the walking stick, before ducking out of the way again.

Stella had just crossed the road when she heard a car approaching and paused to see who it was. To her relief it was Mr Tyler and another man who looked like a workman in rough, muddy clothes. She ran back up the garden path to them, shouting, 'Some men are trying to break into the cottage. Gabriel and Silas need help.'

The workman was out of the car and off round the back like a shot.

'You keep out of the way, lass,' Roy warned and followed him.

She didn't protest but as he ran round to the other side of the cottage, she crept after him, stopping at the corner to peep carefully at what was going on.

When they saw two more men arriving, one of the intruders yelled, 'Look out!' and tried to run away. He shoved Gabriel at the young man, sending them both falling over, and managed to scramble across the wall into the field.

The other man punched the workman and sent him crashing into Mr Tyler. Avoiding them, he set off running round the cottage towards the front.

Hoping she was well enough hidden by the ivy, Stella gripped the umbrella by its bottom end and waited.

Her luck was in. The intruder glanced hastily over his shoulder as he came towards her, so she had time to thrust the umbrella handle out in front of his lower legs. She managed to hook one and send him falling headlong on to the path, roaring with fury.

She let go, thinking it prudent to jump away from him, relieved that by this time Mr Tyler and Silas had turned back. They caught the intruder as he tried to get up. He fought to get away and was so strong it took the workman's help as well to hold him down.

She saw an old clothes line hanging from a post and as she grabbed it, Gabriel limped across from the kitchen doorway and brought out his penknife to cut it. She left him wiping his bloody nose and rushed across to give the piece of rope to Mr Tyler.

The intruder continued to struggle like a wild creature, but there were enough men to hold him till he was tied up hand and foot.

'We'll let the police deal with you,' Roy told him as he stood looking down at him, panting.

'What for? Trespassing?'

'With violence. And—' Roy sniffed. 'What's that smell?' He felt inside the man's pocket and pulled out a package, holding it by one corner and smiling grimly. 'They might arrest you for attempted arson as well, and that's a much more serious offence.'

The man lay still. 'I never done nothing.'

'But you're carrying a rag soaked in paraffin and a box of matches, all wrapped in greaseproof paper. There's already been one attempt to set this place on fire and why would anyone carry something like this unless they planned to try the same thing?'

The man glowered at them, saying nothing further.

Roy turned and smiled at Stella. 'You're a brave lass, and a clever one. You did well to trip him up and then to think of the washing line. I'll always want you on my side in any fight.'

She nodded. The anger was still flowing through her, but it was mingled with satisfaction now because she really had made a difference and helped to defend her future home.

She was worried about Wilf though and hoped desperately that he and Jericho were all right. Whatever they were facing in Backshaw Moss, please let them be safe.

Wilf and Jericho arrived at the first street of the slum area just as one of the men shoved Gwynneth away from her possessions so hard that she fell over. By the time they got out of the van, the bully had picked up a small pile of plates and deliberately smashed them on the ground, laughing at her wail of anguish.

There was a group of people standing nearby but no one came forward to help Gwynneth get up. As Lucas moved towards his mother, the second man grabbed him from behind and punched him in the kidneys, following that up by kicking his legs from under him with a big, heavily booted foot as he struggled to get out of the way.

Jericho was out of the car in seconds, running towards his brother. Wilf hastily fumbled for a tool from a box of oddments behind his seat, muttering, 'Good!' as he found himself holding a wooden mallet. As he followed Jericho towards the bullies, he held it behind him.

One of the men laughed. 'Here comes another fool. Let's hope he can give us a bit more fun than the other two did, eh.'

Even as the man was speaking, a stone whizzed out from behind a corner and hit him on the shoulder. The person who'd thrown it dodged back before anyone could see who it was.

'You'll be sorry!' the man roared. 'We'll find out who did that when we've finished with these weaklings.'

There were cries of 'Shame!' and 'Leave her alone!' from

various parts of the crowd and a couple more missiles were hurled in spite of the threats.

As the man turned towards him, Wilf brandished the mallet and his opponent hesitated.

The noise of people yelling masked the arrival of the police car and Deemer got out quickly, holding his truncheon, with his young constable following suit.

'Police! Stop at once!' Deemer yelled.

Wilf moved back, letting the mallet hang by his side again.

One of the men yelled, 'Can't catch us, you old fool!' at the sergeant and the two of them made off.

Deemer signalled to the constable not to try to follow the bullies and stood smiling in the direction they'd taken. He clapped the young policeman on the shoulder. 'It's all right, lad. I know one of them. I even know which part of Manchester he lives in.'

He turned to find out exactly what had been happening here and growled in anger at what he saw.

Gwynneth was sitting beside her pitiful pile of belongings, sobbing desperately and clutching the two halves of her mother's cake stand.

The crowd started to thin out as people tried to get out of the way, but Deemer roared, 'Stay where you are, you cowards. You outnumbered them. Why did you do nothing to help her? Constable, arrest anyone who tries to leave.'

Jericho went to bend over his mother and help her to stand up.

She clung to him, still sobbing. 'What are we going to do, son? Where can we go now?'

Wilf went to join them. 'You can come and stay in our house for the time being, Mrs Harte.'

Jericho looked at him sharply. 'Will Mrs Morton let us do that?'

'I'm sure she will when she hears what's happened. She's

a very kind lady. There's a big attic that isn't being used, where those who aren't keeping watch can sleep. And your new home will be ready soon. We're pushing the work forward as quickly as we can, because Mrs Newby is just as eager as you are to move in.'

Gwynneth turned to look sadly at their pitifully small pile of belongings and spoke in little more than a whisper. 'We didn't have much and they broke things on purpose, even my mother's best plate.'

Wilf watched her put the two pieces of it in her pocket. His heart twisted in pity at the sight of her pain.

'One day, you'll have a nice home again, Mother. I'll find a way to make a better life for you, I swear I will. And I can mend the plate.' Jericho looked pleadingly at Wilf. 'Can you take her home in the van, Mr Pollard, with whatever of our possessions will fit?'

He gestured to the piles of oddments that betrayed their poverty all too clearly. 'If you could come back afterwards for the rest of the things from our room, the ones that are worth salvaging, anyway, we'd be even more grateful.'

'Of course I can.' Wilf offered his arm to Gwynneth. 'You come and sit in the van, Mrs Harte, while we load your things into the back of it.'

'Thank you, but I'd rather help.' She went to start sorting things out, passing them to the men till everything still salvageable had been retrieved. Only then did she get into the van with Wilf.

'We'll settle you in Mrs Morton's house until your new home is ready,' he said gently.

She turned to him. 'Are you sure Mrs Newby will still want us to live in her cottage?'

'I'm absolutely certain of it.'

'They'll come after us again, you know, and maybe damage her home. That horrible man won't be satisfied till he's driven me an' my sons from the valley as an example to others.'

'They've been trying to damage her house already, but we stopped them. He wants the land it's on. With more people nearby, it'll be easier to keep watch over it, so you'll be a help to her.'

She brightened slightly at that.

Deemer came across to them in time to hear the last few remarks. 'I'll help make sure no one hurts you, Mrs Harte. It may take me a while to catch the man who's ordering this done and put him behind bars, but I know who he is. And in the meantime, we'll do our very best to keep you safe.'

He turned to Wilf and added in a whisper, 'We had a bit of luck. I know who one of those men is and where he lives. I'll ask a colleague over there to bring him in for questioning, which he'll be glad to do. I'll get more pieces of my jigsaw puzzle from him, see if I don't. When I've got enough information to trap Higgerson good and proper, I'll strike. And that time is coming closer, I promise you.'

He watched Wilf drive away before turning to the sullen group of people who hadn't risked trying to get away with the constable standing over them. 'We'll take all their names now, constable, and find out where they live and what they saw.'

But as he'd expected, everyone claimed only to have seen the last part of the incident, involving the arrival of the police.

They couldn't very well pretend not to have seen that, could they?

But one man winked at him across the crowd, tapped the side of his nose, making a swift gesture of rubbing two coins together.

Deemer nodded at him and mouthed, 'Later.' If he had to pay out of his own pocket for information, he would. This was England and this was his valley, where his job was to uphold the law. In his book that applied to rich wrongdoers as well as poor ones.

Jericho waited patiently for him to finish, then asked, 'Can you please come and check that we're leaving the room clean, sergeant? I'm sure Higgerson's agent will try to keep the rent he owes us by claiming we've left it in a mess.'

'Is it worth a few shillings to get into a legal battle with the owner?'

'It's not worth the money, but it's well worth the satisfaction of standing up to him. You don't give in to bullies, not ever.'

'You're a brave chap and I'll vouch for you if needed. Lead the way.'

When they'd checked the room, which was as clean as possible in such circumstances, Deemer helped carry down their last few possessions, got into the police car and said quietly, 'We'll go back via Croft Street, constable, just to check that everything's all right there.'

He hoped the man who'd signalled to him would come and offer more information. Every bit helped.

What Deemer found at the cottage meant he had to spend another hour sorting out the aftermath of the other incident. But at least this time, thanks to Tyler and his men, he had a prisoner and by hell, he'd make sure he got the whole tale out of the fellow.

Though if this resembled any of Higgerson's other attacks, no one would have seen or done anything that linked any of this to him. It was galling how the fellow managed to cover up any traces of what he'd done by keeping people terrified of him and using men from outside the valley to attack decent people, damn him.

This sort of thing happened all over the world, from what

Deemer had read in newspapers and magazines. Dishonest rich people got away with unconscionable acts.

Well, not here. He was going to clear his valley of this filth, if it was the last thing he ever did. Or die doing it. He had only a few years to retirement but he intended to make them count.

He was glad the new council was making a start on the same problem, coming at it from another angle. Reg Kirby was a good man, and as patient as Deemer when he wanted something doing. The two of them shared information occasionally on the quiet.

Yes, Deemer thought, there was more hope with Reg in charge than there had been under the previous mayor. He didn't think he was mistaken about that.

One day . . .

Wilf drove Gwynneth Harte back to his home and the minute Mrs Morton found out what had happened, she said she was more than happy for all the Hartes to stay in her house.

Gwynneth looked at her dubiously and then at Mona, who was standing near her mistress. 'Are you sure?'

'Of course I'm sure. Wilf, dear, go and bring Mrs Harte's things in.'

'The straw mattresses aren't very nice. I think we'd better sleep on the floor tonight till we can make new ones.'

Mrs Morton nodded. 'We have some old flock mattresses up there, I think. You can use those.'

'You're very kind.'

'Well, dear, being kind pays off sometimes. I was a lonely old woman and because I helped Wilf, I now have a house full of people and two children to help raise. I'm happy to help you as well.'

Wilf popped his head round the door. 'Shall I put their things in the attic?'

'Yes, of course. There's plenty of room up there. And there are some mattresses and old blankets too.'

'Good. I didn't fancy bringing the straw palliasses in and leaving a trail of straw and mud everywhere.'

'We can make others.'

'If they're needed.'

'And we can afford to pay you some rent,' Gwynneth offered.

'I'd rather you helped Mona in the house. More people make more work. Oh, my dear!' She put her arm around the woman who'd begun weeping again at this further kindness. 'Is something else troubling you?'

'No. I'm crying out of sheer relief. I don't know whether I'm on my head or my heels today. Earlier on I was happy when Gabriel showed me round the house across the street. Our new home will be so wonderful after Backshaw Moss. Only,' she mopped further tears, 'when I got home, I found my possessions being thrown into the street. They smashed my mother's plate on p-purpose.'

Mrs Morton put an arm around Gwynneth's shoulders and felt her struggle to control herself, so just kept making shushing noises and waiting for her to calm down. 'I can glue the pieces of plate together. I love china and have mended some of my family's stuff.'

Gwynneth stared at her. 'You can?'

'I can try.'

'Thank you. Oh, thank you. This is all so wonderful.'

Wilf had been standing near the door, listening and smiling. He'd known he could rely on Mrs Morton. 'I think this is yours too, Mrs Harte.' He held out a Bible. 'It's muddy and battered, but I think it still has all its pages.'

She took it and clutched it to her bosom. 'I thought I'd lost it. Oh, I'm so glad to have it back. It belonged to my grandmother's family. Reading it is my biggest consolation when things go wrong. Um—' She looked back at Mrs Morton. 'You won't mind if I still go to the Methodist chapel?'

'Why should I mind?'

'Some people do. They only associate with their own congregation.'

'Well, I'm not like that and I don't mind at all.'

Wilf was glad he'd found Mrs Harte's Bible for her. She and her sons had had a hard time and Mrs Morton would be able to glue together the pieces of that fancy plate of hers. Better to have it with cracks showing than not at all.

Decent people helped one another.

One day, Higgerson would get his comeuppance!

He went back to the van for the last load of household oddments and took them up to Mona, who had now taken Mrs Harte into the attic so that they could work out how to re-arrange it.

He was glad he'd noticed the Bible lying in the mud. Some people derived a great deal of consolation from their religion. For him, it was hard work and learning new skills that had pulled him through the bad times. And people. Kind people made a big difference to the world.

Best of all now, he felt there was real hope for the future with Stella. He didn't know whether he could father a child with her, because he never had with Enid, but that would be his most precious hope apart from marrying her.

He saw his children peeping out into the hall through the half-open kitchen door and waved them back. 'Stay inside the house, my loves. I'm just helping a lady to move into your attic.'

They nodded and he went out again to return to Backshaw Moss for the last of the Harte family's possessions.

He saw the shame on Jericho's face at how shabby their last things were, bundles of who knew what wrapped in old sheets. 'Let's load up quickly, lads, and get your things back then we'll see what else we need for tonight.'

'We can sleep on the floor,' Jericho said. 'We don't want to trouble anyone.'

'Where's the trouble? Your mother will no doubt lend a hand with the housework and I'll feel safer to have people around to make sure Mrs Morton and the children are safe.'

Jericho's face brightened at that. 'We'll find our own food, then. That'll save you a bit.'

'It'll be easier if we all cook and eat together.' He saw the shame still lingering on his companion's face and sought in vain for a way to persuade him to accept help. 'Let us do this for you. We all understand how cruel life can be.'

Jericho sagged and closed his eyes for a moment or two. 'Eh, you're a kind man, Wilf Pollard. One day I'll find a way to pay you back for this, though.'

'No need. Just help someone else in your turn.' Wilf clapped his companion on the shoulder and turned to get into the van. 'Come on. Let's get away from this horrible place. It should be knocked down, every last tumbledown house.'

'Higgerson will never allow that. He makes too much money from the rents. It's a proper little goldmine.'

'I agree. No wonder he's trying so hard to keep it as it is. But he'll make a mistake one day, you see if he doesn't.'

'I hope you're right.' Jericho had overheard things which told him there were moves afoot to bring that man to justice, but he kept that to himself.

Wilf didn't pursue that, either. Surely one day the scales of justice would tip in favour of decent folk? From what he read in the papers, the job situation was slowly improving in the south and surely it would start to improve in the north, too?

'We'll get there.' He clapped Jericho on the shoulder and his companion nodded.

Jericho tried to keep believing the hard times would end. He might have been too young to be called to fight in the Great War, and thank goodness for that, but he hadn't missed the troubles of recent years and he'd had to leave school early, something he regretted greatly.

He looked sideways at Wilf, who had also had to make his way, and who had now succeeded beyond most chaps' wildest dreams. If Wilf could manage, so could he, whatever it took.

27

R eg frowned as he looked round the council chamber. He was starting to worry that Mrs Dentry and Charlie Willcox hadn't arrived yet. Charlie was usually one of the first here.

There was the sound of someone arriving, but it was one of Higgerson's cronies. Nasty little twerp, that one was, and why was he smirking tonight?

It was galling. Reg might be mayor, but he needed the presence of all those who usually supported him if he was to gain the special grant and make a start on cleaning up Backshaw Moss.

By the time everyone else had arrived, he was getting seriously worried about the remaining two council members. Something was wrong, he knew it was.

'Aren't we going to start, Mr Mayor?' Higgerson drawled, in that annoyingly slow voice he used when he felt he was in a winning position.

One of his friends sniggered.

'Let's give our colleagues a few more minutes,' Reg told them sharply.

Shortly afterwards there was a sound outside and Charlie came in, tie askew, hat missing and a tear in his upper jacket pocket. For once his cheerful smile was missing and he looked furiously angry.

Everyone gaped at him.

'What happened to you, Charlie lad?' Reg asked.

'I was attacked as I was getting into my car near the shop. If two of my regular customers hadn't happened along, I don't know where I'd be now.' He stared down at his clothing. 'I think I'll hire a bodyguard to get me to the next meeting.' He looked across pointedly at Higgerson and added, 'I'm determined to get this plan passed, you see. Even more determined now.'

There was dead silence in the chamber.

Reg hadn't missed the smirk on Higgerson's face when Charlie came in, even though it had quickly vanished.

Before he could start the meeting, more sounds were heard in the hall and Mrs Dentry came in, looking shaken and pale. She too had damage to her clothing and her hat was slightly awry. She was clinging to the arm of Sergeant Deemer.

'This poor lady was attacked as she walked along her own street,' Deemer announced, his arm still supporting his companion. 'Fortunately she called for help loudly enough for her neighbours to hear. They chased away her attackers and phoned the police station.'

'I knew how important tonight's voting was so I still wanted to come and . . . ' Her voice quavered and she had trouble continuing.

'So I was happy to escort her here,' Deemer finished.

'I don't know what the town is coming to when this sort of thing happens to decent folk,' one of Higgerson's main cronies said, but he looked smug rather than regretful as he added, 'Ladies really shouldn't be out on their own after dark.' He gave her a pointed look and she shrank back.

'Mr Willcox was attacked too,' Reg told Deemer. 'Shouldn't gentlemen be out on their own, either?'

'Most gentlemen can take care of themselves, unlike the weaker sex.'

Reg let out a scornful snort at this old-fashioned remark.
'More likely, someone wanted to stop them both getting to
this meeting.' As he let that sink in, he exchanged a grim
look with the man next to him. Henry Lloyd was one of the
town's lawyers and a very shrewd fellow, and Reg was sure
he hadn't missed any detail of Higgerson's reactions.

'Perhaps we should ask the good sergeant to wait here until
the meeting is over so that he can escort the lady home,'
Todd suggested.

'We can't have outsiders attending a council meeting,'
Higgerson said at once. 'Especially as this is a rather confi-
dential matter.'

'I'll wait in the lobby,' Deemer offered.

'I'd be very grateful for your escort home again, sergeant.'
Mrs Dentry tried to pin her hair back into her bun with a
hand that was still shaking, and Leah went to help her.

Reg waited until the sergeant had left the room then
declared the meeting open. He hoped Deemer would eavesdrop on them.

It was hard to keep the discussion on track but he managed
to make progress through the necessary steps, in spite of
regular objections about anything and everything by various
members of Higgerson's clique.

They ended up agreeing by a majority of two on a plan
to clear one of the worst alleys in Backshaw Moss and put
the rest of this special grant towards setting up a proper
sewage system for that area. This would mean draining some
of the boggy ground to the east of the slum area, from which
the word 'moss' came to be in its name. The land had never
been drained properly, probably because Higgerson hadn't
owned it all and had no plans to build there, due to the very
uneven terrain around it.

What had eventually been decided ought to gain them
the special starter grant, especially if the proposal was

accompanied by an outline of a plan to clear Primrose Lane afterwards, the ironically named worst part of the slum.

Whoever had chosen flower names for the streets, Reg thought sourly, must have been mocking the valley folk. It was a long time since any wildflowers, or indeed any vegetation, had been seen in that notorious group of dwellings.

Leah and Todd walked out afterwards with Charlie and left the sergeant to escort Mrs Dentry home.

As they stood by Charlie's car, Todd held his brother-in-law back for a moment. 'We'll follow you home, just to be sure. Drive very slowly, especially on that stretch bordered by fields between Birch End and Rivenshaw, and pull to a halt at once if you see anything suspicious on or near the road ahead of you. I'll keep watch on your rear.'

'Thanks. I'll make sure I have a bodyguard for the next meeting, though I don't like having to do that. What the hell is happening to our valley?'

'Higgerson is happening. We thought with Rathley dead, there would be less trouble. Instead, Higgerson has taken over some of his projects and outdone him in wickedness. But I think he's overreaching himself using all this violence to get his own way.'

Leah nodded her head sadly. 'And yet nothing has ever been tied to him.'

'Not that you could prove in a court of law, anyway. I put my trust in Deemer for getting the necessary evidence one way or another,' Charlie said. 'He gets *that look* on his face whenever Higgerson is mentioned. He's proved in the past how tenacious he can be, and he'll do it again.'

'It won't be easy.'

'No, but I think Higgerson underrates him, probably because he wasn't living here when Deemer was first working in the valley, and that may be his undoing. Now Deemer's our sergeant that gives him more power. He'll be the fellow's undoing, however long it takes.'

'I hope you're right.'

Halfway up the hill to Birch End, Todd noticed in the light Charlie's headlights cast ahead of them a shabby van parked by the side of the road, half-hidden by a wall. There was no reason for anyone to have stopped there, because there were no farms nearby.

'I don't like the looks of that,' he muttered under his breath, wondering if he should have led the way up the hill. 'Pull over, Charlie lad.'

The van began edging forward and the leading car slowed down abruptly and stopped on the verge.

'Thank goodness!' Leah muttered.

Todd drove past it and stopped. 'Go and tell Charlie to stay where he is, then get into his car, Leah.' When she hesitated, he added, 'Hurry up! I'm going to stop near that van. I have the steering wheel to hold on to if I have to brake suddenly, but you'll be safer with Charlie than in the passenger seat.'

'Be careful, Todd, love.'

'Mmm.' He waited till she'd done that before moving his own car slowly forward and just before he got to the van, he suddenly swung it round to park it sideways across the narrow road, blocking off access for the van to drive downhill to Rivenshaw. He didn't intend whoever it was in the van to get away easily.

An innocent person would have got out of the van to ask what was going on, he felt. No one got out of this van, though, and the driver had a scarf hiding the lower part of his face.

He watched as it edged forward a little more, stopped for a few seconds before reversing back into the gateway. It swerved out suddenly on to the road, narrowly missing Todd's car then going in the other direction, and accelerating till it was moving up the hill far faster than was safe on a narrow, winding road.

As it neared the first bend, Todd saw headlights of an approaching vehicle, but the van driver must have been paying more attention to what was behind him than in front and didn't seem to notice the approaching danger till it was too late.

A small lorry came round the bend and the van braked hastily, trying to pull aside to avoid it. Only it had been going too fast for its driver to keep control on the rough ground at the side of the road and it was still going fast as it ran headlong into the dry-stone wall that edged the field.

Todd drew quickly to a halt beside it, worried because there was no sign of movement from inside the van. He found the driver lying sideways across the front seats, not moving, his head bloody.

Wrenching the van door open, he began to drag the driver out. Suddenly the man proved he'd been faking unconsciousness by punching Todd, sending him sprawling backwards on to the ground.

But the lorry's driver had also stopped his vehicle and run to join them, and he was big enough to grab the man and hold him until Todd could come to his aid.

'Are you a lunatic, driving like that on this road?' the lorry driver demanded, twisting the man's arm behind his back so that he yelped in pain when he tried to get away.

'Daniel Pollard! I was never so glad to see anyone.'

'What's going on, Todd?'

'I think this fellow has been paid to drive Charlie Willcox off the road. Someone is trying to stop certain council members from voting for a plan put forward by the mayor to start clearing Backshaw Moss. They attacked Charlie on his way to the meeting and clearly they were after him again on the way back.'

The man lunged sideways suddenly but Daniel and Todd were both strong enough to keep hold of him. Blood was still running down his cheek but he didn't seem seriously injured.

Leah got out of Charlie's car and came to join them. 'Here. Take my scarf and tie him up. I knitted it myself and it's good, strong wool. He won't be able to break it.'

Charlie had been staring at him and said slowly and clearly, 'I recognise your face. You're one of the men who attacked me earlier this evening.'

'Never seen you before.' The man continued to struggle but they managed to tie his hands behind him.

Todd smiled grimly at their captive, then asked, 'Your house is closest, Charlie. All right if we take him back there? We can phone Deemer to tell him we've got a present for him. Daniel, can you keep hold of him in my car if we find something to tie his feet? I'll bring you back here to get your vehicle afterwards.'

'I can drive our car to Charlie's,' Leah put in. 'Daniel can take him there in the lorry while you keep an eye on him.'

Daniel grinned. 'My pleasure. And I've got a few pieces of rope, so he won't get away. I'll have to get on my way afterwards, though, because my friend's waiting for me to take his lorry back and I have a lift arranged back up the valley to Ellindale. Will you be all right if I leave you to it at Charlie's?'

'Oh, yes. Deemer will be delighted to take him off our hands, I'm sure. I don't think Higgerson will do anything to help him get out of this.' He glared at their captive. 'You'll be charged with dangerous driving at the very least, I should think. And if any of the people who helped Charlie recognise you, Deemer will be able to charge you with the earlier assault as well.'

The man mustn't have known that Higgerson would not

help him, because he sagged and lost all his defiance, looking very unhappy now.

They locked their captive, still tied up, in the sturdy stone outhouse devoted to storing Charlie's coal supply while he phoned the police station.

Deemer's wife answered. 'He's not here . . . Oh, hold on, I can hear something. Yes, he's just driving back up the street.'

As they'd expected, the sergeant was delighted to be called out again for this reason.

They left the driver of the van locked in Charlie's very sturdy coal shed until Deemer turned up a few minutes later in the special police van that had a locking rear compartment, accompanied by his constable. He listened to their explanations, handcuffed the man and locked him inside his vehicle.

Leah looked at the scarf he was holding out to her. 'No, thank you. I don't want to touch the thing now, let alone wear it.'

'I'll put it in the poor box. Eh, I'm going to enjoy questioning him. Well done, Todd. That was quick thinking. And just between you and me, it looks as if I have a man wanting to sell me some other information about Higgerson. Well, I think that's what he wants. He sent a message that he'd come to my back door later tonight.'

'Do you think he'll know anything helpful?'

'He's from Backshaw Moss, so he might well. People there see a lot of chancy goings-on. It's worth listening to what he has to say, worth a shilling or two if it's useful information.' He looked at Charlie. 'Take care how you go until we get this sorted out, Mr Willcox.'

'Oh, I will.' Charlie gave him a wry grin. 'One good thing: at this rate half the unemployed younger men in Birch End will be finding work as bodyguards.'

When the sergeant had gone, Todd accepted Charlie's

repeated invitation to try his new port while Leah and Marion enjoyed a cup of cocoa. Fortunately, the visitors had a live-in maid who looked after Leah's son, so they didn't have to rush back.

Todd enjoyed the port and agreed that it was good, but refused a refill and waited for his wife to finish sipping her cocoa. 'Deemer was right about one thing,' he said thoughtfully. 'We'll need to be extremely careful how we go until this is sorted out. Leah, you should be all right in Ellindale. There are enough people in the fizzy drink factory during the day to keep you and our lad safe.'

He turned to their host. 'It's going to be more difficult for you, Charlie. You're out and about half the time, so you'll need protection.'

His friend shuddered. 'Don't worry. I'll make sure I get help. I'm no fighter. Do you need me to find someone to keep an eye on you as well, Todd?'

'Thanks, but no. I know one or two chaps in our village that I can call on and they'll be glad to help me with the car repairs and keeping the cars I'm selling looking clean and shiny. I'm thinking of building a shelter for them, to show them off better whatever the weather. Can't do it till this trouble is over, though.'

'Higgerson's a cunning devil.'

'So is Deemer,' said Todd.

'Still, don't let your guard down.'

'I won't, I promise you.'

Charlie nodded. 'With a bit of luck, it'll all be over in a few days.'

Todd didn't think so but he intended to be very careful. He'd come through the war and he'd come through this, too.

Late as it was when he got his prisoner settled, Deemer reported what had happened to his superior officer, who sounded rather dubious about a wealthy gentleman like Higgerson being behind so many troublesome incidents. However, he did grant Deemer permission to phone a friend who was a sergeant in Manchester and see if they could together bring in the man who'd been part of the attack and possible arson attempt on the cottage.

As he put the phone down, Deemer's stomach growled but he didn't let himself deal with his own needs yet. Something within him was burning to sort out these troubles. He was worried in case it grew worse and people for whose safety he was responsible got seriously injured, so he picked up the phone again.

His friend in Manchester was at home and took down the details, happy to oblige because he knew the man in question from a scar on his chin. The fellow had been a thorn in his own flesh for a good few years and if they could get him locked away, it'd save a lot of future trouble.

When Deemer had finished his call, he nodded in satisfaction at his wife. 'I can have my meal now and I'm more than ready for it.'

'Sit down. I've been keeping it warm for you.'

He was only part way through a plate of cottage pie and boiled cabbage when there was a knock at the back door.

His wife stood up to answer it and he said, 'No, don't go!'

She looked at him in surprise at his sharp tone.

'From now on, you'd better look to see who it is before you open the door after dark. The situation is going to get worse before it gets better, or I'm a Dutchman.'

She stepped back and let him open the door.

He found the man from Backshaw Moss standing there, thin shoulders hunched against the cold, with no overcoat, only a threadbare jacket and a faded woollen muffler.

They studied one another, then Deemer said, 'You'd better come in. You don't want anyone to see you standing there.'

'Thanks, sergeant.'

Deemer took him into the kitchen and the man stopped in the doorway to stare at Mrs Deemer.

'It's just my wife. Could you give us a minute or two, love?'

She nodded and left the room.

'Sit down. Tell me your name.'

'I'd rather not, if you don't mind.'

'I do mind. I don't do business with folk unless I know their names.'

'Patrick O'Brien.'

The man was eyeing the plate of food so hungrily Deemer got another plate out and scraped the last of the cottage pie from the dish on the stove on to it. There went his midday meal for tomorrow. 'Get that inside you.'

'Really? Thanks.'

The sergeant had never seen a plate of food cleared so quickly. He pushed his own half-full plate aside. 'I'll finish mine later. I'm supposing you've got something to tell me, Patrick.'

His visitor looked so scared, only desperation could have brought him here today, Deemer decided as he dipped into his pocket and brought out two half-crowns. He set them on the table but kept his fingers on them. 'Tell me.'

His companion leaned forward and though they were the only people in the room, he spoke in a near whisper and looked back over his shoulder a couple of times.

Deemer nodded in satisfaction and pushed the coins towards his visitor, who scooped them up and slipped them in among his clothes quickly, like a magician at a stage show.

'Any time you can find me some more information as useful as tonight's, Patrick my lad, there will be another five bob for you.'

The thin, haggard face brightened still further. 'Thank you, sergeant. And I'm grateful for the meal. It meant a lot to me that you bothered to give me something to eat.'

'Eh, I'd like to feed a lot of hungry people, but I'm only one man and I can't afford to. I'm glad to have helped you tonight, because you've helped me.'

He saw the fellow out and closed and bolted the back door, before starting on the rest of his meal, which was now cold.

His wife came back to join him and noticed the empty baking dish on top of the cooker. 'Did you have a second helping?'

He shrugged. 'Not exactly. The chap who came to see me had a stomach that rumbled so loudly I couldn't think straight, so I gave him the rest.'

She came across to sit on his knee, old as they both were, and put her arms round his neck. 'I love you, Gilbert.'

'And I love you, Mattie love.'

They sat cuddled together for a while before he reluctantly let her stand up and got on with writing up some notes before bedtime. His superintendent was a stickler for paperwork and had a nasty habit of turning up suddenly and demanding to see the records. Deemer had learned that always being up to date on these was the best way to keep him on his side.

28

The next week crawled past on leaden feet for everyone working or living in Croft Street, which seemed to have more than its usual share of men in ragged clothes passing slowly along it, stopping to stare at anything and everything.

Birch End village centre was the same, with a few men standing on street corners as usual, huddling in doorways for shelter from the icy winds. But now they were paying a lot more attention to who went past them.

'Something's brewing,' one shopkeeper said to his wife. 'Keep your eyes and ears open as you serve people.'

As they were speaking they saw two men get into a shouting match when a stranger objected to being followed around by a local.

'Take Seth with you if you go shopping today, and leave the children at home,' Wilf told Mrs Morton. She left them at home with Mona, and missed their company and comical comments on the world.

When she came back, Mona asked how things were.

She waited until the children were engrossed in their play to answer. 'It's as if people all over the village know something bad is going to happen, as if storm clouds are gathering and getting closer by the day.'

In Rivenshaw the young constable was sent out and told to report back immediately on anything unusual. He reported to Deemer at midday when he came back to eat his sandwiches that he'd seen Higgerson coming and going from his place of work a few times. 'It's a big house that, isn't it, sarge? An' near the centre of Rivenshaw. He must see nearly everything that happens.' He took another bite and added indistinctly, 'I never seen him looking that angry before, never.'

'Good. Angry men are more likely to make mistakes. You hurry up with that meal and get out again.'

In the early afternoon, Deemer's wife went shopping and reported seeing a bruise on Mrs Higgerson's arm when the poor woman's sleeve rode up as she was reaching for something in the haberdasher's. 'I've seen bruises on her before, but not usually that big.'

'He enjoys hurting people, that one does,' her husband said. 'Must be dreadful to be married to him. She always looks cowed. Just be careful what you do and where you go from now on, my lass. If anyone lays so much as a fingertip on you, I'll not be answerable.'

When he drove Stella home, Wilf got out of the car to see her to the gate, glad she'd let him drive her instead of taking her own car. 'Promise me never to go anywhere on your own after dark, whether you're driving or on foot. Not even if it's in answer to a message that's supposed to have come from me.'

'You think something's brewing, don't you?'

'Yes. And I'm sure they'd not hesitate to hurt you in an attempt to frighten you away from the valley. If I want to let you know something, I'll add a special password to my message.' He whispered it in her ear under the pretence of kissing her cheek, then made the pretence reality.

As he pulled away, he added, 'And keep your voice lower when you speak to people about me or about your cottage. There are eavesdroppers everywhere.'

'We're on our own here,' she protested.

'I just saw a curtain move at one of the ground-floor

windows of your lodgings. Someone there is definitely watching us. Maybe someone's listening as well.'

'That's Mrs T's sitting-room window. She does like to keep an eye on everything. You've seen her do it. Why does that seem suddenly worse than before?'

'I don't know. It just does. I hope I'm wrong, but I've got one of my feelings about trouble brewing. We've been a long time struggling to look after our families in this valley, and I was beginning to think we'd turned a corner. But maybe there are certain people who don't want ordinary men to earn a decent living.'

'And ordinary women, too. Not all women are homemakers. Some have to support themselves, as I've done since I was widowed.'

He smiled at her. 'Sorry. And women too.'

'It's Higgerson, isn't it, at the core of all this?'

'Yes. He's taking advantage of men's desperation to put bread on the table for their families in the worst possible way, using the worst types to intimidate others. We've got him worried, I know we have, and that probably means he's even more dangerous than usual, so just . . . be careful.'

She nodded. 'I will, love. And make sure you're careful too.'

He smiled down at her. 'I will. I've even more to be careful about now, haven't I?' He kissed her cheek again.

As she watched him walk away, she reached up to touch the place where his lips had been, smiling when he turned and flapped his hand at her to tell her to go inside. She was surprised to find the front door unlocked and open just a little. You'd not notice it from the street.

She turned and saw that Wilf was still standing by his van, waiting until she'd gone right inside before moving off again. No use worrying him with this. The door might have been left in that position by mistake, after all.

But she'd never found it ajar before.

Still, even if someone had been spying on them, they'd have heard nothing.

Wilf seemed to think she was in particular danger because of buying the cottage, and perhaps he was right. Yet in spite of that, she wouldn't change the life she was making for herself here in the valley – especially finding him – not for anything in the world.

There was enough light shining from a nearby street lamp into the hall through the windows to each side of the door for her to see the door of the sitting room further down the hall close. The handle didn't make a sound as it moved slowly into place, but she had excellent eyesight. Frowning, she switched on the hall light and made sure the front door was properly closed.

She'd bet it was that Miss Wolton again, trying to eavesdrop on her and Wilf. Well, let her try. Stella would make sure she didn't get any information from her about what he and his partner were doing in Birch End.

Mrs T must also have been watching them, but she didn't think her landlady meant anyone harm. She was just a little nosy, wanting to keep an eye on her household, and was usually cheerful and obliging with everyone.

Stella went into the sitting room, and yes, Miss Wolton was there, as well as two others. She sat and chatted for a while, surprised at being asked openly about Wilf by her.

'My friend says his business is doing really well.'

'We don't talk about business.'

'But he must say things.'

Another woman came to sit near them. 'Did you find your handkerchief, Miss Wolton?'

'What? Oh, yes. I'd dropped it near my room.'

Sure now of who had been in the hall, Stella didn't stay much longer.

It was a relief to get into her own room, but when she opened the top drawer to put her gloves away, she froze and studied its contents because something didn't look right. She always put things in the same place and they weren't quite as she'd left them.

Someone had been going through her things. She had no doubt about that because though they'd tried to put things back in the same way, they hadn't quite succeeded. She had a particular way of folding her underclothing and placing her smaller items along the front edge of a drawer so that they didn't get pushed to the back.

Who had done this? And why?

She checked the other drawers and again felt sure that they weren't quite as she'd left them. Furious, she stormed downstairs and knocked on the door of Mrs T's private room.

She kept her voice low. 'Something's happened and I need to speak to you privately.'

Her landlady looked surprised but held the door open.

When she was inside the cluttered little room, Stella told her what had happened.

Mrs T stiffened. 'Are you sure?'

'Absolutely certain. I'm a bit fussy about where I put my things in drawers and they weren't folded my way, either. Also, one of my petticoats was in the wrong place in the pile.'

'Oh, dear. I'm very sorry about that. I'll sort it out tomorrow. It won't happen again.'

'You believe me?'

The landlady stared down at her hands. 'Yes. Unfortunately. I was asked to give someone a room suddenly and was a bit suspicious because she has relatives in town. But she said she'd fallen out with them and offered to pay extra for the inconvenience. I hadn't realised she would do something like this or I'd never have—' She broke off. 'Leave it with me. I'll make sure the person leaves tomorrow morning when the temporary guests leave.'

'Who is it?'

'Leave that to me and please, don't talk about it to anyone else.'

'I won't. But it's Miss Wolton, isn't it? Why would she spy on me?'

'She has a relative who works for someone who does things like this.'

'Higgerson.'

'Shh! Don't say his name. Just leave it to me. I'll have her out of the house first thing in the morning.'

Stella tossed and turned in bed that night, thinking about the situation.

What had the searcher been looking for? Her bank book? The paperwork to do with buying the cottage? Perhaps. What else could it be? But what good were they to someone else?

Thank goodness she kept them at work in a drawer with a lock. There wasn't anywhere that had felt secure in this room, so she'd kept them in her satchel at first. Then there was an empty drawer at work once she'd filed everything properly. For future use, she'd thought, but she didn't like lugging the papers around all the time so she'd asked Nick if she could use the drawer temporarily. He'd waved one hand and told her to go ahead.

He was such a nice man. She really enjoyed working for him and Todd, but even with the two men's offices to keep in order, it wasn't a busy place and she sometimes wished she had more to occupy her.

She liked the folk she'd made friends with in the valley, didn't think she'd ever met a group of people who worked so closely with one another, cared about their neighbours and families so much, were just plain *decent*. It was an under-rated word, but she thought it better by far than beautiful.

And then there was Wilf, such a special man. She smiled in the darkness. She'd fallen in love with him and his children so quickly. And he with her. How lucky they were to have met!

No one was going to stop her from carrying out her plans. Not long now until she moved into the cottage, where she'd be just across the road from him. They hadn't spoken about when exactly they would marry, but she didn't want to leave it too long.

Mr Tyler was pushing the men to finish work on the cottage quickly and had told her they were ahead of schedule, in spite of attempts this week to steal building materials and intimidate a workman, who'd immediately reported it to his boss. Mr Tyler seemed to have earned their utter loyalty during the many years some of them had worked for him, and thank goodness for that.

Stella filled her time at the office each day, once the work was up to date, by making lists of what she'd need to do, or knitting another warm scarf for herself, because the worst of winter was yet to come. She didn't feel guilty about doing that because there was simply nothing else to do, as long as she was there to answer the phone or deal with customers who came to book driving lessons.

She didn't intend to buy anything for the cottage till she'd moved in and gone through every cupboard and drawer. She was looking forward to doing that once the workmen were out and the place cleaned up.

Sometimes she lost herself in daydreams about Wilf and what sort of husband he'd make. Derrick had been a nice man, but rather boring. She doubted Wilf would ever bore her! He was interested in anything and everything, full of ideas.

And today, to crown it all, she found when she got back
to her lodgings that Miss Wolton had moved out this morning.
Good riddance.

Gwynneth got on well with Mrs Morton and Mona. She'd
been apprehensive, had never lived in such posh surroundings. But the two children broke the ice, playing in the kitchen
or going out for escorted walks up and down the street if
the clouds lifted for a while. She loved children, was longing
to have grandchildren to love, but even Jericho, her eldest,
was showing no signs of courting anyone.

She knew Mona was watching how she worked, but she
wasn't worried about that. She put all she had into any job
they gave her. Well, she hated any form of dirt, just as they
did. It had been agony having to live in Backshaw Moss.

Once Mona had relaxed her watchful attitude, the two
women sat in the kitchen, sometimes with whichever man
was keeping watch that evening. They'd chat quietly about
this and that or leaf through old magazines.

When Mrs Morton invited Stella to come to tea on Friday
evening, Mona, who had shown a fondness for harmless
gossip, whispered that Wilf was courting her.

As if that wasn't obvious to everyone from the way he
looked at her. Well, good luck to them and to all lovers.

It had been years since Gwynneth's husband died and
she'd loved him dearly, missed him still. She was too old to
look for another husband. And who'd want to marry someone
so poor? If she hadn't been ill just at the time Jericho lost a
good job, maybe they wouldn't have sunk so low. But the old
doctor cost a lot and they'd had to sell one thing after another
to get her the help she needed.

She heard Wilf on the phone, talking to Stella from the
sound of it and insisting on going to pick her up that evening.
She didn't blame him. It grew dark early at this time of year

and Mona had told her how someone had tried to waylay Mr Willcox when he was driving home from the council meeting. No wonder Wilf didn't want the woman he loved driving up that same stretch of unlit country road on her own.

She just hoped her sons would stay safe. Jericho was mostly here at the house after dark, and Gabriel and Lucas were across the road. But they were more vulnerable at the cottage.

You couldn't help worrying about your children, however old they were.

29

Wilf picked up Stella, as arranged, on Friday evening and she asked if they could sit in the car for a while, because she wanted to discuss something. 'We could park near the road, if you don't mind. It's cold but I need to know what to plan for and we won't be alone once we get to Mrs Morton's.'

'Fine by me.' He stopped the car near the skid marks where the man trying to attack Charlie had gone into the ditch. He was unable to resist kissing her, then put one arm round her. 'What did you want to talk to me about?'

She took a deep breath, summoning up all her courage. 'When do you think we should get married?'

He looked a bit startled and she wondered if she'd been too forward and should have waited for him to raise this matter. Slowly a smile creased his face – a warm, loving smile – and she relaxed.

'Is there a reason for asking this, Stella love?'

'Yes. Mr Tyler called in at work to say I could move into the house next week.'

'He said he was going to tell you. There will still be a lot for you to do to set everything to rights, but the new bathrooms and electrical connections will all be finished by then, which is the main thing for you and for the Hartes.'

'I've been making lists, but I can't do fully detailed ones until I'm in the cottage and I'd be in the way of the workmen if I tried to do that now. There may be furniture and other household goods I'll need later, though actually, it looks to me to contain too much furniture and far more ornaments than I'd want. And . . . ' She hesitated and finished in a rush, 'Well, the main thing I need to know at the moment is whether to provide just for myself or for all four of us.'

He was silent for so long, she began to worry.

'You're sure you don't mind me and the children moving into your cottage.'

'If we're married, it'll be *our* home. We've had this discussion before, Wilf. I may be bringing more possessions to our marriage, but you'll be the one who'll have to use your skills at doing jobs to bring the cottage up to scratch.'

She looked at him, feeling her eyes well with tears as she added, 'And you'll be bringing me children, who will be a far bigger treasure than a cottage as far as I'm concerned. It's possible you and I may not be able to have children of our own. If we're very lucky, I hope we can, but if not, it'll be even better that we have Ronnie and Peggy, don't you think?'

'I never thought to find such a loving woman as you.' He took a deep breath. 'All right, love, let's get married as soon as we can and hang what mean-minded people say. Before Christmas, if possible. I think we'll need a special licence for that, which will cost more, but who cares?'

She had to ask, 'You're sure I haven't pushed you into it?'

'Pushed me. *Pushed?* No, love. I can't wait for us to be together.'

She let out a long, happy sigh. 'Good. That's settled.'

They sat holding hands for a moment or two, smiling foolishly at one another, then he took his hand away and said, 'We'd better get back now. Shall we tell them tonight?'

'Of course. Mrs Morton and Mona are like family to you, and they're becoming family to me as well. They'll want to help plan our wedding, I should think.'

'And Gwynneth will need to know about the cottage being nearly ready because it'll be better if she and her sons still move in. Let alone, they have nowhere else to go, it'll make the cottage more secure for you and the children.'

She couldn't stop smiling as they drove back to Mrs Morton's.

They smiled again as everyone congratulated them, and then the Hartes looked relieved as she and Wilf assured them that they were still wanted to keep it all as secure as possible.

Late on Friday evening Deemer heard a knock on the back door of his house. He peered out of the window, because a bona fide person seeking help when the police station was closed would have come to the front door. He didn't intend to leave himself open to attacks.

He recognised the way the man outside was hunched against the cold and opened the door to let his new informant in. Only the sod ran off and before Deemer could close the door again, two men who must have been hiding beside the door grabbed him and dragged him, yelling and trying to shout for help, away from the house.

But he only got out a couple of yells because they pushed his face down in the bare damp soil of the vegetable patch so that his voice was muffled. Then someone hit him over the head so hard he saw flashing lights. Everything was spinning around him and all he could do was act as if he'd been fully knocked out and hope they wouldn't hit him again.

He felt woozy, in no state to fight back, but managed to keep up the pretence of being unconscious as they tied him up, gagged him and rolled him behind the shed.

'I hope the fool freezes to death,' one of them said, giving him a passing kick.

Deemer held on to his anger at that and listened carefully to the sounds they were making.

Oh, hell, they sounded to be going back into the house. What would they do to his wife?

He wriggled about desperately but they'd tied him up too tightly to get free of the ropes and the gag was preventing him from calling for help.

Mattie Deemer was upstairs about to get into bed when she heard a knock on the back door. She couldn't resist peering out of the bedroom window to see who had come to the house at this late hour. She switched off the bedroom light first, as her husband had trained her to do – never give away your presence until you're sure you're safe, Gilbert always said.

She was grateful she'd heeded his warning.

Her first instinct was to rush down to help him, but of course she would be worse than useless because she'd seen at least two men out there, and who knew if any others were lurking in the shadows?

Instead, she grabbed the bolster and shoved it under the covers to look as if someone was sleeping there. She couldn't find her slippers in the dark so slipped barefoot up the attic stairs and across its rough bare boards towards the police station attic, a route very few people knew about.

All the time she was shuddering and trembling. What had they done to her husband? What would they do to her if they caught her?

She heard footsteps inside her home and knew she wouldn't have time to open the door to the police station side of the attics, let alone close it quietly before anyone came up here.

She ducked down behind an old trunk at one side of the half-empty space. *Always listen to your instincts,* her husband had said so many times, and something was telling her to hide. The intruders might not come up here, but if they did, she didn't want them to see her, and the white nightgown would give her away.

It was a good thing she had hidden because someone did creep up the stairs and stand at the top, not even trying to breathe quietly. She resisted the temptation to peep and waited for what seemed a long time. Eventually she heard the intruder mutter, 'No one up here.' Footsteps went down the stairs again.

They must think she was asleep in bed. If they'd gone right into the bedroom, they'd immediately have noticed that it was a bolster not a person.

Pressing one hand to her chest – as if that would stop her heart pounding – she carried on across the attic and down into the police station by the other, less obvious staircase, hoping to be able to phone for help from there.

But when she picked up the phone it was dead, making no sound at all. They must have pulled the house phone out of the wall, or cut the wires outside or done whatever was necessary to put a telephone out of order. What did she know about such things?

She heard sounds outside and went into her husband's office to peep out of the rear window of the police station. Two shadowy figures were leaving by the back door of the house, but there was no sign of her husband. What had they done with him?

One of them laughed loudly enough to be heard from where she was standing and the other shushed him. They must be rather stupid to be so careless about making a noise. The one who'd come up to the attic had made no effort to hide his presence.

What had he been laughing about? Surely they hadn't killed her Gilbert? Terror iced her veins at the mere thought, but it also made her pull herself together and she became even more determined to raise the alarm.

She looked down at herself. Barefoot, with her hair in its nightly plait and wearing only her nightgown. Thank goodness it was flannel and not her cotton summer gown, so at least it covered her decently. Fine warrior she'd make, but she had to go out if she was to get help, and if it was embarrassing to be seen in your nightclothes, well, this was an emergency.

She had a quick look around the police station, her eyes more accustomed to the dimness now, and to her relief, she found the constable's mackintosh and put that on. But there were no shoes of any sort, not even Gilbert's galoshes.

Now, where should she go to for help?

That evening, several men slipped into the field next to the cottage but stayed out of sight.

One sniggered and whispered something to the man next to him and a heavy hand clouted him from behind.

'No – damned – talking.'

They glared at one another in the fitful moonlight, then Artie, the man in charge, strode off across the field to continue checking everything.

The one he'd thumped wouldn't dare try to hit him back but when Artie turned round he could see the way the fellow's eyes followed him, and that made him wary. He wished yet again that he could have chosen his own men for tonight's venture and that he'd had more time to plan this. He wouldn't have hired that fellow for a start, nor done things so openly. But Higgerson interfered in everything. The richer he got, the more reckless he seemed to be, as if he felt he could get away with anything.

It'd be better still not to do this at all. Artie was getting seriously concerned about Higgerson's mental state. He'd worked with him for years, because he paid well, but never before seen him get so furious as easily as he had lately, or seen such a wild look in his eyes.

Oh, well, you did what you had to in order to feed your family, and Artie had made a few other arrangements so that he didn't get caught if things went wrong.

He settled behind a tree from where he could watch the house. The lights went on and off in various parts. Two men keeping watch here now, unfortunately, and two others were across the road within easy yelling distance. Three tonight, if Wilf Pollard returned.

Eh, whatever was Higgerson thinking of?

Time to reconnoitre again. He found the way of getting to the front of the cottage that he'd marked out mentally earlier in the week, then jerked back as a car turned into the street. Two people got out of it, Wilf Pollard and the woman he was courting, the one Higgerson wanted to stop moving into the cottage. Damn! He'd come back earlier than they'd hoped.

Artie sighed. Apart from anything else, he wished he didn't have to hurt Wilf, who was a good chap and had been kind to Artie's cousin. But there you were. They'd have to get Wilf out of the picture if they were to get hold of the woman. Luckily, she was only a slip of a thing and would be easy enough to capture and hold.

The plan now was to wait until Wilf and the woman left the house across the road at the end of the evening and pounce. It'd take at least two men to deal with Wilf, and be easier if they took him by surprise. Time for the next stage, positioning his men so that the two guards here in the cottage couldn't help her. They'd have to move up one at a time and be very careful not to be seen.

He gave a grim smile. At least no one would be able to call for police help now. Fred had come back from Rivenshaw and explained about leaving Deemer tied up in his own garden. Artie wished Fred had obeyed orders and tied up the wife as well, but he said she'd been sleeping soundly, so there was no need. Anyway, she'd be used to her husband getting called out at night and wouldn't worry if she woke to find him missing.

Mattie took a deep breath and slipped out of the police station's back door and into the yard. It was dark and windy and there was no warmth in a raincoat, so she was soon shivering. She didn't dare go back into the house, in case someone was still there, so unbolted the yard gate.

Where should she seek help?

As she hesitated, she heard footsteps and two men came into view. She didn't recognise them so edged back into the gateway.

But they'd seen her and stopped.

One came across to her. 'Mrs Deemer? Is something wrong?'

She knew who he was, one of Higgerson's cronies. 'I'm just coming back from visiting a sick friend.'

The other one stared at her. He was still standing in the shadows and her eyesight wasn't very good in this kind of light. Who was he?

What was she going to do? Had she gone straight from one danger into another?

Patrick had hated having to trick the sergeant after Deemer had been so kind to him, but you didn't argue with Higgerson's thugs, not if you wanted your family to stay safe. He ran off as soon as he'd done what they wanted but when he went home, his wife took one look at his face and pointed at him in that way he hated.

'What have you done now, Patrick O'Brien.'

'None of your business.'

She folded her arms. 'When you get that look on your face, I make it my business. I don't like nasty surprises.'

He raised one hand to her and she snatched up the poker.

For a moment there was a stand-off, then he gave in. He hadn't been going to hit her, not really. He hardly ever touched her, unlike some men he knew. He explained quickly what he'd had to do tonight.

She looked at him in horror. 'You left that nice sergeant who gave you a meal for them thugs to hurt. An' I've told you before, I'd rather starve than see you turning into a criminal. If you've helped murder a good man, I've done with you.'

'I didn't. I'd never. They weren't going to kill him, just tie him up and leave him out in the garden. Murder causes too much fuss, an' that Artie doesn't believe in it, let alone want to risk being hanged.'

'That sergeant is as old as my father. He'll freeze to death out there on a night like this. You go back right away and let him loose.'

He looked at her aghast. 'I can't do that. They'll hurt *me* if I free him.'

'They won't know it's you. You can cut him free and hurry back here. I'll swear you never left the house if anyone asks.'

When he didn't move, she gestured with the poker. 'I mean it, Patrick O'Brien.'

So he went outside again, scowling.

When he got near the back of the police house, he waited and checked everything, then crept into the garden. Sure enough, the sergeant was lying behind the shed.

Patrick took out his pen knife, waited a bit longer to be sure no one had stayed to keep an eye on him, before slitting the ropes on Deemer's hands and feet. He'd thought the poor man was unconscious, but the sergeant's eyes opened and he growled in a low voice. 'You'd better stay here. I need to talk to you.'

Patrick jerked away from him.

'I'll arrest you later for being an accomplice if you don't stay here now.'

So he stayed. Couldn't win, could he? But he knew his wife had meant what she said and if truth be told, he'd hated helping them tonight. He too would prefer to stay on the right side of the law.

He just hoped he didn't get a beating from Artie for this.

30

Stella stayed later than she'd intended and was glad Wilf would be taking her home. 'That was a lovely evening,' she said as they got into the van.

When they reached the end of Croft Street and turned on to the lane leading to the main road down the hill, something hurtled through the air and hit the windscreen. Wilf braked and men leaped on to the running boards on either side of the van.

He sounded the horn several times and tried to speed up again, but found his way impeded by more objects and the car slowed to a halt. 'Straw bales, damn them!' he grunted.

By that time, the man on his side had opened the door and was trying to drag him out. Another man joined him and Wilf found it impossible to stop them pulling him from the vehicle.

A third man had by this time opened Stella's door and grabbed her. She couldn't have stopped a big chap like him, so let herself go limp and whimper. He laughed as he got her out and tried to put his hand across her mouth, so she bit him good and hard, then kicked him where it hurt before clawing at his eyes.

Speed, her grandfather had taught her. Do everything you can as quick as you can.

She hadn't expected to succeed so easily and could only assume that he hadn't expected any resistance from a woman.

The pain he was in must have slowed him down and by

the time he reached out to grab her again, she was already moving fast, not even trying to go to Wilf's aid, but running back along the road, screaming at the top of her voice. Footsteps pounded along behind her but that only made her run faster.

She called out loudly for help and along the street doors began opening and men armed with improvised weapons coming out. Wilf had told her the neighbours were always prepared for trouble from Backshaw Moss.

When Jericho came to the door of Mrs Morton's house, armed with the knobbly walking stick, she sobbed in relief and swerved towards him.

He didn't waste a second, pushing her behind him and turning to face the man who'd pursued her.

A bell suddenly began to ring further along the street and more lights came on in houses.

'End it!' a loud voice called and repeated the order. The attackers hesitated, then turned and scattered.

'Wilf's car was ambushed,' Stella told Jericho. 'Just as we got to the lane. They'd set up straw bales to stop it. Two other men were pulling him out of the car.'

'Stay inside and lock the doors,' Jericho ordered and set off running down the street towards the lane, yelling, 'Someone come with me.'

Knowing the stupid plan had failed, Artie ran towards the rear of the cottage. This was the last time he worked for Higgerson. He had enough money to get himself and his family out of town and by hell, he'd have them all gone within the hour.

A man jumped out in front of him – the one who'd failed to obey orders – and tried to swipe him with a cudgel. He managed to dodge the worst of the blow and by that time he was so furious at this attack from someone supposed to be working for him that rage lent him the strength to wrench the cudgel out of his hand and use it on him.

The man fell like a stone and Artie didn't wait to see whether he got up or not, but ran on.

He was over the garden wall and into someone's flower beds within seconds, cursing as he tripped over a spade, but managing to right himself and get away into the posh part of Birch End.

Yells and shouts seemed to be coming from behind the cottage as well as the street but he ignored them. Let the fools save themselves if they could.

Wilf struggled in vain against the two men holding him, who were both big brutes. Then headlights appeared on the road up the hill and they suddenly let go of him and ran off into the fields.

Charlie had to stop when he came to the barrier of hay bales and Wilf staggered across to them and began hurling them aside. 'Keep your engine running!' he yelled as the car door opened. 'They've run off but one of them was chasing Stella down the street. Get back in your car and follow me! Tell your friend to do the same.'

'It's not—' Charlie began.

But Wilf had turned away to hurl aside enough of the bales to get his van out. His engine had stalled and he muttered in gratitude as it restarted first go. He turned it and set off towards Croft Street as fast as he could.

He found a scene of chaos there with two men tied to a tree and Jericho directing the neighbours to tie up another fellow they'd caught. What the hell had been going on here? But first things first. 'Where's Stella?' he called at the top of his voice.

'She's in the house. That woman's a fast runner.'

He sagged in relief. 'Thank goodness. Need any help here?'

Jericho grinned. 'Nah. This was the most stupid attack I ever saw put into action. The leader escaped and they won't say who he was. We tried to phone for official help, but can't get any response from the police station. We're all right, though, and so is the cottage. They tried to set it alight again, but Lucas put the fire out.'

'What's the betting Higgerson's behind this?'

'No doubt about it. He'll have an alibi for tonight, though, and none of the men who carried out the attack will dare point the finger at him.'

Wilf turned as Charlie got out of his car and came towards them. 'Good thing you and your friend turned up.'

Charlie grinned at him. 'They might not have run away if they'd seen it was only me and a tailor's dummy I was taking back for Marion. I'm no fighter.'

Both his companions chuckled and Wilf said, 'Excuse me. I have to check that Stella's all right.'

As he went towards the house, the door opened and Stella came out to fling herself into his arms.

'You're all right.'

'Yes. And I can see that you are.'

Mona and Mrs Morton were staring at them from the hall, and men were watching them from the street. Wilf didn't care who saw him, he kissed her again and held her close.

'When's the wedding?' someone called.

'Soon as I can arrange it!'

Someone else applauded.

In Rivenshaw, the second man moved out of the shadows towards Mattie Deemer and she tensed, ready to run, till she saw that it was the new doctor.

'Oh, thank goodness! Doctor, some men have attacked my husband and I'm afraid he's hurt. Could you—'

'I'm all right, lass.' Deemer came around the side of the house, moving slowly and leaning on a man she recognised.

She gulped and went towards him. 'I thought they'd killed you.'

'No, lass. But I'll admit to a headache.' He gestured to the man standing uneasily by his side. 'They'd tied me up, but Patrick here – you remember him? – found me and cut me free.'

As he swayed dizzily the doctor came forward. 'Can we get you into the house? I think that cut needs attention.'

'I'll leave you to it,' his companion said and walked quickly away.

Deemer studied him with narrowed eyes but said nothing. He knew who it was.

'I'll leave you in safe hands, then, sergeant.' Patrick started to move away.

Deemer ignored his pleading glance and kept hold of his arm. 'I need you to help me into the house.'

Mattie led the way, blushing as the house lights showed her nightgown and general disarray.

But the sight of the blood on her husband's face and neck made her forget that and pull herself together. She hurried to set a kettle on to boil.

'I need to phone the inspector,' Deemer said.

'I think they did something to the phone,' Mattie said. 'I tried to phone from the police station but it's not working.'

He turned to Patrick. 'I'm co-opting you as a special constable. Go and fetch my constable. And see you come back with him.'

Only then did he allow his wife to settle him in a chair, muttering under his breath at the waves of dizziness that kept slowing him down.

'I'll get another constable out of this for our valley, if it's the last thing I do,' he muttered as the doctor washed his hands, examined his injuries and began to dab at the blood. 'We need someone based in Birch End.'

As Deemer's wound was being stitched the constable turned up, followed by Patrick, who hovered near the door, looking as if he wished he were anywhere else.

After a quick explanation, the sergeant told the constable to go off and wake up a neighbour with a telephone, so that he could contact headquarters.

'Sarge, if you'll just give me a minute to look at the phone, I'll see if it's easy to fix. I've a bit of experience with electrical gadgets, and they might just have pulled the wires out or cut them. We could do with a phone working here. There's bound to be some to-ing and fro-ing.'

'Hurry up.' Deemer turned to Patrick. 'Your job is to make sure no one comes in here who shouldn't. I meant what I said: you can consider yourself a temporary special constable.' He looked knowingly at the man. 'You'll be paid for it, you know. Seven and six for a night's shift.'

'Oh. Well, all right.' Patrick stood straighter.

By that time a bandage had been put over his wound and since he couldn't think of anything else that was urgent, Deemer gave in to his wife's urging and agreed to lie down on the sofa, just for a few minutes.

Mrs Deemer looked at the doctor. 'Can you stay a little while to keep an eye on him? He still seems dizzy and I need to go and get dressed.' She blushed as she looked down at herself.

In Birch End, some of the neighbours got together to search for any other men lurking, but the group of villains had vanished, except for the three who'd been captured and who were still refusing to say who had hired them.

Lights blazed in all the houses in Croft Street for the rest of the night, and after Gwynneth had checked that her sons were all right, she helped Mona provide cups of tea for the various people dealing with the aftermath.

Deemer didn't come but his constable turned up and did justice to his excellent training by the way he talked to people to find out exactly what had happened.

Later, two officers from the next area turned up, because the doctor had insisted on Deemer resting and for once the sergeant felt so 'unsteady', as he phrased it, that he'd done just that and called in for more help.

It was growing light before Wilf managed to find time to speak to Stella again privately. He simply put his arms round her and said, 'Thank goodness you're all right. I don't know what I'd have done if anything had happened to you.'

'Thank my granddad, who taught me how to defend myself, and it doesn't hurt to be able to run fast.'

'You're a brave lass. Some women would have had hysterics if they were faced with a man trying to grab them.'

'Not if the man they loved needed help. Most people have the ability to draw on hidden reserves in a crisis, though sometimes it's better to run for help than try to do the impossible. Anyway, Charlie turned up, didn't he? Fancy him driving them away. He's not exactly a heroic type, is he?'

Wilf chuckled, still amused by the incident. 'Turns out they thought there were two men in his car. He was taking home a tailor's dummy for his wife to use for her sewing and had it strapped into the front seat beside him.'

He gave her a rueful smile. 'This has been the most botched-up attack I ever heard of, a real comedy of errors at times. Thank goodness.'

'I don't need to ask who organised it, I suppose.'

'We can all guess. But he'll probably escape being charged for it. The men who've been captured are refusing to say anything except that they were offered money by a man they'd never seen before to do this tonight.'

'Why were they trying to kidnap me, do you think?' Stella asked.

'I think it was me they wanted and they were just trying to stop you helping me. They wouldn't expect a woman to fight back like you did.' He grinned at her. 'I can see I'll have to watch my step with you after we're married.'

'As if I'd ever turn on you, or need to.'

Mrs Morton came to join them. 'We've made you up a bed in my spare bedroom, Mrs Newby.'

'Thank you. I am tired now, I must say. I don't know what Mrs T will think of me not going back to the lodgings again.'

'I'll phone her when it gets light, by which time word of this affair will no doubt be out.'

Wilf consulted his wristwatch. 'It's six in the morning. Roy will be up by now, or at least, awake. He's a real early bird. I'd better phone him before I go to bed and tell him about our little battle. I don't think Higgerson will dare do anything else for a while, though. Do you?' He yawned. 'Let's leave it all to the police now.'

31

A week later, a wedding took place. The bride wore her best suit and blouse; the groom his rarely used and rather old-fashioned Sunday best suit. They were accompanied to the town hall by the groom's children, Mrs Morton and Mona.

They hadn't invited anyone else or told people exactly when they were getting married because they didn't want a fuss made, but Roy Tyler and his wife were waiting for them at the registry office.

'I might have known you'd find out,' Wilf said. Then the two men shook hands and Mrs Tyler gave Stella a kiss.

After the short ceremony, Roy grinned at them. 'Did you think you could get away without some sort of celebration? You've too many friends in this valley for that, lad. I've booked a table at the hotel.'

'It's enough to be wed,' Wilf protested. 'Don't waste your money.'

'Humour us,' Ethel Tyler said. 'After all, it'll look better if people know your friends are on your side.'

When she put it like that, he gave in. He'd do anything to protect Stella. And Higgerson had been keeping a low profile ever since the night of the attack. Every time Wilf thought of how he'd got away with it, he felt furious.

At the hotel, they found other friends waiting for them as well, including Stella's employers and their spouses, plus Charlie Willcox and his wife, and Wilf's brother and wife.

He sighed. 'Here we go, love.'

Stella smiled at him and he followed Roy to the area at the far end of the room where tables were set.

By the time they got to their places everyone was standing up and at a sign from Charlie, they chorused, 'Congratulations, Mr and Mrs Pollard.'

There were some very brief speeches which showed again how well Wilf was regarded, then the bride and groom's health was drunk in the traditional sherry or Leah's special fizzy elderflower drink, according to taste.

Afterwards, as the party started to break up, Mrs Morton leaned towards Wilf and whispered, 'There's food in the cottage and a bed made up. We'll look after the children tonight. I think everyone deserves a special wedding night.'

He beamed at her. 'You're a wonderful woman.'

Taking Stella's hand, he led her out of the hotel, moving as quickly as he could, not wanting any more delay. He found his van waiting outside, with a lad keeping an eye on it, and helped his new wife into it.

As the happy couple walked out of the room, Deemer turned to Roy. 'I'm really annoyed that Higgerson has an alibi, as we'd expected.'

In an equally low voice, Roy said, 'Well, I bet he takes more care what he does in future. He's seen what people can do to defend themselves against outright attacks.'

'We'll catch him another day. I shan't give up.'

'None of us will, Gilbert lad.'

There was the sound of a motor starting up outside.

Roy smiled. 'In the meantime, two people who suit each other down to the ground have got wed, and I'm sure they'll be happy together. Life goes on in spite of the Higgersons of this world.'

★

There was a knot of white ribbons on the door knocker of the cottage. Gabriel opened the door before they could do it and came out to greet them. 'Congratulations, and welcome to your new home. We'll be in our part of the house if you need us, but I don't think you will. Thanks for the furniture, Mrs Pollard.'

'Thank you for keeping an eye on things. We'll be fine now.' Wilf closed the door after them and let out a long sigh. 'Alone at last.'

'Let's walk round the cottage,' Stella said. 'It'll make it feel more ours, don't you think?'

He was happy to do anything she wanted, so arm in arm they made a tour of the rooms on the ground floor.

'It's the biggest house I've ever lived in, Stella love. Like a palace. Fair takes my breath away to think it's my home now.'

'It's felt like my home ever since those dreams. Wasn't that strange?'

'Aye. Who knows how that sort of thing happens. Let's hope you don't get strange dreams all the time.'

'It's the only time it's happened to me. But I feel the same as you about how big the cottage is. It feels like a palace.' She stopped and cocked her head to one side as if listening. 'It feels welcoming, somehow, don't you think?'

'Yes. But most of all, it's you being here that makes it a home for me, my brave lass, not the spooky stuff.'

She blushed. 'I wish you'd stop calling me that.'

'You are brave and you're bonny too. Now, let's go and check the upstairs.'

It was well over an hour before they came down again, hand in hand.

'You're truly my wife now,' he said softly.

'And you're truly my husband, darling Wilf.'

My father in Army uniform

My father was sent abroad to the middle east in 1941 and didn't return till late 1945.
This must be later in that period as he's a sergeant by then, judging from the stripes. So he
saw me as a baby and then not till I was four-and-a-half. I remember a young woman asking
me in puzzlement why he didn't get any leaves. She clearly didn't understand that you don't
get leave in wartime when you're so far from home. He started in Egypt and wound up in
India as his last stop, as far as I can make out. He would never say much about those years.
He was a clerk in the Army Medical Corps. I do know that he and my mother wrote to one
another every single day they were apart and stayed madly in love for the whole of their lives.

Me as bridesmaid

This is the only time I was ever a bridesmaid. I was seven years old, so it was about 1948. I'm the one wearing glasses. I've worn them since I was two so they're as much a part of me as the clothes. This was my mother's cousin's wedding. I remember the bow kept slipping and it annoyed me greatly.

CONTACT ANNA

Anna is always delighted to hear from readers and can be contacted via the Internet.

Anna has her own web page, with details of her books, some behind-the-scenes information that is available nowhere else and the first chapters of her books to try out, as well as a picture gallery.

Anna can be contacted by email at
anna@annajacobs.com

You can also find Anna on Facebook at
www.facebook.com/AnnaJacobsBooks

If you'd like to receive an email newsletter about Anna and her books every month or two, you are cordially invited to join her announcements list. Just email her and ask to be added to the list, or follow the link from her web page.

www.annajacobs.com

This book was created by
Hodder & Stoughton

Founded in 1868 by two young men who saw that the rise in literacy would break cultural barriers, the Hodder story is one of visionary publishing and globe-trotting talent-spotting, campaigning journalism and popular understanding, men of influence and pioneering women.

For over 150 years, we have been publishing household names and undiscovered gems, and today we continue to give our readers books that sweep you away or leave you looking at the world with new eyes.

Follow us on our adventures in books . . .
🐦 @HodderBooks f /HodderBooks 📷 @HodderBooks

HODDER &
STOUGHTON